BLACK FIRE

A TOMMY BLACK THRILLER

WILLIAM KELY McCLUNG

Falling Up

Publishing

ISBN 979-8-9851700-3-0 (paperback)
ISBN 979-8-9851700-5-4 (hardcover)
ISBN 979-8-9851700-4-7 (ebook)

Library of Congress Control Number: 2022912793

Publisher's Cataloging-In-Publication Data

Names: McClung, William Kely, 1958- author.
Title: Black Fire / William Kely McClung.
Description: Midlothian, VA : Falling Up Publishing, 2022. | Series: Tommy Black thriller, bk.1. Also available in audiobook format.
Identifiers: LCCN 2022912793 (print) | ISBN 979-8-9851700-3-0 (paperback) | ISBN 979-8-9851700-5-4 (hardcover) | ISBN 979-8-9851700-4-7 (ebook)
Subjects: LCSH: Special forces (Military science)--Fiction. | Kidnapping--Fiction. | Human trafficking--Fiction. | Thrillers (Fiction) | Military fiction. | BISAC: FICTION / Thrillers / Suspense. | FICTION / Thrillers / Military. | FICTION / Action & Adventure.
Classification: LCC PS3613.C33 B55 2022 (print) | LCC PS3613.C33 (ebook) | DDC 813/.6--dc23.

First Edition: October 2022

For information contact:
kely@williamkelymcclung.com

Book and Cover design by:
John Clayton @ heAring eYe doG CreaTive

Dedication

To the victims of trafficking and exploitation —
Your bravery can't be captured with words,
but help to fill hearts
with the inspiration of your courage.

CHAPTER
ONE

"*H*e *has a talent for violence.*"

What the hell was that supposed to mean? The specificity of words was interesting. They stood out. Caught the attention of people who might care and note such things. People who might want to find out. Not propensity or tendency. *Talent.* A curious choice with entirely different implications. Coming from a psychiatrist who interviewed him twice as a child and added as a footnote on the second report.

That was the thing about reports, even as part of sealed juvenile records. *They were records.* Records because they were recorded and kept—not destroyed. If the psychiatrist hadn't been a retired military officer, they might have stayed buried.

It wasn't something he tried to have any more than he tried to have blue eyes or a thick shock of black hair. Okay, sure, it was partially developed as a child. Nurtured on the streets as a ten-year-old growing up without a family. A sob story in a world full of them. Watching his mother die from an overdose and him shooting the boyfriend that beat them both bloody and fed her habit. *His talent discovered.* The fire, the police, the foster homes.

Then the fights. His talent became useful. Bigger kids found it was a mistake to think they could take advantage of him.

And then he grew. Bigger than some and stronger than most. He was singled out for a lot of reasons. Passed all the tests, mental and physical.

"He has a talent for violence." Then came the training, the wars, the combat missions.

Right now he just wanted to say hi to the man who saw something more and raised him as his own.

And maybe grab a hot dog.

The place looked the same, which made sense—you don't mess with an institution. A small orange Formica counter top. Limited hot dog menu on the wall. Business license. Inspection rating with a 99 circled on the top. Mounted and framed reviews from the Sun-Times and the Tribune. Framed eight by tens of celebrities and sports legends. Ford, Howard, and Hudson. Sosa, Pippen, and Jordan. Obama. All signed to "Big Al."

Beside them, in a place of honor, a group picture of five soldiers. Desert fatigues. Clowning on each other, a couple with shirts off. Elite fitness levels, weapons in hand, and ready to take on the world. Dillon, Jimenez, Crawley, Williams, and Black.

Tommy Black banged on the small silver bell. His hands were calloused and scarred as much as the counter.

A one-man operation, a voice bellowed from the back. "Hang on! Hang on!"

Moments later, Big Al Lobinski himself, *old-country* a generation ago, stepped from the back. His face distorted behind a two-gallon jar of pickles carried in hands the size of baseball mitts that he set near the register. His face filled with genuine delight as he took in the man on the other side. *The son he never had.*

"I'll be damned, Tommy. What a surprise!" Big Al wiped his hands on his apron and lifted the hinged counter top. "Wow. You look great! Look at you, man!"

He grabbed the younger man and shook him affectionately.

"Jesus! Hard as a rock!" Squeezed him with a bear hug that would crush some men. Yelled to the back.

"Scottie! Get out here... See who it is."

Moments later, Scottie, a 10-year old with all concentration on his Game Boy, shuffled out from the back.

"Uncle Tommy!" The boy rushed him, jumped into his arms.

"Jesus. How many hot dogs are they feeding you?"

"I can eat like four!" Swelling his chest in pride.

Tommy set him on the counter.

"Sure. Three times an afternoon." Al set the boy down. "You in town awhile?"

"The weekend. Down to Bragg and back over."

Al looked at the man his son had become. No biological connection, but he'd dare any man to say Tommy wasn't his. The naivete of youth worn away, but as fit as when the picture on the wall had been taken. A few lines around his eyes, caused as much from the sights he'd seen as from age. A man whose pride was worn by others, rarely himself. Like the pride that washed over Al now and filled him with warmth.

"Be glad when you're finished." A familiar refrain. *Twenty years was enough, wasn't it?* "Where you staying? We got all kinds of room." Glanced at the boy on his game. "Scottie can take the couch."

"Probably grab a hotel. Out early and schedule's FUBAR."

"It's no problem."

"Rushing to say hi to some of the guys. I'll try to get back before I leave."

"Sure." Al smiled. The affection genuine, both men knew they didn't have to push it.

"You gonna stop and see Jackie?"

A plea in the big man's voice. If you weren't family, you'd never catch it.

"Wish you would. For me. Just— you'll see." He looked at Scottie. "For a big-time attorney, she can be pretty dumb."

Black tried to keep it light, smiled. "That's pretty much all of us."

A car cruised by—a stereo on wheels. Cranked banda-brass cut like a knife while the heavy, low-end vibrated the storefront windows.

"Yeah, well." Al pounded Black on the back with affection. Rattling bones. "Let me grab you a couple dogs." He lifted the counter and disappeared into the back.

"So who's winning?" Black asked.

Scottie grinned. "Man, I got this!" His fingers flew even faster, showing off.

Black sat on the narrow excuse for a bumper on a black Escalade. Loaner from the DOD. He looked out from the alley behind Big Al's Hot Doggery through the embrace of brick walls dressed in graffiti, like two sleeves of colorful tats.

At first glance, *a really quick glance,* it might pass as Mexico. Rich, saturated colors on every wall. Streets lined with stalls and food carts selling pink clouds of cotton candy, ice-cold Horchata and fruity, neon-colored Licuados. Stores proudly displayed rows of colorful quinceañera dresses on wire manikins along the sidewalks. Music blared from every direction on over-taxed and under-powered speakers—norteño, banda, mariachi, and son jalisco.

The lush black hair of the women and the razor-cut fades of the men were right. Jeans and pointed boots and straw cowboy hats in place. Storefronts and street signs in Spanish.

The first things out of place were the jackets, scarves, and gloves many of the people wore. On closer look, the rosy cheeks and red noses, along with breath condensing in the cold were giveaways.

Black hated cold growing up. Winter had been a bitter knife that cut through the thin, worn-out sweaters and jackets his mother scrounged at Goodwill or the shelters. The clothes made him shiver in shame as well as the cold until Al and his family had brought him in, and given him a home with roaring fires and warm cider and hot chocolate.

Having traveled much of the world, usually somewhere along the equator in full combat gear, and with a couple of extended tours in the desert, he now found he enjoyed the refreshing bite of frost carried on the Chicago wind. The cold rode on currents from the north, across Lake Michigan, and between the towering giants of the Loop into the neighborhoods. It slid past the leather bomber jacket and through his cotton t-shirt. Early winter and he wasn't dressed for it, but Chicago was just a quick stop on his way to warmer lands.

The Windy City—the nickname's origins still argued over by etymologists and linguistic historians pointing to blow hard, pontificating politicians, braggadocio citizens touting the relief of summer breezes during stifling Midwest summers as a way to attract industry, or bone-chilling air racing from the north across the massive lakes and funneled through the downtown's narrow alleys.

The Great Lakes were at least a *sea* in Black's definitions of bodies of water. Twenty percent of the world's freshwater, including the ice caps of both poles. A place of mystery growing up, a hint to the boy that other lands waited to be discovered far beyond the horizon.

He'd petitioned his seventh-grade science teacher in an oral report that they should change the name to the Great Seas.

"Give me your reasons," she had asked.

"Twenty-five-foot waves, oil tankers and pirates ships. They have tides. I know they're small, but they have 'em! And they have seagulls! *Seagulls!* Who are we to argue with Mother Nature?"

Impressed with his facts but not enough to lobby Congress or anything. "So how would you define the various bodies of water?"

"Simple," he said. "A puddle you can step across. A pond you can skip a rock across. A lake you can swim across. A sea you take a boat across. And an ocean—" *it was almost too big to imagine,* "you have to fly across."

"Nice try," she said. She gave him a '*B*' for his research and an '*A +*' for creativity.

It was at lunch, when bigger classmates, the entire backfield of the junior varsity including the quarterback made fun of him, '*they have pirates and seagulls,*' that Tommy got himself suspended.

Black was savoring the hot dogs. He tried to count the versions he'd had around the world. Quickly gave up. Deceptively simple, the Chicago dog stood above the rest in his book. Fifteen thousand on-line reviews of Big Al's Hot Doggery said he was right.

The snap of the natural casing surrounded the all-beef dog dragged through the garden—sweet pickle relish contrasted with crisp dill pickle, pickled peppers, fresh tomatoes and pure, yellow-mustard sprinkled with celery salt, flooded his mouth with flavor and made him smile even as the two men entered the alley and wobbled his direction.

High on something, mellowing their buzz with tall-boys in hand. One fingered his side under his jacket, and both locked on Black like a homing beacon.

Easy money. The gringo was stupid enough to be alone, munching away on gringo food, sitting on the bumper of a gringo truck.

Nicolás was feeling good. The crank still fresh in his system, and though they were out of beer, their next twelve-pack was sitting right in front of them. Maybe dinner too. A nice truck. *Maybe they should take the keys?* Probably give it to them when he saw the knife. Mateo would argue against it. Too much trouble. Too much heat. *Fuck Mateo.* Then again, he just wanted the beer and maybe some pussy.

Mateo finished his beer and drop-kicked the can. It rattled down the alley toward the gringo. Who the hell was this to be sitting in their alley? But then, what the fuck? Even cops didn't give a shit when tourists were this stupid. Pretty much like a withdrawal at the ATM.

"Hey, hombre. Whatcha doing here?" Mateo stepped to the left, a practiced dance with his partner.

"This our street, my friend," Nicolás explained.

Black took a bite of his second dog. It might have been even better than the first.

"Okay."

"Okay? Okay is you owe us money," Nicolás offered.

"Tribute, holmes," Mateo said.

"Okay."

Nicolás took a step to the right, watch his partner do his thing. Looked at the gringo eating his hot dog. Sometimes, they got a look in their eyes when they realized they were in serious trouble.

The gringo didn't seem too concerned yet, but maybe he wasn't getting it.

Black thought he might have to go for another dog. Dinner was a few hours off. Probably pizza with the guys. One thing he'd learned, you took advantage of wherever you found yourself in the world. *And when in Chicago—*

Mateo put a little bass in his voice. Nicolás always found it funny, but it usually worked.

"So cough it up."

Yeah, Black thought. He could probably wait till dinner.

"Okay."

"Okay?" Mateo waited but nothing was happening. "What the fuck? You gonna pay us or what?"

Nicolás fingered the knife, figured he better step in. Maybe the gringo was simple or something. He had a cousin that way.

"This our street, man. You gotta pay up."

Black finished the hot dog. Definitely better than the first. *Damn...* he forgot to get a napkin.

He licked the tips of his fingers. "Sure."

A car started into the alley. Saw the three men in front of them. Two wired as though they were hooked to a car battery, another guy hanging out on the bumper of a huge SUV that blocked the alley. They tried to back up. A horn from the street blasted from behind and startled them. Made them wait.

"This fucking guy is whacked."

Mateo nodded and turned toward the car.

Black watched the two clowns go to either side of the car. The driver glanced at his wife, oblivious, ear to her phone. He was trying to back out but traffic stood still behind him. Everyone in a hurry to get to the next round of lights and continue the crawl. An extra thirty-seconds would be unacceptable.

A train roared from nearby. Steel on steel, the echoes filled all available space and made it impossible to hear what was being said.

Black watched the scene play out like a silent novella. He'd already rated the seriousness on the same level.

Taking charge, Nicolás lifted his jacket to reveal a small buck knife on his belt. The driver scrambled for his wallet, and Black felt for him when he turned to his wife and she rolled her eyes. The man, fighting his panic, said something. She stared at him, shook her head, and finally dug into her purse. Handed a few bills to her husband and returned to her call.

The man paid Nicolás who grinned at Mateo. *This is how it's done motherfucker!*

Withdrawal made, they turned to Black. Sauntered back, feeling their power. Determined.

Nicolás was sobering up. "Okay, man. Cough it up."

"Sure."

Nicolás pulled the knife. "Dude! You see I got a knife?"

"Yep."

"Yep?"

"Sure."

Mateo was pissed. "Motherfucker. What you mean sure?"

"*'Sure'* is I'm not gonna pay you dudes, motherfuckers, hombres."

Nicolás waved the knife. "I swear my God—fuckin' cut you, man!"

Black stared at him.

Nicolás shivered. *Goddammit!* This wasn't going well at all.

Finally—

"Man, give me your jacket!"

It *is* a nice jacket, Mateo thought. Brown leather. Some kind of military patches. Pretty cool.

"Yeah, holmes. Give us the coat."

Black pushed off from the back of the Escalade. Wadded up the wax paper from the dogs and pushed it into Mateo's coat pocket. Mateo open-mouthed.

Nicolás couldn't believe the disrespect. "What the fuck?"

He slashed the knife backhanded at Black. The blade should have opened his throat. Maybe sliced his hands or arms if he got them up quickly enough.

Too fast to see, *certainly too fast for Nicolás and Mateo,* Black grabbed Nicolás' hand and snatched the knife. He twisted the man's fingers backward until the wannabe gangster was up on his toes, then slammed his forearm into the man's face.

Nicolás heard his nose break at the same time tendons tore and bones cracked in his hand, the pain and shock too great to scream.

Black let him go. Nicolás fell to his knees and clutched his face, gasping for air and choking on blood. He looked at his hand, fingers ruined and twisted, already ballooning into something unrecognizable.

Black spun and stabbed the cheap blade into the brick wall beside Mateo's head. The knife snapped in two, slicing through the banger's ear as it bounced off.

Mateo felt the warm blood running from his ear down the side of his neck but was afraid to move. He looked from his partner into Black's eyes. Blue shifting to gray. Expressionless until he smiled.

Mateo thought it was the scariest thing he'd ever seen.

CHAPTER
TWO

The huge Denali pickup bullied its way off the expressway. The towering architectural wonders of the Loop were to the north, holding up the low-lying clouds blanketing the city.

Here, there were no luxury hotels, no high-end shopping plazas nor Broadway-style theaters. Fine dining, overpriced chophouses, and roof-tops with table cloths and fine china overlooking the river were traded for occasional rib tips, or thawed fish fried in recycled canola oil and served on wax paper.

Institutions could still be found, like Rocky's Pancake House, where you could buy a set of tires, one-hundred-fifty dollars for four at the counter on your way out, but a Miracle Mile was far too short a distance for its wealth and affluence to touch neighbor-hoods like Auburn-Gresham, Chatham, and Englewood.

Part vibrant, historical community, and for those who lived in it, part war-zone. Hyde Park and the former President's house were shouting distance away, but in the past few years, it was not uncommon for fifty to sixty people to get shot over a weekend. A long, three-day holiday could double that and would make national news. Like other mass shootings, headlines quickly replaced and forgotten.

Hospital trauma teams worked overtime in the summer months when, to escape the oppressive heat, people sat with friends and family on their porches or made themselves easy targets along the streets, but this was early winter, when people huddled inside and were mostly unseen.

It was still early afternoon. The pick-up rode under sagging, wet blankets of sky devoid of color, poverty so great they couldn't even afford the gray. A hint of flurries danced in the air, and slush from the week's early cold snap lay along the curb.

Dillon slowed the truck. Checked addresses against the clipboard on the console. His truck, three years old, was still worth more than many of the houses. Strange neighborhoods, strange times. A house might be old but immaculately kept, yard tended, shutters freshly painted, a wreath on the door, or an occasional Christmas tree in the window. Their neighbors' homes might be decorated with plywood nailed over windows, graffiti and gang tags on the walls, garbage, and trash instead of grass.

Cars were dominated by ten and fifteen-year-old Toyotas and Hondas, painted in sun blistered blues and faded reds, rocker panels of rusted lace. Add a few oversized monuments to the days when Detroit muscle and luxury were king spread down the streets, but none worth restoring. Mismatched tires and hubcaps the norm. Many sat on dry rotted tires or concrete blocks.

He found the house he was looking for in relatively good shape. Boards protecting the windows, grass brown and patchy under the first snows, but cut short in anticipation for the long winter. Roof patched, garbage picked up. A realtor's lock box on the doorknob and a bank notice taped to the door.

With plenty of parking space to be found on streets cracked and cratered with potholes, some so legendary, children looked forward to summer rains to use them as swimming holes, he rolled to a stop in the nearly frozen trash along the curb.

A woman, just a stick figure even under the fake fur, scarves, and mittens, dragged two children alongside the baby carriage she pushed over the sidewalk. The front-wheel wobbled back and forth, like every grocery cart Dillon had ever pushed, and he sat watching it chatter back and forth like a demented bobble-head until they turned the corner and disappeared.

Dillon, double-checked the address against his list. No real need with the bank notice on the door, but others could be seen along the street that had the same treatment.

He grabbed his little compact camera, shoved it into his pocket. Opened the glove box. Inside, a police-issued Glock 22. As he reached for it, his phone rang.

Took a deep breath to steel himself for what he knew was coming and tapped to answer on his Bluetooth headset.

"Yeah, baby."

Each second of the scratchy voice on the other side carved new lines of disappointment across his once handsome face. He forced himself to listen as long as he could, penance for misdeeds in a former life some might say, though he had plenty to pay for in this one.

He pulled the little device from his ear, dropped it on the seat next to him. Stared through the fogged windshield at the street beyond while the high-pitched buzz of the miniature speaker, like a demonic ant, continued to scream at him.

Outside the truck, a paper cup rolled across the street, jumped the curb and stopped, gathered its strength and cut across the yard, an urban tumbleweed determined to find a better neighborhood.

Dillon watched it, wondering how far it had come and where it might go. Wishing he could go with it. Remembering a time when it seemed he might travel wherever the winds would take him.

Suck it up, Buttercup. Lie down and die or get your goat smelling ass up and move!

He turned off the engine, silenced the little speaker in mid-scream, flipped the door shut on the glove box, and dragged himself out the truck. Pressed the key fob to set the alarm.

The cold was welcome after the sweltering summer. Real winter wouldn't come for a few more weeks, after Christmas and New Years. Last year's was mild, temps averaging in the twenties, but Dillon knew they were due for another apocalyptic, *Day After Tomorrow* winter. Where giant lake-waves froze in mid-air, massive ice-breaker ships were brought in from the arctic to free up the lake's shipping lanes, and multi-story icicles created fantastic crystal landscapes along the coast.

He banged on the door. No answer. Not supposed to be, but you never knew. He listened. Nothing, except the rumble of distant trains carried on the crisp wind.

He worked the combination on the realtor's lock, took out the key.

Opened the door, calling out as he entered, "Anyone in here?" Locked the door behind him. Turned back to the small house. Weak shafts of sunlight struggled through the boarded-up windows, staining the murky room in mottled shadow.

"Hello? Anyone home?" He flipped the light switch to make sure the electricity was cut. An empty house with live wires could be hijacked and power the neighborhood. Checked it off his list.

Dillon moved to the corner. Took a pic. Nothing artsy. The flash fired long enough to show the mildewed walls still standing. Dillon moved to the opposite corner. Snapped another photo.

Moved to the kitchen.

Tried the light switches, double-checked for gas at the stove. Turned on the faucets. Pipes rattled from somewhere outside and then under the floors and through the walls until water sputtered into the stainless double sink. Dillon adjusted it to let the water drip. Made a note. Opened the refrigerator and gagged on the smell, fighting not to retch. A half-empty gallon jug of water, a couple of cheap beers, and some kind of unidentifiable food that had doubled or tripled its mass under the weight of a multi-colored garden of mold.

Dillon took a photo—real invasion of the body snatchers stuff. Afraid to disturb the alien experiment in case it jumped out at him, he gingerly closed the refrigerator door.

He snapped a couple of angles of the little kitchen. Made his notes.

Dillon was on his way to the back when he heard the sound.

His hand was slipping past his jacket and going for his gun even before he tried to decipher it. *Shit!* Still in the truck.

He paused mid-stride. Cocked his head to listen. There! A rhythmic *thump, thump, thump.*

"Hello? This is the bank," Dillon shouted. "Nobody s'posed to be in here. If someone's here, show yourself."

The sound continued. He should have left then. Walked to his truck, grabbed his gun, or called the police.

He'd never live it down if his six-foot-four, two hundred-eighty pounds of African-American veteran cop called for backup on a loose shutter or family of squirrels. *Fuck it—*

He moved the police badge from the side of his belt to the front. "This is the police. Come out now."

Dillon stepped through piss-colored streams of light leaking from the windows in the back.

Listened. There! The sound continued. *Goddammit!*

Dillon pulled out his phone, turned the flashlight app on.

Stepped carefully. Stopped in an intersection of doorways. Pushed one open. Linen closet. Let out a deep breath. *Christ!* Hadn't realized he'd been holding it. He let his chest heave and expand, tried to slow it down. *Remember your training.* Let your diaphragm do the work. Slow your heart. Eight years military, fourteen on the Chicago Police Department.

What the fuck am I doing out here?

Making money for his daughter's wedding. Gonna happen soon. Making sure he could cover his share and more. Just because his ex remarried a couple of steps up didn't mean it wasn't his to do. And the crazy girlfriend, and the— *Focus motherfucker!*

He pushed open another door. The stench of a bathroom without working pipes. Plastic buckets in the tub for piss and shit. The acrid smell made his eyes water, and he shoved the door closed.

Thump... thump... thump... and now, low and underneath it, picking up steam, *uhhhhh.... uhhhhhh... uhhhhh...*

Jesus Christ! In this fucking shithole? *It sounded exactly like—*

Dillon took a breath, shoved open the last door. The room was black. Sound intensified. He lifted the phone's light.

A rail-thin black man, arms corded in wasting muscle and a relief map of veins was hanging on to a tall wooden dresser across the room. His naked torso shone from exertion in the phone's light, his pants bunched at his ankles, his lips white with a froth of foam like a racehorse coming down the stretch.

He grunted and humped away on the wooden dresser, slamming his pelvis into it.

Dillon slowly stepped backward on the creaking floor. The crazed man jerked his head up, startled from the light but on a five-second delay. As crazed and bloodshot as any Hollywood zombie movie, his eyes locked on Dillon. Both men frozen until—

The man grabbed for a gun and threw the dresser aside with near-superhuman strength. Stood just feet away from Dillon—naked, his wilting erection a raw mass of bleeding flesh, pus weeping eyes impossibly wide, gun outstretched and aimed at Dillon.

Jabbed the gun at Dillon. Gestured toward the overturned dresser. "MINE!"

Too late to run, Dillon dropped his phone and charged. The man stepped forward to meet it but stumbled on his pants and fell into Dillon's arms. Dillon's big hands grabbed for the gun, tried to wrestle it away. The man twisted and turned but held on. Jacked on adrenalin, Dillon pounded the man's face with one hand while trying to control the gun with the other.

Dillon dwarfed the other man, but his attacker was amped on drugs and insanity. They crashed into the wall, smashing deep into the drywall.

BANG! The gunshot lit up the room and startled them both, tore into the ceiling. *BANG BANG!* Super-heated gas and gunpowder scorched both their faces.

The man's head was just inches away, and Dillon realized in horror, the man was trying to bite him—the foul breath warm on his skin—the broken teeth grazing him and trying to rip flesh from his face.

Dillon spun with his full, two hundred-eighty pounds to slam the man into the wall. Again. Lifted him and smashed his head into the low ceiling, and then back against the wall.

Something cracked inside the man. Dillon could feel more than hear it, and the man went limp.

He kept hold of the gun, and let the naked rag-doll drop at his feet.

He staggered outside, almost made it to the truck before he dropped to his knees. Fell onto his back. Tried to breathe. Let his heart slow from a million beats per minute to a thousand. Suck it up, Buttercup.

Dillon opened his eyes and stared at the featureless sky, letting the flurries rest on his eyelashes. Let his tears and emotion wash over him, then rolled over to purge the rush of adrenaline and throw up.

Gun still in his hand, he backed away on all fours and made it to his feet. Bent back over to allow his knees to catch up. Watched his breath take shape beneath him. Looked up at two little boys across the street, bundled against the cold. Staring at him.

He made it to his truck. It took a couple of tries to get the key in, and a couple more to get it started.

CHAPTER
THREE

She lay on the luxurious bedding, reveling at the feel of thousand-thread-count Egyptian cotton.

Her smooth, dark skin in contrast to the arctic white of the rich duvet—her long, thick mane spread like a headdress across the pillow. Dared herself to close her eyes ten seconds and not fall asleep.

"Get up. Get up. Get up!"

She groaned and rolled from the bed determined to kill her friend but grabbed a glass of champagne and pushed past the delicately embroidered sheers to the balcony. The breeze felt as inviting and luxurious as the sheets. She gasped as she stood by her friend and took in the view.

"I know, right?" Two girls—one dark and one light—both beautiful, looked in awe at the night draped above the endless Indian Ocean. The gentlest of waves lapped at the beach, while the ocean beyond reflected the moon and a million points of starlight unfiltered by man's hand.

"I mean, it has to be the same one right?"

Billie was so sincere and the moon did seem massive, but Sam had to laugh.

"Yeah. Pretty sure there's only one."

"Well, maybe we're closer or something out here," Billie said.

Sam smiled. "Yeah. Maybe."

Sam clinked her glass with Billie's. Returned to the sky.

"I think the moon is the same distance. The stars seem closer because the air is cleaner," Sam said. She pointed to the Southern hemisphere's most famous constellation.

"That's the Acrux—Alpha Crucis. And that part?" Billie tried to follow her finger. "Those five are the Southern Cross. See that one? It's one of the youngest in the whole galaxy, and the closest star to our planet. Alpha Centauri."

"Wow." Billie shook her head in awe and then confusion. "Is the moon upside down?"

"Sure is! Almost. It's because compared to our position back home, we're upside down."

"Crazy!"

"And that point of light, right there, is Jupiter. And I think that one's Saturn."

"The crazy part is how you know everything," Billie said.

Sam shook her head and laughed. "Not everything. But I know I love you." The two girls bumped foreheads.

They looked at the sky. "They look like diamonds," Sam said.

"Speaking of—" Billie held up a pair of diamond pendant earrings. "Wear these tonight."

"Really? They're beautiful."

"You're beautiful," Billie said.

"Do you think he'll ask?"

Billie laughed. "Come on. You know he will!"

Sam bit her lip. "He better or you're sleeping with me tonight."

"Don't tease me, Sam."

The two girls kissed lightly and giggled.

"Yeah, right. As if you'd give up hard dick for a night. Plus, you kick like a mule!"

Billie laughed. "Okay then. Hard dick it is!"

Billie downed her champagne and stepped inside to retrieve the bottle. Filled both their glasses. They touched glasses and leaned out over the balcony. The parking lot and the beach beyond five stories below.

"This is all so delicious. I can't believe we're here!" Billie said.

"Your mom's cool—what did your dad say?"

"About shacking up with Allan on a tropical island for a week? Get fucking real."

"I like him."

"Allan or my dad?"

Billie laughed. The delight so genuine, it would be hard for anyone not to fall in love. But this was Sam's night, and she glowed with happiness.

"Both," Billie said. "Not at the same time or anything. Your dad is way too macho for that!"

Sam laughed. "You're incorrigible." She glanced across the balcony and Billie followed her eyes.

Two rooms over, a handsome man with a drink in hand, leaned on his balcony. Sam guessed him to be about forty. He had a head of thick blond hair above an unlined face that looked like it spent a lot of time outdoors. He was fit—an athlete she guessed or maybe even a model. His defined jaw softened with a small smile of open appreciation for the two girls.

It was when he raised his glass in a silent toast to them that Sam thought his eyes, gun-metal blue, looked cruel and predatory.

Both she and Billie raised their glasses to return the toast as a woman stepped out to join him. *Truly stunning,* Sam thought. Early twenties, mixed-race like herself, and the best of both. Her naked arms long and graceful as were her hands and neck. The dress she wore, French couture—as if she had just stepped off the runway. She had no need for the elegant jewelry she wore to draw the eye across every curve and line.

She leaned over the balcony. Further. Even further. Sam held her breath as it looked like the woman might fall.

The man dragged her back, his strong fingers digging past faint bruises on her arm, and forced her close. He crushed his lips to hers, never taking his eyes off of Sam. The woman gave no response or reaction until finally, he pushed her away.

She glanced at the girls with eyes so sad and hopeless, Sam felt her heart stop and had to tell herself to make it beat again.

The stunning young woman went back inside. The man finished his drink and followed her in.

Both girls shivered. "Creepy," Billie said.

CHAPTER
FOUR

The truck sat on the street in the coming dark. To the right, a large church. Iron gates and gray stone. A few steps leading to a huge red double-door. Stained glass in most of the windows, colored Plexiglas replacing broken panes. Closed now, but on Sundays, it could be a place of comfort and the singing inside a joyous celebration.

To the left, two floors of brick townhomes along two blocks of manicured lawn. A virtual oasis of Section 8 housing surrounded by crumbling infrastructure and burned-out homes. Three blocks down was an abandoned school, five blocks up was an abandoned city. Boarded-up stores and beauty salons, sealed-off office buildings and storefronts, and banks with entire walls and roofs missing.

This was a land that time forgot. A casualty of the civil rights movements of the sixties, raped by outside political expediency and inside corruption. Whored out as a shining example and then buried in embarrassment as the failures of colonial expansionism were brought to light, and eyes once again turned inward.

Industry and hope moved on, leaving the older residents to wonder why their country had abandoned them, and the younger with seething anger and resentment of authority to be both tempered and fueled by drugs and violence and passed on to their children.

No movement in the pick-up, but at another angle, someone might have noticed the vaguely human-shaped shadow behind the fogged windows.

Dillon stared out, seeing nothing. If asked, he wouldn't have had any idea how he got here, or how long he'd been sitting in the cold. The last thing he remembered was throwing up and looking up at two little boys bundled in matching snowsuits, oblivious to their runny noses, standing across the street and staring at him.

The truck was cold, but he didn't feel it. His breath condensed in thick clouds, but he couldn't see them.

He watched himself through the eyes of the little boys. A big man, doubled over, clutching his chest and desperately trying to catch his breath. The man staggered, tried to steady himself. Raised his eyes, looking right at him.

Dillon—*the boy*—was frozen in place. Shaking. He couldn't understand what was wrong with the man. Why he couldn't move, couldn't shout, couldn't run for help? Why was he here? *Watching him?*

He turned to the boy standing beside him. Felt a silent scream bubble up from somewhere inside—*the little boy was gone and in his place was now his sister.* Her tears ran as freely as his own, snot dripping from her nose. Riveted on the man. Their small feet rooted to the ground.

Dillon, the boy, looked back at Dillon, the man. Across the street, and yet the boy could see his reflection in the man's eyes. Felt the man's tears as his own, running down his cheeks. Felt his little chest tighten as a fist clenched and crushed his heart. Felt his view dim while he watched the light fade from the man's eyes. The big man lost strength, and fell face-first to the ground.

Dillon watched again as his father died in their front yard from a heart attack. Forty-two years old, a year younger than Dillon was now. Dillon seven and his sister nine. Too young to understand. Too scared to do anything but hide.

It took two days to find them. Alone and dehydrated and nearly frozen to death in an abandoned house.

Clutching each other, terrified and convinced they must have done something so wrong, so terrible, God had taken their father away.

A determined pounding. A deep, muffled thud... *thwump thwump thwump.* Dillon tried to resist it. He just wanted to sleep. *Thwump thwump thwump.*

It took all his will to open his eyes. Tried and failed. Maybe one eye at a time. Left or right? *Suck it up Buttercup.*

Okay, okay. Left eye. A bit of light. The windshield opaque with frost. Crystallized abstracts beyond. If he could capture that view exactly as it was, he could probably sell it for a fortune. *Fugue State Number One.*

Right eye—*open!* The blocks beyond lit with a single working street light over the entrance to the abandoned school.

Turned his head to the right. Glanced at the church. Dark. Gates locked. No redemption offered or comfort given. *Thwump thwump thwump.* Turned his head to the left. *Thwump thwump thwump.* His girlfriend, Rina, face distorted in rage, phone in one hand, banging on the window.

"You don't hear me calling you, motherfucker? What the fuck is your problem?"

Oh, just sitting out here watching my pops die again. For the billionth time in my life. Dillon turned back to the front. Closed his eyes.

"Oh, no you don't! Where the fuck you been? You know what time it is?"

If he kept them closed, she'd go away, right?

"You gonna ignore me? I've been calling four fuckin' hours!"

She banged the glass with her phone to emphasize her point.

"You s'posed to drop me off at the motherfuckin' church, and now you gonna just sit out here and do what? What the fuck you doing? Jerking off with some trash-bag hoe on your phone?"

Dillon's low, weary voice carried through the glass. "Not now, baby."

"Not now, *baby?*" She beat on the glass, hurt her hand, and kicked at the door. "We need some groceries up in this mother-fucker. I'm home all day, you leave your goddamned socks and underwear on the floor? You s'posed to be some bad-ass cop, and I got to pick up after you like a motherfuckin' child?"

Dillon opened his eyes and looked at her. Screaming in rage, mouth impossibly wide, voice fading.

"You better open this fuckin' window and talk to me!"

Flecks of spittle gathered at the corners of her mouth. Front tooth chipped, but she wouldn't get it fixed. Thought it made her look tough. Give her some kind of cred in the clubs with the other bitches. *Yeah, sure.* Real tough, he thought. Sloppy drunk and slipped on the stairs to bust her mouth.

Who the fuck wanted a sloppy drunk snaggletooth bitch?

She kicked the door again. Dillon let his eyes drift toward his hands. Both shaking but one with the cheap-ass gun he had taken from the zombified crack head. *What a piece of shit.* Grips cracked. Cheap finish scraped and scratched. Rust eating the barrel. Looked like it had been cleaned exactly never.

"You know what? Fuck you! I ain't even movin' till you get your fat ass out here and act like a man."

Dillon rolled down the window.

She stared at him. He stared back but saw nothing. *Heard nothing. Felt nothing.*

"You gonna sit there like some pussy-ass motherfucker?"

She spat at him.

He lifted the gun and shot her in the face.

CHAPTER
FIVE

The music pounded under the shamanistic power of the DJ. He held the writhing bodies under his spell; twisting, turning, pushing, and pulling their passions for and against each other into a transcendental frenzy. Lights flashed, strobed, and danced in time to multi-colored lasers crisscrossing man-made fog. Expensive designer fabrics and smooth, sun-drenched skin slid against each other, the friction of sexual tension and wanton abandonment multiplying in the tropical heat.

Sam's gyrations were comparatively innocent and that much more enticing because of it. She turned from Billie, and danced her way toward the perimeter of the dance floor; the two men keeping their eyes glued to her every undulation.

Hunter, a former triple-A outfielder, shoulders and forearms showcasing his former talents while his midsection hinted at the three years absent from the field, nudged his friend Allan.

"Don't think you're getting out of this one, buddy."

Allan grinned. "Who'd want to?"

Sam slipped past the bodies on the dance floor and reached for Allan. Hunter downed his drink and headed for Billie. Allan pretended reluctance and made Sam work to drag him into the pulsing crowd.

The music magically shifted and the dance floor, a single collective organism, adjusted with it. Billie was grinding her ass into Hunter who did his best to hang on and match her rhythms.

Sam moved into Allan, reveling in her power without knowing she had it. She loved the look of lust and utter puppy dog devotion in his eyes. Thick blond locks, always errant, like a Kennedy or Redford, tumbled over his brow, dripping sweat onto tanned cheeks that in turn ran in rivulets past a squared jaw and onto a broad chest. The face of a powerful Wall Street broker or future Congressman for sure, and with the current Mayor of one of Connecticut's wealthiest towns for a father, the path to politics his for the wanting.

His dancing was somewhere just north of spastic dad-dance and like the same, oblivious to his lack of rhythmic ability. She thought he was the sexiest thing she'd ever seen.

The hostess felt naked, the man's eyes stripping her already skimpy costume, roaming and probing each cleft and curve. Her job three nights a week the past four months, she was making more keeping her clothes on here than she did taking them off in New York's high-end strip clubs.

Now she spent her days immersing herself in Creole culture, and diving among the splendid coral reefs while letting the memories of the abusive asshole she left behind with a kitchen knife and forty stitches in his chest fade from her life. She felt violated for the first time since moving here. A thousand bodies gyrating gigawatts of energy around her, and still, she felt a shiver as she opened two more emerald bottles of Krüg Grand for the table.

Christiaan Kronmüller openly eyed the girl. The more he took in, the more his hand dug into Lina's leg.

She didn't wince, not so much used to the pain itself as to the idea of being in pain when she was with him. He was a cruel man in many ways and yet would have been surprised to find that she found him so.

She turned from the embarrassed hostess to the three girls fawning and draping themselves over the two men Christiaan had invited. Though she was only two or three years older, she couldn't think of them as anything but girls.

Not prostitutes, but certainly pros at working men around their fingers, trading sex for high-end parties, drugs and expensive champagne, high-end fashion, and fast cars.

And what the hell, the sex might have even been good, if sometimes rough and a bit one-sided. They knew nothing of love and so had little to compare it to except earlier fumblings at romance without the current benefits from entertaining powerful gangsters.

Lina didn't know the men, though she had seen the one with the badly healed scar above his eye once before at the ranch. The other was new to her, but had the same brutish manner expected with Christiaan's friends.

The hostess looked away from the man's gaze and took in the rope-like muscles of his forearm, flexing, and contracting with effort. Though she couldn't see his hand under the edge of the table, she could feel his grip on the woman's leg as if it were her own. Afraid of seeing herself in the abused woman's eyes, she finished filling glasses and left them behind, shuddering as she left.

Kronmüller, unfulfilled, watched her leave, his hand squeezing hard enough to make Lina cry out. Inflicting physical pain, in this case, to the woman he loved, was as pleasurable as stroking himself. It was just a little pain, not as if he'd flayed the skin from her back or sliced off her breasts.

Lina was the love of his life. He would never abuse her in those ways. He dreamed of starting a family, children to hold and love, his woman by his side, hand in hand taking on the African bushveld.

Lina pushed away, sliding along the plush leather sofa. "Excuse me. I'll be right back," she said.

"Don't be long," Kronmüller said. She started to reply, stopped herself, nodded, and slid off the seat.

His eyed followed her as she cut across the dance floor. Nodded to another table where two huge men watched his every move.

They nodded back, and surprisingly graceful for men the size of small tankers, rose to follow her.

The crowd parted for them in time to the music, moving out of the way to avoid being crushed.

Kronmüller kept his eyes on her until he caught a glimpse of the two girls seen earlier from his balcony. One blond and blue-eyed, her figure on open display and gyrating in a wanton display of sexuality. Grinding, thrusting, slamming her hips back and forth in a jackhammer parody of the wild sex she was certainly hoping to find later in the night.

He dismissed her as quickly as the other five-hundred women on the dance floor. But the other—*mixed-blood*—he thought. Like Lina, her European features softened by African heritage, the figure generous in enviable proportions, her color a deep pecan independent of the sun.

Whereas Lina, the love of his life, was a woman, this was still a *girl*. He drank her in until the crowd flowed back into the wake his bodyguards left behind.

Lina ignored the gaggle of women in the restroom. A huge, single mirror spanned the full width of the room above spotless marble sinks where Lina stared at her reflection.

Here, unlike the reds and orange beams shining across the textured walls of the stalls, and the flattering club lighting over the massive floor to ceiling mirrors on either side of the doors, the light was bright and pure, *daylight spectrum,* allowing the women to touch themselves up beneath the most critical eyes.

Lina tried to control her shaking, brought it down to a barely perceptible tremble. Looked into her own eyes, and tried to enter the looking glass. Willed it so. Felt her grandmother's spirit calling her. Could feel the pull and embrace, *was almost there—*

"You don't have to stay with him."

Lina looked at Billie standing beside her, looking back at her in the mirror. Her lips quivered, and she tried to cover by reaching for her lipstick. As the color slid across her lush lips, Sam reached out to reassure her but stopped when she saw the fresh bruises.

"We'll help you get away. You don't have to stay with him. We'll help you. My boyfriend has powerful connections, political connections, and we'll help you, I promise."

Their eyes connected in the mirror.

Sam's full of hope and promise. Lina's frozen in acceptance and despair. Lina smiled sadly and walked away.

Sam bit her lip and looked to Billie and shrugged.

Billie looked back at her in the mirror, replacing her reflection with the afterimage of the sad, elegant woman. She had a flash of Sam in the same position of torment and fought the tears the vision brought to her eyes.

The two girls hugged each other and went back to the club.

The bartender slid the double Ciroc Ten vodka across the polished concrete bar. Kronmüller intercepted it as Lina reached for it. He gulped it down and shoved her into Ringer, one of his massive, tanker-sized bodyguards.

Billie slipped past them, crashed into Kronmüller, dumped a full glass of red wine down his thousand-dollar shirt. Gave him her most innocent smile. "I'm *so* sorry—"

"Bitch!" Kronmüller shoved her away.

The other tanker ship, Grip, grabbed her arm and jerked her back, pulling her off her feet and pinning her arms.

Kronmüller started forward when Sam stepped in and slapped him. Even before she registered his reaction, he slapped her back, spinning her head and knocking her to the floor.

A huge security guard, even bigger than the two bodyguards but noticeably softer, started across the floor. He caught the eyes of his boss and was waved off.

Lina broke away from Grip and knelt to help the American girl up.

"You're in danger," she whispered. "Leave this place now."

Sam let Lina help her to her feet.

Ringer shoved Billie at Hunter who caught her in his arms and pulled her behind him as Allan stepped toward Kronmüller.

"Who the hell do you think—" Grip slammed him in the gut, knocking the wind out of him. Allan staggered to his knees, gasping, fighting for air.

Hunter started forward but was almost pulled off his feet as Billie frantically jerked him back. He took in the two massive bodyguards, thought better of it, and let himself be pulled back into her arms.

Sam did her best to help Allan, still struggling to breathe, to his feet.

Kronmüller reached for Lina, grabbed her by the arm, and pulled her to him. Sam lurched forward, spitting at the man.

Lina looked back at her, a look Sam would later play over and over again in slow motion, the beautiful face composed, but eyes brimming with infinite sadness.

CHAPTER
SIX

Mike Jimenez had been a homicide detective for exactly seven weeks. A single day before his partner, Jack Crawley accepted his own promotion.

They'd been tasked with their second slaying, a cut-and-dried domestic that was turning out to be anything but, already on track to break the annual average caseload of four homicides that each of the city's one hundred homicide detectives would try to solve. An impossible equation illustrated by their official arrest rates in less than a fifth of those cases. Convictions an embarrassingly smaller percentage still.

Federal task forces and university academic studies had tried to understand why Chicago's closure rates were so low, and conclusions were mixed. Growing violence, increased disparity of wealth and the mistrust of authority, further fragmentation of gang structure, and growing competition for a dwindling pie of illicit drug profits. Add in social media posturing, access to cheap weapons, political party finger-pointing, systemic racism, and the complexities increased exponentially.

Jimenez was now looking at their third case. A teenage boy lying across the sidewalk and front yard of a small, Southside bungalow. Thirteen—fourteen. A fresh pair of Jordan Black Cement on his feet. Stick-and-poke ink on the back of his neck proclaiming his gang affiliations.

The trail of blood splatter twenty feet away, a stripe the last ten feet of sidewalk up to and under his body told the probable story of being hit in a targeted drive-by, staggering under the onslaught, then crawling toward his house. At least three entry wounds in his back—they'd maybe find more when they turned him over.

Broken windows of a car in the driveway with two ragged lines of bullet holes in the passenger side from two separate streams of fire. Assault styled semi-automatics confirmed from dozens of 9mm shells left sparkling on the dirty street. It was doubtful forensics and an autopsy would add anything new.

A woman was wailing nearby and being comforted by neighbors who somehow had seen absolutely nothing. Three young boys, visibly shaken but fronting, doing their best to look tough and hardened even with the tears in their eyes, stood across the street watching the police and their every move.

Crawley approached a potential witness, an inconsolable twelve-year-old girl who was quickly surrounded and silenced by family and friends.

First on scene, their case whether they wanted it or not. The ambulance and a half-dozen other police cars visible, speeding in from opposite directions. Emergency lights and sirens flashed and blared. People on the sidewalks and yards came from houses along the block, many to gawk and stare, others on cell phones and filming, determined to catch the police doing something they could share across the social media networks.

Police jumped out of their cars, taking control of the street, allowing the medical examiner to get through, when Jimenez glanced down at his phone.

He struggled to hear over the escalating noise, tried to make sense of the words coming from the other end.

Crawley was directing the uniforms when an unmarked pulled up and two plainclothes dicks stepped out. Both older, both part of the order of cops who had given up on accomplishing anything years ago, going through the motions long enough to lock their pensions. *What the fuck was this?* A kick in the balls is what it was.

Jimenez was pale, which was saying a lot for the Colombian. He turned toward his partner, circled his finger around in the air, *wrap it up*.

Crawley joined him at their car.

"What's up?"

Jimenez tossed him the keys. "You drive."

Jimenez met Crawley twenty-four years ago. Fort Benning. Same path. Basic training. Infantry, then Airborne.

Growing up less than twenty miles from each other but it wasn't until Ranger Assessment at Camp Darby, Fort Benning, Georgia, that they met. Crawley goaded, begged, and challenged Jimenez enough to get him through the Combat Water assessment while Jimenez returned the favor for jump school and Airborne to form a friendship that survived past the ten years of deployment in the 75th Ranger Regiment.

They had saved each other's lives dozens of times, were best man at each other's weddings, Godfather to each other's children, and joined the Chicago Police Department together eight years ago.

As part of the Ranger's deployment in Afghanistan, and later assigned to the Special Operations Group working out of Kabul, they had become friends with another hometown boy and future Chicago cop, Elijah Dillon.

And though only a Captain at the time, all three later served on a secret joint-task force under now Major Tommy Black.

Less than ten miles from the first crime scene and yet it already seemed a different world, colder, more forbidding. Ice crunched under their tires as previously thawed streets began to refreeze.

They saw the clouds of breath from the anxious crowd lit up with the reds and blues from two dozen emergency vehicles. Police cars and cruisers, two stout BearCat G3's with SWAT emblazoned on the sides, a half-dozen unmarked sedans and SUVs, lights strobing and flashing and filling the night.

The ME's wagon, ambulances, and two fire trucks stood ready as did a half-dozen news vans and crews, their antennas and satellite arrays telescoping upward into the gently falling snow.

Jimenez recognized at least two of the breathless reporters in front of broadcast news cameras speaking to their respective viewers. Jack Rivera and Helen something—rival networks, poster boy and girl for news stations everywhere. Two dozen cops tried to enforce a perimeter of flimsy yellow Police Line - Do Not Cross tape. The crowd was still growing—the entire scene further broadcast on Facebook and Twitter, Snapchat, and Instagram.

A uniformed officer lifted the tape for them, and Jimenez and Crawley stepped through.

"Command?" The uniform pointed toward one of the BearCats.

They both started in that direction when Jimenez saw Dillon's ex-wife, Holly, arguing with a uniformed officer. Costumed like an escaped mental patient—heavy wool coat hastily pulled over bright flowered pajamas, toy-blue rubber galoshes on her feet, a scarf wrapped around her head in a hurried attempt to tame the wild strawberry-blond hair that looked like she had been hit by lightning.

In a way, he supposed she had. Jimenez had always liked her, and she'd become friends with his wife. Though she had to sometimes fight the bigotry and prejudices against their interracial marriage, she loved Dillon and made it work, at least until their daughter had made it out of school and into college.

He never knew what had happened, life he supposed. Not his place to ask. She'd moved on, remarrying and moving to the toney Northern suburbs. The tears and concern on her face said more than words ever could—that Dillon would always be a part of her life.

Dillon had also moved on, albeit with a frenzied, three-year streak of one night stands that ended a year ago with Rina, the one they would all have bet against. The one he had moved in with. The one now lying dead on the street.

Jimenez scanned the rooftops. Counted two SWAT team snipers, knew there were at least three or four more somewhere unseen. Like the tow-behind light towers and Lentry lights, the news cameras and smartphones—all trained on Dillon sitting motionless in his truck.

Dillon paralyzed. Running it through his mind. The images came faster and faster, replaying the past six hours at impossible speeds until it was a single image of light, a frame frozen in one blinding flash of the gunshot. The image fizzled and his mind would go blank, a synaptic short-circuit, then start over again. Somewhere, behind it all, he sensed the growing entity of the crowd, could feel the energy like a storm growing around him. It made him feel infinitely small. *Infinitely lost.*

Crawley climbed the metal steps into the BearCat. Two long desks, dozens of radios and phones, a wall of live monitor feeds. He imagined it looked not dissimilar to the interior of the news vans and their crews except filled with some of the department's highest brass and crack technicians.

Deputy Chief Rosenberg glanced at Crawley, frowned as if someone was passing gas in the confined space, and went back to giving orders on radio. "Stay until my order. Blue is the primary shooter. No one else fires. Exception command *ALL GO.*"

He turned to Crawley. "Where's Jimenez?"

"Outside. Sit-Eval."

"The situation is your other buddy is completely fucked up! We've made repeated attempts to communicate. Negative on any measurable response," Rosenberg ranted. "I'm told you all know each other. Army ass-buddies overseas. Now which one of you has a better chance of bringing this situation to a successful conclusion?"

Crawley had to swallow it down to keep from being suspended.

The question affirmed everything Crawley and most of the officers thought. That the entire force suffered from a lack of respect from the top.

It was obvious to him, even if he was only partially right, that Rosenberg had found his position as a political animal, not of the rank and file, and certainly not from serving or gaining leadership experience in any capacity serving overseas.

"I'd have to say Detective Jimenez would have a better chance. Sir."

Jimenez was on his way to command when he sensed an instinctive shift in the crowd. Tommy Black stepped from a black Escalade.

Holly turned as the crowd parted to let him through.

She pushed forward, wrapped her arms around him. She held tight, the iron body and strong arms wrapped around her the lifeline she was praying for.

"Jesus, Tommy. What are we gonna do?" She fought her panic and lost. "Did he really do it? I mean— *Jesus!*" Started to laugh, couldn't stop. "We all wanted to shoot her, but..."

Her laughter broke apart and morphed into bone-wracking sobs. He held on until she suddenly pushed him away.

Grabbed his head, hands on each side of his face, forcing him close. "You bring him back, you hear me? You owe him that. You talk to him and bring him back."

Jimenez saw Black kiss her on the forehead, step under the tape and inside the perimeter.

They shook hands. "Glad you're in town."

"Let me talk to him."

"Not so sure about that, Major. Need to clear with brass. Might happen. Rosenberg's an ass, but he's not stupid," Jimenez said. "At least not all the time."

Rosenberg stomped down the steps toward Jimenez.

"Mike!"

Black watched the exchange for about five seconds. Long enough to hear the Commander shouting, "I don't give a shit who he is! Keep him behind the perimeter or get him the fuck out of here!"

It played out for about twice that long before Helen Matticks sensed a new twist to the story. At five-five and a hundred and fifteen pounds, she was able to surprise the six-three, two-hundred-fifty pound cameraman when she grabbed and turned him and his camera on Black striding toward Dillon.

The cameraman glanced back at her with new respect and then focused on Black.

Black looked down at Rina. From this angle, looking down at what was left of her face, it wasn't pretty.

"Dillon."

The big man turned his head. Tried to focus. Black back-lit in the dazzling spotlights. Flash-backed to a thousand years ago. A small stone cell carved into the rock. Iron bars. Kabul. Afghanistan. Desert shit-show at the foot of the mountains.

"Ahh, Jesus, Major. Guess I'm really in the shit now."

Black stepped around the pool of freezing blood. Pulled off the bomber jacket, placed it over Rina's head. Stepped to the window.

"Yeah. Looks like it."

Dillon looked as lost as when they first met.

Dillon's entire team killed in a market bombing during what was supposed to be routine reconnaissance, Dillon alone emerged unscathed. Brass could only look the other way for so long as the big man spent the next month drinking and brawling, taking on locals, fellow soldiers, and the military police that came to arrest him.

The two uniforms with 75th Ranger Regiment scrolls on their shoulders and MP bands on their arms went down to massive, crashing hooks lobbed by the six-four, two hundred and sixty pounds of pissed off, inebriated infantryman that threw them.

Black, out with his own team at the base camp watering spot, stepped in to help, took a crack across the jaw that felt like it tore his head off before he stepped back in, feinted left, ducked under a giant swing, kicked the man's leg out to bring him down to size, and launched a blinding four-punch combination that put the big man on his back. Lights out. Bruised and bloody but mostly intact.

Black had returned the next day to interview the fellow Chicagoan in the brig. Entered the cell and shook hands with the confused Sergeant. "That was a hell of a punch."

Dillon tried to remember the night. "I'm sorry, Sir. Did I hit you?"

Black grinned. And rubbed his jaw. The two men sat. "You want to go home?"

"Sir?"

"Is that what you want?" Black asked. "Right now, it's what they're thinking is best."

"Thought I knew what we were doing here, Sir. Thought maybe this one was different. You know? From the wars our fathers fought." The big man visibly shrank in the small metal chair. "My team. I hate to think they died for nothing. Just wish I knew where all this was going."

He spoke so sincerely, so innocently, Black was caught by surprise. Looked down at the folder of records in his hands. Every detail memorized the first time he'd read them.

"Says here you're from Chicago."

"More or less. About twenty-five miles out in Gary, Indiana."

"Former murder capital of the U.S."

"Yes, Sir. But it's pretty peaceful now. Most people are already dead," Dillon said. He smiled at his own joke. A toothpaste-commercial smile in a broad, handsome black face without guile or agenda, and Black saw the man that would later become an integral part of his elite team and one of his closest friends.

It was a year later, after Black had taken a bullet for him, literally and figuratively, that Dillon pledged himself to the cause, ready to follow his commander into the fires of Hell if asked. Black never asked. He charged in first and men followed willingly.

Success in their secret war wasn't published or shared, even with the men who thought they served in the same offensive.

Their objectives were defined by secret Congressional committees, their missions *suggested—not assigned,* by men in Washington, Langley, and nearby Springfield, Virginia.

"She just wouldn't stop," Dillon said.

Black looked at the gun in Dillon's hand. Nine millimeter, polymer-framed, semi-automatic Hi-Point. Squat and ugly. Cheap. Made to let the masses carry a gun. Reliable enough if you took care of it, but cheap enough to abuse and throw away. If you could afford a cut-rate smartphone, you could afford the gun.

"Lot of people worried out here."

"Holly?"

Black nodded.

"Fuck," Dillon said. "Don't tell Sam, okay?"

"Okay," Black said. "Think she might find out though. She at school?"

Dillon shrugged. "On break. Her honeymoon. Not that she's married but thinking he's gonna pop the question. Tells her mother, but I'm not supposed to know anything about it. You believe that shit? My baby all grown up?"

Black ran it back in his mind. Then again fast-forward. When she was born. Her second birthday. Keeping Dillon calm, and driving ten-year-old Samantha to the hospital with a broken arm. From cute kid to stunning young woman. High school. College. Grad school. *No, he really couldn't believe it.*

Dillon brought him back. "I didn't mean to do it," he said. "Or fuck. Maybe I did. She just wouldn't stop."

Dillon looked at Black. Saw him looking at the gun. Without warning, he put it to his head. Barrel to his temple. He pulled the trigger.

The crowd reacted, a murmur and collective exhale, but nothing happened.

"Jammed," Dillon explained. "You believe that? Cheap piece of shit."

Dillon looked out at the cops and crowd surrounding him. Holly was out there somewhere. He was glad he couldn't see her.

"Maybe we should go in," Black said softly.

"I can't do it."

"Yeah, you can."

"Been thinking it out." Dillon calm. "It's not the "ten-by," or the fucking trash I gotta live with. We got that shit out here. It's Sam. I can't face her."

"She'll forgive you," Black said. "Holly already has. Saved her from doing it herself."

Dillon shook his head. "I should never have fucked that shit up. Holly's the best and I just fucked it all to hell. The fuck was I thinking?"

"Come on, Dillon. They love you."

"I can't do it, Major. Could you?" Dillon's eyes welled with tears until they overflowed and ran down his smooth, broad cheeks. "I'm sorry, Tommy. I really can't."

Black watched his friend struggle. Strafing rounds and mortars exploding, outnumbered a hundred to one, shrapnel leaving its mark on all of them, but still, he'd never felt so helpless. He looked to the crowd. Could feel them waiting. The police watching his every move. He'd counted five snipers as he stood talking to Jimenez. Easy to spot as he knew where he would have placed them.

Though impossible, he felt he could look past the spotlights and see Holly's eyes boring into him.

Was thankful Sam was somewhere far away.

"Where's your service weapon?"

Dillon looked at him, the fog clearing as he repeated the question in his mind.

"Ahh—Jesus." He glanced at the glove compartment. "Oh, man. I'm all kind of fucked up." Dillon's tears stopped, and the million-dollar smile was back.

"Goddamn, I love you, Tommy. I loved all you motherfuckers, but you? You're my brother. My *real* brother. Made me family. Always loved you."

Black swallowed hard. "It's gonna be okay."

Neither could speak. Trying to cram in another lifetime of respect and brotherhood into the moment. Dillon put his fist up, Black met it with his own.

Both men croaked out a whispered, "Tuskers." Neither knowing what else to say. Finally—

"You think we ever did any good out there? I know we tried, but—" Dillon said. "The shit we did—you think we ever did one thing good?"

A question he asked himself a hundred times a day. A thousand lately. He had no answers.

"You're gonna look out for her?"

Black barely got the word out. "Yeah."

"Promise me."

"Good as done, D."

Black looked at his friend. Locked in every line and shadow. Shared each breath and heartbeat. Finally, nothing left to say.

"Okay. See ya," Dillon said.

Long moments. Black struggled. Reached out to put a hand on the big man's shoulder, stopped himself in mid-air. Maybe neither one of them deserved that comfort. Turned back to the crowd and walked away.

The crowd and police went quiet. In Black's mind, it was beyond silence, an infinite void he stepped into.

He found Holly, staring at him with a fury he forced himself to meet. Fire in her eyes, a preview of the hell that waited for him. No quarter—no forgiveness. As if the moment had already played out. As inevitable as the passing of time.

Black was almost to her when the gun went off. Anyone watching him wouldn't have seen the reaction, but the sound ripped at the fabric of his soul. The reverberation tore at his heart and he struggled to breathe.

Holly falling as Black scooped her up and rode out the storm.

"What the fuck have you done?" Her body shook and fury became hysteria. People backed up, the pain too close. She kicked and clawed. "What the fuck have you done?"

Black held on, absorbing her heartbreak as his own.

CHAPTER
SEVEN

The ocean and sky seemed one, joined as a single infinite expanse until the morning light changed them back into two separate elements. The horizon where they met was soon defined by a thin ribbon of red light as the sun considered rising. Streaks of pinks and purples radiated from a field of the palest yellow announcing its decision and raced forward to chase away the night.

Sam lay back against Allan's chest, feet from the gentle waves where tiny crabs surfed on the sea-foam across the white sands, then sprinted on drunken little legs back up the beach. Cooler currents danced and whispered among warm ocean breezes and caressed her cheeks. A favorite pair of well-worn jeans, a thin t-shirt, and one of Allan's dress-shirts. She absorbed his every breath, made his rhythm her own. Went deeper and tried to sync their heartbeats. *So close—*

She gave up and pulled off the diamond pendants, pushed them into her pocket, then lay back against him. She loved the way her head fit between his chest and shoulder, and pulled his arm tighter to lock herself in.

The sun burst over the horizon with an explosion of color, the pinks and purple fragmented into impossible variations, the water a kaleidoscope refracting the light. Her breath caught as she tried to take it all in.

"The best thing about being on American time is staying up all night to see this," she whispered, as much to herself as him.

Allan said nothing. Continued to stare at the water. She could imagine he might still be embarrassed by the club, though that seemed silly. The man had been a giant—but she loved that he'd stepped in without hesitation to defend her.

"You okay?"

"I've got something to tell you," Allan said.

"Okay."

Curtains closed, the room lit only by the thinnest sliver of morning light edging past them. Billie and Hunter lay across the bed. Exhausted from the travel, the club, and the altercation with the gangster and his men.

Hunter acted pissed at her for stopping him from taking on the bodyguards, but she knew it was all an act. No sane man would have taken them on. He hit the bottle harder than she was expecting, but then again, this was new to them. She'd thought to repair his ego in her own way, stripped off her clothes and curled up beside him. Hunter was out before his head hit the pillow.

Billie's legs jerked and kicked. It was enough to wake her up. It took a moment to remember where she was. Second day here and the jet lag was starting to hit. Nine hours difference. She glanced at her cell phone. Five-thirty in the morning Mauritius time meant two-thirty in the afternoon back home.

Wow! She was really here—across the world on a tropical island. Sam's boyfriend had the money and Sam refused the invitation until Allan had offered to bring Billie along.

The couple had been together for just over a year, and had been discussing the next steps. Sam wanted Billie there to share and celebrate the moment. Business-class tickets—way beyond any domestic first-class she'd ever flown—and a suite in a luxury hotel. And though she only met him a week before they came, his friend Hunter was good-looking, a lot of fun, and seemed to be a genuinely nice guy.

She slid her hand across his chest, let it drift lower. Let herself explore. Not hard, but *full*. Plenty to work with and make her happy, she thought. And as he'd proved on their second date, while not exactly good in bed, more than willing to learn. *At least when he was awake.*

She slid naked from the bed and padded to the bathroom. A nightlight added a soft, pale green glow. She sat on the toilet, looked at the alien reflections she cast in the glass walls of the double shower, and peed. Flushed and rinsed her hands and checked her breath while making funny Martian faces in the mirror. Froze. A soft noise from the bedroom. Nothing ominous— just *strange*. Out of place.

Billie grabbed one of the beach-sized bath towels from the heated rack and pulled it to her, the comfort of a luxurious Turkish towel for armor. Opened the door.

A huge shadow stood over Hunter. The silhouette of a silenced gun in his hand. The bed pooling in shiny black blood, the apparition fired the silenced gun two more times into Hunter's head.

Billie was frozen. Trying to process what she was seeing. In no hurry, the apparition turned to her. Raised the gun. She tried, but couldn't scream, couldn't breathe, couldn't move. The gun coughed and spit twice. She fell and never would again.

Ringer stepped close. Looked at the blood seeping from the two holes in her chest. Put two more in her head.

Sam was waiting for him to get up on one knee, pull out a ring, and propose. He looked so lost and forlorn. She tried to help him.

"Anything you want to talk about?"

It took him a minute, and she let him work in his own time.

"This is not easy for me, Sam."

"You're already married," she joked.

Long moments, trying to find words. "Yeah."

Sam laughed. "Yeah, right."

Allan didn't say anything. She looked in his eyes and it started to sink in.

"What?"

"I'm sorry, Sam. I didn't mean for it to happen. It just—" his voice cracking. "I fell in love with you."

"What?" She pulled away and jumped to her feet, tried to steady herself, afraid she'd throw up. "So you— *What?* I'm supposed to be some sort of side-piece when you weren't fucking your wife?"

He rose to his feet. Reached for her.

"Sam—"

She jerked away. "Fuck you, Allan! Who the— Get the fuck away from me!"

She stormed away, heading toward the water. Splashed for ten steps into the surf, then stomped back, her tears did nothing to put out the fire raging in her eyes. She slapped him. Hard. Her fury almost taking him off his feet.

"Fuck you, Allan."

She pushed past him and headed toward the hotel.

His heart broke for her. He loved how everything seemingly touched her in some way, but yeah, he supposed she was right. She was meant to be a fling, an affair he kept secret while he worked things out with his wife. She was beautiful, exotic, and challenged him just to keep up. Not a chance in hell his father, grooming him for a congressional run, would ever accept what he'd consider her less-than-perfect pedigree.

He rubbed the side of his face, worked his jaw to make sure it still worked right and watched her disappear around the hotel's sculpted privacy hedges. With no idea how he'd make this right, he started after her, trudging through her footsteps in the sugary sand.

Words ran through his mind of what he might say, how he might convince her to stay. They played forward and backward like a newscast at triple speed and didn't even make sense to him.

As he stepped past the overhanging frangipani, from the sand onto the paved path, he saw her. Her feet a foot off the ground, kicking and struggling, as Ringer held her in one giant hand and muffled her screams.

Incongruous to anything he could have imagined, his brain short-circuited and stopped sending signals.

He froze in mid-stride and then it was too late.

Grip lunged at him from the side, stepping past him to avoid the blood as the blackened tactical blade in his hand stabbed rapid-fire into the future congressman's chest. The impacts themselves would have been enough to put the man down, but the knife penetrated past muscle and bone into heart and lungs, and blood exploded from each wound.

As Allan began to fall, Grip stepped gracefully to the other side to avoid the blood, slashed the American's throat, and let him drop.

Sam tried to scream but was quickly losing strength as Ringer's hand shut off all hope of breath or sound. She had a glimpse of Allan falling before Grip pulled out a syringe and jammed it into her thigh.

Her world began to fade. Her last sight was Allan's blood seeping into the sand.

CHAPTER
EIGHT

The boy sat across from the detectives at a metal table bolted to the floor. He didn't remember their names, didn't hear them when they introduced themselves, too angry to care. The woman was looking at naked pictures of him. Polaroids. Clinical lighting. A variety of angles and distances. He wasn't embarrassed—not the first time strangers examined him, and he was getting used to it.

The man in the rumpled suit asked questions. The boy registered them but didn't answer, already turned inward. He was counting backward from a thousand in multiples of four while working multiplication tables of seven until they met.

He wasn't a math genius or even trying to be. He just liked the idea of being able to do two things at once. Like playing the piano with one hand while drawing a picture with the other. Not sequentially. But concurrently. Two separate functions meeting in the middle and allowing his actions and reactions to be guided by both simultaneously and without conscious thought. He wasn't sure how it might help him—for now, he just needed the challenge. It was a skill he would later apply in many ways.

Detective Cole looked at the pictures. Two-inch wide welts that cut into the skin, some a half-inch high, crisscrossed his back, upper thighs and buttocks, painting the pale, white skin with black and purple stripes. A dark bruise in the shape of a large fist planted in the center of his chest and knuckle prints imprinted on his ribs.

Angry fingerprints on his arms over faded bruises of yellow and brown.

She traded reports and pictures with the man. An earlier time, almost a year ago. Second-degree burns on his palms, a broken collarbone, the bruises of hand prints around his throat.

Father unknown. Mother just fifteen years older than the boy himself. He'd been taken away from her twice.

The mother was an addict. Crack, alcohol, and heroin. Anything to enter an alternate reality, even for just a few hours or minutes. An abusive biker for a boyfriend who fed her habits and occasionally pimped her out, and who when he got tired of beating on her, turned to the boy.

As far as Cole was concerned, she was as guilty as if she'd swung the belt.

It was an earlier time and children were kept with their mothers. Even if she was a monster, she had her moments of sobriety and her plea in the courts saved the State from paying for foster care.

Cole looked up at the boy. Ten years old. He had to be in pain. Both physically and emotionally, but you'd be hard-pressed to know it. If he was angry, he didn't show it. Seemed perfectly normal, which under the circumstances, according to the doctor who first interviewed him, meant he probably wasn't.

Years later that would be amended.

"He has a talent for violence."

Black sat on one side of a short metal table bolted to the floor. Across from him, the Chief of Detectives, Bill Mathews, yellow legal pad, digital recorder, and a thin manila folder, sat quietly, trying to figure out how best to proceed.

"I know it's been a long night. As you can imagine, Major, this is a nightmare for the department, so you're going to have to bear with me."

The night was over long ago, and morning was fast becoming noon.

Black said nothing.

"The fact that you served together, or rather he served under you, doesn't tell me much or concern me. Your file is so thin, I know I'm not getting the full picture here. What does interest me is all the redacted, blacked out shit in your file. You want to fill me in?"

"Couldn't if I would."

Mathews tried to put the words in order. "What?"

Black smiled. "Chief. It's not happening."

Mathews was unnerved and trying to figure out why. The man across from him was handsome. Not like a model, unless it was for an Army recruitment poster. Thick, dark hair with the barest filaments of silver, and clear, blue eyes that looked directly at you when either of you spoke. A thin scar above his right eye—if you looked close, another one high on his forehead at his hairline. He wasn't big, but he certainly wasn't small. The records in his hand said a shade under six feet and two hundred pounds. His hands thick, as were his forearms. Not huge but—tempered. Corded ropes of muscle that ended at knuckles pounded into solid battering rams. Calloused and scarred. Forty-three, just a couple years younger than Mathews himself.

When Mathews looked at himself in the mirror, he knew the man staring back looked at least ten years older, maybe fifteen on a night like tonight, whereas the man across from him could probably lie and knock at least seven or eight years off his ID.

Mathews was divorced—*what veteran cop wasn't?* His current girlfriend, a yoga teacher and part-time astrologer would have said it was the man's aura, a confidence that emanated like a magnetic force. He didn't look intimidating, but his files said otherwise.

He'd heard of men like that in the service. Never actually met one—one of the alpha dogs let off the leash to lead the pack—but suspected he had now.

"Had to try."

Black nodded in sympathy. Smiled again. Mathews grinned, felt himself being won over. *Fucking charming bastard too.*

...

A BMW entered the parking lot. Parked in the Official Parking Only spots. An attractive woman, maybe thirty-five stepped out.

The wind caught her thick blond hair. Pulled at the dark overcoat.

The severe business suit, patent leather heels, and black Coach messenger bag framed her beauty more than hid it. She crossed the parking lot toward the squat, uninspired police station.

Outside the room, watching through the ubiquitous one-way glass, Rosenberg, Jimenez, and two high-ranking uniformed police officers watched on. Just in from the preliminary press conference. They wore enough ribbons between them to outfit any scout convention. They watched both men and heard the conversation through the digital speakers.

"What I don't understand is why you didn't order him to surrender his weapon?"

A door opened and the woman from the BMW joined the men watching on. Jimenez tipped his head in acknowledgment. She returned it with a tight smile. She could feel the other men looking at her. Used to it even if she couldn't understand it. Determined to not let it get in her way. They followed her gaze back to the interview.

"He's a civilian." Black caught himself. "Was a civ—"

"Or at least try to talk him out of blowing his brains out?"

The expression never wavered but the energy inside the room changed and Mathews backed away.

"We're done here," she said.

Rosenberg was taken aback. "We're done when I say we're done."

She pulled a few papers from her bag. "We're done," she said again.

Rosenberg barely glanced at them. Handed them back as though he was afraid of catching something.

She smiled. Looked at Jimenez. Let the warmth back in her blue eyes. "Mike."

He reached out to shake her hand gently. "Jackie."

And she walked out.

The three-story police lobby was bustling. The marble floors and columns designed as they had been since the Greeks and Romans held court to multiply every sound, to add gravitas to every footstep and whisper.

Cops and attorneys knew their parts; complainants and victims figuring it out as they went.

Major Tommy Black and Jacqueline Lobinski crossed the wide, gleaming floors toward the exit.

Crawley was escorting Holly into the building when Jimenez intercepted them and tried to steer them away. Holly shrugged his hands off and strode toward Black. Jackie hung back in respect.

"You stay the fuck away from me and my family. You hear me?"

Black didn't try to stop the slap, let it hit with all her fury.

Jimenez and Crawley both winced at the impact, Jackie gasped, and a dozen people jerked and spun at the sound.

"You stay the fuck away!

CHAPTER
NINE

More than a thousand years of culinary evolution from Phoenician flatbread to 16th-century Nepalese paper-thin street food, brought by European immigrants to the Americas, a way to feed the working man on his way to or from the docks and factories, culminated in the birth of Chicago's deep-dish pizza.

Like the controversies of Edison or the Wright brothers, the actual origins of the invention itself might be questioned, but common agreement was that deep-dish pizza as we know it was first served as early as 1943 at the Near Northside Pizzeria Uno started by Ike Sewell and Ric Riccardo.

Though Malnati's family assert while working as an employee for Pizzeria Uno, it was Adolpho "Rudy" Malnati's genius that originated the recipe, the dish arguably reached its current heights when Burt Katz, known for naming his business with literary references, *The Inferno, Gulliver's* and *Pequod's*, introduced his caramelized crust, stuffed pizza to the Northern Chicago suburb of Morton Grove.

Eventually, a second location opened in Lincoln Park, and the small chain sold to Keith Jackson where further, subtle adjustments were made to the recipe. This was the pizza that Black and Jackie waited on.

Black sat with his back to the corner. He'd been looking forward to one of his favorite foods with Jimenez and Crawley and Dillon, their go-to spot the rare times he made it to town. Now it was relegated to nourishment.

He'd meet with Jimenez and Crawley a bit later, try to make some sense of this after he got some sleep.

Like any soldier who had seen combat, they each had their own fears—demons they tried to keep buried in their own ways. Demons they never put names to, afraid that would bring them up from the dark, out of their souls, and into the world around them where they could infect all they cared for and loved. Black was sure they'd never really know what happened, but maybe they'd prove him wrong.

Jackie sat across from him at the high-top table, turned just enough that she could twist to the door every time it opened while talking to him.

"Dad said you might be calling," she said. "And Scottie was thrilled."

She was as smart and beautiful as he remembered. She had helped him heal. Gave him purpose growing up, someone to protect besides himself. Brother and sister. Filled with joy at seeing her now, the warmth and pride he felt for her in total contrast to the dark cloud over his heart.

He scanned the other tables in a poor attempt to hide his emotions. A lunch-time crowd. Hipsters and students. Out-of-town conventioneers on the Windy City Pizza Tour. A table with four cops. Another with three steelworkers in hard hats. People piling up to the bar to watch an early game.

No one else would see it, probably not even Al. Certainly not his men. Jackie had always been the one person who could read him. "She'll forgive you, Tommy."

"Not sure I will."

She jerked her head toward the sound of the opening door. Light slashed across the dark wooden floor as a group of hipsters piled through to grab a few beers.

"Sorry. I'm just a bit jumpy," she said. "This is just all so unreal."

Tommy could read her just as easily. "Why did he want me to talk to you?"

"What? Dad? No. Nothing. I'm sure he just wanted you to say hi." Her eyes flitted around the bar. "It's nothing. Dad's just a bit paranoid these days."

"Bullshit," Black said softly. "He's the toughest, least paranoid guy we're ever gonna know. So what's going on?"

"Nothing. Really. I—"

The waitress, an undergrad at nearby Du Paul, brought out the three-inch thick pan of pizza. "Careful, it's hot." She served them each a slice. Bubbling cheeses, lean Chicago sausage, the famous caramelized crust, more a lasagna that anything one would find in the Mediterranean or even New York.

"Can I get you anything else right now?"

"No," Jackie said. "I think we're good."

Jackie took a drink of red wine from her glass and started to dig in. Black smiled at her, shook his head, and cut into his own. He was thrilled he could even taste it. Delicious. Heartbroken he'd never share it with Dillon again.

"I guess you're in town for a few days. Sorry it's like this. Rosenberg reached out to your commander or admiral or whatever, and you're here until he finds some answers or they decide otherwise."

"Yeah. I spoke to the CO last night. Dillon was never under his command, but we want answers too."

Jackie took another drink of wine. She knew that tone. Knew that no one could dig their heels in more than Tommy.

"You're not a cop here, Tommy. You need to let the department do its job."

"Sure."

"Tommy, the military has no say in this. It's a civilian matter."

"Okay."

"Okay?"

Black shrugged. "Okay."

They both knew better, but Jackie knew it was hopeless. Maybe Dad could talk to him.

"So you gonna fill me in?

"Tommy, come on. There's nothing—"

"YEAH!" A shout and Jackie's head snapped toward the bar. They watched the replay of the pass and dunk that brought the small crowd at the bar to its feet. Slapping palms and pats on the back as if they had run the play.

"Okay—Jesus." She pushed her plate away. "You're both trying to mother me to death!"

Black said nothing. Waited. She traded her near-empty glass of wine with his, still full and untouched.

"Okay, okay." Took a drink. "I have a client. Murder—capital one. A couple of open questions but prosecution found a witness that puts him at the scene with what tuned out to be the murder weapon."

"And?"

"'*And'* is the witness is gone. My client hinted—no—he said it. Said it was going to happen. Told me not to worry about it and carry on. And now the witness is missing and my client is back on the street. A massive bail that I never thought he'd cover, but he did. Still have the trial coming up and all, but—"

"Happens all the time," Black said.

She nodded. "Yeah. It's my job to defend him. That's my job. And I am."

"But?"

Jackie looked at him. "I know he's guilty."

"That's not your job."

"Yeah. I know. And—not threats exactly. Hints really. Nothing overt but I know what he's saying. If the case goes bad for him."

She took a small drink. "Maybe I'm just making it all up. You know—making too much of it. Too many late-night movies."

She downed the wine.

"It sounds like it," he said.

Put his hand over hers. Her hand trembling. It felt so small to him.

"I'm sure everything is going to be fine."

CHAPTER
TEN

By the mid-1850s, Port Louis, capital of Mauritius, was the busiest and most important shipping center of the Indian Ocean. Progress first meant steam took over from sail and the port wasn't deemed suitable for the increased tonnage. With the opening of the Suez Canal, the importance of the island's harbor and shipping lanes quickly dwindled.

Soon, the Mauritius shipyards smelled little of the sea, but rather an unpleasant fog of brine and dead fish marinated in a variety of petroleum-based fuels and solvents. Waste and garbage tossed into the water. Diesel exhaust and lubricants for the steel added to the stench.

Depending on which warehouse district you were in, exotic spices might fill the air. Some streets pungent with Indian turmeric and Chinese garlic, others sweet with Madagascar vanilla and Indonesian coconut.

Tonnage was replaced with tourists. More tourists meant dollars for clean-up. Brightly colored shops and markets. Nearby eateries and coffee shops. Soon, the Mauritius melting-pot cuisine, Chinese and African, Indian, and French, from the street stalls and cook-stoves sprinkled throughout the labyrinth, could be tasted on the air.

Sam could neither see nor smell any of it, her mind locked in terror as she lay on a dirty concrete floor. Eyes covered, only a hint of light came through the cloth. Mouth gagged with a dirty rag, the smell of oil and chemicals mixed with her fear brought the sharp taste of acid and bile to her tongue. Hands and feet bound with thick, twisted wire and then looped together, she couldn't quite reach the blindfold or gag.

Something small and furry slid by her naked feet, and she jerked away, thrashed on the floor, her screams muffled and useless. The wire dug in cruelly and it took all of her will to make herself stop. Tried to catch her breath. She tried to slow the pounding in her chest. The shaking of her limbs. Couldn't do it but did her best to quiet her breathing so she could listen.

She had the impression of boats sloshing on the water and birds in the air somewhere far away, closer to the harbor, but here, sound was dominated by machinery. She thought she heard what must be a container crane across the bay. Giant twenty and forty-ton containers banging into each other as they were stacked on ships made ready for distant locations around the globe.

Men were talking close by. She heard words, a bit of laughter, maybe a curse, but it was a mixture of French and local Creole and useless to her. At least two, maybe three. Not young. Their footsteps sounded heavy. Boots on the feet of big men. The echoes and reverberations told her she was in a large steel structure, somewhere on the docks. A warehouse in the shipping yards maybe.

She heard a steel drum, rolling on its edge across the concrete, but with no reference, had no idea what it could be. Coming closer. With her limited senses, magnified through the amplifier of fear, it sounded like a train that would crush her under tons of steel. She thrashed again, twisting and turning, cringing away from the sound until the wire cut into her flesh. The noise stopped and she forced herself to lie still.

The presence of someone nearby. Thick, sour breath touched her cheeks as she heard them squat down beside her. She tried to control her shaking but knew they were staring at her, eyes exploring her body. Her skin crawled and she fought not to throw up.

The blindfold was untied and roughly pulled away from her eyes with a flourish.

Blinded by the sudden light, she squeezed her eyes shut until the spots faded and the muscles tired. She slowly opened them again.

The man stood and looked down on her. He could have spared her the knowledge of what was happening, but he liked to see the look in their eyes. Welling with tears, sometimes pissing themselves, their responses so uncontrollable they had once— *it was only one time*—had a girl who died on the spot. Her heart just stopped he supposed. Maybe it took a lifetime in her mind but was near-instantaneous to him. Her eyes opened, flitted around the room, settled on his black and yellow-toothed grin, drifted upwards to his dull, black eyes, and then—*just stopped.*

Now the man, Whank, always waited to see if it might happen again.

Sam didn't die, but maybe only because she couldn't imagine what was happening quickly enough.

Three men. All hard, worn faces. Eyes like sharks. Little reflection, cold and dead of feeling. Big men, the thick muscle that comes from a lifetime of back-breaking hard, manual labor.

Tiaan picked up a welding torch from a workbench, and she watched with growing horror as he adjusted the oxygen and acetylene valves, lit it with a *whoomph*, and began cutting the lid off a steel drum. She pulled away as the sparks rained down and bounced across the floor.

He worked his way around the edge until the third man, Heinrich put on heavy leather gloves and slid it off. It bounced on the floor, spun round and round till the ringing died out.

Tiaan and Heinrich turned to her, and she again started screaming. The gag kept most of the sound in, but she protested the assault with every ounce and fiber of her being. Twisted and turned, ignoring the blood that seeped around her wire bindings.

They lifted her off the floor and stuffed her in. Whank with a digital camera. Snap! Another and another. He caught a great one of her absolute terror just as the others fitted the lid back in place.

Tiaan fired up the torch and began welding it back on.

Screams were muffled behind the steel, and her pounding sounded to Whank like one of the steel drums played at the festivals. A unique Mauritian fusion of imported African Sega and Jamaican Reggae called "Seggae."

As the steel melted back together, the sounds of her struggle settled. They'd give her a moment. Finally, silence. They waited until the final useless attempt began with what in her mind was an all-out twisting, turning, thrashing, kicking, pounding from inside the drum. Since the space was small, just thirty-five inches high and twenty-one across, protest was limited. Not for the first time, Whank thought, the women never sounded that upset at all.

Heinrich picked up a three-pound hammer and an iron railroad spike. Punched a hole into the top of the drum.

Sam shrank away from the screeching steel. The sound ripped into her brain as light and air flooded the small opening. Like looking through a pinhole camera, the image beyond distorted in the refraction of air as the man reached forward and slammed the hammer down again. And again. Three holes, an inch in diameter, her only connection to the outside.

"PLEEEASE! DON'T DO THIS! LET ME OUT—"

Heinrich picked up a bucket of water. Dumped it on top. Sam screamed anew, the wet and cold startling her. Her voice already as raw as her wrists and ankles.

Heinrich pounded on the lid with his fist. "Shut up! Not one more sound. This is water. Drink it. Piss in it. Do what you want. You make a fucking sound, one fucking sound, and next time it's acid."

Sam whimpered and shrank as far away as she could. Just inches available in the fifty-five-gallon drum. Unable to process what might come next.

Tiaan started up a forklift and spun it toward the steel drum.

CHAPTER
ELEVEN

Jackie shot herself with the rusty little trashed-out gun. The Hi-Point 9mm. It tore half her head off, and then she handed the gun back to Jimenez.

He'd done it twice and was starting to look bad. Eye torn from his skull, a flap of scalp hanging down, a massive divot in the side of his head. No longer the handsome Latin cop.

Crawley wasn't even recognizable. Only the brass nameplate on his shirt told who he was. Or maybe more accurately, who he had been. He put the gun on the floor, spun it around on its side.

It stopped on Holly. She was laughing so hard when she pulled the trigger she missed and when she went to do it again they all jumped on her to wrestle it away. "Not your turn!"

She pouted and fussed, but Dillon pulled her close, his blood dripping down on her for a wet, sloppy kiss. They pulled apart and looked like they both had been shot.

They spun again. Black was the only one who hadn't yet gone, but he was sure this would be his turn. It spun and spun, like one of those spinner widgets that had swept the nation, but it stopped on Dillon again. He grabbed for the gun, put it to his temple, and smiled.

"Okay. See ya." Pulled the trigger. Part of his head blew off, splattering the others, and he turned to Black. Grinned, shattered teeth, half his jaw missing, and unable to keep his tongue in his mouth.

Black screamed in his dream and woke up.

Covered in sweat. The sheets wet, pillow damp. Black had only laid down a couple of minutes ago... five or ten at the most. Checked his watch. Five hours had passed.

Threw off the blanket, padded naked to the shower. Turned it on as hot as he could bear and stood under the water until the small room filled with steam. Dialed down the hot water until only the cold, just above ice in the winter-cooled pipes, cascaded down his head and broad shoulders. He shivered, forcing himself to take it. Five minutes. Ten. He slowly let the hot back in the mix until his shaking stopped. Lathered, rinsed, and dried off.

He had stopped on the way to the hotel at an Army surplus. Not exactly state-of-the-art military issue. Partly stocked with rejects, cheap Chinese knock-offs of U.S. military gear. Some older, decommissioned uniforms. First-grade paratrooper boots from the seventies and cheap tactical knock-offs stocked from the past few years. There was plenty to choose from.

The vet behind the counter, Vietnam, 101st Airborne '67 and '68, blind in one eye and missing part of a leg, looked at the ink, looked in his eyes and looked at his choices. He hobbled to the back, reappeared, and replaced a couple of items. Rang it all up for five dollars, pushed them into a black canvas rucksack. Black thanked him, slid three-hundred dollars across the glass counter top, and walked out. It had all taken less than fifteen minutes.

Black stood naked and stretched. It took twenty minutes to feel normal. Fuck elite. He felt old. Did a single push-up to warm up the muscles. Two minutes down, two minutes up. Let the rest of the moisture from his body evaporate before getting dressed.

Black on black on Black. He smiled. A real comedian. Missed his calling.

The vet had traded the well-worn paratrooper boots he'd grabbed for an almost new pair of Danner 8" tactical. Desert brown. Size eleven and a half.

He slipped them on and was thankful to the vet for looking. They hugged his feet and ankles and were radically better than any military issue boots made in the seventies and eighties.

He sprayed them down with a can of black concealment paint. He wasn't trying to make them pretty, he was going hunting.

The Escalade parked in the shadows. Easy enough as working streetlights were few and far between on this side of town. Most houses dark, many boarded up. Dogs barked to each other over the roar and rumble of a nearby train and the constant, distant hum of traffic.

A dark-gray Charger Pursuit pulled up beside him. Crawley in the driver's seat. Slid down his window as Jimenez went to the trunk and pulled out a large black duffel bag. "You know this is not a good idea."

Jimenez walked around through the falling snow and slid in the Escalade's passenger side.

"I know we lost family last night," Black said. "I know I'm not waiting for something to happen to Jackie."

Crawley nodded. "I get it. But how you think it's not going to point at you?"

"You think I give a fuck?"

Crawley looked at him. He was supposed to arrest him, at least try to stop him. Maybe that was the choice Black faced the night before with Dillon. They were family and by extension, so was Jackie. He knew Black wouldn't hesitate to do it for him. For any of them. Crawley had sworn an oath, but he'd sworn an earlier one to Black. Knew that both he and Mike not only had the Major's back but would be first through the door if he'd let them.

"Let me park."

Black turned to Jimenez. The cop was opening the duffel bag.

"Once you're in, we can divert maybe ten, fifteen minutes. That's about it."

Black didn't bother looking in the bag. Overkill. He didn't need much. He knew what he'd asked for and knew Jimenez wouldn't bring less.

"Done one way or the other by then," Black said.

"No halfway on this one, Major."

"Never is."

Crawley let himself in the back. Handed Black a thick file. Black used a small tactical penlight to scan it. Didn't need to know the details, only the faces.

Clarence "Mookie" Williams, Gib Parsons, Maino Johnson, a couple of other mutts. Mugshots for each. Black and whites with glib expressions, ink on their faces, and murder in their eyes. Rap sheets. As bad as it gets without being put on death row. Looked again at Mookie's face. Teardrops inked under his eyes, affiliations high on his neck.

"This is crazy," Crawley said. "No recon, no back-up."

"These guys are as dangerous as any of the T-men we dealt with," Jimenez counseled. "And probably just as armed. What's our plan?"

"No *'our plan'*. You've done your part."

"That's bullshit." Jimenez was genuinely pissed. And disappointed.

Crawley caught it. He was torn, though relieved for Mike's sake. His partner had a wife at home to think about.

"So what's *your* plan?"

"Three men walk into a bar," Black said. They waited. "One man shoots the other two."

"Jesus. That's it? That's the plan?"

Black smiled. "A work in progress."

"Major. I— I don't know what to say," Crawley said. "We lost family. Shit's not supposed to happen. Not here, not at home. I know you two were close, but—"

Crawley stopped himself. Looked out the window. These streets were a war zone for many, but paradise compared to some places people in the world had to live. Places he had walked into and sometimes crawled out of.

Their team had walked through fire with Black leading the way. As rough as it had been for him and Mike, the shit they'd seen and taken on in the heat of the battle, he knew it was nothing compared to what Black had done to lead, and then after, to protect his team once they were dissolved.

Their successes were legend, for the enemy and their own, hinted at and spoken of in whispers. Only a small part of it documented. The less proved and recorded, the less that might bite some past or future politician in the ass. Their mission, as successful as it was, maybe too successful in some ways, was told to stand down and disband. They were no longer a part of this or the last administration's global strategy for peace and prosperity.

They heard the RUMINT, the mixture of rumor and hard intelligence that informed most military decisions, but even now, they could only guess at what the Major was still doing there.

Black caught Crawley's eyes in the rear-view. Looked at Jimenez. Affection, respect. Brothers in every way but blood. And that had been spilled and shared, keeping each other alive just to do it all again. Defying death and keeping hell away just a while longer.

Fist bumps all around.

"Tuskers." Repeated by Crawley and Jimenez.

"Tuskers."

CHAPTER
TWELVE

O pium is still harvested much the way it has been for 6000 years. A small knife is used to slice and score the poppy, usually in the cooling afternoon, and by morning, the resinous, milky white sap, or what the Greeks called poppy tears, secreted by Papaver Somniferum, is gathered.

Found in stockpiles of gathered seeds and pods in Neolithic caves across Europe—Greece, France, Spain, as far north as Sweden, it was perhaps first cultivated by Sumerians in Mesopotamia and traded by Phoenicians across the Mediterranean.

The Egyptians in the time of Tutankhamen smoked and traded with Athens and Rome, while Alexander the Great and later Genghis Khan helped spread the poppy across Persia, and into India and China.

First confined to priests and mystics for its euphoric, mind-altering properties and to allow them to dazzle audiences with their ability to ignore pain, it soon became a tool for the warrior class where its use was primarily to ease the agony of battle wounds and injury.

By the time Britain was conquering the world, many of the poppy's medicinal effects were being explored and documented in university and hospital texts, and it soon made its way to the masses.

Friedrich Wilhelm Sertürner, a comparatively uneducated but curious pharmacist, was first able to isolate the organic alkaloid compound that he named morphine, after the Greek god of dreams, Morpheus.

By the mid-1820s, standardized doses were being manufactured by several sources, including an apothecary in Darmstadt, Germany, owned by Heinrich Emanuel Merck. His descendants would later found the pharmaceutical giants Merck and Company, and Merck KGaA.

After the syringe was being manufactured reliably, injectable morphine became the standard for reducing pain and was prescribed for a wide range of maladies; pain, sleeplessness, schizophrenia, hysteria, chronic cough from emphysema and tuberculosis, and even opium addiction.

Perhaps first brought to the Americas in quantity by the colossal influx of indentured Chinese immigrants, opium soon found its way into popular culture and everyday life in various forms including the wildly popular Laudanum, marketed predominantly for women and children, but it was morphine that first addicted Americans and along with alcohol, led to the Temperance Movement and later, Prohibition.

As the primary tool for both battlefield surgical and post-surgical pain management during the deplorable conditions of Civil War hospitals, as many as a half-million veterans of the American civil war became morphine addicts.

The ten-fold increase in the euphoric properties of morphine over raw opium increased ten-fold again in 1874 when Alder Wright, a chemist in a London hospital further refined the opioid alkaloids into diacetylmorphine.

Heinrich Dresler, a Bayer Laboratories chemist, further tested and refined the new semi-synthetic drug and by 1898, Bayer began producing and marketing the drug as a new analgesic and cough sedative.

Originally touted and trademarked, now wiped from the corporate annals, they named the powerful opium derivative Heroin, from the Latin *heroes,* for the feelings of power and exaltation it imparted.

Selective breeding of the poppy greatly increased the phenan-threne alkaloids—morphine, codeine, and thebaine. The latex cultivar of modern Papaver bracteatum, or Persian poppy, with its beautiful eight-inch scarlet flowers, while not producing morphine or codeine or other narcotic alkaloids, produced the thebaine commercially extracted for the raw material that serves in the synthesis of Oxycodone, Hydrocodone, and other semi-synthetic opiates fueling the supply of over 300,000,000 prescriptions written each year in the United States alone. Of course, the opioid crisis in America was followed by a rapid increase in related overdoses, and by 2018, more than 70,000 deaths a year were being attributed to its use.

Imagine a football field of poppy flowers. 1.32 Acres. Each football field producing approximately twenty pounds of raw opium. Now imagine 400,000 football fields. Spread throughout the 50,000 square miles of fertile valleys of the Hindu Kush and guarded by 25,000-foot peaks.

In Afghanistan, incisions are made with the nustar, a specialized knife with several blades just millimeters apart to score the pods in the afternoon. The sap is collected the next morning. Raw opium can be sold to merchants on the black market but is often refined into the more profitable morphine base.

Increasingly, Afghanistan and the Taliban became vertically integrated heroin producers, not only growing and harvesting the poppy but facilitating and participating in the refinement into morphine and heroin, reducing the weight and bulk to facilitate smuggling.

Crude laboratories, as simple as a few barrels for mixing, jugs of precursor chemicals, a generator and a simple press, create a sticky brown paste that is pressed into bricks and dried in the sun, reducing bulk and weight by up to ninety percent or further processed into crude heroin which is two to four times more potent and much more valuable.

Worldwide, illegal drug trade generates over 400 billion dollars a year. An estimated sixty to eighty billion of that comes from Afghanistan, where eighty-five percent of the world's opium is grown.

From taxation and protection rackets of the farmers and smugglers, with banking entities and their investments into both legitimate and illegitimate businesses, the Taliban profit from every step of the illegal trade.

Regional governments likely underestimate the Taliban's overall income at 500 million a year while intelligence sources within the NATO-led mission Resolute Support place the number higher, upwards of two billion U.S. dollars annually, with as much as sixty percent of that generated by opium.

Just as traditional Chinese rice routes became banking conduits for the Thai and Burmese heroin that financed much of the CIA's secret and illegal war in Laos and Cambodia, the long-established trade routes used by the Taliban are the same ones used for most of their other illegal smuggling operations.

Attractive to local farmers, hashish cultivated across an estimated 50,000 acres yields nearly 4,000 USD in profits per acre, depositing another 100 to 150 million in their coffers. Even the smuggling of western cigarettes sold on the black market to India and Pakistan, fetch four to five times the Afghan street market price and bring as much as an additional 150 million a year.

Kidnappings and extortion of citizens in Afghanistan and Pakistan, as well as Westerners, NGOs, and others, are lucrative and perhaps earn upwards of another fifty million.

And of course, arms sales. Portions of the arms supplied to Pakistan in as much as 40 billion in aid from the United States, ostensibly in the fight against terrorism and to promote stability to the region, end up in the hands of Taliban and rebel warlords in Afghanistan, and the bullets fired in the bodies of Americans, their partners, and their NATO allies.

Afghanistan was officially designated a Narco-State. A country whose economy is dependent on the illegal drug trade, creating regional and international implications across human, economic, and political security spheres. The fluid banking, the bribing and intimidation of corrupt and susceptible political figures—the military, judicial, and banking institutions across the region, made the efforts that much more expensive and harder to plan and coordinate.

In the quest to bring down Al-Qaeda and the Taliban by cutting off a primary source of funding to the fundamentalist Islamic insurgency, the Administration worked with highly placed Afghanistan counter-narcotics officials and regional partners to create a plan that would target and indict Taliban narcotics kingpins.

Later, as part of the fluid strategy to stabilize the region, deals were made with Iran, Turkey, Pakistan, and Syria, but with pressure from Senate and House Intelligence Committees, the newly formed task force was summoned by the then-deputy chief of mission and told to stand down until further review.

In secret meetings outside of Kabul, a former U.S. battalion commander and then NATO Special Operations Commander, Colonel Jordan Stevens was asked to create a small, direct-action operational task force that would bypass extradition and indictments to target and disrupt the production supply chain as directly as possible.

Stevens recruited one man, already becoming a legend in covert-ops, who in turn was tasked to create the covert team.

The man recruited and trained just eight men, a select group of Special Forces operators including Rangers Recon Scouts Sergeant Mike Jimenez and Sergeant Jack Crawley, and Infantry Master Sergeant Elijah Dillon.

The small team, Tuskers, named after the toughest and most fearsome of all European beasts, the wild boar, formed under the command of then Captain Tommy Black.

CHAPTER
THIRTEEN

Black drove the Escalade around the block, entered an alley that ran parallel to the overhead tracks of Chicago's Green-line. The train roared overhead on its way to Ashland and 63rd, but Black cut across South Loomis, past Ogden Park, and toward 71st.

He cut through another alley, paused. No one following him. Not that anyone had a reason to—yet.

He pulled back onto the bigger streets, passed another church. His fifth in ten minutes. This was the kind of neighborhood that warranted a lot of prayers. Turned on a smaller street not much different from the others. Some houses boarded up, while others sat broken and abandoned and couldn't be bothered. A few cars, a burned-out SUV. He turned off his lights and let himself coast into the shadows.

Snow began to fall in earnest and made it difficult to see. Three inches on the ground and temperatures still dropping. Random working streetlights lit large, wet clumps torn from the night skies, while reflections from the towering giants in the distance created a soft glow that was perfect for his purposes.

Put his phone on vibrate. Grabbed the items taken from Jimenez's duffel bag. Zipped his jacket. Pulled on a pair of black gloves. He needed his hands working, not frozen.

Black stepped out—a black wraith moving silently through the alley toward another street.

Crawley cruised past an abandoned elementary school. Children and teachers exchanged long ago for overgrown weeds and useless chain link fences. Anything deemed of value had long been scrapped and sold, while books and maps and globes still sat on the desks and across floors with the overturned chairs.

Battered lockers and hallways were used as canvases for mostly unimaginative taggers, while needles and beer cans replaced bats and balls.

Jimenez thought he saw a family of coyotes, bitch and pups, moving through the snow toward the cover of the crumbling walls and broken windows.

Crawley turned the corner and slowed down. A shit street for sure. Abandoned homes, overgrown lots, more discarded cars. On the opposite corner, a darkened market. Beside it, two storefronts. One for rent and one with a banner proclaiming Grand Opening—Jashanna Dance Studio.

Next came the alley, then an abandoned two-story house painted in brilliant oranges and reds, peeling trim in greens and blues and with entire passages of both the Bible and Koran hand-lettered on the walls.

The next building was brick and stone, a four-story gray-stone surrounded by an eight-foot fence topped with coiled razor wire. One obvious way in, a half-ass metal gate opening to a broken walkway leading to the house. Lights on and visible on the first, second, and third floors. A few Christmas bulbs hanging off the windows and randomly draped over unkempt bushes.

On the porch, door open behind them, two huge men. Either one as big as Crawley and Jimenez together. Both with enough metal to double as Christmas displays or pretend they were players.

Neither hiding the M4's in their hands. They eyeballed the cops from behind huge blue clouds of smoke and white breath as they cruised by.

"What's his plan?"

Jimenez shrugged. "You know he makes the shit up as he goes."

Crawley threaded his way through the cars parked on both sides of the streets. A new AMG GTR, two hundred-thousand with the custom wheels and stereo. A couple of new BMWs, a couple of high-end SUVs, same customization—wannabe hip hop style.

Further down the street, a two-year-old four-door sedan. Black, with chrome hubcaps instead of custom rims. Jimenez took in the radio antennas along the roof-line. Snapped his eyes toward another further down the street. Then a black Ford van. Tinted windows. More antennas.

"Christ! It's a fucking conga line out here," Jimenez said.

"Special Needs could make these fucks."

They cruised the street as slowly as possible, passing an empty agency car, plates screaming FBI for anyone who knew how to read them. Then another, at least two men behind the tinted glass, and then the van. Number of agents unknown.

Crawley grabbed the radio as Jimenez dialed in a new frequency.

A crackle of static and the squelch of feedback, then, "Central. This is David Jackson Zulu. Over"

"Go ahead. Over."

"Maurine? Is that you?"

"Yeah, Jackie boy. You calling 'cause you miss me?"

Maurine was only five-four, but well over two hundred pounds, and had hair the color of a fire hydrant teased into some kind of 50s style 'poodle cut' that she thought made her look hip and retro. Crawley was sure *no one* could miss her.

"Hey. We're doing a look-see at Ohio Adams. Can you tell me if there's a half-ass Fed Op going on that nobody bothered to tell us about?"

"Nothing on the field watch. Let me see what I can find out."

Jimenez twisted his head back toward the walk-up.

"What the hell is the Major doing?"

"Christ!" Crawley peered out through the snow. "I thought he was going in dark!"

A man from inside the van with a 400mm lens saw Black come from the alley, walk through the snow, open the sad little gate, hanging at an angle on its broken, rusty hinges, and approach the four-story brick building.

Two more men watched the same scene play out on the bank of surveillance monitors stacked along the inside of the van. The rest of the equipment was state of the art—cameras and mics, visual and audio recorders.

In the dark and strobe-like falling snow, Special Agent Warren Michaels, the only one old enough to know, thought it all looked like black and white animation from the early days of television.

"Be advised. We have what appears to be an unknown white male," Michaels turned from the monitor to the other men. "He's white right?"

They stared harder. Special Agent Richard Jackson on the camera and Special Agent Rafael Rodriguez sitting on a seat beside Michaels. Shrugged. Being *special* didn't make it any easier to see.

Maybe a bit of profile but never face-on to the camera. They saw the man pull off his gloves as he approached the gate, and push them in his pockets. Yep, white. Rodriguez nodded.

"An unknown white male approaching the target."

In the fed car, two more agents, both in similar two-for-one discount suits and ten-dollar ties, strained to see through the snow. Danny Kooser, with a nearly useless shotgun mic aimed out the window, headphones on, a telephoto up to his eyes, while his partner, Carmine Biela, stared through a Night Optics Gen II monocle, dialed down to zero to contend with the blast of ambient light reflecting off the snow.

"Roger that."

Biela traded the two-thousand dollar monocle for a hundred and fifty dollar pair of Bushnell's to watch Black go through the gate and walk toward the two giants. Biela spoke into the radio mic.

"UNSUB approaching the door. Might be here to move the package."

"And get himself killed," Kooser added.

Black pulled his hands out of his pockets, making sure he wasn't seen as a threat. The two behemoths, six-four, six-five, seven hundred pounds between them, might have been great college linemen. Maybe even co-captains. Probably offense, Black thought. They didn't move right for defense.

With the unlikely name of Casper, the giant on the right tilted forward. "The fuck you want?" Yeah. Holding their ground. *Definitely offense.* Tackles or guards.

"I want to talk to Mookie."

"Who is you, white boy? You a cop?"

That's it? *White boy?* Okay. Not college. *Maybe* high school.

"Do I look like a cop?"

Deon looked him over. "Exactly like a cop."

Casper looked up and across the street into Kooser's camera. "You with those motherfuckers?"

Black didn't need to look. "Fuck no," Black said.

Deon took a hit from a blunt the size of a Cuban cigar, let it out slowly. Casper glanced at the van, thought about it. "Go on. Get the fuck out of here."

Deon, from behind the cloud of blue smoke. "What the fuck you want with Mookie?"

Casper irritated with his co-captain. "There ain't no *'fuck you want with Mookie.'*"

Gestured with the carbine, in case Black didn't see it. "You a ignant motherfucka out here. Mookie don't talk to ignant motherfuckas."

The warmth beckoned Black from inside the open door. Voices, male and female. A bit of laughter, maybe some moaning.

A television somewhere. He wondered if he should just shove the carbine up Casper's ass and pull the trigger.

Deon determined to get to the bottom of this. "You a reporter?"

When his brother had been killed walking back from a junior-high basketball game, reporters hounded his mother until she gave them a sound bite they played over and over until the next shooting—not even a day later. A little girl sitting upstairs with five other little girls at her first slumber party. A drive-by pray and spray.

"You wired?"

"Yep."

Casper frowned. Not sure how this changed anything, but Mookie did like the spotlight. "Let me see," Casper said. Again used his weapon to make his point.

Black unzipped his jacket. Slowly opened it up for them to see. Both men's eyes went wide, and they started backing up.

"I want to talk to Mookie."

CHAPTER
FOURTEEN

Crawley and Jimenez made their second loop as the two men let Black through the door.

"What the fuck?" Jimenez shook his head. "How the fuck he pull that off?"

The door closed behind Black and the two cops swiveled to the Feds as they passed.

Both agents stared back.

"Looks like we have local dicks on scene," Kooser relayed into the mic.

Michaels came back over the crackling radio. "Be advised. UNSUB—white male, six feet, entering premises at Ohio Adams."

"This is fucked," Biela said. "What about CPD? Definitely made us."

"Looks routine. They'll call it in and move on."

Kooser agreed. "And what if UNSUB's the buyer?"

Michaels came back, "Stay alert.

The two cops passed the van, still unable to see movement inside, but could feel themselves being watched. Crawley glanced at his partner, "What a clusterfuck."

Crawley forced himself to keep driving, his mind racing overtime. Did the Major know the target was under federal task-force surveillance? How could he? DEA? No. Vehicle plates pointed to FBI. Or ATF. *Fuck—maybe all three.*

How the hell had Black talked himself inside? And how the fuck was he going to get out again?

Black entered the walk-up. A dim vestibule with a steep staircase on the left. A long hallway made up the right side—doors on either side for its entire length. The two giants retreated and Black bumped the door shut behind him.

First door on the right open, lit inside with a sparse strand of intermittent-blinking Christmas bulbs on the windows, ratty furniture, and a few hypes lounging on a stained, scary-looking sofa. A couple were helping each other shoot up, while two others shared a crack pipe.

"Be cool, man," Deon said.

A door on the left side of the hall opened, and a skinny chick, dirty cropped t-shirt and panties, scratching at the scabs on her face, crossed the hall. Meth-head zombie walk, ignored the three men and fell onto a bare, soiled mattress in the first room.

Black still held his jacket open, the threat enough to keep the men at bay. A web belt crossed his chest. On the belt, two hand grenades. Black's thumbs looped through two shoe strings looped through the pins.

Black reached for Casper's weapon. The man backed up, watching the shoestring pulling dangerously at the pin, tripped on the stairs, and fell back on his considerable ass.

"Shit man! Okay, okay." He handed over the assault rifle. Black put his hand out for Deon's. The man thought for a moment, searching for a way out of it. Gave up.

Black took the gun. "Where?"

"Third floor," Deon said flatly. "No way you is getting out alive, motherfucka."

"I'm okay with that." He gestured toward the open room on the right and backed the two men in.

Meth Chick was wrapped around a skinny, semi-conscious girl on the dirty mattress. Like two pieces of tangled spaghetti.

She looked up—eyes not focusing, brain not quite processing as Black goaded the two giants into the room.

"Fuck y—" the words not out of Deon's mouth when Black shattered his face with the butt of the carbine. Deon's head rocked back.

He reached up to catch the blood and his teeth as he dropped to his knees.

Lunging forward, Casper's massive arms reached for Black in hopes of crushing him. Three-hundred fifty pounds versus two hundred. Black let himself be pulled in.

The giant looked into the eyes of death looking back as Black drove the tactical blade up through his throat and into his brain. The light in Casper's eyes faded quickly, and Black jerked the blade out, stepped to the side as three-hundred fifty pounds crashed to the floor, and toppled over.

Deon's eyes locked on the grim reaper above him. Shaking. Trying for control but failing. He wasn't ready to die, and fought for words through the fear and the blood streaming from his broken nose and mouth.

"You ain't gotta kill me, man."

Black considered. He was here for Mookie. "You get one chance. Take it."

The big man watched as Black slipped off the grenade belt, tossed it to Meth Chick.

Black moved aside and let the man lumber to his feet and lurch into the hall. Black reassessing the man's potential. Could have been a running back. Pro Bowl material. The man bounced off the staircase, recovered, spun in place, did a stutter step, and crashed out the door.

The door opened and one of the giants burst out, blood pouring from a busted face, slipping on the snow, and tripping down the steps. Got his feet under him, sprinted toward the street.

"What the fuck is this?" The FBI men watched on telephoto and monitors as the man crashed through the gate, tearing it completely off its rusted hinges, and took off up the street.

The agents in the car watched Deon heading right for them. Biela on radio. "What the— Do we scoop him up?"

"Fuck that shit!" Kooser said. "I don't need him bleeding all over the fucking car."

Michaels and the two in the van watched him on monitors. Deon made his way to one of the hip hop SUVs and was soon fishtailing and sliding up the street.

The other two agents in the van shrugged and waited for Michaels. He ran it through his head.

"Maintain positions."

Halfway up the stairs to the second floor. Outside edge of his foot, heel to toe, thankful for the tactical boots. Moving on the treads closest to the wall, aiming for quiet. Needn't have worried. Though the outside of the building was rough, partly from neglect and partially from design, hiding the nefarious operations inside, the construction was done at a time when people took pride in their work and the structure was solid.

Black came onto the second floor, clocking the security cameras embedded in the ceiling as a shirtless man came from a room and entered the long hall. Radio in one hand, M10 compact machine-pistol in the other as he tried to buckle his pants. Registering the strange white man coming up the steps when Black's knife, invisible in the dim light, spun across the thirty feet of hallway and into his throat.

The shock and force took him off his feet, and he crashed backward into the windows.

So much for quiet—

Black raced toward an opening door. Slammed a punch into the first man coming out that broke the man's jaw and bounced his head off the door jamb. Black spun and snapped an elbow back into the face of a second man trying to exit the room, shattering cartilage and bone.

Pivoted on his right leg and threw a kick with his left that he drove through the first man's knee, then backhand chopped the throat of a third man, crushing the man's windpipe.

The man dropped his gun and clawed at his throat as Black turned back into his first two attackers.

No immediate threat from the first.

The second man pushed past the blood and pain of his broken nose and tried to bring his gun to bear. Black threw a blinding combination. Palm strike, hook punch, elbow. The palm strike put his thumb in the man's eye, ruptured the eardrum, and shattered the man's cheekbone. Black's hook shattered the man's wrist, snapping the radial bone.

The downward elbow strike crashed through muscle and tendons and dislocated the man's shoulder. The man gasped in pain and his gun bounced on the floor. Black pushed the now useless arm up and slipped behind him, wrapped his arms around the man's throat, and then dropped forward—his weight snapping the man's neck.

The third man still struggled for air, his eyes locking on Black and the guns that lay at their feet. Black ducked under him, grabbed, spun, and lifted the man long enough to pivot and toss him down the stairs.

The man crashed and tumbled to the first-floor landing.

The first man lay on the floor, holding his knee and groaning in shock. Black mercifully kicked him in the head and put the man out.

Black crossed the length of the hallway. Pulled his knife from the throat of the dead man stuck with his ass hanging out of the broken hall window, wiped it off on the man's pants leg. Passed an open door, a young naked woman passed out on the bed.

Turned the corner and climbed the stairs to the third floor.

Same layout. A long hall with windows on either end. Doors on the left and right, another flight of stairs at the end leading to a fourth floor. Signs of renovation. Lath and plaster replaced with modern drywall, new hardwood floors, new hardware, and recessed lighting. Same cameras in the ceilings.

Mookie watched Black on a 110-inch 8K monitor, the center-piece of a modular display that took up fifteen feet of wall. The expansive room, formed from one-half of the entire third floor, was surprisingly stylish. Raised twelve-foot ceilings and gleaming hardwood floors. Besides the poster bed and welcoming furniture, well-lighted contemporary art and textile hangings, displayed blown glass, a saltwater aquarium, a thirty-year-old Bechstein grand piano, and half-a-dozen vintage pinball machines.

Gib and Maino joined him, and after watching the man on the screen destroy the first level of his security team as if a spinning, slashing, whirling dervish of death had been set upon them, Mookie now watched the man come up to the third floor.

The three grew up in the most violent neighborhoods of one of America's most violent cities. Murder a part of the daily struggle.

All three then fought for their lives with other violent offenders from those same neighborhoods in some of the most demeaning and vicious lockups in the world. Same dynamics—hidden behind bars. Places where men, despite the public outcry and promises of reform, became subhuman to survive. Places Mookie thrived but vowed to never return.

Mookie had never admitted fear before, to himself or others, but watching this play out in real-time, he felt—*something*.

"What the fuck he want?"

"Let's kill the motherfucker and ask him later," Maino said.

Mookie was fine with that. Like the witness to the murder they'd neutralized. He liked that word. Expanding his education. He didn't kill or murder people anymore. He *neutralized* them.

Gib ran toward a control panel in the walls. Scooped up an AK47 as he went.

Maino crouched at the far end of the room, standing near a door with an AK of his own, while Mookie picked up a gleaming nickel-plated Sig P226. Fifteen rounds of 9x19mm parabellum.

No need to chamber a round, always ready to fire.

His hand on the switch, Gib nodded to Maino, waited for Mookie.

...

Déjà vu. Black crested the stairs to the third floor. A myriad of smells. Grass, along with something stronger, sharper. Hashish. Asian food. A rancid smell of burning plastic laced with urine and the smell of sewage. A muffled television heard from a room somewhere on the left, the repetition of a video game further down the hall. The right side of the hallway sounded, *or maybe just felt,* quieter. Cavernous.

There'd been no time for intelligence or recon. Black was relying on instinct.

Instinct was a combination of internal processing of sensory minutia and genetic coding. Without thought to slow him down, the lizard part of his brain, millions of years of encoded survival data, let his body move in ways that defied logic or computational reasoning. He once tried to unravel it. That got him shot and landed him in a Taliban prison cell.

Experience had taught him to rely on his subconscious as much as anything he might give himself credit for as rational thought, and instinct was telling him that the rooms on the right side of the hallway, away from the rancid odors, was Mookieville.

Bound to be more guards, Black dove toward the door on the left as the lights went out and the darkness exploded with gunfire. His full weight and momentum let him shatter the thick wooden door and brought him inside a room.

Blinded by the comparative darkness, a man silhouetted against the television's glow got off a few rounds before Black tackled him.

Instinct, not even sure there was a man in front of him until the gunshots went off. No thought, no technique, no time. He used all his momentum to tackle and drive the man across the room until they crashed into a wall. More shots raked the wall, and he felt the exploding gunpowder and heat against his face.

He smashed the man's head against the wall. Again. The man was strong but caught by surprise. Black let his fingers dig and gouge at the man's eyes. The man screamed and Black smashed his forehead onto the man's nose. Flesh and bone exploded under the onslaught, and as the man's head flew backward, Black launched himself into the air.

The man bounced and staggered off the wall as Black came down with his full weight, driving his elbow into the man's spine. The man's vertebrae separated, his spine snapped, and he dropped like a stone. Black scooped up the TEC-9. Felt the weight. Maybe twenty rounds.

Maino sprayed bullets from down the hall until he emptied the mag. Rounds ricocheting and going through walls. Nearly blind and deaf, he stumbled down the hall as he slapped in a second magazine.

"WHERE ARE YOU MOTHERFUCKER?"

Black moved silently toward the broken door, pressed himself against the wall. Heard Maino dragging himself closer.

The windows at the third story hallway were lighting up from the outside. Glass shattered and semi-automatic gunfire ripped and echoed into the night.

"SHOTS FIRED SHOTS FIRED!" Biela screamed into the radio.

Kooser grabbed the mic. "Move in. Move in."

"Negative!" Michaels's voice shot back. "Maintain your positions." Michaels was responsible for their safety too. They were a fucking surveillance team—techs and computer geeks. Not the men you put in the middle of a fire-fight. "Back-up is on the way. Repeat. Maintain your positions."

Kooser half-way out the door. "Fuck that!"

Biela jumped out behind him, slipped, and fell hard. Cracked his head on the car door and hit the ground hard. Dazed and bleeding, he staggered to his feet and tried to run after Kooser. He found it hard enough to breathe the icy cold air, running on the ice with leather shoes was impossible.

...

The third-floor lights flicked back on. Blinding after the dark. Maino fumbled and dropped the magazine.

Black on the other side. Heard the mag hit the floor. Adjusted his position. The TEC-9 pressed against the wall.

He heard someone yell out. "You good?"

Maino bent to pick it up and yelled back. "Yeah. I'm good."

Black fired. Twelve 9mm rounds ripped through the new drywall. He stepped from the room. Blood dripping down the walls.

Gib at the doorway in Mookieville.

Mookie screaming. "CUT 'EM!"

The entire building went black, the glow of city streetlights and snow fighting to get inside the grimy windows.

AK in hand, Gib took a deep breath, peered around the doorway into the dark hallway. Jerked his head back, eyes crossed and glazing over. Black's nine-inch tactical blade buried to the hilt in his forehead.

Gib turned toward Mookie and fell into the room, his AK raking the walls in an explosion of sound, bullets, plaster. Rounds stitched a line across the monitors and the giant LCD screen exploded in a shower of sparks.

Black stepped into the room, felt for the wall, and flipped the lights back on.

Mookie stood in the middle of the cavernous room, his nickel-plated P226 pressed against the head of a young girl. No more than twelve, eyes bright and clear against her dark skin, accepting of her fate and perhaps welcoming the release. Watched Black materialize through the haze of gun smoke like a magician on stage but with a submachine gun in hand.

"Stay the fuck back or I'll blow her motherfuckin' head off."

Black strode toward the man without hesitation. The man who destroyed countless lives. The man who thought he was above the law. The man who threatened his family.

"Stay the fuck back or I swear I'll —"

Black dropped the TEC-9. In the instant Mookie watched it fall, Black pulled his 1911 Commander and fired. The heavy .45 barely moved in his hand but the 230-grain hollow point exploded from the custom four and a half-inch barrel.

Mookie's head exploded—the atomized mist of bone and blood filled the air and settled to the floor.

Black lowered the gun. The waif-like girl stared at him—a man dressed in black, gun in his hand, both of them covered in blood.

Trembling, fighting tears, she bolted toward the door. Black reached for her, but she was slippery with Mookie's blood and darted past. Raced barefoot up the stairs.

Crawley and Jimenez saw the flashes upstairs as they came back around the corner. Slowed the car and saw Kooser and Biela slipping and sliding their way up the sidewalk toward the house. Not dressed for running in the snow—the faster they moved, the less progress they made.

Crawley gunned the powerful engine, slid the squad car over the curb, bounced over the sidewalk, and into the gate. Cutting off the two agents.

Further down the street, Michaels and Rodriguez were out of the van, pulling breakers with FBI stenciled on the back over their vests.

Jimenez shouting on radio, "—10-33. Need immediate assistance. Shot's fired. Ohio and Adams. Repeat. Officers need immediate assistance—"

"—FBI!" Kooser yelling as he and his partner came around the car.

Crawley made it up the steps and to the landing. "Chicago PD! Stand the fuck down!"

Biela waved his service weapon, trying to catch his breath.

"Back the fuck away! This is a federal directive order—"

"You back the fuck away!" Jimenez joined Crawley at the top of the steps. "Chicago PD has lead."

Squad cars, with light bars and dash strobes bouncing off the snow, their arrival announced with sirens screaming in the night, turned onto the street from both directions.

The FBI van scraped the side of Crawley's Charger, bounced up over the curb, and crashed through the eight-foot fence. Metal on metal, razor-wire sprung free and sparks flew across the van's roof and windshield and brought them all to a momentary stop.

Black could hear the cops and agents arriving and arguing downstairs. He took off after the girl and stormed up the stairs.

The girl crying and pulling at a locked door. She sensed Black behind her and spun. Mute but eyes pleading. She moved aside and Black's foot rocketed into the door, shattering wood and tearing metal from the frame.

Crawley and Jimenez were still arguing over jurisdiction, gamely slowing the Agents down. Uniforms were exiting their cars and joining the fray as Kooser, Biela, Rodriguez, and Michaels crowded their way in.

They saw the broken man at the bottom of the stairs. Fell back, and pushed their way into Meth Chick's room. Slipped and slid and stumbled over the big corpse.

Casper lay in a pool of blood reflecting the intermittent-blinking Christmas lights.

Beyond him, Meth Chick and her skinny girlfriend knelt in the center of a dirty mattress, their eyes glazed in fascination and wonder as if trying to analyze and grade the most precious jewels in the world.

Cradling the two steel-jacketed grenades, Meth Chick gazed at her worshiping girlfriend and smiled, filled with love, then finally seemed to recognize they were no longer alone.

Fingers tangled in the shoestrings, the shoestrings looped through the pins, she lifted the grenades as if talismans against the invaders.

Kooser tried to swallow. "Ma'am. Don't move."

...

Black stood frozen. Anger. Adrenalin. Horror. In front of him, a dozen young girls, colors of the rainbow, as young as six and as old as fifteen. All rail-thin, panties and thin cropped or torn t-shirts, ribs and bruises showing. The mists of their breath billowing in the dark against the cold, helping each other to prepare for whatever new horror awaited.

As his eyes adjusted, he took in the few ratty mattresses. Threadbare blankets in the freezing room. A makeshift toilet of plastic buckets. Wire dog crates. A couple of slight, fragile girls lying inside.

They saw the tears welling in his eyes. Could feel the air vibrate around him as he fought the memories and emotions that bubbled up and cascaded through his soul.

He saw their fear and doubt, could feel it as his own. Saw himself through their eyes and knew he must look like Death itself.

Voices and arguing from below drifted up the stairs. Black dropped to his knees, set down the .45. Emptied his pockets. An extra mag, two knives, his phone. Laced his fingers over his head and waited.

The girls began helping others from the cages. Huddled together for warmth and trying to comfort each other. Thankful but confused at the apparition on his knees. The girl from downstairs took a step forward and pointed at his phone.

Meth Chick watched the cops trying to back out of the room, stumbling over Casper and the sticky puddle of blood.

Casper had never been nice to the girls, taking advantage of their weakness, pay-for-play drugs for sex, and nearly tore her girlfriend in half. Thought it was funny he was so big he tore their insides. *Now, look at him.* Dead. Casper the friendly ghost. No— not friendly. Not nice at all. She laughed. Now just a pile of meat.

A fat fucking dead ghost.

She saw the wide-eyed men looking at her, filled with fear. It made her laugh harder until she gave in to her hysteria. Suddenly stopped, lurched at them. Laughed as they shrunk back and she pulled the shoestring.

Nothing.

She started laughing again.

Kooser slowly reached for the grenades. Cautiously took them out of the girl's hands. Duds. Empty props used as paperweights and gags. *Real fucking funny.*

Black and the girls heard the men from downstairs coming closer. A herd of tactical boots and leather shoes clomping up the stairs and clearing the lower rooms. Could hear them shout as they discovered more bodies.

Black followed the girl's finger to his phone, lit up, and spinning on the cold wooden floor. A name on the screen. HOLLY. He hesitated. Reached out and put it on speaker. He could feel as much as hear the stampede of cops coming up the final staircase.

"Tommy? You there?"

He could hear Crawley and Jimenez arguing with the Agents over who should take the lead. Jimenez calling for restraint and to be first onto the fourth floor. Losing the argument as the FBI forced their way past. Just steps away, outside on the landing and preparing to enter.

"Tommy?" Black heard the gut-wrenching fear in her voice. Looked at the window behind the girls. Thirty feet away.

"Tommy?" Crying. "Sam's missing."

Decision made. The girls sensed his thoughts, parted as he rose, and watched him sprint across the room. Hit the glass at full speed as the cops tumbled over each other into the room.

Kooser getting a shot off as Jimenez pulled his hands down. Both running past the girls to the window.

Lower and further away than he remembered, Black hit the second-story rooftop of the building next door dreaming he'd roll gracefully across the rooftop, and sprint off into the night.

Instead, unable to see beneath three inches of heavy wet snow, he skidded, crashed, and tumbled, his weight and momentum breaking through the forty-year-old tar shingles and rotted beams.

The rooftop gave way, helping break his fall as a loose nail ripped at his side. He slammed through a rotted wall further slowing his momentum and found himself almost on his feet standing on the second floor.

Gulping for air, his entire rib cage burning in agony, deeply bruised if not broken. Black once tried to tackle a Humvee head-on. This was worse. Forced his lungs to push past the pain. Checked his side. Blood spilled over his fingers from a six-inch gash, but he'd live.

Black stumbled down the rotted staircase to the first floor. A dazzling light show of colored police strobes bounced across every outside surface and reflected off the trampled snow. He watched through the torn siding and broken windows until the officers, shouting and getting instructions on radio, began pulling out service weapons and turning toward the building he was in.

He squeezed through a gaping hole in the back wall and faded into the night.

CHAPTER
FIFTEEN

The Panamanian freighter, Adventuress, tossed and rolled. The 115-meter ship, loaded at 2500 metric tonnes, cut through the Indian Ocean waves on its approach to the island much the way Portuguese, and then French sailing ships had in the mid-16th century.

At nearly a thousand square miles, the island is home to a mix of French, Indian, Tamil, Chinese, and African descendants, many of their ancestors brought in as slaves from Madagascar and Mozambique primarily to work the coffee plantations owned by the French East India Company.

Fifty-seven hundred miles away from its European Mother, Réunion Island remains as an overseas department of France and an outermost region of the European Union with all the rights afforded to the union's citizenship for the island's 800,000 inhabitants.

Sam was in Chicago, curled up in her bed, fighting for warmth under thick blankets and fighting the tug of consciousness that threatened to bring her back. The blankets were heavy, wrapped around her, protection from the cold, but she couldn't move. The blankets of thick, quilted down became thick, heavy snow, and quickly melted.

Drenched and threatened to drown, yet she couldn't rise. The water sloshed and splashed around her. Her waterlogged mattress slowly sank into a shallow bath of warm, fetid liquid as her skin became a sponge—the water *alive*—moving and crawling and seeping into her pores.

She woke with a start, but without light, first thought she was still asleep, caught in the dream. It took moments to realize the nightmare was her reality. Gasping for air as she desperately tried to adjust her body.

Though able to untangle some of the wire wrapped around her hands and ankles, there was nowhere to go, no way to relieve the cramping in her arms and legs which threatened to tear muscle from her bones. Twisted to move her head toward the glimmer of hope the three tiny holes afforded her. Pulled in what she could of the moist ocean air, fought to control her breathing. Knowing with every fiber of being that she had to keep her fears and panic in check.

Gave in. Screamed until she passed out.

The ocean now calm. Points of light millions of light-years above matched the bright dots that spread and danced across the small island's interior mountains. The Panamanian captain steered the ship toward the port lights of Saint-Denis where tall, insect-like gantry cranes stood patiently to pluck and load treasure to and from the waiting ships.

Manifests filed and signed as bored inspectors left the ship after the most cursory of glances, monster-sized cranes began the task of off-loading the first of the ship's cargo.

Forklifts and trucks soon maneuvered through the narrow alleys formed by stacks of twenty and forty-ton containers, moving and further organizing the crates, drums, and boxes.

The wide steel forks slid beneath a wooden pallet, lifted a stack of steel drums, and carried them toward a cavernous warehouse. Another man hit a switch that opened the steel dock doors, and the forklift rolled in.

The pallet set down as another man cut the metal strapping that held the drums in place. Two men moved drums out of the way, while a third man reached for another. Marked on its side with a yellow X, three one-inch holes punched in its lid.

He rolled the heavy drum across the floor toward a wooden workbench. Turned on a hand-held angle grinder, put on a plastic face shield, and began cutting off the top. The spinning abrasive disc chewed through the metal with a shower of sparks; the tearing, grinding sound of carbon fiber and aluminum oxide on metal filling every available space.

The grinder stopped. No erudite French spoke here; the only communication between the men was in a bastard Creole. The man switched the worn disc for a new one and finished cutting off the lid.

He used his foot to kick over the drum. One of the others reached for the helpless woman, guiding her past the sharp metal edges. Her body too cramped and weak to stand, another stepped in and the two lifted and dragged her toward shadows at the back of the warehouse.

Terrified, wet, cold, weak—Sam was too scared to speak. They pushed and pulled her toward a large industrial shower room. Shoved her in and she crumpled to the tiled floor. No strength to protest when one of the men reached for a thick fire hose. Another man turned the faucet and a battering ram of cold water slammed her against the tiled walls.

The four men stood watching the forced shower. No banter, no joking, no leering. Meaningless to them as any other piece of meat.

CHAPTER
SIXTEEN

B lack couldn't get comfortable but the plane wasn't designed for that. It wasn't designed for passengers at all. The little sleep that overtook him might have been worse than none. He was hungry. His side throbbed and burned.

He'd abandoned the Escalade. DOD plates with embedded RFID chips. Might as well slip the handcuffs and leg chains on himself and make his reservations at Guantanamo. Not that they wouldn't move him to one of the off-grid black sites. Maybe build one just for him where nobody could hear him scream.

They wouldn't want to *retire* him. Might miss out on life-changing, career-making information. Not that he had any they couldn't get on their own. He was a soldier, *not a fucking spy,* but they'd want to make sure. Might take them a while, but they'd find out eventually or at least report that they had. No. Easier to feed him three squares and keep him buried somewhere in case they had to dig him up again.

He wasn't trying to escape—Black had no illusions or equivocation about the law and what he'd done. Right and wrong and the law were entirely different matters, and he could live with himself. He needed time to find Sam, bring her home safe. Then he'd turn himself in and let the courts, the system he'd sworn to defend, even if it had sometimes abandoned him in the past, sort it out and accept whatever judgment they visited upon him.

Black was improvising, formulating plans as he went. Jumped on a train. Lots of CTA cameras, but he was confident he could make himself blend in and the best chance of them not all working was on the Green-line. A haggard, working-class man on his way to or from work for the night shift, or one of the city's five-thousand homeless people. Dressed in all black, limping, and favoring his side; he figured he looked the part.

If you didn't look closely you wouldn't see the blood, and if they did, most people wouldn't want to get involved.

The middle of a snowy night in Englewood. The only other white man he saw this deep was arguing with an imaginary jury about how his ex-wife was entirely responsible for the holocaust and the destruction of six million Jews, and therefore not entitled to alimony or child support for any of their three Springer Spaniels, one of which acted suspiciously like he might have some Border Collie in him.

Black couldn't make sense of all the leaps in logic but turned to look as the guy's deep, gravelly voice sounded so much like Nick Nolte he thought it might be him, rehearsing a role and riding the train as part of his process. Not sure if Nolte was a method actor or riding on his train, and after turning to look at the man, buried inside a Malibu, California hoodie, still couldn't call it.

He wouldn't call it acting, but his ability to compartmentalize his tasks on a subconscious level allowed him to observe and mimic those around him with uncanny accuracy. At six feet, he could stand tall and project a slim, well-built man at least an inch taller. Add boots, and he could make people guess him at six-two or three. Round his shoulders, pull his head down, compress his posture, and people put him at five-eight or nine and pegged at two-twenty or even thirty.

Even with blue eyes, his dark hair and frequently tanned skin meant he could be mistaken for any of a dozen nationalities.

It was all a lot of effort, and he wasn't putting much into it either way right now. He was counting on the fact people tend to not want to look too closely at their fellow riders, unless they happened to be a beautiful woman which he decidedly was not.

Got closer to downtown and forced himself to start paying attention. He sat up straighter. Projected a different level of confidence. A couple of men got on. On their way to work. A couple students, the two girls really into each other or just trying to stay warm. Three wannabe thugs stomping the snow off their boots. Flashing metal, staring everybody down.

Next stop, a mother and daughter boarded—a pretty Hispanic woman of about thirty and her daughter—already a tall, willowy beauty of about ten. The kind of young beauties used to being harassed.

He smiled at the mother, just enough to let her know he was on their side, and they could count on him. They would make good cover if people thought they were together. She smiled back, distrustful but hoping he could back up the confidence he was giving off if they needed him. She took in the other passengers, scooted by the thugs, and pulled her daughter into the seat in front of him, crowding together with their arms looped around their many packages.

He could hear the mother's quiet conversation with the daughter. On their way to the mother's sister's house. A place to spend the upcoming holidays. His thoughts flashed to the girls on the fourth floor. Hoped they'd soon have somewhere loving to go, someone to look out for them in their future. Was glad the mother in front of him would never have to have her daughter taken and abused by the men he'd visited tonight.

They got off two stops later; one smartphone lighter, but otherwise unmolested.

At least four people in this city would give their lives for him without question, but he couldn't contact anyone of them. Couldn't put them in danger more than he had.

Jackie was going to be furious, as much about him not trusting her to deal with the threats on her own as anything he'd done. Big Al would be worried but proud of him. Saved him from having to take action, if not with his own hands, then one of the many people who owed him from the days he walked his own beat.

He knew Crawley and Jimenez would be okay; only pissed he didn't wait to let them help.

The phone was perfect. Too inexpensive to have the high-end security that would prevent him from using it. He called Holly.

She answered before the second ring. "Hello?"

"Don't speak. We have ten seconds." He waited to make sure she understood. No sound but for a quickening of her breath. "Where?"

"Mauritius. It's an isl—"

Black disconnected. Took out the SIM card. Wiped down the phone. Left it under the seat. Got off at the next stop.

Snapped the chip in two and dropped it into the slush, then hailed a cab. Would cost a few dollars, but he could get a ride east out of the city. Make it to an interstate truck stop. Find a ride out of Gary or Merrillville. I-65 South to Kentucky.

Louisville. Nobody looking for him there.

Who the fuck escapes to Louisville?

On his fourth flight, in the air twenty-nine of the past thirty-six hours. Left Louisville with a retired Naval pilot, the father of a boy he saved fifteen years ago on a Kuwaiti oil field. The father was now the private pilot for a retired CEO of a major transportation concern and the quick flight across the northern U.S. border was made in comfort on an otherwise empty seven-seat Cirrus SF50.

Picked up a Southern Air cargo plane that stopped in Kulusuk, Greenland on its way to Kenya. Grabbed another transport plane to Madagascar, and was now on another cargo plane to Mauritius.

The plane smelled strongly of vanilla. The owners, the parents of a woman he'd once had an affair with, had once asked his recommendation for a security team to protect their vanilla crops.

At six-hundred dollars a kilo, more than the price of silver and with over five-hundred million USD in exports, the surge in price compounded by a devastating cyclone created a need for high-end security from pirates and extortionists across the island. It seems their previous security firm was both.

Black had spoken with the errant firm and helped convince them that it was in their best interest to resign. He then reached out to a few people he thought might enjoy a radical change from their current scenery for a cushy job on a Pacific island.

Black stayed long enough to remind the girl why it would never work, besides the fact he found out she was engaged, then made it back to Afghanistan in time to find his team was being disbanded.

He now sat in the jump seat, the rear of the plane stripped and empty. With nothing to absorb the sound, it rattled with every adjustment and course correction.

The pilots usually flew alone, but this wasn't the first time they had an unidentified passenger. The plane hauled crates and transport boxes of dried and cured vanilla beans but occasionally contracted to haul *unspecified* cargo. Part of the deal the owners had made with their new security firm.

"Don't know who you are. But somebody likes you."

The girl, still single, was on holiday in Vienna, which let Black off the hook for anything that might slow him down. Her parents were only too thrilled to help out, as thankful for him breaking off the romance as they were for his efforts to protect the family fortune.

The co-pilot twisted enough to see Black eying the cot bolted to the wall.

"We're usually flying routes west of here. Longer flight times. Still have about 90 minutes, but bunk out if you want. Looks like you could use it. Or there's coffee in the galley."

"Thanks."

Black unbuckled and headed for the galley.

CHAPTER
SEVENTEEN

S am dropped heavily on the floor of a dark, twenty-foot steel
container. Without strength to resist, she lay still while a man
with huge bolt cutters entered the open door and stood behind
her. He waited, but she was afraid to move. He kicked her lightly.

She rolled over and looked up at him. He might have been
handsome but offered no expression or animation to his face. Eyes
steady, he contemplated her without malice or comment, which
frightened her even more.

He nudged her again, and her eyes went to the wicked-looking
bolt cutters. Slowly lifted her bound hands. He cut the remaining
wire bonds from her hands and feet, kicked the wire out the door
as he turned and left.

She was too weak to protest as heavy steel doors slammed shut.
Clung to the narrow shaft of light sneaking in before she heard the
latch and locks snapping shut from the outside. She could hardly
make herself move; scared but thankful to be alone. This time,
without bonds, and in a space large enough to move and stand in.
Small holes had been drilled through the metal and her eyes slowly
adjusted as her mind again began to race.

What did these men want? Here because of the man at the
club? It was his men who grabbed her. His men who attacked
Allan. There could be no doubt that Allan was dead; the knife
moved too quickly for her to see, but she'd seen blood arcing
across the air, the sand wet with red.

What of Billie? Was Hunter also lying with his throat cut somewhere while Billie was left alone and scared, wondering what was happening to her? She thought of the beautiful, exotic woman, thought of her words. *'You're in danger now.'* Yeah, no shit.

Saw the infinite sadness in the woman's eyes as she'd turned back to her.

Had she known? Was she too a prisoner? The obvious abuse, the bruises, the utter disdain the man demonstrated, and yet, the woman held herself—*what?* Above it all? Outside it? As if the cruelty of the man couldn't touch her.

She was overwhelmed with a premonition. Deja vu but from the future, looking back to this moment looking forward. Could she possibly hope to be as brave?

Sound from behind startled her. Sam scrabbled backward across the rusted steel floor, her back pressed tightly against the door, eyes boring into the blackness.

Long moments. A slight shuffling sound. Naked feet on steel? Terrified... and then... a small hand stretched forward from the black. A small plastic cup offered.

More movement and as Sam's eyes and ears adjusted beyond her fear, she could make out a child's face. Then another. And another.

Another hand—a chunk of stale bread.

Sam pulled off the wall, scooted forward, reached for the cup. Water. Grabbed at the bread. Suddenly starving. More children, a dozen. Boys and girls, six to fifteen, moved forward to surround her.

CHAPTER
EIGHTEEN

The pilots had ignored him, unsure of who and what he might be. Better to have as little interaction as possible rather than say or do the wrong thing. Black stepped from the plane and crossed the tarmac, overlooked by any official government scrutiny.

The planes and jets behind him, Black stepped from the bright tropical sun past armed guards outside the huge hanger doors and into a cavernous, dimly lit structure. Stacks of pallets and wooden crates scraped the metal ceiling struts stretched forty feet above him.

Stenciled or stamped on their sides, writing in any of two dozen languages. Inventories and manifests stapled or taped to keep track. Black had been in many such warehouses before and knew that spread among the inventories were enough arms and munitions, rocket launchers and missiles, to outfit a considerable army. Destined for trade and payment around the globe—part of the efforts and back door dealings of a dozen three-letter agencies in as many countries.

That he found himself left alone here was a testament, as were the clandestine flights that brought him here, of the relationships and respect that men who knew of him held for him. Others had received cryptic phone calls or judged his face and stature against rumors and stories they'd heard whispered, and knew that it could only serve their interests to allow the man his space.

Black passed through, happy to let them think whatever they liked as long as it facilitated his goals. Legends were mostly bullshit, even his own, but they sometimes could be useful. Somewhere in these stacked crates were some of the tools he'd want to have at hand, but he wouldn't compromise any of the men here by asking. He would find what he needed elsewhere.

He stepped into streets alive with color and shape; bleating horns of competing delivery trucks, forklifts weaving in and out of traffic and darting in and out of the warehouses and factories that lined the roads, merchants and cooks hawking stacks of Day-Glo colored fresh fruits, steaming chicken and fish curries, and flat, iron skillets over burning coals cooking the ubiquitous dhal puri.

Black pulled out a few American dollars, letting them flash as he bought a pair of the savory flatbread pancakes, folded and stuffed with seasoned yellow split peas and chutney.

"Ici Monsieur. Taksi pou anboche." A chorus of similar offers and the taxis inched and jostled for position and his attention.

A small, banged-up pick-up truck caught his eye. Black ate his snack as he walked across the street, dodging and slipping between the shifting cars and trucks, and without negotiation, slid into the passenger's seat.

CHAPTER
NINETEEN

The plush Beechcraft Bonanza soared over the Upper Karoo, dancing on warm currents rising from the arid grasslands.

Distant red plateaus melted with shimmering heat waves into the horizon and the bleached out sky above it.

Kronmüller reveled in the new plane's responsiveness and his talents in flying it, turned the stick and dipped his wings to watch his shadow race across the backs of a herd of elephants lumbering through clouds of dust as they crossed the southern wetlands now suffering from drought. A harem of Springbok shifted direction as one, running from the sound of the single prop engine racing overhead, then shifted again toward the distant Matroosberg Range and the possibility of late spring grasses sprouting beneath the mountain shadows.

Not for the first time, he thought of flight, not just of the plane but of his person, leaving this dried-up world behind. The forty-gallon tank and nine-hundred miles of range weren't enough—soon he would investigate adding tip tanks and another twenty gallons per wing. Knowing the increased range was there would be worth the cost, even if he never took advantage of it.

The plane set down on a loosely defined runway of hard-packed bushveld and was soon joined by two Range Rovers that taxied the last six hundred feet beside it until he stopped.

Kronmüller stepped from the plane. Dressed more for the clubs than the bush—designer shirt and slacks. Exhilarated from the flight.

He let himself into the first of the Range Rovers, on the ground but still high from the flight.

"The world from above is an amazing place."

Grip smiled despite the reminder from Kronmüller that they came from different worlds. Kronmüller from the sky, the rarefied air of lineage and wealth. Grip from the earth, blood and sweat and shit. The rich and the poor. Kronmüller mostly treated him well. Let the prick have his petty digs.

"Welcome back, Mr. Kronmüller. How's the new plane?"

"Barely needs me." Smiled back at the huge bodyguard. "Any idiot could fly the damn thing."

Grip headed across the savanna.

"Lina?"

Kronmüller never failed to ask; his obsession always displayed and getting worse.

Half of Grip's job seemed to be keeping tabs on her every move. "At the house."

"My father?"

Grip shrugged.

"Fuck it," Kronmüller said. "Let's get this over with."

Mid-morning on a summer's day; Kronmüller and Grip walked across the hard-packed dust. No wind to stir the air, Kronmüller could feel his Versace shirt sticking to him, rivulets of sweat running between his shoulder blades and pooling at his lower back.

Sure, he could dress in something more appropriate, be a fucking farmer like his father, or go naked like the savages, but like everything else in his life, he worked to bend the elements to his will, not be broken by them. Part of that he knew would involve jumping in the plane with Lina and flying as far away from here as he could.

A group of workers stood some distance away from Ringer and a powerfully built older man. White-haired with skin like polished leather. *Ouderling*—the Elder Kronmüller.

Ringer nodded a greeting, but Ouderling kept his eyes lowered, locked on Zama as if relinquishing his gaze might give the man the chance to escape.

Obsidian black skin made red with Karoo dust, the naked man could be twenty years either side of fifty. Hands and feet tied and lying at the roots of a scraggly Mopane tree. The man was covered with insects, eating and crawling in the ragged welts and ripped flesh from a horrific whipping. Flies swarmed in his drying vomit and the bloody liquefied excrement that leaked from his body. Broad lips and nose broken and distorted, eyes swollen shut.

Kronmüller tried to hide his disgust. The smell was making his eyes tear, and he fought the rancid bile that rose to the back of his throat. Grip stood beside him, as resolute as stone, awaiting orders should they come.

Ringer threw a bucket of water on the feces. Kronmüller watched in disgust as his father knelt; his thick, calloused hands sifting through the waste. It took a moment, but he rose with a small, unpolished diamond; nothing more than a small, dull stone in his hands.

"Dust to dust, but somewhere, a gem."

Ringer held out the bucket and Ouderling washed his hands in the remaining water. Examined it in the bleached light of the overhead sun. Looked back down at the hapless man.

"I don't mind you trying to steal from me. I expect it. Even respect it. You're trying for a better life for yourself and your family. But to do it with so little imagination? That's an insult I can not forgive."

Ouderling turned to his son, pushed the diamond into the pocket of his designer shirt. Wiped and cleaned his hands on the expensive fabric. Daring his son to do more than stand with quivering lips and hate-filled eyes.

The two bodyguards and the dozen laborers watched father and son. For an instant, it seemed Kronmüller might break. Grip watched, impressed that he didn't. Sooner than later he knew, he would have decisions to make, life and death decisions, on where his loyalties and future lay.

Ouderling turned at the huffing of a distant pride of lions. Five cats—three females, a juvenile male, and the huge pride male, the coarse black mane framing its massive head, frozen in splendor, locking eyes with the elder Kronmüller. Man and Beast, locked in a battle of wills. One, with two hundred years of hard-fought legacy to back his claim to the land; one, with millennia. Neither one moved.

After what seemed hours but in reality, could only be seconds, Ouderling turned to look at his workmen, then the two body-guards, and finally, the tortured man at his feet.

"We'll leave it for the gods to sort out." He pushed past his son and walked toward the second Range Rover.

CHAPTER
TWENTY

Black folded himself into the front of the little pick-up, knees pushed up against the cracked and worn dash. Tried to put the seat back, reached for the lever beneath the seat.

"Sorry, Boss," the driver said cheerfully. "Stuck."

"Pull over."

The slight young boy appeared so heartbroken, Black tried not to laugh. Brown eyes blinking as if he'd been slapped, the smile flipped over in a tight frown, but he jerked the wheel with no regard for the traffic stacked up behind him and pulled over. The street erupted in blaring horns and brassy bleats of protest.

Black got out, reached under the seat. It took a moment, the lever really was stuck. He didn't want to break anything, but not in the mood to do yoga the entire drive. Seconds later, the seat slid back a foot and Black climbed back in.

The boy's smile was back, an infectious grin. "Wow, super good, Boss!"

The boy leaned on his horn and forced his way back into traffic.

Black held on and took a moment to assess his driver. *Maybe* old enough to have a driver's license, dressed like a walking load of laundry, every color and pattern imaginable.

"Air not working." He flipped the fan switch up and down a couple of times to prove his point, waited for a response, hoping Black had a fix for it too.

The boy pulled and jerked at the steering wheel with his skinny brown arms, using his slight body weight to keep the pick-up moving mostly in a forward direction. The truck had given up its power steering about the same time the rear bearings had started to seize. Braking took multiple pumps of the pedals, pushing whatever fluid remained back into the hydraulic lines enough he could bring the truck to a stop.

The boy kept up a non-stop chatter; a Tarantino-style monologue that explained the island's storied history: the pros and cons of the candidates in the upcoming Mayoral election, the projected weather for the next ten days and the effects of Western industrial manipulation of third-world climate change, and the fight for dollars and tax credits from the burgeoning film industry. At times he would drift in and out of French, or deliver entire passages in Creole, before realizing Black was ignoring him and possibly not understanding the full genius and cleverness of his dissertation.

"Tu parles français?" the boy asked. No answer. "You want English only? No problem. Speak good. YouTube. Many TV. Netflix. HBO."

They threaded their way through the industrial streets; warehouses and delivery trucks, steel hand carts laden with goods stacked and tied ten feet high, merchants with their wares spread on the sidewalks and negotiating prices on everything from nails and screws to baskets overflowing with glistening sardines.

"How you like my city? Really great, huh? Honeymoon top spot. You bring your wife. American? American number one! Where you from mister? New York City?"

"Chicago."

"Chicago? My kind of town! The Windy City. Home Obama. Chicago Bulls. Michael Jordan. Chicago Cubs. Blackhawks."

The boy took a quick breath, navigated toward a more touristy part of town. Colorful street stalls, food stands, local trinkets, oily smoke from the coals, and salt from the ocean in the air.

"Where you go? You need hotel? Best price for Chicago."

Black let the smells, colors, and sounds seep into him. Soon they were close enough to the water that young beach bodies, board shorts, and micro bikinis, were fearlessly cutting back and forth through the cars, open-top jeeps, motorbikes, and bicycles.

"You need girls? Ali knows the best place. Girls number one. Ali know everything! My name Ali. Flotte comme un papillon—" Threw a quick double jab, cross. "—sting like a bee. Ali Bomaye. Your friend Ali find what you need." Caught his breath. "What say you need, Mister?"

Black had called a friend, now with INTERPOL, and asked her to dig into the local news, the hospitals, and morgue.

Sam wasn't mentioned by name but instead reduced to being a girlfriend, a possible local, seen in the company of Allan Chamberlin, son of Xavier Chamberlin, head of a prominent New England political family, and was being quietly sought for questioning. The murder was being downplayed and kept silent, but she'd given him the location of their hotel where he'd booked a room for himself in the name of John Clayton, homage to the first book he'd read.

"I need a gun."

A light switch thrown; Ali's eyes narrowing in concentration, his mouth twisting in thought. Continued driving but started taking surreptitious glances in the mirror, the boy's stealth about as clandestine as a hammer in the head, taking in the details of the man sitting beside him. The clear blue eyes, the thickness of the shoulders and forearms, the powerful hands—knuckles calloused and pounded flat.

His clothes gave little hint. Black had exchanged his bloody Chicago clothes for new everything in Louisville. Burned and buried and traded for trendy tactical boots, jeans and t-shirt, and a simple canvas bomber jacket. Clothes that belonged to the Naval pilot's son. Not perfect but close enough. He needed to pass for a tourist or a local, not look like he was storming the beach.

"You need a gun cowboy? You need a gun Rambo?"

Ali waited but the man just looked at him, giving no hints.

"Ahhhh... Bond. *James Bond*. This serious shit."

Black did his best not to laugh at his new friend.

Twenty-six miles away, southeast of the capital, a British Airways jet out of London-Gatwick landed on a Sir Seewoosagur Ramgoolam International Airport runway. Named after the Mauritian leader who won independence from the British in 1968, and later served as the fledgling nation's Governor-General and first Prime Minister. The passengers soon departed Gate 26 and began making their way toward baggage, customs, and ground transportation.

Two men were met by airport security and whisked past all other inconveniences, their service weapons still on their persons from the flight. Regulation haircuts and discount suits were only a part of the full persona that screamed as much as any placard they could have carried—FBI.

Met outside by their Mauritian liaison and counterparts.

Michaels reached out his hand. "Special Agent Warren Michaels and this is my partner, Special Agent Rafael Rodriguez."

"Jack Gauber, Mauritius Police."

"Pete Curpen. Special Operations."

Shaking hands all around before Gauber led them to a black Land Cruiser.

Bags put in the trunk, Gauber took the wheel.

"Good flight?" Curpen asked.

Curpen took the front and let the agents pile into the back seats.

"Long," Rodriguez said. "Eight hours to London. Twelve hours here. I'm sure isolation at the end of the world has its advantage but access is not one of them."

"Hence the isolation," Michaels added, not unkindly.

"*Hence*," Rodriguez repeated. He found much of his older partner's English vocabulary *quaint* and *whimsical*. That Michaels spoke four languages, including French, Russian, and Turkish, while Rodriguez added Spanish and Arabic, was one of the reasons they'd been fast-tracked to investigate the American's murder.

No one knew where this might take them.

Being part of the Chamberlin political dynasty, albeit nothing greater than a territorial governor a hundred years ago, but one that continued to make generous party donations, meant you had the full weight of the government's highest investigative arm should you request it. And Allan's father had.

Their help—not only the FBI's but the help of Michaels and Rodriguez personally requested. The case in Chicago was an absolute cock-up and still ongoing, just getting started, albeit with a new direction and focus after the discovery of the children. The fact that they were successfully recovered made the agents instant bureau superstars.

A missing girl, even if she was the mistress of the politician's son, with the bullshit logic that she was also from Chicago where they'd realized a successful outcome, put them on a very short list. Michaels knew their superstar status would only last until the next unsuccessful outcome, but for now, after twenty years, he was on the fast track.

"Then you'll be happy to get to your hotel," Gauber said. "I'm sure you'll find it adequate. Even here, at the end of the world."

Ali turned left off of Queen Street onto Corderie. Pulled over and let Black get out. Black paid him and started toward the Central Market.

Ali counted the money and grinned. Americans, always the most generous.

"Chicago, how will you know?"

Black spun long enough to answer him. "I'll know."

Ali shook his head, disappointed to not be invited on what he could only imagine was going to be a grand adventure. Who knows where it might have taken him? The island was too small to hold his dreams, but at fifteen, he knew he had plenty of time. He pulled from the curb, seeking his next fare.

...

Michaels's thoughts were still on Chicago. Who was the man who had stormed his way into the house and taken out a half dozen thugs and their murderous drug lord? *'Taken out'* was being generous.

A war zone. And yet, no *civilian* casualties. Two-dozen children they hadn't known existed. The endpoint for a trafficking ring that stretched from Miami, San Jose, and Juarez to across the seas.

It would take time to sort out; half the girls didn't speak English. Two were from Nigeria—Benin or Tonga maybe—West Central Africa for sure. Others from across the States. How'd they ended up in Chicago? In that house? Who was the man? Why had he come? Too many questions. Questions they couldn't begin to answer mucking about on an island at the end of the world.

The policeman pulled out into the exit lanes and headed to the A10.

"Any new developments?" Rodriguez asked.

"Nothing yet," Curpen said. "We'll get you to your hotel. Sit back. We're about twenty miles out and it might not be as bad as Chicago—that's where you're from, right? The Windy City. But we're a small island. Just over a million, most of it centered around Port Louis. Traffic can have its challenges."

"We have you at the bay," Gauber said. "The waterfront was redone some years ago, and you'll be in the thick of it. Restaurants or room service at the hotel, or plenty of places to eat nearby. Mauritius has some of the best food in the world, so be adventurous."

The FBI agents took in the passing landscape. The dense, active development hiding the sparkling ocean on one side. Lush mountain and forest on the other.

"That sounds great," Rodriguez said. "When will we see the updates?"

"After your flights from Chicago and London, we thought it best to let you rest and bring you up to speed first thing in the morning," Curpen offered.

Rodriguez was thankful but Michaels was fighting to keep his frustration in check.

"That sounds good. I'm sure it can all wait till then."

Black was tired. Could feel the lack of strength in his legs. Drained, he walked through the endless rows of boxed vegetables and exotic fruits. Could feel his back cramping and shoulders tighten as he passed tall stacks of colorful Indian and Chinese fabrics. His side ached and felt increasingly hot. His chest tightened each time he thought about Dillon. Gave in to his heavy eyelids for a moment as the rich perfume of spice and herbs washed over him; turmeric and garlic and thyme, vanilla, cardamom, and clove.

The market transported Black across the world to the Chatuchak Weekend Market in Bangkok, then back again into the Grand Bazaar in Istanbul. Central Market was only a fraction of their size, but so was the population.

Each with their own flavor, each with their own smell. Bangkok with its smoky incense, grilled pork, pungent fish sauce, the underlying festering sewage floating in the canals and rivers, the exhaust from the motorbikes and tuk-tuks with occasional high notes of Jasmine and orchids and roses from the flower markets. Istanbul, with rich coffee and tea mixed with cloying, blue smoke of the hookah, raw fish and new leather, sweat from the bodies and exhaust from the vehicles of the city's twenty-two million inhabitants, all cooked in the salty brine of the Bosporus Strait.

He realized how hungry he was and thought to grab some food. Tired and hungry. But— *something else*. He didn't dare define it, learned long ago not to try, but he *recognized* it.

The first hint of some deep, intrinsic energy that began roiling up from somewhere inside him. Intuition, the patterns and threads weaving his future in the tapestry of fate, wrapped around him like one of the silks and batiks the merchants were selling on every corner. He couldn't yet see where it might take him, but was filled with an overwhelming conviction his life was about to change again.

Black gazed at the market in wonder—no longer looking at it from the outside but rather standing inside it, cloaked in infinite possibilities. The surrounding crowd oblivious. Black smiled.

Thirty meters and five aisles of goods away, a woman was looking at him. Responding to his goofy grin he supposed, she smiled shyly and turned back to the cloth she was bargaining for. Black turned to his task, afraid to let his gaze linger lest he be distracted. It took all his will power not to look back at the beautiful, exotic face imprinted in his mind.

Truth be told, he had some idea of where he was going and what to look for. He'd made a couple calls on a secure sat-phone when he'd stopped in Greenland to organize his travels. He'd needed a place to start, and equally secure calls had been made on his behalf.

Black made his way toward an ancient, raisin-faced woman selling hundreds of exotic and custom blended teas. Black accepted a small, steaming sample.

"Mesi, Mama." She sat back down and waited for him to search and hopefully make a purchase. Caught by surprise when he continued. "Mo noir dans mo bonhère, mo rouz dans mo malhére?"

The old woman took another look, disappointed in herself that she'd missed it. Yes, it was all there if someone looked, but the kind, handsome face and the warmth of the blue eyes had thrown her off.

She answered his riddle—*I am black in happiness and red in my grief?* "Cévrette." *Prawns.* She gathered her feet beneath her, willed her legs to straighten, shifted some of the weight to a hand-carved walking stick, deep purple Padauk wood topped in gold.

Moments later, a young man, not much more than a boy, her grandson Black thought, stepped out and presented a riddle of his own.

"Mo rouze dans mo bonhère, mo noir dans mo malhére?"

Black smiled. He recognized the pattern more than the words. *I am red in my happiness and black in my grief.* Black answered with, "Lagrain café." *Coffee bean.*

"Come," the boy beckoned Black toward the back.

As Black stepped through the hanging fabric that made the door, the young man spun in place with a seven-inch blade arcing at Black's throat.

Black twisted as the blade went by, blending with the thrust and intercepting the knife as his knee shot forward to crush his attackers thigh. The younger man buckled. Black spun him, wrenched his arm back and brought the knife to his throat.

"No! Please!"

Black looked at an older version of the man whose life he held in his hands.

"He was only testing you," the man pleaded. "He's just a boy."

Black shook his head. He'd been an instant away from opening the boy's throat.

"Stupid way to do it." Black let the boy go, stabbed the knife backward deep into the wall.

"Jayren, leave us."

Jayren backed away, rubbing his arm and throat. Looked down at his hand. A trace of blood smeared across the back from the hairline cut under his jaw.

"Father, please. I can help."

"Zafferes mouton napas safferes lion," the man said firmly. *Sheep business is not lion's business.*

Jayren glanced at the knife, half of its blade buried deep into the solid wood of the wall, and left them on their own.

"My name is Angelo. Thank you." The man, sixty Black guessed, bowed and seemed genuinely contrite. "Please. Tell me what you need."

"Something heavy. A 1911 or a G21 would be ideal."

The request confirmed everything Angelo would have guessed. "I can come close. Come."

Angelo led Black across the market to a small building. It seemed like it might fall until he unlocked three nearly invisible locks on its heavy iron door.

Black entered past the thick reinforced concrete walls as Angelo closed and locked the door behind them. He heard the man flip a switch and moments later, weak fluorescents buzzed and flickered on. An empty room. Angelo smiled.

He removed a key from around his neck and moved toward a lock nearly invisible in the middle of the wall. It turned smoothly, and he slid the entire wall aside on precision bearings that let the man move the wall with minimum effort.

Dozens of guns were on display. Handguns and automatic carbines. Submachine guns and a .50 caliber Barrett sniper rifle. Boxes of ammunition.

"You're a dangerous man."

"No. At best like my son. But I've seen my share."

Black reached for a Glock G21 SF. Two boxes of .45 Precision Tactical. Two knives. If he needed more, he was in real trouble.

CHAPTER
TWENTY-ONE

Sam felt the container being lifted, swaying to what she guessed as fifty or even a hundred feet into the air. With her fear, it could have been the moon. She could smell the change in the air. Hear the distant machinery.

Most, not all, of the children gravitated toward her, reaching past each other for a comforting bit of contact. A young boy, maybe six or seven, lay asleep, shivering feverishly in her lap. Others lay beside her or leaned against her back and shoulders. As the container lifted, eyes welled with fresh tears, lips quivered and hands trembled. Afraid and terrified as the children, Sam was old enough to know the horrors people visited on each other.

That they were alive was a good sign—they had value, though seemingly no more than livestock, a pig or a fowl. If they had reached their destination, it was just in time. The small amount of food they'd shared was gone, and as of a few hours ago, the water. Their captor's rationing and timing were that much more frightening because of it. They weren't the first.

The whine of steel cabling on a massive winch reverberated through the dark container as it was lowered. The lighting enough Sam could see fresh tears spring to more than a few eyes. Children crave and thrive on order—it's part of what she studied in school. She only could guess at whatever horrors conspired to bring them here, but this was anything but routine.

The container swayed and spun. Nauseated from the dark, the stifling heat, the rancid odor of waste and fear. Sam was thankful her stomach and bowels were already empty and fought to control her shaking.

The steel hit bottom with an earth-shaking thud.

She could feel it. Off the water and onto land. The sounds and vibration changed. How long had it been? With no clocks, no real idea of day and night, she'd lost track of time. In other circumstances, she might have gauged it by hunger or sleep. Nausea and terror distorted both. It may have been days, weeks. She felt her arms. Her breasts. No. Not long enough to lose significant weight. A couple of days at most. But too fucking long. Her fear turned to anger. Who the fuck were these people to treat them like this? What the fuck did they want?

The children started to stir. They could hear the machinery of the docks outside. The release of cabling. An indistinct murmur of what must be voices and shouts. English. A strong accent. She made out a few words. Her mind flashed to the club. The few harsh words exchanged between the giants and their boss. South African, Allan had said.

The latches and hinges shrieked and groaned and the two doors that formed the end of the container creaked open.

Sunlight flooded in, blinding Sam and the children. To their light deprived eyes, the change was a physical assault that attacked with stabbing needles of pain. Sam rubbed her eyes with her fists until the spots faded enough to open.

Turning to the back of their prison, she could see there were more children than she first thought. Two dozen, maybe more. Boys, girls. None older than fifteen. Two small figures, her impression was of two girls, lay still and unmoving at the back of the container. Her eyes flooded with tears, and she turned back to the open door.

Two men stood back lit in what seemed to be afternoon sun. Blackened in silhouette, bloused fatigues, and combat boots. In front of the spots dancing in her eyes, she could see assault rifles in their hands.

"Get out! Get out! Get out!" The men shouted and the children, weak and scared, did their best to file past.

Though her eyes were still adjusting, her impression of the first was he was little more than a boy himself, while the other was a man of forty.

The older man slapped the feverish boy on the back of his head as they passed, knocking the child down. The boy-soldier then prodded him with his rifle and kicked him forward as he stood.

Sam rose, helping the boy to his feet and standing protectively beside him.

The two guards stood, staring her down until the boy-soldier reached forward to grab at the sick child. Sam slapped his hand away and the boy jabbed at her with his rifle.

Another man slipped in behind him, cuffed the boy-soldier on the side of his head, knocking him into the steel wall.

The boy bounced off and spun in anger.

"Gann uit, tietkop!" The man shouted.

The boy started to bring his rifle up but thought better of it and slunk off.

She tried to hide the trembling, hoped she somehow looked defiant and not terrified.

The man smiled, stepped aside, gesturing gallantly for her to pass.

Sam stepped from the shadows into the day.

Camissa, the *"place of sweet waters,"* is the ancient Koi name for the land made fertile by the flow of water purified in the hydrological subsystem of one of Earth's oldest mountain ranges.

Six hundred million years old, nearly ten times the age of the Himalayas, the table-topped mountain dominates the landscape and shelters the city Dutch East India Company settlers first established as a halfway station on their routes of commerce from Europe to Asia and named The Cape of Good Hope.

With plentiful freshwater canals dug for irrigation, fertile soils, and ample timber for ships and settlement, the town thrived. Soon, non-Dutch settlers began arriving; first, the Huguenots, fleeing religious persecution, and then the French and British.

By the mid-eighteenth century, farms and industry were thriving and setting the stage for one of the world's most enduring legacies of separation and segregation, such that imported slaves, mostly from Java and Madagascar, already outnumbered the Europeans.

Carved into the city's urban form, the newly named Cape Town utilized natural barriers and politically calculated man-made infrastructure to create an affluent, whites-only center, surrounded and serviced by the poor black and coloured labour forces, and separated by divisive buffer zones of harsh scrubland, railways and highways, rivers, and valleys.

The five-ton truck rumbled past the high whitewashed walls and electrified fences from the city center, soon leaving the decorative gates and manicured lawns behind.

Wide, dusty township streets lined with a thin facade of neatly matched brick and render houses with their bright and cheerful orange pan-tile roofs erected years ago during the 2010 World Cup, hid the endless jumble of shantytown shacks and debilitating poverty from a cursory glance and the outside world.

Two children in her arms, two more sharing her lap. Sam twisted from the open, appraising gaze of a young guard, made hard by generations of impossible hardship, struggle and war, and made cocky by the Chinese-made AK-47 in his hands. She peered through the wooden slats of the cargo bed.

A woman and three infant children sat and waved from a ratty, once-red sofa in front of a dilapidated, but active market. Men, women, and children on foot along the road—a stream of bicycles, sometimes with three and four balanced on the front and back, navigated the deep ruts and potholes.

A group of barefoot children tried to ride a skinny cow along the open sewers—cheers and laughter quickly fading as the truck continued grinding toward the distant mountains.

The young guard peered through a hole in the canvas roof of the truck bed. Said something to another guard across from him. Speaking Zulu, the dental clicks and pops of the musical language echoed the raindrops beginning to dance on the canvas roof.

The two guards laughed and looked back at Sam, perfect white teeth on display in grins that looked anything but friendly.

CHAPTER
TWENTY-TWO

B lack walked along the strip of white sand; a postcard with turquoise water stretching into the horizon on one side and the intermittent shade of the Casuarina trees on the other. The air was soft—warm, gentle, and perfumed.

A hundred meters ahead, a couple walked on the beach. Two hundred meters behind him, small groups of people were heading into the water, launching boards for windsurfing or paddle boarding.

He regarded his hotel, eight stories of concrete and glass on the other side of a high privacy hedge. Large balconies in every room faced the ocean. Windows on the sixth floor with obvious yellow crime scene tape across their balconies, ostensibly to stop Spiderman if he was in the neighborhood.

A path led from the beach toward a gap in the hedges. Hastily posted signs: NO ACCESS - PLEASE USE OTHER WALKWAYS. Crime scene tape, MPF—SCÉNE DE CRIME, blocking the path from both directions.

Black saw dozens of footprints in the sand leading into it. Any recoverable or forensically valuable prints would have shifted in the wind, and he wondered if casts had been made. Black had no idea of the resources the Mauritian Police Department would have at their disposal but assumed it would be adequate for most circumstances. This couldn't be considered one of them. Over a million permanent residents with at least that many tourists each year. Less than fifty homicides per annum, less than five kidnappings. And never the murder of the son of a prominent American political family.

Black assumed the FBI would come. With extensive resources in nearby Africa and the Middle East, they kept busy investigating endless terrorist attacks on American assets and potential suspects. Black was confident that Xavier Chamberlain wouldn't settle for less.

It was likely they'd be tracking him as well. He hadn't planned on his assault on the drug dealer's house being watched and filmed by the FBI. He hadn't planned on anything.

The dealers had been a potentially lethal threat to his sister, and so he hit them as hard as he could before they even knew he existed. Not much of a strategy, but it served him well in the past. His objective had been to take out Mookie and his men, and in that, he'd been successful. He hadn't been confident or worried about getting out alive. Now, of course, there was more to do before he could let himself get killed or apprehended.

Black had done his best to move quickly and avoid their cameras, but they were the FBI. It might take them some time to unravel, and the young, rescued children would complicate things, though he guessed that must be the reason the house was being watched. Child-trafficking. He knew of such horrors, but children in cages? In the U.S.? *In Chicago?*

Mookie and his thugs got off easy. He could count on Crawley and Jimenez to run interference, but they could only get away with so much. No, it wouldn't take the FBI long, and they likely wouldn't be alone.

He was now AWOL. Given orders to stay in Chicago as local police retraced Dillon's footsteps, he could add military police and any of the other international agencies that could expect and receive INTERPOL coordination. Black didn't expect any of the people who helped him get here to go further out on a limb or to deny anything but full cooperation with all authorities.

But he also knew no one would be extending themselves on behalf of a young African American girl here on holiday, the *girlfriend or mistress*, of the fair-haired son of said political dynasty.

Dynasty was a stretch, but the headlines would write themselves, and for at least the next few months, they may as well have been the Kennedys. No one would care or consider if she too was a victim, perhaps even before she arrived here. A girlfriend was an embarrassment to the family, and the daughter of a questionable and now disgraced Chicago police officer too much to think about.

Black didn't know much about Sam. Not really. He'd been gone too long. He'd had time on the planes across the world to try to remember each moment. Time enough to know he spent too little time with her and anyone else he'd ever cared about. He remembered her filled with the spark of wonder and curiosity, of the generosity and compassion that rendered her truly beautiful.

Sam graduated from high school a year early. Majored in psychology at Northwestern. Earned her masters at Emory. The last he'd heard, she was looking for a doctoral program in child psychology and development. The kind of woman the world needed more of.

He also knew she was the joy of Dillon's life. That Dillon was his friend, his brother. That she was that one thing that made anyone who met her know there was hope, even for a fatally damaged killing machine like Dillon, which is how they would paint him—*someone like Black*—to create and do something good.

He knew she was as close as any child he would ever have of his own. He knew he loved her.

Black was forty-three. Had plenty of all too willing female companionship, probably more than any one man deserved, though much less than he could have if he'd taken advantage. The same thing that drew men to his command drew women to his bed. Best not to analyze it too much.

Figured he'd been in love exactly twice before. First, when he was seven. A girl whose name and face he'd never forgotten, and then again when he was twenty. Blond hair, blue eyes, and a laugh that still echoed in the recesses of his heart.

His inexperience rendered him incapable of sharing more of his violent childhood than he had. She held him through the nightmares, helped teach him to control and channel his impulses, if not into something good, at least into something that might be *made good*. Still, she'd wanted to know and understand more of the past than he was ready to face.

Like most young couples, they drifted apart, her to save the world within the framework of the law; he with a study of chaos, less and less with the mathematical possibilities of a classroom and more and more on battlefields around the world.

There were the other, confusing affairs; where the women's pursuit clouded reality and made one pause. Like the vanilla princess of Madagascar. Like an exotic, half-Italian, half-Puerto Rican girl he met in France who turned out to be married to a Sicilian mobster. The Don suspected but could never confirm the affair, but after he'd hit and abused her one night, he'd been found dead with a broken neck in the very stables built for her wedding present.

Investigations pointed toward him being thrown from a horse, a huge black stallion named Heller, though no one could ever remember him riding. The girl soon inherited the mobster's empire, and Black forced himself to leave rather than be a part of it.

For the most part, he'd never let himself have the kind of serious relationships that would let him think someone *could* love him.

He'd had glimpses, small windows into what might have been, maybe in another life, but vowed to never do what had been done to him. To let his weaknesses and excesses torture and torment those who cared for him, destroy their sense of hope, and drive them to embrace their darker impulses.

Black only knew that if Sam was dead, anyone with any part in it, no matter how small, was going to pay. If she was alive, he'd apply all of his resources, *all of his talents,* to bring her home safe and live the life she deserved.

Black stood in the middle of the crime scene. A small, sandy bit of path leading from the beach to the hotel. The beach and vast ocean on one side, the hotel and an expansive parking lot on the other. The hedges where he stood had been planted and cut into a maze for privacy, the intricacy mimicking an English garden.

Black had seen the initial police report, forwarded on by his friend. Blood, a lot of it, soaked into the sand. Throat cut. By itself, it didn't tell much. He hadn't been able to see the autopsy report or photos. They might have told him a lot. Killer to killer.

He heard voices and stepped toward the parking lot. A handsome, dark-skinned hotel porter, his red vest trimmed with gold buttons and velvet lobby cap, the island's colonial roots on full display, was helping two men put their golf clubs in the trunk of a large sedan. Black watched them until they drove away.

Two men, one to kill Allan, one to grab Sam. He could see her struggle. She was young and athletic. Cross-country and tennis before devoting all concentration on becoming an academic star. But they would be professionals. She'd kick and struggle, but have a large hand over her mouth. Probably drugged. They'd want no noise.

Why the girl? She came from a middle-class family at best. There was little chance of garnering significant resources or money from her. The man would have been the better choice. So—not money—not ransom. Revenge? A jilted lover? Or something to do with the Chamberlains? She'd only been here a day. How much trouble could she have gotten into?

Black watched it again. Ran it through his mind. Two men. Professionals. He needed to see the American's autopsy reports.

Black studied the hotel. Her two companions killed in their room on the sixth floor. A part of it all. Greater risk for—what? Greater reward? Sam. Three dead—Sam missing. Taken. *Alive.*

CHAPTER
TWENTY-THREE

K ronmüller stepped from the shower, finally clean, dried off, dropped his towel on the floor.

He'd stripped off the filth he'd worn in the front drive, the twelve-hundred dollar Versace shirt soiled with Zama's excrement, his pants, underwear, and the handmade shoes, and had them burned as the maids and gardeners watched on. He felt no more self-conscious standing naked in front of a staff of servants than being seen naked by the livestock or a pet; the cattle or one's cats or dogs.

Now he stood in front of his dressing room mirror, one entire wall, floor to ceiling. Unmoving, staring at his reflection. Only at his eyes, not at his lean body—some would call it a swimmer's physique. Hip bones and broad shoulders, lean abdomen with strong arms, and powerful legs.

He lived on a godforsaken farm in the middle of the Little Karoo, a mostly arid desert extending to the fertile valleys and foothills of the Swartberg Mountains, and so had done very little swimming.

His father's idea of sport was rugby or hunting. Kronmüller loathed both and probably for that reason. Never a star, but his brother Joffire had played well enough in the football leagues to stir his father's interest. Enough to stand apart from Kronmüller's lack of prowess on the field.

He knew how to hunt and shoot—dragged along by his father and brother to bring down everything from the mighty elephant and elegant, loping giraffe, to apex predators like the lion and cheetah. If asked, he wouldn't have known whether he hated the hunt—the heat and dust, the animal entrails and blood—or only his father and brother.

Instead, he hiked and trekked as a boy across the Karoo, exploring and searching the land, not for diamonds and trophies for the wall, but for fossils and signs of early life in the boundless expanses of exposed sedimentary strata in what once, millions of year ago, had been a vast swamp basin of the Gondwana.

There, as a young boy, traveling with a Basarwa servant and his teenage son in the deep gorges and river basins, along the foothills of the Karoo Koppies, as far as the Bushman Lands to the west and the Lesotho Highlands to the east, he first found fossils of common marine animals, trilobites and starfish.

Inspired, he later found evidence and remains of the Triassic mammal-like Thrinaxodon and Permian predators like the saber-toothed Rubidgea, an eleven-foot beast with teeth even longer than those of the mighty T-Rex.

He thought to pursue the study at university, at prestigious Witwatersrand or the research-intensive University of Cape Town. Instead, his father insisted, demanded, he pursue political science in Pretoria, thinking the boy would one day take his rightful place in South African politics and government.

The younger Kronmüller had no desire for the fight in returning power and prestige to the white ruling class from which he came. Nor did he want to follow his brother into the military. After skirting most of his mandatory conscription, he instead fled to live with an uncle in Germany for a year.

Occasional visits as the year stretched into two, and after his brother was killed, stretched into three. Instead of being hardened and educated as his father hoped, it was there that the sometimes weekly escapes to Berlin and Paris, Brussels and Amsterdam, first exposed him to a world of excess—exclusive parties and high-end clubs.

The endless girls, alcohol, and drugs, as well as his fetishes and predilections, soon created a longing for people closer to the land of his birth. A place where he could experiment and explore without castigation or reprisal with the peoples of his own continent. Not the white-bred Boer women, those of the closed Afrikaans upper-class, carefully cultivated from their original Dutch stock like his whore of a mother, but more often, the forbidden Kaapse Kleurling, known in Africa as Cape Coloureds and the exotic, Asian blooded Cape Malays.

Kronmüller gazed at the eyes staring back at him in the mirror. Stoic. Steely. Breath calm, heartbeat steady. Wondering if this was the face his father had seen or was it the one he found on the verge of panic and tears reflected from his dreams and nightmares for most of his life.

He turned and padded toward his closet, bigger than some of the house servant's apartments. Opened the mirrored door and caught a glimpse of the terrible scars that covered his back. Like his nightmares, another gift from his father.

He would cover them with something beautiful, something his father would absolutely hate; Prada or Balenciaga. Then find Lina... or perhaps look in on the girl.

Sam tried opening the heavy wooden door. She kicked and pulled at the ornate doorknob. Heard it lock from the outside. Spun and pressed her back against it to take in the room.

If she hadn't been a prisoner, it would have been beautiful. Dark, gleaming hardwood floors. Heirloom Persian rugs. Textured walls delicately inlaid with ostrich shell. Richly saturated, contemporary paintings and textile art on the walls. An elegant sitting area with luxurious fabrics paired against classic lines of furniture. A huge, gleaming master bath beyond. Imported silk drapery in front of giant windows.

Drapes and sheers billowed and she ran to the windows. Leaded glass panes. Iron bars. She pulled at them, her mind not yet willing to accept this new chapter of her capture.

She spun back to the room. Took in the bed.

Sam was too horrified and too inexperienced to recognize the designers or imagine the true cost, but a dress and fine lingerie were displayed across the luxurious designer bedding. Levi's and Victoria Secret she knew, not these, but she recognized the signature red soles of the ivory ankle boots, still in the box and laid at the foot of the bed, and knew they alone cost a thousand dollars.

Slumping against a large, antique wardrobe, she wrapped her arms around herself and struggled to stem the tears. Fighting against the images racing through her mind, the opulent display on the bed terrified her as much as the steel drum and shipping container.

CHAPTER
TWENTY-FOUR

The waterfront hummed with the sounds and vibrations of a tropical paradise readying itself for the night as the sun began its descent, dodging in and out of clouds waiting to rest along the horizon. Neon was starting to buzz and hum and come alive, adding to the island color.

Tourists, sunburned and dehydrated from their days on the water and beaches, began to come en masse to the busy development for their evening's entertainment. For some, to try their luck in the casino. For others, the allure of shopping or the variety of restaurants and street stalls; still others, refreshment in the bars and lounges of the upscale, four and five-star hotels.

The woman sat by herself under one of the cafe's colorful umbrellas. She ordered and was turning from the young waiter as Black sat down.

"Excuse me," she said. Lightly.

"Don't even try." Smiling.

They appraised each other. Took in details. Black, the way he had been, though she noticed he'd showered and changed his shirt.

The woman unpretentious in walking shorts and t-shirt. Long and lean muscle gave shape to her smooth, sun-bronzed arms and legs, while a small, gold locket sparkled beneath her throat. If she wore make-up, he couldn't see it, yet was sure she'd be at home on the set of a Hollywood movie or some glamorous, high-end fashion shoot. A fraction over five and a half feet, so not a runway model, but nothing overdone and everything seemingly in perfect proportion.

Thick, glossy black hair, eyes just as dark, and set with amusement beneath lashes naturally lush and full.

Hard to know, but early thirties he guessed. She chewed on her lip enough to slow down the smile tugging at the corners. Finally ...

"You hide it well," she offered.

Black waited.

"The gun."

"And you. The watching. The following."

A shout of surprise, a few *oooh's* and *ahhhs*, a round of hearty clapping as a small crowd responded to a street performer and his sleight of hand.

"I wasn't trying to hide. And I wasn't following *you*," she said.

"The man three tables behind me," he said. "Another at the end of the row."

She liked the way he set his mouth to temper the triumph yet couldn't hide the delight dancing in his eyes. Forced herself to turn away. Glancing from the man behind him to another studiously looking down at his phone. She'd missed that one.

"Local informants. They play all sides. The one behind you is Rícard and the weaselly looking one on the phone is Gustave. They were interested in you, and I was interested in why. Though I have my guesses."

The waiter returned with a bottle of South African Beeslaar Pinotage; a unique, fabulously dark red wine, notes of oaky cocoa, toasted vanilla, and cedar, with a finish of lush plum, cassis, and boysenberry. Set down two glasses. Poured a taste for her approval.

She smiled, as much with her eyes as her mouth, as Black took in the two glasses. A shrug, the tiniest bit of movement to her shoulders. "I'd been hoping you'd join me."

Somehow sweet and shy, probing and questioning, yet knowing and full of the confidence Black responded to.

"For a drink?" he asked.

"For starters."

"And then?"

She tasted the wine. Nodded her approval, and the waiter poured both glasses.

Taking the moment, seriously considering it.

"A cause," she said. "It's why you're here. It's why the others are interested in you."

Special Agents Michaels and Rodriguez stood behind two couples checking in to the hotel. Two Germans in their seventies, worn from their travels and ready for rest, and a young couple in their twenties, the accent placing them from central Spain, maybe Madrid or Toledo.

The young girl excited to be on holiday, oblivious to the rest of the lobby crowd and the two agents behind her. Her boyfriend couldn't stop sneaking glances at the two men who looked like cops, wore it proudly like their discount suits, to see if they were interested in him.

He couldn't know that unless he pulled out a gun and started shooting or announced a bomb around his chest, that they weren't. Still, Rodriguez couldn't resist giving him a steely, hard jaw stare just for fun. The couple was finally checked in and the young man hurried his girlfriend away.

The girl behind the polished granite counter greeted the agents with an infectious smile; learned and practiced at an early age for sure, but refined in some hotel-desk smiling school, and in this case, passed with flying colors. *Top of her class.*

"May I help you, Sir?" Her voice musical. French with a hint of Creole.

They flashed their credentials; picture IDs and shiny badges that almost matched the gleam of the hotel receptionist's toothpaste-commercial-perfect grin.

The badges were enough that her eyes quit smiling for just a moment, but to her credit, she never lost the hint of perfect teeth and the upward curve of her perfect lips.

"Give me just a moment, and I'll call my manager."

...

"Who's interested?" Black asked.

"Your American FBI for one."

Black's reaction was to *not* react. Which was enough. She liked that he was such an open book—*he'd be a terrible liar*—and she enjoyed being one up on him.

"You didn't know?"

"I knew it would happen," he said, "but maybe not this fast."

She smiled again and the sun came back out. Raced backward up from the sea and lit her face. He told himself to ignore it. It wasn't that special. Not really. Lots of women smiled. Even at him. Always had. Probably just a trick of the light, a lack of sleep that lowered his inhibitions enough that the simple gesture now quickened the blood in his veins.

He couldn't be sure, but if his display of ignorance could make her do it again, it might be worth checking out.

"I'd like to think they're here for more than a politician's son," she said. "But that leaves you or the girl."

Back to work. "What do you know of the girl?"

"More than I know of you, but still... You come here through circuitous channels. Buy a gun. Local eyes and ears track you, and the FBI arrive." She searched his eyes. An infinite blue reflecting the deepening sky. "The real question is, are you the good guy or the bad guy?"

"Just a guy."

"Maybe. Maybe yes. Maybe no."

She sipped her wine. Eastern European he thought. The black hair, the tone of her skin, and the hint of Slavic blood in her high cheekbones. Her eyes seemed to look past him, into him. *Yeah, perhaps a gypsy.* Already on her crystal ball and casting some kind of island voodoo on him. Trying to see into his blackened heart.

Good luck with that he thought—anything once there excised and buried long ago.

He grunted. Shrugged. It earned another smile.

"Maybe you don't even know yet," she said.

Black was at a loss. Yeah. She saw a lot.

"Yeah. Maybe."

The Agents took in the room. Presumably, it was like dozens of others in the hotel except, in this case, it had all the signs of an active crime scene. Tags and Post-its stuck to walls and lamps and doors, tape on the floor, every surface marred with fingerprint dust. Yellow crime scene tape across the windows and blocking the balcony. Sections of carpet and bedding cut away and removed for further analysis, as if they might replay the events.

Michaels knew they were scheduled to come back the next day with Gauber and Curpen and be given full updates and status reports, but he wanted to see the room on his own.

The man, Hunter, had been shot four times, twice in the head, evidently while he was sleeping. Michaels vaguely remembered something about the man when he'd been brought up from the minors to the big show in Philly. A future star third-baseman and a sensation with the bat, hitting close to .400, sending three pitches over the wall in as many games. A blown-out knee, ruptured meniscus, put a stop to that and the man soon faded away from a *"might-be"* to a *"might-have-been."*

The girl was a childhood friend of the other girl, unclear why she was there, but he could guess. His daughter had a phase where she took advantage of her looks and charms and took off to Europe and South America for several extended holidays. Of course, part of that was rebellion against daddy and his conservative, stick-in-the-mud notions of propriety and Midwestern upbringing. That she finally got it together, earned advanced degrees in nursing, and was now happily married with two beautiful children was something this young lady would never experience.

All signs said she was coming from the bathroom, half in, half out, watched her boyfriend get shot, and then took four slugs of her own. Nine millimeter, same weapon. Two in the chest, two in the head. Professional, certainly military training—the headshots unnecessary in this case but drilled into some military training programs.

The first question was, were they both targets? If not, who was the primary, and who was the collateral? There were bound to be other questions, but the biggest perhaps; motive. Why kill them at all?

Rodriguez made his way to the balcony. Beyond the flapping plastic yellow tape; a couple more floors and balconies above them, the half-filled parking lot far below, a narrow strip of sugary white sand, the setting sun, and endless ocean.

"How'd they get in?"

It was the same question Black asked himself when he stood in the room two hours before. He'd checked into his suite, a floor above and down the hall. Slipped over the seventh story balcony, scaled the decorative facade, and made his way on the narrow ledge to this one. Doable, but not easy. No signs of scuffing or abrasion, so Black had been the first.

It would have only needed one man to take out the couple, presumably after an intense night of celebration and sex. Initial reports scanned while on the plane put the incident at four or five in the morning, so no pretense of room service. A key would have been the cleanest, which meant it was given to the killer, or he had sophisticated electronic tools and training. He knew the assassin was professional. The job was too clean and silent to allow for anything else. Except at the very highest levels, the skill sets of covert entry and murder rarely intersected. It was never like the movies. No, whoever it was, inserted a programmed card key and walked in.

Michaels turned from the bathroom. "Tox reports show he'd of been pretty out of it, but the key had to come from somewhere."

"Means someone knows something," Rodriguez said. "We'll find them. You want to hit the club or wait till morning?"

Getting his second wind, Rodriguez looked annoyingly refreshed. The Desi Arnaz of the FBI. Michaels wouldn't be shocked if the handsome Cuban broke into his nightclub act as Lucy came popping through the door.

Michaels scanned the room. A full suite. An easy guess that Chamberlain was paying for it. This was the kind of room that could eat up a year's salary in a single week, but not that much better than the rooms he and Rodriguez had been given at another nearby luxury hotel.

Gauber and Curpen, or at least their department, were going all out to make sure the agents were comfortable. Respect? Or a way to buy complacency?

A hot shower and bed would be welcome but could wait a little longer; the jet lag hadn't hit him too hard yet. Back in Chicago, they would have been in their early morning routines, stuck in traffic or doing paperwork in the office, and fighting over the last cup of burnt coffee.

"You good for the club?"

"Oh, yeah," Rodriguez said.

"Let's grab a bite and do a quick walk-through."

The food would either wake him up or put him out, but it would be good to visit the club without the babysitters.

"So do I get to know your name?"

"You don't already know?" she asked. "I thought you'd use one of your high-level agency contacts to tell you."

"Nope." He'd thought about it. Would have been simple enough. Snap a picture and send it on—fifteen minutes of waiting. "Seemed easier just to ask."

She liked the way his eyes looked at hers. Not probing, not searching. Content to take in the surface as much as anything deeper. Sharing the wine had been the most intimate evening since before she could remember.

Jesus! Just what she needed. Fall, even for a moment, for an American vigilante, or spy, or soldier, or whatever he really was. She'd find out soon enough, but by then she could be sure he'd be gone.

"Nicola."

The name washed over him. Three notes of a single chord. He hoped he didn't look like a simple schoolboy, one he never had the chance to be.

The light in his eyes letting her know he was smiling even before his mouth caught up. "It's nice."

The name confirmed his first thoughts about her origins, though didn't narrow them much further. Her response about the agencies, her knowledge of him, deepened the mystery that much more.

"Hungry?"

"Starving," he said.

"Let me get the check and let's get out of here."

Ricard watched the two move through the crowd. Who was this American and what was he to the woman? It would seem they knew each other, perhaps intimately. He of course knew of Nicola. She was someone to be feared for lots of reasons, but none that concerned him. No reason she would know who he was.

He'd never admit it out loud, but he knew he was much too low on the totem pole to have ever crossed her radar, and so did little to hide or blend in. The streets filled. No one knew he existed, which of course, is what made him good at his job. He dialed his phone.

Gustave answered, "Ouais?"

"Keep your eyes open. I'm going to make the call."

"Je te tiens."

They walked through the thickening crowd in the middle of the wide street. The night alive with laughter and two dozen languages. Easy enough to recognize some; English and Spanish, Italian and Russian, Tamil and Hindi, Yoruba and Afrikaans, all peppered with French and Mauritian Creole.

The air alive with texture; the gentle Indian Ocean breezes carrying the smoke and aromas of an eclectic mix of foods and spices from the street vendors and coal-fired cooking grills lining the markets. The ever-present dhal puris, curries and chutneys,

super-sized vegetables roasting on the coals, sweet fruits and pungent chiles, Chinese noodles and Indian vindaye, curried fish and
steamed dumplings.

They pretended ignorance to the two men following and
shared a large flatbread topped with spicy prawn curry and deep-
fried samosas. Nicola grabbed for an intensely hot, fish vindaye
served over rice. Black was glad when she suggested a local beer to
wash it down, and then let him try deep-fried sweet potato cakes
filled with coconut and vanilla.

"Let's confuse them," she whispered, then slipped her arm
in his, leaned her head against his shoulder as they walked. To
anyone watching, they looked like any other handsome couple on
a lover's retreat.

Her hair fragrant with hints of vanilla and cinnamon,
subtle enough to make him wonder if it were the spices or truly
the way she smelled.

She burrowed in closer, and he wondered if she was cold, her
t-shirt little defense against the island breezes and early evening.
Rain would be coming. He took off his jacket and draped it over
her shoulders.

For the briefest of moments, their skin touched. His calloused
hands and the smooth bare skin of her neck and shoulders. She
hoped he thought the slight trembling was because of the falling
temperatures. This was stupid—he was little more than a thug.

First thought; he'd come to avenge the politician son's murder.
She now knew he was looking for the girl but had little idea of
why or what she was to him. Had no idea of how far he might
be willing to go. Then again, he'd traveled ten thousand miles
to be here.

But she liked the way he looked at her when he spoke; direct
and without artifice. Equally, she liked the way he looked at her
when she spoke. As if her words were the most important thing in
the world. It was stupid, *that was the word for it,* but tonight, for a
few minutes, she wanted to forget that she'd never see him again.

...

Gustave hung up. It was his contact that put them on to the American. The contact resented his father not trusting him, not bringing him further into the business. Gustave had reached out, asked the boy to let him know if anyone suspicious showed up. Shady types, cop types, military types. Especially an *American*. Of course, anyone coming to an island and buying a gun was suspicious, and it was about the timing as much as the who.

And a day later, an American shows up. Could easily be a cop. Or military. Looking for a gun, which certainly made him shady. Gustave called Ricard, who could be a tool, endlessly trying to assert control, and then constantly probing to see if he had it. But this job really couldn't be any easier—*stay in the shadows and follow the guy*—and the money was good.

He watched the girl break away from the American, head toward the public toilets. Ricard said the girl could be dangerous, though he didn't specify or hint what that meant. Just not to take her for granted. *Jesus.* Like an explanation would be too much for him to absorb.

The American stood talking to a street vendor selling wood carvings to the tourists. He let himself be led toward the back. *Just what an island girl wanted.* Gustave wished he had someone to wager that the American would return with one of the ridiculous wooden ships as some kind of present for the girl.

He could see Ricard on the phone—the girl had disappeared to the toilets—the American was somewhere in the back of a street stall.

Gustave suddenly just wanted to get paid, and call it an early night.

He'd scored some chocolate chip cookies—*heroin mixed with ecstasy*—and had a certain girl of his own who'd be only too willing to show her appreciation for the favors.

A powerful arm slipped from behind his neck and crossed his throat, pulling him back as it cut off the blood supply on the left carotid artery. His hands clawed without effect at the iron cords of muscle locked across his throat, then flailed the air in desperation.

All thought of the American, the money, and the girl vanished. Instead, fear, panic, and confusion. In his mind the torture was endless. In reality, the struggle was brief—*seconds*—and as Gustave lost consciousness, Black set him down to the pavement and leaned him against the wall. To anyone passing, a drunk sleeping it off.

Black hoped taking the little weasel out for a moment might escalate things. Like buying the gun, it was more about introducing himself to the less savory elements of the island and putting himself in a position where he could ask some hard questions.

He saw the other man, the one Nicola called Ricard, in an animated conversation on the phone. He had little doubt that whoever was on the other end would be revealed soon enough.

Black watched Nicola return, gliding through the crowd, as effortlessly as the island breeze. She smiled as she saw him, sad and sweet, some reserve and regret, and he wondered if she regretted the night, but knew he didn't have time to investigate it. Maybe in another life—it seemed this one was already chosen for him.

Black was glad he had a mission, which is how he thought of it. A mission. Missions had objectives. Objective: find Sam and bring her home. Objectives kept him clear, let him channel his efforts past distractions. Like the one now walking toward him.

No one knew more than he how fast life could change. It was part of what he was trained to do. He pulled a trigger and four seconds later the life of a man a thousand meters away was over. One night in Chicago, and dozens, maybe hundreds of lives, had irreparably been changed forever, including his. Some made better, some worse, some just over.

Maybe it was the coincidence of feeling his life was at a crossroads that made him pause, but he knew he was on a finite timeline. He knew he had innate talents and honed skills. That somewhere out there was a young girl who needed them. One he promised to bring home. One he was willing to give his life for.

Even though he most times fought against it, he also understood he was human. No better or worse than any other, no more or less deserving of life and happiness. Like the food, it only took a moment to hit your senses, and for your brain to process it and tell you that you wanted more.

He also knew he wasn't the kind of man that could be loved. Had it affirmed since he was five years old. But that didn't stop him from moments filled with the rare taste of it.

It could all be confusing. Best to never think of it. Concentrate on the mission. Focus on the objective.

Nicola slowed, reluctant for the intimacy of the evening to end, gentle and unexpected, and that much sweeter because of it. She knew little about this man; could reach out to those same agencies to find out more. And she would, *albeit in a more direct way,* but she knew he was a good man. Damaged in some way; she could recognize it as easily as an infant recognizes another. But he wasn't evil.

She had experience with evil men, and Tommy Black, Tommy, was not evil. That he had the capacity for violence, she had no doubt. It was written in the way he moved, the intensity with which he took in everything around him, but he was maybe a better man than he could know.

She felt his focus slipping away. Some intrinsic shift in energy and rhythm, a subtle vibration that set off the alarms she kept in place for herself, bringing her back to reality.

"So what's the plan?" Her voice betrayed her frustration. Had to fight herself to not give in and kiss this sad, confused man, explore his lips with her own, search for a truth beyond any words he might say, any act he might commit.

The recognition of her emotions surprised her, but she was unable to stop. "You make yourself a target and beat the answers out of anyone who shows up?"

"It's worked before," Black said.

"What about when they're better than you? Better armed or in greater numbers? This is their territory, or theater, or landscape, or whatever you call it. These are violent people. They've proven that."

"I get by."

Nicola felt her anger growing. She'd been around violent people, those with bad intentions, for most of her life. First, as a child in the middle of an endless war. Then, in the aftermath, as a young girl. It got worse for her long before it got better. *What the fuck was wrong with people?* Why was violence such an easy answer?

"I get by." Three words said simply and truthfully. In a world where death was the reward for mistakes and failure.

That he moved as gently, as warm against her as the moments before was confusing. And frightening.

She looked up at the lighted sign across the street. La Caravelle.

"Mauritius is not big. If he was trying to impress her, they would have ended up here." She hesitated, unsure of what to say. Slipped him a business card. Smiled sadly, already missing, if not him, then the idea of him, and afraid it showed in her eyes. "Stay alive and find me after."

She kissed him lightly on the cheek and walked away.

CHAPTER
TWENTY-FIVE

Black stepped into the hellish vacuum of the club. Light, sound, and temperature controlled by the engineering and arrogance of man and separated from the island paradise beyond its walls. The energetic, sometimes obnoxious crowds in the streets far preferable in Black's book. Early, and Hell was still being tweaked and dialed in for the night.

Two sound technicians worked with the DJ on getting the bone-shaking bass of the sound system just right, while a light artist programmed his latest laser show, the lights reflecting off mirrors and computer-controlled diffraction gratings for maximum visual effect, and to ensure the complete epileptic meltdown of anyone susceptible.

A few condemned souls, oblivious to the laserist's artistry bouncing over them, sat at the nearly empty bar or scattered around the massive room nursing overpriced spirits, hovering over their glasses with both hands to prevent them from vibrating off the tables while numbing themselves against the inevitable onslaught of desperation.

Of course, some people came for the fun, and a few might find it, but in Black's experience, few and far between. The rest would be left to try harder, their desperation to keep up leading them to an endless feedback loop of failure and disappointment drowned in drink or distorted with whatever mind-altering drugs were on hand.

A dozen people, impossibly young and beautiful, worked diligently behind the bar, getting ready for the night, a few souls followed his lead, and wandered in slowly from the outside.

Black sat at a high-topped table beneath the shimmering nebula of the laser lumia above him. The colors changed from green to blue to red and back again as the light show was further adjusted. A waitress, little more than an exotic sprite, glided through the shadows, changing colors in time with the lights, then disappearing within the strobes until magically appearing directly across from him. He wondered if it was a trick they actually practiced, its smooth execution a requirement of the job.

"Hi. What can I get you?" Asked with a Mauritian patois.

"Water."

Her face fell. The lights froze long enough for him to see she was still young and beautiful, just disappointed. Black pushed across a one-hundred-dollar bill.

"Keep it." And just as quickly, the smile returned.

"Be right back." She turned and headed to the bar.

Black watched her go, the glide adjusted for effect with swaying hips and an extra bounce in her step. He smiled and shook his head in wonder.

The room was huge, ceilings lost in the shadows above, and a balcony partially circling and outlining a second floor. Brass railings and velvet ropes sectioned off to form the VIP area, where high rollers could demand and expect expensive bottle service, and servers like his sprite could make hundreds or even more in a single night.

The entrance to what might be a kitchen to the left of the bar, restrooms to the right. A heavy door back to the far left. Not marked with a mandatory EXIT sign above, so perhaps leading to private rooms or offices.

Hard to see along the dark ceiling amid the flashing lights, but Black knew security cameras would be trained on every inch of floor and the bar, keeping an eye on customers and employees alike.

A few more people trickled in, the endless night of the club linked to the real world outside.

The waitress brought back a bottle of Icelandic spring water, no doubt bottled from one of the local island springs running down from the volcanic mountains. Black hadn't spent enough time in Iceland to know if their clubs served high-end *tropical-island spring water*.

"Thanks. What's your name?"

"Jamirra," said brightly.

"Nice place. Do you work here every night?"

"No. About half the week. Three or four nights," she said. She glanced at his hands. No sign of a ring. Big smile. "American?"

"Guilty."

"You look like a soldier. Or a cop."

"Yeah. I have that look."

She cocked her head, an artist considering her final adjustments. Satisfied. Smiled. "It works on you."

"Guess I'm stuck with it. I'm not a cop, but I am looking for someone."

She hesitated, just for the briefest of moments, but the smile returned. "Aren't we all?"

"Yeah. I guess so."

Jamirra looked around. The place still empty. No one close enough to hear and no one else to make money off of. "You're looking for someone here?" A hint of hopefulness.

"Not sure. But maybe," he said. "You heard about the murders a couple of days ago?"

She sighed. "You're sounding more like a cop."

"Nope. Promise. "

"Okay. It's not like I know anything, but they were here."

"The cops?"

"Well, sure. But no. The Americans. He was some famous politician, right?

"I don't know about famous, but enough there'll be more cops for sure. But I am looking for the girl and I'm not sure anyone else cares enough to."

"Yeah. I can imagine. It's sad, but happens all the time." She looked around again. "Even in paradise. Girls go missing. Guys too I guess. Young kids. And if you're not rich or famous, no one cares. She's like a girlfriend or something?"

"More like my daughter. One of my closest friend's daughter."

"Like your goddaughter," she offered.

"He died, and I want to bring her home."

She frowned, then shrugged.

"I really don't know anything. I had the night off. But my roommate worked. She said there was a fight at the bar. Not the first time. It's a club, right? Some asshole and his bodyguards. Lots of people, I don't know if you can call them gangsters, but rich people anyway, bring their own security and—" she looked up at a giant of a man looking their way.

"I think Oscar was here. He's a good guy. I think he would have tried to help but sometimes the rich ones get a pass." The enormous man stepped from behind the bar. Not as huge as a house, but at least a garage. "I better go."

"Thanks, Jamirra."

She smiled. "I hope you find her." She clasped him warmly on his forearm. "I know you will."

The big man was almost upon them, slowed by a quick conversation at another table. She pointed to his glass.

"We're an island, so we've got plenty of water," she said cheerfully. "I'll check back on you in a bit."

She turned and slipped by the giant, almost under his arm as he reached out to shake Black's hand.

Black reached out to return the greeting while sliding another hundred across the table. More magic tricks, the money disappeared in one hand as his other grasped Black's.

"Two minutes," squeezing to make his point.

Black had no hope of squeezing back. It was like grasping a cinder block. Still, his own hand gave little and it earned him another minute.

"Oscar. What can I do for you?" Affable. A baby's face lit with a genuine grin. If ever there was a lovable giant, this might be him. Hiding out in the islands.

"Maybe three nights ago. A young woman. Black. American. Beautiful. Some kind of fight at the bar."

"Not that I know about."

"Oscar. Jamirra says you're a good guy. Would've tried to help but maybe backed off by your boss."

The giant looked around, the world's biggest kid making sure no one else was listening. Turned back and shrugged.

"He's an asshole, but he's the boss."

"Been there," Black said.

"Listen. I really can't help you."

"Yeah, you can. Look. I get it. You tried to do the right thing. I only want a name."

Oscar scanned the bar. Black gave him a moment. His baby-faced features twisted while he decided if he should talk. Conflicted but ready to get it off his massive chest.

"I've seen them in here before, but I'm new enough I don't know the name. I wanted to smash them. The two guys were big. His security I mean. Hard asses for sure. Not sure I could take them." The gentle giant hesitated. "I mean, probably not. I'm big, but I know the difference. Still, when the other guy hit the girls—"

Oscar watched Black's face darken. "Slapped the one, I guess the one you're talking about, hard enough to put her on the floor. I don't care if he is some kind of big-time gangster. That's not right. You don't hit women. That's not what I signed up for, you know?"

"I do know."

"Those guys are the ones got killed, huh?"

"Yeah. Pretty sure."

The door opened and more crowd pushed their way in. Shouts and laughter.

"You think I could have maybe changed something? You know? If I stepped in?" The giant looked like he might cry, obviously torn. "Maybe I could have done something."

"You were right, your instincts, but like you said, smart enough to know the difference," Black said. "One thing changes, then everything can change, but I don't think you could have done anything to have stopped what happened later."

Oscar wasn't convinced. It would take him a long time to get over it. Black couldn't help but like him.

"The girl is missing. I'm going to bring her home."

Oscar looked at Black. His eyes. The set of his mouth. His hands. A couple of fine scars over his eyes. Handsome, but all of it carved in stone.

"You're one of *those* guys, huh?"

Black hesitated. He knew what he was. "Yeah."

"I don't know the name. But SA I think. I heard them speak. I can point you to the boss."

"Good enough."

Michaels and Rodriguez let themselves be pushed into the club along with the rest of the crowd, early enough in the evening there was no cover charge. They'd stopped to eat in the hotel. Neither adventurous enough to risk their stomachs on unknown dishes. They settled on beef imported from South Africa—grass-fed and free from the hormones of American cattle—and fish caught off the island's coast. The steak cut with a butter knife and fork; the fish grilled and served with coriander, saffron, and fresh chillies over rice.

Hours away from capacity, but dozens of people were beginning to crowd the bar and a few tables. Servers running to and fro, racing around the room. Music playing, lights flashing. A giant of a man, maybe the biggest Rodriguez had ever seen, heading through a heavy steel door toward the back with another man.

They took a table near the still empty dance floor. Rodriguez raised his arm to get a server's attention, but needn't have bothered. Another appeared from the mists to take their order.

Michaels knew they looked like cops. They would sit for a moment, try not to appear too aggressive, and find out what they could. His partner's good looks and Cuban charm would do them little good tonight, and the food and radical time change was hitting them hard. Nothing worthwhile would happen and no information would be gained. A waste of time they didn't have. They both needed sleep.

Paul Bradley—*the boss*—the club's general manager, sat at his desk, the room cramped with piles of paper and bulky steel file cabinets along one wall while a bank of monitors for the security cameras filled another. Club command center.

He had copies of the police reports and forms his employees filled out. Courtesy of a little bird down at the station. That the Americans had got themselves killed meant little to him. It didn't happen here and the connection wasn't proven. Nothing in these reports or the tapes he'd turned over to say otherwise. And it wasn't like tourists would quit coming. If spun right, in time, the publicity would add to the club's allure.

No successful club owner in the world could afford not to have a good working relationship with the police. Minor altercations and occasional all-out brawls were expected. Mix sweaty, pheromone rich bodies gyrating in close proximity, stir in alcohol, cocaine, and whatever designer chemical concoction passed as the drug du jour, add bone-shaking music and seizure-inducing light shows reflected across machine-made textured air, and you were bound to stimulate peacock-like displays of inflated egos. Blood flowed, women swooned. Nothing different in three million years. Of course now, just as likely for the men to swoon, and blood flow was usually reduced to a few bumps and bruised egos.

La Caravelle attracted its share of high rollers. The kind of men, and a few women, who could afford to consistently drop thirty to fifty thousand a night on having a good time, meant attracting some less savory types. Where they made the money they spent was no concern of his.

No, the danger to the club came from the scrutiny of the tax auditors. The club walked a delicate balance that could easily be toppled. Paul Bradley's job was to walk that tightrope and make sure that didn't happen.

He reread the incident reports. Fucking South Africans. You don't punch out a girl in the middle of a club. An American girl at that. He had no love for Americans in general, but still, it had been a tough call to hold back his own security man from stepping in. He didn't worry about social media broadcasting the event, he paid a lot of money to ensure the club stayed an absolute dead zone.

Signal jammers meant social media and the Internet were useless here. Inhibitions dropped and more money flowed as people realized their actions inside the club stayed free of instant sharing and broadcast. That might come later, the next day perhaps, a camera in every pocket, but by then, people generally a bit more sober and their posts a bit more considered. No. He'd been worried about the boy.

Oscar was a gentle giant whose job was to intimidate with his huge stature, not mix it up with battle-tested mercenaries who would have torn him apart. No doubt the boy would have jumped into the mix, but then they'd have had to carry him out. Wouldn't that be a sight for the medics? They'd need a bigger wagon. He couldn't explain why, but he felt some affection for the boy— his wife's nephew—and a responsibility to keep him safe.

Fucking gangsters. He didn't know or care if they were responsible for the murders. Not his job. Only for how they conducted themselves under his roof. Still, he wouldn't put it past Kronmüller.

He'd seen his share of tough guys, both wannabe and truly scary made men from a half-dozen different mobs. Italians, Chinese, Saudis, and Nigerians. Put them on an island in the middle of the Indian Ocean where they thought they could do what they wanted with impunity.

That was the club business. Walk the line. Predict and meet the needs of those who supported the enterprise. They paid the employees and kept the lights on with their ostentatious expenditure on the floor while paying the owners and managers their salaries with private requests and considerations under the table.

The South African was a psychopath. A wildcard—and Bradley didn't make his money gambling with wildcards. He'd need to audit his books and remove or justify any expense he'd ever taken from the man. What a pain in the ass. He had some long nights in front of him. Hopefully, the man stayed away for a while. Better yet, fucking forever.

Bradley scanned the monitors. Early. The predicted storms had held off and the club was filling up nicely. He watched the bartenders a moment.

One of the new girls had caught his eye. His wife didn't mind; it kept him from pawing at her. She hadn't let him touch her in more than five years. It had been double that since he'd wanted to. Bradley glanced at another monitor focused on the hall. What the hell? Oscar, his bulk filling the lens of each camera as he passed, leading another man in his direction.

Black stayed slightly behind Oscar, his size preventing them from walking side by side in the hall.

"It would be nice if I could talk to him alone," Black said.

The giant turned as Black handed him a couple hundred more. "I can do that."

Oscar moved aside and hung back as Black passed him and reached for the door.

Michaels and Rodriguez were paying their tab. Coming had been a mistake, accomplishing nothing, but they might as well minimize it as much as possible. Get some sleep and liaise with the Mauritian Police tomorrow.

Then they saw Curpen, his focus on another man at the end of the bar.

The man waved to the police officer, jerked his chin toward the steel door. They watched Curpen thread his way through the crowd, his hand sliding beneath his coat in a move they could only interpret one way.

The man pulled the door open, and Curpen followed.

The man, as broad and stout as an English stove-pipe, rose from his desk as Black came through the door. Black smiled broadly, reached out his hand to shake.

Bradley hesitated, confused, but offered his hand in return.

"Can I help you?"

Black's hand grasped the boss's in a bone-crushing grip, locking it in place as he continued forward, lifting and letting the same arm crash forward, the point of his elbow smashing under the bigger man's sternum. As the air went out of the man, Black jerked his hand down and forward, pulling Bradley off balance and then as the man staggered, lifted his arm back up and spun him, using the momentum to run the man face-first into the monitors.

Face twisted sideways against the glass, nose bleeding, "What the fuck do you want?"

Black released him and Bradley spun to find Black's .45 pushing against his forehead.

"What the fuck? What do you want?"

In another place at another time, Black figured he'd still dislike the man. Coarse—a pudgy face dominated by small, deep-set black eyes glittering with avarice above a broad, oft broken nose. The blood that flowed from it now slowed by a bramble of hair growing from each nostril. Unshaven, the kind of heavy beard that grew in a matter of hours. He stank with fear and stale sweat, his clothes and breath rank with cigar smoke.

"Blonde. South African. Hits women."

The man stammered, spittle flying. "Man, I don't know what—"

Black pulled the steel barrel away only long enough to rap it across the man's mouth, and then shoved it back against the greasy forehead. More blood, spit, and broken teeth.

"One chance. Three seconds."

The beady eyes wide. Taking in the calm but steely blue eyes staring back at him. As scary as the gun. Counting down in his head. Three, two—

"Okay! *Jesus Christ*— Kronmüller. Christiaan Kronmüller."

Black considered shooting him here. That idea lasted about a second. Thought about pushing the barrel through the man's skull. That lasted a couple more.

"I want the girl. Let him know I'm coming." Pulled it away long enough to slam it against the man's temple. Moved back as the man crashed to the floor.

Oscar was on his way back to the main club, his bulk filling the hallway. He took his struggle through the narrow hallway as a sign and made his decision. He needed a better place to work.

He turned the corner, the door in front of him opened and Curpen, he knew the man's name from the past two days of police asking questions, stepped into the hallway. Closing the door behind him.

Oscar looked down at the Sig 9mm in the policeman's hand.

"Can I help you?"

Oscar lurched forward, his back on fire. Spun.

Ricard stood in front of him. Oscar looked down at the bloody stiletto clutched in the man's hand. He reached forward, thought to crush his attacker, but the smaller man was ferret quick.

He darted forward and under the grab, stabbed three rapid-fire thrusts into Oscar's mid-section then danced back as the big man watched his blood spilling from his guts to the polished concrete floor.

Oscar tried to turn back to the cop, but slipped in the blood and crashed to the floor. He watched as Curpen cursed and turned back toward the club.

Black glanced at the monitors. The security cameras recorded on disc. He had no doubt the police would have taken the relevant video. He glanced around the small office. Nothing of value.

He'd use other sources to find out what he needed to know about the South African. Kronmüller.

He stepped into the hall as Ricard sprinted past him, bloody knife in hand. He reached out, clutching for the assassin's throat, but the weasel slipped past. Black ran toward his new huge friend. Oscar. The gentle giant lay in a growing slick of crimson liquid. For the first time in his life, Black could match the amount of blood to the body. He knelt down, afraid he knew the answer.

Curpen stepped back into the chaos of the club. What were the two agents doing here? He'd no time to ask—had been told to prevent the American from talking to Bradley, but this was spiraling out of control.

"This way!"

He pulled his gun again, crashed through the door, and charged back into the hall.

Black searched for a pulse. If it was there, it was faint, but he could see the blood leaking from his new friend pulse in time with what must have been a still-beating if very weakened heart.

The door crashed open with three men behind it. One with a gun and two more going for their own. The recognition that they were cops, the FBI Nicola warned him about, was near-instantaneous, measured in milliseconds. Black had been around such men all his life.

He was sprinting toward the back when two shots rang out, the concussion amplified in the sterile hallway and followed by the whine and ricochet of bullets bouncing past.

As he neared the corner, he rolled, bounced off the walls, and lurched to the side. It was physically impossible to dodge a bullet after it's fired, but he wasn't about to become a steady target. Two more shots drowned out the shouting and confusion he heard behind him.

Black slipped around the corner as slugs tore into the walls around him. Bradley, the club manager staggered from his office with a gun in his hand.

At this range—charge a gun.

Black crashed into the man, slamming him back into the half-opened doorway. They both staggered back. The boss with broken ribs and a shattered scapula, gasping for air that wouldn't come, and Black tripping over him in the narrow confines.

He tangled and fell, scrambled back to his feet and darted for the back door. More bullets flew, the ear-splitting CRACKS bouncing off the walls and filling every bit of space in the halls yet he heard the distinct sound of a bullet ripping through flesh.

More bullets from Curpen's gun. Bradley clutched at his throat and fell to the floor. The two agents made it to the corner as Black crashed into and sprinted out the door into the night.

Curpen rushed toward Bradley as Michaels watched Rodriguez turn toward to the giant. The hall floor filled with blood—surely the huge man was dead.

Curpen felt no emotion, only the sensation of warmth as Bradley's blood pulsed past his fingers. Nothing he could have done anyway. He watched the light go out of the deep-set, beady little eyes and waited for the man's final raspy breath, and the trembling shudder as he died.

No doubt it was his bullet that had torn through the man's throat—but that could be handled. What were the American agents doing here in the club? What did they know? That was the problem with all Americans in his experience. They never followed the rules, even when so clearly laid out for them.

And what about this fucking Major Thomas Black? NATO Special Operations Force. *Another fucking American*. It hadn't taken long to figure out who he was and get a good idea of why he was here. He was going to be more of a problem than they'd thought.

Michaels stood between the two fallen bodies. "Dead?"

Curpen stood. "Yes."

Michaels looked from the dead man at the cop's feet to the blood on his hands.

"The big guy?" Curpen asked.

They turned and walked back, Curpen trying to spin the events.

Michaels couldn't concentrate on anything the man said. His mind was on the man who escaped. Watching the tape roll in his mind—running, dodging, rolling, twisting. Power and grace—the movement of an elite athlete.

If they added an Olympic event for running from gunfire, the man would be team captain. It made absolutely no sense, but Michaels knew he'd seen him before. Just seventy-two hours ago in the streets of Chicago.

Rodriguez hovered over the giant. Nothing else could describe him.

Later, they'd learn his name, and that he was six-eleven, three-hundred ninety pounds. For now, he was *the giant*.

A member of the club's security team was frantically calling for help on one of the club's hard-wired phones. Two more kept the crowd away while they cleared the door.

Rodriguez was doing his best to stem the blood. Failing. He looked up at Michaels. Mouth set; grim, but hopeful. His eyes telling his partner the huge man had a chance. Not much, but a chance.

CHAPTER
TWENTY-SIX

Sam stood in the shower. Steaming water cascaded over her head and ran down her back, and still she shivered. Unable to think. To take the next steps. To strip off her filthy clothes. She tried rubbing the rich bar of soap into her t-shirt, to wash and rinse the jeans she wore while keeping them on. Harder than she thought.

She slowly calmed and began forming a plan. She'd strip, wash the clothes and put them back on to let them dry against her skin. She pulled the t-shirt off. Rubbed the thin fabric with soap as the bathroom continued to fill with steam until she almost couldn't see her arms in front or her legs beneath her.

The cleaning would never be perfect, the t-shirt irreparably stained and torn. She washed and wrung it out, hanging the shirt over the glass door before tackling her jeans. Tried to pull them off. Not easy, taking all of her strength as the wet fabric clung like another layer of skin. Pants around her ankles, she slipped and fell, crashing hard and undignified to the slippery shower floor. Wriggled them off. The heavy fabric much harder than the t-shirt to wash and rinse by hand.

She stood up and watched dirt flow from the fabric into the drain. Sand from the island. Rust and oil from the barrel. Dirt from the shipping container. Dust from the truck. Her hands and forearms exhausted by the scrubbing and wringing. She tried to straighten the denim, making room on the door for them.

Panties were easy. The fabric fine enough she thought she might actually get them clean. She rubbed until the fine threads began coming apart in her hands.

Once naked, relieved to be out of the filthy clothes, she was again lost. Panicked. She began rubbing her skin with a vengeance. Reached for the shampoo. Washed and rinsed her hair. A second time. A third.

Afraid to open the door, but she knew she couldn't stay here forever. Stepped from the shower, grabbing from a high stack of huge, luxurious towels and dried off, rubbing her skin until raw and the caramel color of her skin turned pink.

She traded the wet towel for a dry one, wrapping it tightly around her. Turned back to her clothes, dreading the effort of putting them back on. She lifted the jeans from the door, reached into the pockets. Pulled out the two diamond pendants. *Billie!* Was she somewhere close? Going through the same torture? Afraid to make the trip on her own, Sam had convinced her friend to come. She shivered, her bones rattling from the pain in her soul as she fought not to throw up.

Sam slumped to the tile floor and cried.

Sam wasn't ready to die. She couldn't explain it, but she knew that dying here wasn't her fate. Nothing could ever be the same, but whatever happened, whatever trials she might face, she would live. Somehow, some way, she'd get home.

She wiped at the tears, took a deep breath. Pushed the door open from where she sat. The steam swirled around her like a ghost and fled to the larger room.

The dress and lingerie waiting.

Ouderling sat behind a massive desk, the legs and apron carved with masterful depictions of African tribal life. The room itself, huge. Fourteen-foot ceilings, wainscoting, and hand-carved crown moldings. African Rosewood and Rhodesian teak. Rare books and big-game trophies.

Christiaan, the younger Kronmüller, paced on the hand-knotted Isfahan Persian rug. He slammed his hand against the polished wood walls. Ouderling laughed at him.

"Goddammit it. I'm not a child!"

"You will not blaspheme in my home," Ouderling bellowed. "Now sit the fuck down."

Kronmüller stomped back and forth, seething in rage but with nowhere to vent it, quickly deflated and plopped down in one of the silk embroidered Queen Anne chairs. Exactly like a child.

Ouderling moved to a shelf cabinet and pulled down two cut-crystal tumblers. Poured them both drinks, a thirty-year-old Balvenie. Placed one on the desk before his son and then stalked the room behind him with the other

Both men were trying to calm themselves down. Kronmüller, he didn't think of himself by his given name anymore, hadn't since being addressed exclusively by his last name in boarding school, drank deeply of the dark amber liquid, the buttery smooth Scotch wasted against his anger.

"At least your brother fought against his instincts and joined the army."

"Bullshit. He was conscripted like the rest of us. He only embraced it to be with his black moffie because you couldn't stand to have queer son."

"Do not speak of Joffire that way! None of it's true!"

"What are you going to do? Beat it out of me? Change the family history? Of course it's fucking true."

Ouderling threw his drink against the wall, the glass shattering and shards bouncing into Kronmüller's face. He blinked but didn't flinch. Ouderling watched the blood trickle down his son's cheek like a trail of tears.

Lina sat on the stairs, listening. No secret to her that the Elder hated her. She wasn't pure. *Tainted, sub-human—a mutt, a dog, a baboon.*

She'd heard it all and worse. She knew her days were few—whatever her time left, limited.

The deep, guttural voice of the Ouderling came up the stairs to her as if he stood at her ear

"Your sickness has infected your brain. Your thoughts are a cancer grown from your perversions. So no—there is no beating it out of you."

Ouderling poured himself another drink, sat behind his desk. He fingered the gun he kept tucked in his belt, a semi-automatic Dreyse M1907. An immaculately kept antique. Regarded his son. A disappointment—not the legacy he'd envisioned, but all that he had. His son stared back at him with ill-disguised malevolence.

"Fuck the help when you need to, but you'll sell your American nigger with the others. And you'll stop this nonsense of breeding with your klonkie bitch or I'll have the baboon chopped up and fed to the hogs."

CHAPTER
TWENTY-SEVEN

Held hostage under whatever cover the city could offer, the promise made by late afternoon clouds now delivered in blankets of pelting rain. Heavens split with a roar—the jagged, split-second glimpse beyond the skies shook the earth beneath in protest and her tears fell harder still. Surely as wet as Atlantis itself, even the light took refuge. Streetlamps and neon, windows from the stores and hotels squandered their rays until such time when the storm might pass. No taxis to be found, but an occasional car surfed the streets as the gutters and storm-drains struggled to keep up, throwing high wakes behind them as they slid and sloshed through rising waters.

Black walked. The inundated walkways and roads disguised his stagger. He could have been another drunk, having spent his money and leaving himself with no other way to get home. Walk or drown. The storm offered neither respite nor sympathy.

He crossed a dark intersection and the waters, rushing from the highlands back to the sea, nearly took him off his feet. His innate sense of balance saved him, and he continued, shivering, wet from the sweat pushed from within as well as the torrential rains without.

In the formless shadows, one could sense the city beginning to thin. Behind him, the huddling contract of life waited to emerge as the clouds raced each other across the dark sky.

In front, more felt than seen, any hint of light and warmth taking refuge from the storm, Black could feel the gravity of the distant mountains pull him forward. The dark side of the island beckoned, and he lurched forward to meet it.

And then, as violent as it came, the heavens sealed the breach and the storm raced out to sea. Black turned on the hillside street to look back. The air still charged, every color electrified and exaggerated, the coast glowed in the distance with the last of the setting sun.

Black could make out streets, their signs, and the dark structures around him. Here, light was tied to economics as much as the elements. Houses and markets lit with candles or oil as often as electricity; streetlights saved for the tourists and their dollars far behind and below him.

Sound returned. Voices. Laughter. The barking of a dog, the distant wailing of a child.

Ahead, a three-story structure of weather-beaten timber and planks stood as if fashioned from a shipwrecked galleon. A couple of generously proportioned women in the doorway flirted with a couple of men. The scene and figures timeless, maybe playing in an endless loop since the island's discovery for all he knew. Soft yellow light, and the hint of music beyond guided Black forward.

The top floor no doubt an apartment, or maybe several; perhaps the local brothel. A flicker of candlelight, golden beams danced on the tin ceiling above and washed over the street below. This, the side of town where living on top of each other was ofttimes a literal description.

Music, an African-laced Creole, sprung from open widows echoing back and forth down the wet streets and narrow alleys.

Above the door, the weathered sign with the fighting rooster stenciled on it announced the pub's name as Bantam. The men and women moved aside with raised eyebrows, and with a seemingly random mixture of accents and languages, asked amongst themselves about the wet stranger.

Black entered, his shoes squishing and sucking rudely, as wet as if he'd just been plucked from the sea.

The first floor was a market, mostly dark. Rows of canned and packaged goods visible on neat and tidy shelves. A glass counter and an old-fashioned cash register off to the side.

Black took a deep breath. Turned to the steep wooden staircase. Took time to convince himself he could make it.

The pub was surprisingly lively. A dozen men and women sat talking and laughing around a heavy round table, a book shoved under one leg to keep it steady. Six mismatched bar stools were occupied. A middle-aged couple, as shapeless and doughy as unbaked bread, slow danced, holding on to each other and swaying in slow motion even though the music was fast and energetic.

Nothing stopped as he entered, yet except for the music, it was as if a dim switch had been pressed, and the sound levels of every conversation and movement dropped by half.

A man perched on a stool turned from the center of the small, crudely hewn bar, took in the bedraggled stranger, then stood and offered his seat.

"Thanks." With the single word, Black's accent announced his origins, and the room's sound dropped further.

Black let himself settle on the creaking stool.

"Getcha bière?" Already pulling one out of a small metal chest filled with ice.

Black nodded and the bartender cracked open the bottle, blessedly ice cold.

He reached for it, his arm moving in slow motion. Closed his eyes, thankful for the cool contact of his hand on the bottle. Took a long pull.

The man behind the bar, impossible to guess his age, as hard and spare as if carved from a piece of drifting ironwood, raised his eyebrows in question to Luke. The elder man's bushy white eyebrows and a full complement of whiskers coming from his nose and ears to blend with the wiry thicket on his face lifted his chin toward Black's side.

The bartender leaned over the counter to look. Blood seeped from Black's side and dripped onto the floor.

"You're not faring well, mon ami."

Black set the bottle down. Fished in his pocket.

Did his best to spread Nicola's wet business card across the bar and fell off the stool.

Gravity suddenly increased and Black found it difficult to move, the weight of his arms and legs too much to overcome, his chest pressed down against his lungs, his breath too shallow to fill them.

He felt a dozen hands grab at him. The pain blossomed as they lifted and turned him over, his face now pressed into a wooden table, scarred and beaten even more than he was. Could hear voices of concern above him. He needed to let them know he appreciated their worry and generosity, but he was fine.

He just—felt—so—heavy.

He tried to understand why. Ran it through his mind. Backtracked.

Perhaps he'd absorbed the water from the rains, his arms and legs sodden and now doubled or tripled in weight. He'd just lie here until he dried out a bit. Then he could explain it to them.

He willed his eyes to open. It took some effort but eventually, one eye obeyed. Well, nearly. A hint of soft, warm light leaked past his eyelid. Only a moment, but he was sure he'd seen it. Light meant he was alive, didn't it? Maybe if he lay still, it would come again.

He waited. No more light, but he could hear faint, distant voices. He wanted to talk to them, tell them he'd been shot before. That this wasn't too bad. That should be obvious. He was here and hadn't died. This wasn't how dead feels. There were subtle differences and well, the truth be told, he'd been dead twice before. It wasn't so bad and this was nothing like that. Once was peaceful and once was—all manner of opposites of peaceful. It didn't have to be such a big deal.

Lots of his friends had been shot. You either lived or you died.

So much of it depended on luck. He'd held men in his arms as their luck ran out, leaking past his hands and spilling to the ground. *Others?* One man he knew shot in the head with an AK-47 and yet the round somehow circled his skull under the skin and exited from behind his neck. *Physics in random motion produced random outcomes.* Hadn't even fallen. A few stitches and a band-aid.

Black had been shot twice before. Once, a round ripping a narrow furrow along his thigh as straight and clean as a sword. The second time could have been bad, the round had entered near his front hip, bounced off the bone, somehow missed his organs and lodged millimeters from his spine. *Physics in random motion produced random outcomes.*

Airlifted in a UH-60 Blackhawk to a MASH unit, and after a lengthy debate among the surgeons, the surprisingly quick surgery left him with an expected six-month recovery and painful rehab. Black cut it in half by doubling up on the pain, but that was more about being captured and tortured by the Taliban rather than any heroic rehabilitation efforts on his own.

Black felt himself drift. Strange he thought. How he could be so heavy and yet floating so lightly as if on the ocean. He felt his heart slowing down. Saving his strength. He'd sleep a bit and then let them know he was fine. No reason to worry. It was strangely peaceful. Like a sensory deprivation tank, the pain so total there was no room for other sensation.

The voices faded, the hands cutting away his clothes dissolved. No light. No dark. It was—*something else*. Soon, full of awe and wonder, he found he no longer needed to breathe and could finally let his heart rest.

CHAPTER
TWENTY-EIGHT

S am stood at the windows of her room. She couldn't see well in the unevenly lit night, but watched the man storm from the house and drive away in what she thought might be a modified Land Rover. She hadn't seen his face but was sure it was him. The man from the club.

She watched until the dust and gravel settled. Couldn't see where he'd come from, her window view only showed part of a huge stone and timber house. She now realized that the room she was in, on the third floor, might be a separate guest house, facing the back of the main house and not attached at all.

Trying to determine the landscaping and the house layout while trapped within one room wasn't easy. She could see hints of other buildings, barns or stables in the near distance. A tall granary. A large water tank.

Sam had been here for two days. Fallen asleep from exhaustion and woken twice to find food and water. Breads and cereals. Fresh fruits and yogurt. Bottled mineral water. That she hadn't seen or heard anyone enter scared her. She realized they, she assumed it was *'they'*, had been watching her. Waiting until she slept. She had tried to fake it, pretend until someone came, but eventually had fallen into a deep, dreamless stupor. Perhaps she was being drugged. Something in the food or water, but she knew she couldn't afford not to eat—she needed her strength for whatever awaited.

She had yelled down during the day toward what she assumed were maids and workers, men and women who studiously avoided looking up at the room. One woman, a girl really, certainly younger than she was, had glanced up at her pleas as she crossed the expansive courtyard. The girl, ebony skin and long, liquid arms wrapped around a basket of laundry, made eye-contact and looked stricken as if they both had done some egregious wrong, and then hurried away before she was found and punished.

What could it all mean? Some things obvious and some things not. Kidnapped by the man on the balcony. But for what reason? And who was he? The man's bodyguards had brutally murdered Allan. Was he a target or just in the way of abducting her? This couldn't only be about the altercation in the club, but either way, the man was unhinged. Allan was dead. So she assumed Hunter was too. *Where did that leave Billie?* She feared the worst for her friend. Could feel it. Wanted to cry and grieve but forced herself to concentrate.

They were in Africa. Maybe Cape Town. The glimpses she had during her transport fit with what little she knew. Or nearby. Somewhere north of Cape Town. Three thousand miles from where she was supposed to be. She could almost laugh. Where she was *supposed* to be?

Allan had set her up. Expecting what? She'd be so overwhelmed and thankful for the trip she'd forgive him for the two years of lying to her and cheating on his wife? Sure. Thanks, Allan. Having a great time.

She should have seen the signs. Let her dad run a check or run the sheets or whatever it was when cops wanted to know all the dirt. She had tried on her own. Admittedly not very hard—blinded by his charm—so different from anything she had known. He had zero social media presence and shockingly little information on the Internet. Daddy, the Mayor, had spent considerable effort to ensure his son stayed a blank slate until the complete strategy for his future was in place.

Her father was a cop. Chicago. She hadn't told him about the trip. Didn't want to hear it from a man making the fucked up choices he was. What was he thinking? *Rina was a bitch.* The nicest way it could be said.

But Allan's death, his murder, would have been broadcast. Probably the world knew by now. That meant her father knew where she wasn't. Not in Chicago working on her dissertation and not shacked up with Allan on a tropical island. She could picture the rage he'd be in. Watched the fantasy in her mind of her father smashing the South African gangster. Strangling him. Shooting him. There'd be nothing left when he was done.

Her father could be scary. He was a big man. A cop. Army vet. Special Forces or something hush-hush. But would he have the resources to find her? To save her? She couldn't imagine that part.

Who would come to save her? *No one—that's who.* She was on her own. She was young and smart. She had to eat and sleep and stay strong for whatever came next.

Sam slept. Her dreams filled with Army men and her father and Uncle Tommy. A fantastic submarine that somehow turned into an airplane, and they all dropped from the sky, their parachutes floating down. Tanks rolled in and bombs went off. Aimed at the house. She screamed but no one listened. The girl in the courtyard glanced up at her. Their eyes met and Sam screamed at her in warning. The girl waved. Gave a thumbs up. Everything would be fine. Then a tank belched and the girl exploded. Chunks of flesh splattering the windows. Sam cried in her sleep and woke to the sound of a gentle knocking at her door.

She jumped from the bed. Stared at the door in dread. Looked for a weapon. Lamps and figurines. The spoon from her breakfast. Maybe she could break the water glass and use that.

A key turned in the lock, the tumblers clicking and sliding against each other, amplified in her mind as if played through a high-end stereo.

She grabbed the glass and the spoon, pulled back toward the bathroom, ready to lock it behind her, and make her last stand.

The door pushed slowly open, darkness from the hall behind it. Slower still, a face peeked from around it. The beautiful woman from the hotel and club!

Sam dropped the glass to the floor and rushed toward her.

"Help me."

"Shhhhhh." The girl turned and locked the door behind her. "I'm trying."

Both women stopped. Measured each other. Still girls as much as women. Both beautiful. Both mixed race. Both dressed in someone else's taste in expensive out-of-place fashion.

They could pass for sisters—though one was assured and calm while the other stood with bone wracking tremors that threatened to take her off her feet.

Sam wrapped her arms around herself, trying to hold herself together; her hands clenched so tightly they turned white. "What is happening? Why am I here?"

"Come," Lina guided the American to sit at the foot of the huge bed. "We don't have much time. You have to listen to me."

CHAPTER
TWENTY-NINE

Tommy was in the motel room. He was Tommy and he was Black. It made sense. He was Tommy Black. He wished the boy he was could have asked the man he became for help. Was sure the man would have done his best. He would have at least tried.

He could see the pea-soup-green walls. The little, orange plastic chair. The yellow, brown, and green curtains. Hideous, mottled diamond patterns woven as punishment in some curtain weaving hell. They kept the Arizona light from beating past the broken air conditioner. The fan rattled and banged loud enough no one could sleep but it meant the windows had to be kept closed in trade for the few degrees of coolness offered.

His mother solved that by shooting heroin or getting drunk enough she passed out. She'd lay on the stained sheets and sway-backed mattress where she'd shake and sweat but rarely stir until the asshole she called her boyfriend, a three-hundred-pound, heavily tattooed, hairy beast she referred to affectionately as *her* asshole, would come back from whatever Peckerwood meth lab in the hills he was supplying muscle for, and climb on top of her.

Sometimes she'd wake up, and sometimes she wouldn't. He didn't seem to care much either way. He'd pull her panties down, if she had any on, and climb on top. Tommy would hide in the bathroom, doing planar calculations—simple trigonometry functions—with the stained tiles of the floor while running the shower and sink to drown out the grunts and groans from the other room.

Tommy had watched his mother take the money, emptying the cheap backpack and leaving it lying on the floor. He knew it was stupid. Stupid and wrong and dangerous. There was enough she wouldn't have to trick to score the brown powder she'd cook and shoot behind her knees or between her toes. She left him locked in the room, ten years old, but was back in less than an hour.

Reeking of sex and stale, sour sweat, cigarettes, cheap whiskey. Still, she wanted release and by the time she was sucking the dirty liquid from the spoon into the yellowed syringe, acrid smoke swirling around her, he had grabbed the motel key, a couple of dollars off the particle board dresser and went to get a soft drink from the little truck stop across the street.

Tommy crossed the parched two-lane highway. Walked under the jangling bell into the store. He walked to the back, then stopped to watch the reflections in the cooler doors as an excited young couple popped in for cigarettes and snacks, laughing and flirting and laughing some more, making this a pit stop on their trip to the west coast.

It's exactly what his mother had promised Tommy. Escape from the bitter northern winters and a new beginning with oceans of sunshine. Not hooking up with a three-hundred-pound biker and giving blow jobs in the trucker's parking lot for a few grams of Mexican brown.

He was suddenly overwhelmed with the thought that they had one last chance, the chance of his young lifetime, waiting to be grabbed and wrestled into something better. He rushed back across the highway, nearly getting flattened by a tractor-trailer, tripped and fell on the broken motel parking lot pavement, and burst back into the room.

Black watched the boy try to wake his mother up. Tommy convinced that if they could leave, if he could convince her to go to California like she said they would, before Asshole got home, they had a chance.

She didn't move.

He pulled and pushed, shook her, and tried to drag her from the bed. Nothing. *This was not the time to be sleeping.* He grabbed a cracked plastic glass of water and threw it on her. Nothing. Tommy became frantic, pulling at her arm, his small hands digging into flesh permanently marked with dark track marks and scars. Nothing.

He almost didn't hear the huge bike roar its way off the highway, but the motel's cheap block construction shook under the onslaught until the bike sputtered and coughed itself quiet.

Asshole burst through the door, already drunk or high or both, dropped a duffel bag on the chair while tripping on the empty backpack. He growled as he scooped the backpack from the floor like a bear grabbing a salmon, saw it empty, and bellowed a roar of his own. Grabbed Tommy's mother from the bed, oblivious to the fact that she was probably dead and threw her against the wall.

Crawling over the bed, Asshole knocked over her still-burning cigarette perched on the chipped edge of the window seal. As he stalked her and came to grab her again, Tommy threw his body forward and tried to tackle him. Seventy pounds of boy against three hundred pounds of man. Asshole cuffed the boy in the head and sent him cartwheeling across the floor.

Black watched again as Asshole grabbed his mother from the floor, slammed her into the wall again and again. Something cracked and something broke and the pea-soup-green walls were stained in red. Black watched as Tommy crabbed backward, scrambled to his feet, unzipped the duffel, and pulled out Asshole's .357.

No hesitation, but it took all the boy's strength to pull the trigger.

He missed wildly as the powerful gun bucked backward, opening a cut across Tommy's forehead, the thin scar above his right eye still carried on the man today, but the boy held on. Blood ran from his head, pooled in his eyes and dripped to the floor, but Tommy held on.

Asshole spun where he stood, tossed the broken rag doll of Tommy's mother across the bed, and glared at the boy through a haze of acrid smoke.

"You little cum spot! Drop the fucking gun!" Asshole unbuckled his belt and jerked the long leather strap free—the belt sliding and hissing like a serpent through the loops of denim.

The cigarette smoldered against the curtains. It took a moment to decide, raced like Hades' imps across the errant threads and worn fabric and paused as if recognizing the hellish diamond landscape, then attacked with all-out ferocity. The synthetic fibers of the drapes went up like cotton soaked in gasoline.

As the enraged biker came from around the bed, the belt buckle whistling in warning through the smoke-filled air, Tommy steadied the big gun with his skinny arms and squeezed the trigger again.

A fist-sized chunk of flesh exploded from Asshole's throat and painted the wall behind him. The biker crashed backward, his hands clutching his neck and finding only ravaged meat. His knees buckled, and he fell against the wall, his hands overflowing with blood, eyes full of rage and disbelief as he slowly slumped to the floor and died.

The flames hit the cheap wallpaper, raced across the walls, and roiled across the ceiling. Plaster blistered and fell, the cheap TV exploded, the bed caught fire, and still the blaze hungered.

Tommy dropped the gun, grabbed at his mother, tried to pull her from the bed. Used his feet to brace himself against the bed frame and with new-found strength, managed to drag her off.

Tommy pried the door open, fell back as fresh air rushed over him to fuel the fire.

Hands reached for Tommy, pulled him away as he screamed and fought to go back in, fighting through the flames for his mother's arm until he was dragged into the parking lot.

A wall buckled and collapsed on itself while flames raced to the adjacent rooms. The motel room's door, an entry to hell burned into Black's soul forever, clawed and snapped at him with teeth and forked tongues stretched far into the parking lot.

Sirens blared, and as Black watched, firemen pulled up. A half-dozen police cars and an ambulance screeched to a halt. The EMT's fitted an oxygen mask to the boy's face. Tommy, the boy, sputtered and coughed, pushed it away as the motel began to fall.

Black, the man, gasped as the building collapsed into a roaring inferno of flame, smoke, and exploding embers.

"He's back!"

Black could hear voices, far away, maybe in another room. He was fighting to extract enough oxygen from his shallow breaths to make them worthwhile. *Maybe I'm underwater or floating in outer space* he thought.

"Putain de merde! That was touchy."

"No sign of a bullet. Could have a couple broken ribs. Lots of blood though."

"We've got more blood coming. Heart's steady."

The voices faded more.

"He's a strong bastard."

"Looks like he got lucky." They took in some of his other scars. The angry bruises and the fresh rip in his other side.

"Let's get some antibiotics in him, we can start with Cefotan, and keep the fluids coming."

And later. "I think we've done all we can. We'll keep an eye on him and let him rest."

The club came rushing back. Cops and FBI. Oscar and Ricard. Sam and Nicola. Bullets flying, ricocheting down the halls. The sound of a bullet ripping flesh.

Physics in random motion produced random—fuck it—Black fell asleep.

CHAPTER
THIRTY

The hotel rooms were a disaster, the door between them opened to create one larger suite. Beds unmade, towels over the door. There would be no maid service today. The desks and tables of the one had been pulled into the other so that they could work in one room. A photo printer had been set up and was churning out papers, reports, and photos that were being taped to a wall.

Two men and one woman perched behind laptops, extra computer monitors, police scanners, and satellite modems along with the additional equipment to keep them secure. Clement and Julius were twenty-eight. Camille was twenty-five. Another woman, Alix, her task to coordinate the others and organize the rapid influx of information coming in, pouring coffee and keeping them supplied with Red Bull, had just turned twenty-three.

All four were attractive; Camille had done both catalog and runway modeling in Europe as a child, and all four as excited as they were determined.

Alix answered the house phone. She listened and hung up three seconds later. Thankful her on-again-off-again girlfriend worked at the front desk.

"They're on their way back up," she relayed. "What do we have from the hospital?"

Julius hit a key on the laptop and disconnected his call. Was just about to tell them when Special Agents in Charge Michaels and Special Agent Rodriguez came into the room.

He liked saying their full title. It somehow elevated their assignments, but he'd been admonished to call them by their last names only—the same as nearly any cop anywhere in the world.

He turned to the American agents. "Looks like the security guy will survive it. Oscar Buteryn. Damage to his liver and likely lose a kidney, but hanging on."

"Good," Michaels was moving to the printer and sifting for photos. "I'm not buying that this guy," he held up a grainy black and white picture, a second-hand frame grab from the hotel security cams, "takes time to stab a man four times and *not* kill him."

Rodriguez had shot it off his phone as Curpen and his minions scanned the club's security tapes. The Agent caught little more than a blur before they were shooed away with the promise of the entire tape when they came in later this morning.

Could have been Bigfoot for all the good this did. Still, something about it—the senior Agent knew he was forcing his imagination to reconstruct details that just weren't there. It was Curpen's gunshots and the graceful, athletic movement of the man fleeing the scene that triggered the memory, but the idea seemed impossible.

The man in Chicago—*why the fuck would he be here?* How even? They had never seen his face, only a vague shadow entering the walk up, and then the silhouette of a man diving out of a four-story building. Michaels had made it to the window in time to see the man rolling across the nearby rooftop, as nimble and fluid as a circus performer, dodging bullets and bouncing off the club's hallways before disappearing out the back.

The two Agents had gone to the club to get a sense of the energy, and to absorb any obvious staff dynamics without the colored commentary of their Mauritius liaisons.

What they got instead was a dead club manager, a seriously injured giant, conflicting stories from the servers and bartenders, a fleeing suspect who may or may not have committed six murders in Chicago as they were in the tail-end of an eight-month surveillance operation, a bullshit story from the island cop who was supposed to be supplying them all necessary means and information on the murder of a prominent American politician's son and his companions, and the possible kidnapping of the daughter of a deceased, decorated Army veteran and Chicago cop.

Both dead on their feet, too tired to digest the story Curpen was feeding them, they made it back to the hotel. Michaels put a call into the Midwest field office requesting everything that had been accomplished in Chicago in the past three days. All reports, interviews, ballistics, DNA analysis of the blood samples pulled from the broken building next door, and especially any photos or enhanced video. Then he passed out.

Rodriguez spent the same amount of time in his room to arrange outside support, private contractors who occasionally worked with both the FBI and Interpol. As long as they didn't work for the Mauritius Police Department, he'd be happy.

They wakened to the sound of Alix Liáng knocking on their doors. It took the agents a moment to remember where they were. Additional time in Michaels's case to decide not to shoot whoever was banging on his door. Alix introduced herself and then the other three. The four stood politely outside for the ten minutes it took the agents in their respective rooms to shower and dress.

Once inside, they received a five-minute briefing of their tasks. Alix, the youngest, but obviously the one in charge, her position won by her intellectual gifts and the sheer force of her personality, directed the others in setting up cases of electronics and computers.

They first tapped into the hotel's Wi-Fi, amplified, and rerouted their connections. The hotel's host company would have been shocked at the bilateral connection speeds generated with the help of Alix's own proprietary software.

Michaels watched without comprehension. Being tired had little to do with it—he'd grown up with rotary phones. "Okay. It seems like you know what you're doing," he said.

Alix smiled. "Give us a few minutes, and we'll be connected to anywhere in the world." Not the same as having access, but she didn't say that part. They weren't elite hackers but could go places most people couldn't, and it was deep enough for the type of jobs they got hired for. They'd camp in the hotel room to act as the highest level of technical support for the two agents, and digitally pursue any ideas they might have.

Rodriguez scanned the room. He was just a few years older than the contractors but thought they looked like the dream cast of a teenage cop show. He grabbed Michaels's arm. "We're set for MPD in less than two hours. Let's leave them to it, grab a bite downstairs, and make a plan?"

"We've got a pretty good idea of what you want," Alix said, "and enough to get started. All field and after-action reports from the Chicago operation. All concurrent police reports on the same. Background on Chamberland and Hunter. Same on Billie McClusky and Samantha Dillon. Any hospital admittance reports from the past twelve hours. Word on the security guard. All points of ingress and egress for the island, last ten days. Manifests for the same."

"That's a start," Michaels said. "We'll be able to give you more direction once we've talked to MPD. Hopefully the tapes from both incidents and the hotel." He grabbed for his jacket. "Do what you can to get us info on Gauber and Curpen as well."

"Start with Curpen. If he's connected in any way to any other incidents of either murder or abduction, we want to know. No matter how obscure, anything stands out at all, we'll want to know," Rodriguez said. "Track down any partners he's had in the same time frame, and see if anything pops up there."

"Let's go for the usual suspects. Banks accounts, holdings, travel, romantic relationships," Michaels added.

"We'll be back in twenty— No, let's make it thirty. Call it zero nine hundred."

"You guys need anything?" Michaels asked.

Alix was pulling out snacks, making coffee. "We're good." Clement held up a six-pack of Red Bull and smiled. Reached for another.

"We'll be back," Michaels said. The agents left to grab a quick breakfast.

The selections of the hotel's free continental breakfast weren't that unusual, but the quality exceptional. Soft boiled eggs, freshly baked breads and croissants with a wide variety of spreads and chutneys, an array of fruits that would have dazzled on any table in America.

Welcome to a tropical island with the cultural influences of Indian and Malay, African and French, Chinese and Portuguese cuisines. The plan to make a plan became concentrated on drinking the exceptional coffee, rich and fragrant, undertones of vanilla and cinnamon and chocolate, and waking up.

Breakfast over, it was time to work.

"Keep us up on Buteryn. We'll want to talk to him before MPD does," Michaels said.

"Could be hard," Alix said. "They've got officers on the floor and at his room."

Rodriguez smiled. Three hours of sleep, some calories from the hotel buffet breakfast, a hint of his Cuban charm back in place. His best Desi Arnaz. "Yeah. But we're FBI, and we have the dream team on our side. You'll figure it out."

She smiled. "Do you really think we're on sides?"

"Hopefully, we'll know in a couple of hours," Rodriguez said. "But something feels... off."

"I admit we're on fumes and running to catch up. You're here for technical support, but you're all highly intelligent," Michaels said. "You coax the best from machines that others use to send emails and connect on Facebook. So you're intuitive. We need that. We need your impressions as much as your skills. We're here to solve the brutal murders of at least three American citizens, and bring what might be the abduction of a fourth to a successful recovery and resolution. We're not local. Don't know the players, their records, or even if we're playing the same game. So for now, yeah. I think we're on sides."

"Sorry we're so vague," Rodriguez said. "Do what you can. Whatever you can think of to get us up to speed."

Julius' fingers danced over his keyboard. Hit the return with a resounding, definitive punctuation. "This is interesting," he said. Transferred it to one of the two flat screens they had pulled from the hotel walls and set up for just this purpose.

Photos, police reports, news station broadcasts, newspapers. Dillon's murder-suicide.

"What are we looking at?" Rodriguez asked.

"Four days ago. Chicago. Murder-suicide of a Chicago police officer."

Michaels frowned. "Yeah. The night before our shit hit the fan. We were pretty caught up."

Clement summarized the headlines. "Happened outside of Chicago in the officer's resident town of Gary, Indiana. Ex-Army. Chicago PD for 10 years."

"Yeah. A lot of factors at play there," Rodriguez said. "Some of these guys are wound pretty tight."

The screen kept filling up with clippings and photos. Edited news station video from the major channels played in separate windows.

The thing is," Camille said, "the officer's name is Elijah Dillon."

It took a moment to sink in.

Camille was bringing up further background. She transferred it to the other big screen. Army records, college transcripts. Photos.

'—decorated Army veteran and Chicago cop is survived by his daughter—'

The dry notation from the Chicago offices made it seem like something written years ago. *Exactly why they were here*, Michaels thought. To put boots on the ground and faces to the names.

It was all in front of them, or at the least, a huge part of the puzzle, waiting for the pieces to be put in order.

"Jesus Christ," Michaels said. "How'd we miss this?" '*We*' as in FBI.

They all shrugged. Alix not wanting to say the obvious. *They hadn't.*

Michaels glanced at his watch. "Damn, we need to get out of here. Get everything you can on this. Background on the girl, friends, past relationships." Looked back up at the big screen. Something gnawing at him.

News footage played. A dozen police cars, SWAT team snipers, command center trucks, the growing crowd of onlookers. The black Silverado with the cop sitting inside. Another man ignoring the police perimeter and crossing the street to speak to the cops.

They watched it play. The man covering the dead woman with his jacket. Speaking to the big cop. Walking away. The news station tastefully editing out the actual gunshot. More compelling than any Hollywood fiction, the agent forced himself to pull away.

Rodriguez watched his partner watch the video. Something was going on in that head of his. He'd learned to pay attention.

"Okay. We're out of here. Get what you can."

"If they don't jerk us around too much, we should be able to come back with additional threads to pursue," Rodriguez said. "So be ready."

"We're on it," Julius said.

"We've got some ideas." Alix smiled. "Thanks for the trust."

The Agent looked around. *Yeah, teenage cop show.* Mod Squad. Dazzling smiles, perfect hair. Confidence and competence. Writing their scenes, waiting for direction.

"Okay then," Rodriguez said. "We'll be back."

CHAPTER

THIRTY-ONE

Morning came, clear and bright, the island's air cleansed by last night's violent storm. Nicola rolled over, took time to breathe it in, kept her eyes closed, and tried to identify the components of the rich, tropical perfume.

The former hotel was only a few hundred meters away from the entire Indian Ocean. Boucle d'Oreille, the national flower, lay dormant this time of year, waiting until summer and fall before the reddish-orange flowers bloom, but orchids—more than sixty indigenous species found across the island—added their sweet scents. Hibiscus and Bougainvillea, Red Anthurium, and Frangipani. Delicate sugar cane flowers carried on the wind, Impatiens, exotic Birds of Paradise. The rich soil and peat of old-growth forest. Ocean brine for sure.

Eyes still closed, she could tell fruits had been sliced and waited for her on a nearby table. She couldn't separate their components by smell, but her imagination filled in as she knew there would be at the least pineapple, mangoes, papayas, and lychees.

Sunrise long over. A lazy day. The house was just beginning to stir, and lying back in the bed felt as delicious as any breakfast she might find. She let her mind wander to the other side of the island and wondered how the children were. How Aleeza was doing. The beautiful child was so small, still traumatized from whatever horrors she had witnessed in her young life, but Nicola had seen glimpses of her true personality and spirit emerging.

Nicola hated to be away for the night, but knew what she did here was also important. The open children's shelter, more realistically an orphanage, on one side of the island; this secretive, hidden women's shelter on the other. No phones or Internet could be found here, though the women were encouraged to engage with the world whenever they felt they were ready. Nicola tried to come once a week and bring her laptop. Helped the women look for jobs and more permanent housing when they were ready.

She put a lot of effort into making sure the women could stay as long as they needed. She knew only too well the mind-numbing fear and terror they'd felt. Here, they were safe from abusive husbands and boyfriends, safe from family members and even religious persecution; the women here as likely to be Hindu as Christian, Buddhist as Muslim.

Of the seventeen women who stayed here, most had children. They could be heard stirring and giggling in the huge common room outside her door. Originally a private resort hotel, it had been bought and donated in appreciation for a young woman Nicola had rescued from the woman's husband's strict, fundamentalist family. Each of the seventeen women had their own private room and then shared four rooms of baths, showers, and toilets. No men allowed. This was a place of refuge.

Nicola knew she needed to get up. She had a few small gifts to pass out. Supplies to be ordered. Groceries to purchase and inventory. Medical supplies and procedures to arrange.

She'd been caught in the storm before it climbed the volcanic mountains and sped out to sea. Fighting the wind and rain on the motorbike, little more than a scooter, had completely worn her out. Phone service on this part of the island relied on mom-and-pop satellite dishes tapped into spotty data towers. The storm had knocked out her chance to check in with Ruth, and she was lucky to have made it into bed before passing out. She would call soon. Not the first time it had happened.

She took the moment to replay last night, before the storm. Her hours with the American.

Had he found the information and direction he needed at the club? Maybe he'd already left the island, off on his Quixotic quest to find his friend's daughter. That was a rare loyalty and said much about him. She knew she was just hours or minutes away from finding out everything else there was to know. No one could truly hide anymore. She found herself dreading the search. Loathe to discover he was not what she thought. Maybe just a construct of her imagination.

It took some effort, but she sat up, forcing herself to break free from zombie-mode and rise, heading to the showers and toilets. She crossed the room, her steps made as small and with the least amount of effort as she could make them, and yet still move forward. Glanced at the small table. Mango and papaya, freshly baked bread, soft-boiled egg, dried fish, and a glass of some blended fruit and yogurt.

She smiled and shook her head. Marie was new, had been there less than a month, and was already taking over the kitchen. She had admonished Nicola both times they'd talked. "Miss Nicky, you are skinny too much!" A few of the other women agreed and it seemed they had conspired to fatten her up.

She scooped up a piece of mango and grabbed a towel. Fifteen minutes later, the hot water selfishly run out, she dried herself until her skin felt polished. Now dressed in jeans, a t-shirt, and sandals, she sat at the community dining table with some of the women.

"Eat, eat."

"Maria. I can only eat so much."

"Well, maybe in little time. You want something, I make you. You just let me know."

Another woman, not even forty, her voice permanently raspy and strained from the trauma that made her seek out the shelter, piped in. "Maria. Leave Miss Nicky alone. She's beautiful the way she is. If she wants to be too skinny, let her be."

She turned to Nicola. "Don't worry. You look fine. Not skinny, just a little bit. Like a movie star." She smiled. "Will you stay the night?"

"No, I don't think so," Nicola said. "I'll miss you, I'll miss you all, but I need to get back. And don't forget your appointment."

"Yes, Mom," the woman said smiling. The woman was ten years older, but like half of the others, if not calling her *Miss Nicky,* had taken to calling her *Mom,* poking fun at the way she kept on at them.

"Day after tomorrow, right?"

"Tomorrow!" Nicola exclaimed. "You know it's tomorr—" She caught the women laughing at her. She stopped herself and shook her head, joining in.

"I make you coffee," Maria said, bustling off toward the kitchen.

It would be nearly four hours later, the morning just over when Nicola signed off on her chores.

She climbed on the small motorbike, her laptop and Maria's bagged lunch pushed down in her backpack, and purred away.

She would stop at a cafe on the way home, give herself a couple of hours on the computer if it took that long, and then get ahold of René. Nicola was hoping he'd been able to copy the reports she'd asked for, maybe even the videos. It would be too much to ask that they'd been entered anywhere into a proper database or scanned into records. Records that she could hack her way into. Besides, René liked playing spy.

Nicola had been at it for three hours. Had drunk so much coffee, she had to pull out one of the croissant sandwiches Maria had made for her to settle her stomach.

What she had dreaded, finding out Black was not the man she was hoping for, had turned into exhilarating, if at times, frustrating exploration. He was not the man she had thought he was. He was more.

She found reference to his childhood. Mother deceased. Father unknown. Juvenile records sealed. It didn't take her long to unravel some of that.

His father, credited as Henry Black, had been killed while robbing an underground Italian social club in Chicago's Edison Park. A nondescript hole-in-the-wall storefront, the espresso machine, and daily lunch social hiding afternoon card games of briscola and scopa. The beautifully rendered cards were as old as the men who played and winnings sometimes soared to as much as a hundred-thousand dollars. All in good fun, they traded it back and forth day after day, but Henry Black didn't make it out of the parking lot, and little Tommy was left without a father at the age of four.

His mother, a full-time junkie and part-time prostitute, had managed to hang onto the boy until he was ten and then got herself killed in a motel fire outside of Hope, Arizona. Nicola didn't need to dig into various hospital records and reports of abuse to understand what the boy had been through.

She took note of references to the court-ordered psychiatric evaluations along with the applications by the state to place him in foster care. Understandable. The boy had witnessed his mother's death and may have witnessed the murder of what was reportedly her abusive boyfriend.

The three-hundred-pound biker had been a frequent guest of the Arizona State government, both the prison complex in Tucson and the Arizona Department of Corrections in Perryville. He'd been muscle for one of the ruthless outlaw motorcycle clubs, their ranks filled by radical right-wing hate groups and felons, supplying protection for the lucrative meth lab pop-ups the gang ran and the drug's transportation into Southern California, Nevada, and Utah.

The biker had been burned so badly an autopsy had been impossible; witnesses reported gunshots and it was suspected he'd been shot and killed first, the fire a cover-up, most likely by a rival gang or dealer, the murder weapon a recovered .357 Magnum.

His mother's mother had petitioned to bring the boy back to Chicago. By the time the paperwork processed and the boy landed at Chicago's Midway airport, the grandmother, only fifty-three herself, had passed away from acute liver failure, and he found himself a ward of the State of Illinois.

Young Tommy Black was bounced from foster home to foster home, the stays sometimes lasting only weeks. Along the way, more reports of abuse, hospital visits and records, the requisite psychiatric interviews and evaluations, IQ and aptitude tests. He scored near the highest levels on every test given including the Otis Lennon School Ability Test and a subsequent Stanford Binet Intelligence Scale with a particular ability for math.

It was at fourteen, picked up for trespassing, he first came to the attention of Police Sergeant Konrad Alwin Lobinski. Then again for brawling on a Red-line Metra Train. The veteran patrol cop had seen something in the boy, and less than three months later, Tommy Black had gone home to live with Big Al and his eight-year-old daughter, Jacqueline, where he stayed until the two accelerated years of school at Northwestern University.

The first frustrations in her search came with his initial psych evaluations. Sealed. That made sense. They'd been as a juvenile. None of that would have begun to slow Nicola. Where Black had scored near the top of every measurable test, Nicola would have been somewhere considerably north of that, off the charts. The problem came that the evaluations had been sealed and moved to his military records and files.

Again, not much of a problem for her—procurement and development committees might guess and narrow it down to a half-dozen names, but they'd never know that it was Nicola Alexandrescu who had written and programmed much of their security and encryption software and procedures.

She found copies in the databases easy enough. Almost nothing could be read. Redacted. Line after line of blacked-out type. A single hand-written notation left in the margin. *'He has a talent for violence—'*

Weird. The reports most likely could be found in their original form at deeper levels. It would take some time to break in—a challenge she had built into the ever-adapting artificial intelligence engine she'd written for the Army's encryption.

The question was why? She tried to imagine the circumstances that would make the military want to hide juvenile psych evals. Who were they hiding them from? Foreign or domestic or both? And then, back to the *why?* She didn't care to read them, that seemed too invasive, a violation of trust that she imagined they'd established. Now, it was only because the world's most powerful government said she couldn't.

She did find a reference to the doctor who had made the initial evaluation. A retired Lieutenant Colonel who went back into private practice. She searched for and scanned his records. Impressive. Army, Airborne. Lt. Col. Jeffrey Gallagher, M.D. White Sands, New Mexico.

Black had been ten. It took a minute, but she found his next evaluation, just before he turned thirteen, already in the Illinois State system. Arrested for fighting. It seems while protecting another young boy from schoolyard bullies, Black had taken on four older boys and had somehow broken one's arm and another's nose. Black was removed from the foster home he was staying in, and placed in the Mercy Home for Boys and Girls. Another evaluation had been ordered. The psychiatrist who examined him—Jeffrey Gallagher, M.D.

She jumped ahead. He would have had another evaluation to get into the Army's Officer training program. Lt. Col. Jeffrey Gallagher, M.D.

It made no sense to her, but she could go back to that. He lives with the Lobinski family. Graduates from high school with decent if average records but is at the top of the charts on his SATs.

Takes an unnecessary ACT and scores a perfect thirty-six.

She scanned his University records. Finding his groove. A hundred credits, about three years of work in less than two years. Near perfect scores.

He joined the Army. Did basic training at Fort Knox, Kentucky. Then Airborne School—basic paratrooper training, at Fort Benning, Georgia. Further training. Rangers. Two tours in Afghanistan, a tour in Botswana, and it was back to school. Black finished his degree, majoring in math, from Georgia Military College in Columbus and reported for Officer Training School back at Fort Benning.

Already fast-tracked, now it got interesting. Lieutenant Black, 75th Regiment, Army Rangers, was loaned out for the full eighteen-week program at the DEA Training Academy in Quantico. Then six months training with 1st Special Forces Operational Detachment-Delta at Fort Bragg, North Carolina.

Two years later, a Delta Force Captain, he's leading a joint DEA/NATO Special Operations Group task force targeting Taliban narcotics kingpins, ostensibly to arrest, extradite, and bring to trial those who funded much of the Taliban's growing insurgency. They had three years of near-legendary success before the operation was shut down, pulled out from under Black and his team in the middle of operations.

Two of his eight-man team were captured, Black shot in the back while saving the other five.

Nicola scanned the after-action reports. Most of their operations were redacted, pages after pages of blackened out text and handwritten notations, but due to the testimony of his team, Black was put forward for a Distinguished Service Cross in a highly classified, secret ceremony held in Bagram Airfield. Facing a long, painful recovery, a bullet removed near his spine, with the very real prospect of early retirement, he then sat in the military hospital in Landstuhl.

Three months later, Capt. Thomas Black drops off the planet.

Not that hard to figure out the broad strokes of what happened next. The two captured soldiers, part of Black's elite team, sergeants Mike Jimenez—Ranger, and Calvin Williams—Delta, escaped from their Taliban prison at the same time Black, supposedly recovering somewhere on holiday in Europe, was captured by the same.

No mention or readily available report on what he might have endured, but three months later, he escaped during an American led bombing attack near the Taliban stronghold. Two months after that, he walked with a group of four-hundred refugees across the border into Baluchistan Province, Pakistan.

She knew NATO. The Peacekeepers. The good and the bad. Could imagine at least some of the horrors Black must have seen in his years of service; he was old enough to have been there when they had found her.

She checked. Somehow thankful he wasn't. Overlapping timelines, but he'd been somewhere in Africa—Cameroon and Equatorial Guinea and then Botswana. Two years in Thailand and the Philippines. Then brought back to the Middle East, now a Major, before disappearing again—more covert ops.

Nicola tried to reconcile the records and documentation of this elite, violent killing machine with the blue eyes and gentle touch of the man she'd met the night before. The intelligence was there. The confidence and intensity, but she had no doubt he was broken in some fundamental way, and now she could understand why.

She could sense his struggle to find meaning in who he was and in the things he did, but that was his burden to carry, not hers. While much of his past mirrored her own, she had no desire to fix him.

He has a talent for violence. She could accept him as he was— for everything he was and everything he wasn't.

She doubted she'd ever see him again, couldn't imagine why he might ever come back, but if she had the chance to help him in his quest, she would.

CHAPTER
THIRTY-TWO

Images and impressions, full of sound and light and smell, started slow but soon raced in a dazzling montage across billions of neurons at synaptic speeds.

He knew better than to interfere. Let them play out until the neurotransmitters ran dry and they came back under control, then he could slow them down, allow further mental processes to compartmentalize and put them in logical order. He lay still and let them play, but it took time. Maybe days. Eons. Milliseconds. He couldn't be sure. Maybe the rest of the world was already dead and fossilized. Or maybe he was still on the floor of the island pub.

Black slowly let his hand slide forward in the bed. It took more effort than he was expecting. He touched his chin. Unshaven. Let his fingers push upwards to trace the hairline scar above his eyes. So fine most people would never see or notice it, but his fingers could feel the two-inch ridge over his right eye. The heavy .357 had bucked and crashed into his forehead, rocking his head backward and splitting the flesh above his right eye. He'd hung on. Pulled the trigger again. The scar was still there. That nightmare had been real.

Moving his hand and the arm it was attached to was curiously painful. He replayed the events. *Oh, yeah.* It made sense.

He'd been shot.

He tried to imagine the various traumas that were visited on him. The bullet had ripped through his back, oblique enough it only bounced off a rib, tore through the intercostal, and kept going. The shockwave separated part of the cartilage from his left rib cage, while the micro-rupture of the sub-scapular artery meant he lost a lot of blood.

Black took the time to picture each additional effort his body would need to repair the damage. He was convinced if he broke apart the complex metabolic processes necessary for the rebuilding of the various tissues, he could speed up the healing. Like any complex machine, he could redirect resources and efforts, better manage and direct his body into hyper-efficiency. True or not, he'd certainly had his practice.

Events back in order, body in a state of active repair, Black knew he couldn't lie here forever. He commanded his eyes to open. Eyelids slid right up. All working correctly. Light flooded in as it should and in front of him sat a little girl. Shut his eyes. Okay, he was still dreaming. Anything made sense in dream logic.

Opened them again. She was still there. Sitting in a chair. Beautiful. Huge brown eyes under bangs of blue-black hair looking at him with open curiosity. Little legs not close to reaching the floor. Three or four he guessed. Black hit by the thought that he hadn't been around children enough to know.

Looking beyond her, Black could make out a large room. A few dim shadows moving about, milling around a counter. Maybe preparing a meal. As his eyes adjusted and the light came back in, the shadows softened with golden light, and he realized it must be late afternoon. He could hear voices—children. He focused until he could pick out individual words.

The girl jumped up. He'd have to turn his head to keep her in view. That seemed like a lot of effort. Just as he steeled himself for the task, she blessedly returned, now followed by a woman. Short, wide, he'd guess sixties, nearly bald and the little that remained fashioned into a fuzzy buzz cut. He was used to those.

"Major. Welcome to the land of the living."

Black did his best to right things, struggling to sit up. She reached out to help him.

He looked at his arm. Started to pull the IV out.

"Not sure I'm a Major anymore, but —"

"Take it slow. And my people tell me you're still in the Army. Probably just long enough to get court-martialled."

"Well, something to look forward to." She watched him ease the IV from his arm. Reached for some gauze left on the nearby table. Helped him tape it down.

Black tried to stand. It took a moment. The woman reached out her hand. Cool and dry. Surprisingly strong. "Ruth or Ruthie."

"Tommy."

The little girl clung to her legs. She tousled the girl's hair. "And this little bundle is Aleeza."

Black smiled at them both. "Hey, Aleeza."

Ruth stepped close, took Black's arm, and guided him across the floor toward a large open kitchen. Soup kitchen aesthetic. The small group of children, from maybe eight to seventeen, worked at a long wooden counter, cutting vegetables, mixing sauces, stirring giant pots on an industrial stove, laughing as they pounded and fashioned some kind of bread, wide and flat, and making the warehouse-like room smell like a home.

They glanced at him shyly and returned to their tasks. Their chatter too low to make out but still carrying the excitement having a guest can bring.

Black was doing better, gears fitting their cogs, belts turning their wheels, and found his legs would support his weight.

"The toilets and showers are in there. You should find everything you need. Then we can get you some solid food and catch you up."

Bringing Ruth up short in surprise, Aleeza reached out for his hand. She watched the little girl lead Black across the floor to the door.

Black entered, and the door closed silently behind him. An industrial-like locker room. Rows of steel cabinets on one side.

Wooden benches. Meticulously clean sinks and mirrors. The room further divided. Hommes and Femmes. Black entered the men's side.

More sinks and mirrors, toilets, and showers. A stainless steel shelf above one sink had gauze, tape, antibiotic ointment, plastic wrap. A disposable razor. Clothes; an old shirt and work pants, close to his size. New socks and underwear.

It was a challenge, pushing the limits of his limited range of movement, but Black pulled off the large gauze pads and tape from his back and both sides. Stitches under all three—they had taken the time to clean and sew where he had jumped and fallen through the broken rooftop in Chicago. Both sides and his back a mass of discolored flesh and deep bruising.

Not a comic book character, but he always healed well. Still, his life could be mapped in the thin stripes and uneven mending of flesh across his frame. He peered closer at the stitching. Professionally done. He'd ask about that later.

CHAPTER
THIRTY-THREE

Michaels was trying not to explode. Literally. He knew he needed to calm down, his heart wouldn't take much more. It was mid-afternoon, and he was tired of being jerked around. They'd arrived at the Mauritius Police Department on time, were informed Curpen wasn't there, running late. *May I get you some coffee, Sir?* No more goddamned coffee. *Would you like something to eat, Sir?* No! He wanted some fucking information.

Gauber apologized for Curpen and introduced Michaels and Rodriguez to the Police Chief. Detectives and patrolmen. Dispatch and traffic and fucking janitors. Finally, a briefing room with the half-dozen police technicians. Except for the uniforms instead of trendy island fashions, not that much different from the ones they'd left back in their hotel rooms. No Curpen. A tech picked up a call. *He's on his way, Sir.*

The agents knew they were guests, but there had to be limits. Michaels was checking his phone, making sure he had the Ambassador's number at hand, was getting ready to hit the buttons, when the head of Special Operations introduced himself and his assistant. *We've arranged a lunch for you, Sir.* One of the island's finest restaurants.

Rodriguez did his best to calm his partner down and smooth things out. Michaels was immune to his Cuban charm, but he turned up the wattage of his million-dollar smile for the benefit of both the S-Op Chief and his assistant.

Lunch was amazing—a circus of flavors. This was Mauritius. One of the island's finest restaurants. Michaels couldn't taste it.

They were driven to the murder scene at the hotel, having to pretend it was their first time. They saw the beach, taken to where Allan was killed and presumably the girl abducted. Confirmed there were two attackers. Footprints in the sand had told the story—one to take out the future Congressman and one for the girl. No sign she was killed. Then into the hotel suite and the steps taken and progress made for forensics to support and contribute to the investigation.

Mid-afternoon transitioned into late afternoon. They were guided back into the briefing room at the station with the promise Curpen would be there. He was.

"Sorry about that," Curpen said. He seemed contrite. "We're following up on some leads at the port. More to do, but we think we now know how he got in."

"Looks like a cargo plane, produce, out of Toamasina. Most times, vanilla shipments back and forth, but we've suspected them of ferrying illegals and even agency assets," Gauber said.

The Agent's faces registered nothing.

"Madagascar," offered one of the techs, an earnest, fair-haired, freckle-faced lad named Nicus.

"Madagascar," Rodriguez repeated as if it all made sense. "Sure, Toamasina. Madagascar."

"Who's *he?*" Michaels demanded.

"Sorry. Let's back up a sec." He turned back to one of the techs. "Liz. Can you bring up the photos?"

Here, the monitors were built in. Servers and storage, tape machines and optical recorders, all capable of being fed from the efforts of the entire police department but sorted by the techs manning the controls.

Liz, an array of short braids tipped in scarlet sprouting from her head like a rambutan, hit a switch and the room's biggest monitor, a sixty-inch flat screen, filled with shots from last night's streets and market.

Several shots popped up, gradually beginning to concentrate on a single man. They couldn't see his face yet, he was always caught turning away, but Michaels took in the stature and physique, the way the crowd deferred and seemed to part for him. Michaels felt his pulse quicken.

"I have several men posted throughout the city. A bit more than informants, we keep them on retainer. They're able to keep their eyes and ears open in ways that are much harder for us and in likely places where someone might show up," Curpen said.

"What are the parameters?" Rodriguez asked.

"To look for anyone who looks like a contractor. Military or private. Official or shady. Especially for an American. Asking questions and or interacting with several known sources of information and or weapons."

"A pretty big leap."

"Not really," Gauber said. "In our experience, limited as it may be in these situations, there are at least as many unofficial channels pursued as official." Gauber shrugged. "In light of your recent success, we know the victim's father was able to hand-pick and request your efforts. We thought there was a very real possibility he might send back-up as well."

"And of course, the girl," Curpen said. "Someone was bound to be looking for her. Or if involved, knowing or suspecting you were coming, to monitor your progress and cover their tracks."

The pictures began showing more of the man's face.

"One of our informants picked this man up outside the market," Curpen said.

"We have several people on a watch list, and our man watched him make contact with a known arms dealer. Small-time," Gauber explained. "Not a place to arm an invasion or anything, but enough to supply someone with higher-end handguns, ammunition, and bladed weapons."

"All of which we now know this man purchased," Curpen added.

The photos, taken with some skill, finally caught up with the man as he stopped to talk to a woman at a cafe. She was strikingly good-looking, dark-haired, and exotic. Maybe Italian. Another shot of the man. It was better. Another. A close-up. This one could have been a portrait.

Michaels knew it was *him*.

"So who is he?"

Darr, his face a composite of the racial and cultural influence of the island, manning the latest INTERPOL database of facial images, popped up long enough to answer. "Give me just a few moments."

The images flew by on the screen, the biometric data program mapping, and analyzing faces. The trick to speed and accuracy was to program the search parameters to help the software limit the scope of its over a billion fully mapped images, sometimes further drawing on and reconstructing from another three billion partials and fragments.

"For now, we're concentrating on Americans."

The other screen was still filled with shots of last night's market.

The surveillance photos began focusing on the woman. Young, beautiful, exotic. The combination made it hard to determine her age. Late twenties, early thirties. The informant recognized her beauty too, the shots verged on fetish and suddenly felt invasive.

"Who's the girl?" Rodriguez asked. He saw Liz look up and smile. He hadn't meant to sound so smitten.

"Easier. Nicola Alexandrescu. A local do-gooder." Curpen said, unable to hide a trace of resentment.

Liz was more enthusiastic, and her respect increased as she spoke. Michaels watched her fingers fly over her keyboard. Dozens of images, reports, newspaper articles, and academic papers hit the screens, much too fast to keep up with, but she gave a running commentary.

"Romanian national. Orphaned during the war. Trafficked and sold along with seventeen other—" Liz paused, voice choking.

A group photo of about a dozen young girls—one couldn't have been more eight or nine. "Rescued by NATO forces outside of Belgrade. Alexandrescu was placed with Child Spring at fourteen."

A dozen grainy black-and-white photos showed an abused child. Close-ups in lurid detail highlighted the dark bruising on arms and legs, a black-eye, and hand prints around her small throat. In all shots, her small, malnourished body.

More photos streamed by, documenting her social integration and recovery.

"Scholarship to Bucharest Academy of Economic Studies, minored in political science and completed her Masters in Computer Science at University Politehnica," Liz said. "And she added her doctorate at ETH Zurich."

Even Darr stopped what he was doing. "That's umm—that's like the MIT of—well, everything that's not MIT."

Liz read out the title of Alexandrescu's dissertation. It elegantly illustrated their point. "The Use Of Three-Dimensional Artificial Intelligence Models In Generative Adversarial Neural Cryptography."

They all took a moment to digest what it meant. No clue. But all with the same conclusion. Alexandrescu was a genius.

"Yeah, well. She's a pain in the ass," Curpen said. "We've had run-ins with her before. Usually, over the women she saves."

The photos showed a confident, self-assured woman. Beautiful by any standards.

"So what's she doing in Mauritius?" Rodriguez asked.

The photos were catching up. Nicola smiling, standing arm and arm with an older, heavyset woman, a group of children surrounding them. Newspaper headlines. *'Law Professor Opens Children's Center.'*

"Looks like she works with this woman. Ruth Blanton. Former Law professor. UC Berkeley."

"I'm starting to feel like a moron," Rodriguez said.

Michaels smiled. "Understandable."

"FBI doesn't really seem like underachieving," Liz offered.

Smile back on his face, directing the wattage at the helpful tech.

Liz went back to reading. "Blanton's an outspoken advocate for children's rights. Helped to pass a couple of laws for stricter guidance in foster care and adoption. Left UC in 2003. Lived and worked in Hague for a couple of years at the U.N.'s International Court of Justice. Left for health reasons. Applied for immigration in France, lived a couple of years in Paris, and then shows up here about ten years ago."

"Got it!" Darr. Brought the matched identity forward. "Black. Henry Thomas. Major, U.S. Army. Currently assigned to NATO."

Photos and military records filled the screen. Commendations, promotions, lots of blacked-out type. The records and photos came up fast, impossible to keep up, but keywords stuck. Orphaned. Chicago. Special Forces. Delta. NATO.

"Go back, go back!" Michaels couldn't hide the excitement. The images and photo-scanned records froze. Darr started to back them up in reverse. "Right there!" *Chicago.*

"Find out when he last entered the country," Rodriguez said. Clarifying. "The U.S."

Nicus scanned and pulled up records. "Flew from Chania, Crete, with stops in Athens and Munich. Entered Dulles on Lufthansa Flight 414 on the 17th."

Airport surveillance. Black's face frozen on video as he cleared U.S. Customs at Dulles. Easy smile—not a care in the world.

"A week ago," Gauber said.

Nicus's nimble fingers jumped over some more keys. "No record of him leaving."

"He has family in Chicago," Darr read.

They all turned to see the new images. Picture of Lobinski in Police Blues standing beside an eight or nine-year-old girl and a fourteen or fifteen-year-old boy. Posing. Another shot of the boy on the big man's shoulders, the girl held in one huge arm. Police uniform traded for an apron. Laughing. Dressed Chicago dog's in both of the children's two hands. Big Al's on the sign above them.

The boy, now a young man. Army uniform. The girl graduating from college. The soldier clowning with his team in the desert. The girl at her law school graduation. The soldier, captain's bars, military dress, rows of medals and ribbons. Dozens of people piled close to congratulate the girl. Cops and attorneys and soldiers. Black and Dillon and Jackie and a young Sam.

"Isn't that the Chicago cop?" Darr brought up more records. Photos. The Chicago newspapers. Photos of Dillon.

Gauber looked around the room. "So it's safe to assume he's here for the girl?"

Michaels turned to his partner. "What was the name of the defense attorney for Clarence Williams?"

Rodriguez had an enviable memory for names. Especially for women. Locked in the vault if he found them attractive.

"Jacqueline," he scanned his metal database, "Lobinski."

"Who's Clarence?" Nicus asked.

"Five nights ago, Chicago," Rodriguez said. "We're at the end of a two-year case and eight-months of surveillance. Drugs, prostitution, child pornography. One of the myriad end-points for a tracking ring we know originates from somewhere in Nigeria."

"They smuggle the girls to Italy, France. Apply for asylum. Put them to work while they fuck with the courts and the paperwork. Sell what's left to third party traffickers."

"Clarence—Mookie—is up on his third murder beef. Skated on the other two, but the case looks solid," Michaels said. "A twelve-year-old girl. Strangled. Multiple fractures in both arms and legs. Found strung up on a light pole in front of the local church."

"A half-dozen Miranda violations when the local dicks grab him up. Everybody knew who the fuck he was," Rodriguez explained. "Hires a big firm and she's up in the rotation. A win for him. She's bright. Talented. Lose-lose for her. She holds his hand through the courts or ends up with her ass in a crack with the Bar."

"Sounds like they should have put a bullet in his head," Liz said, still looking at photos of the children.

"Yeah. I get it," Michaels said. "But not the way it works for us."

"So—what?" Gauber asked. "You think this guy— He's what? Her brother? He pulls the trigger for you?"

Curpen nodded. "Makes sense to me. Comes home from whatever black-bag bullshit your government has him on to visit the family. Finds out little sis is in deep with the wrong fucking guy and plays big brother."

"And kills six people on the way," Gauber said.

"Good for him," Liz said. Darr was seeing a new side of her. She shrugged. "They deserved it."

"And so now he's here," Nicus asked. "For what? For the girl?"

"Maybe. So what's the common denominator here?" Gauber waited.

"Trafficking? Same as Chicago," Liz offered.

"No," Michaels said. "Not the same. But maybe close enough."

"Fuck it. I say we just let him run with it," Rodriguez said. "At least he gets shit done."

"What the fuck are you saying? We let him run free?" Curpen was pissed. "That's your fucked-up system. Not here. You export your psychos, and we have to clean your shit up. This is my island."

"Sure. We've seen your cleaning," Rodriguez taunted. "Spray and pray and see where the bullets land."

"If that's what brings him down," Curpen said. "We know he tried to kill the club's security guy. Shot the club manager."

"No," Michaels said. "We don't know he stabbed the security man. Oscar. I don't buy it. Doesn't even make fucking sense. The only shots we know anything about came from your weapon. Where are our copies of the ballistics reports? And the tapes from the security cameras?"

"You'll get them when they're ready."

"Not good enough," Rodriguez said.

Curpen ignored him.

"And the security guard?" Michaels asked. "We want to interview him now."

"Last time," Curpen said. "You need to remember you are guests here. You'll get access when we give you access."

Rodriguez was off his feet. "This is fucked."

"Look," Gauber said. "We've got three murders to solve. Four— five, counting the club. And the clock may be running out for the girl."

"The girl could be anywhere in the world," Curpen said. "We don't even know she's innocent in all of this. Jilted lover. Kills her boyfriend. On the run. Probably with the psycho."

Rodriguez rolled his eyes. "Give me a fucking break."

"What the hell do you know?" Curpen exploded. "We read the reports. We know who you are. They didn't send you here as a reward. Six murders? You're a fucking embarrassment, and they want you as far away as possible. You're here twenty minutes and think you have it figured out?"

"Looks like it only took Black that long."

Curpen and Rodriguez faced off.

"Gentlemen," Gauber stepped between them. "I think we're done here for now."

Curpen ground his teeth. "Yeah. I know I am."

"I suggest we take a break," Gauber said. "Count on meeting again first thing in the morning."

"Yeah. Go back to the circle jerk in your hotel room," Curpen said.

Rodriguez smiled. "Better than getting fucked in the ass in here."

Michaels was pulling his partner out. Turned to the techs. "Thanks for your help."

Liz pissing Curpen off when she smiled at Rodriguez.

Gauber tried again with Michaels. "Tomorrow's another day."

Michaels let his breath out. Not hiding his frustration. Returned the handshake. "Let's hope it is for the girl."

CHAPTER
THIRTY-FOUR

The boy, too scared to move on his own, was pushed toward the platform. His tears reflected off his dark skin under the harsh spotlight. He was maybe ten, slight as ten-year-olds often are, new white underwear and nothing else.

The camera clicked and the strobes went off, his trembling body frozen in profile.

A woman grabbed at him and spun him the opposite direction—her cracked and aged hands, the colorful dress and tribal head wrap in total contrast to the young, nearly naked boy. She pulled back and out of frame just as the flash went off.

She stepped forward and clutched his shoulders, turning him back to face the camera. FLASH!

She ushered him off as another woman pushed a young girl forward to take his place. New white panties, glistening coal-black skin. The woman's hands dug into the narrow shoulders and positioned her, stepped back, and let the camera capture her beauty and defiance.

The young girl, no more than twelve, as slim as a reed, turned on her own and waited for the strobes to fire.

Sam was led into the stables. Ringer's hand, *the hand that held the knife that stabbed Allan,* dug into her arm as he pushed and pulled her toward the platform.

It only took an instant for her to take in the makeshift photography studio. Set up near the middle of the stables, a soft gray backdrop hung behind a small wooden platform that created a stage. Umbrella reflectors and strobes, a newer digital camera on a professional tripod.

Half a dozen scared and confused children, boys and girls, maybe six to fourteen, stood in their new white underwear on the far side of the stage.

Sam watched an old woman pull a young boy from the group of ten remaining children on the nearside. She winced as the woman needlessly dug her hands and long nails into his shoulder and positioned him.

Behind the camera, an older man, bent and slight, cleaned his glasses with a soiled handkerchief and waited until she finished.

A young man sat off to the side. Came across like any of the hundreds of studious, nerdy college students she had known, manning a laptop where the images were being fed.

Sitting in a high-top director's chair as if on a macabre movie set, sat the man from the club—*Kronmüller* she knew now—the one who had knocked her to the ground and killed her friends. Sitting beside him, an older man. It was obvious from their respective posture that no love was lost between them but the strong, sharply defined features confirmed he was the younger man's father.

Behind them was the other massive bodyguard, the one she'd heard called Grip. *The one who had grabbed and drugged her.*

Kronmüller started up when he saw Sam. Shock and anger and concern on his face. Now he understood why his father had decided to sit in.

"Sit the fuck back down," Ouderling spat under his breath.

Sam took it in. The studio setup. The scared, nearly naked children. The father chastising and bullying his son. Their mutual hatred on full display.

Lina had filled her in—Ouderling, *the Elder*, and Kronmüller, *the Son*—not enough love between them to be called Father, or the son by his given name, Christiaan. The deep-seated enmity exacerbated by the younger's obsession with beautiful mixed-race women who by the standards of the father, were inhuman, not fit to live or breed.

Ouderling glared at her. Even under the harsh lights and with the African sun baking the fetid air of the stables, she shivered. Wearing the sheer dress over the expensive lingerie and the ridiculous Louboutins, she felt as naked as the children.

Tears of rage welled in her eyes, but she'd be damned if she'd wipe them away or turn away from his glare.

"The tears are a nice touch," Ouderling said. "Might even raise the price."

The powerful bodyguard shoved her toward the back of the group waiting for their time in front of the camera.

CHAPTER
THIRTY-FIVE

"So who is this guy?"

Mock jealousy to hide the real thing. René handed her a folder, kissed both her cheeks, and threw his leg over the seat as Nicola moved to the back of the little motorbike.

"You read the files?"

He shrugged and grinned. "I *peeked*. Dangereux mon amour."

She slipped the folder into her backpack.

He kick-started the bike, left the police station, and they darted into the slow-moving island traffic.

At twenty-five, he was a boy. Slight and smooth. The deep brown eyes of a doe, eyelashes longer and thicker than most women. In their one-time tryst, an unexpected but perhaps inevitable night two years ago, an inexperienced but thoughtful lover. Gentle and concerned. Unlike anything she had known or experienced, the boy had filled her emotional needs for a night even if not her physical.

She had to shout over the traffic and the bike but knew no one could hear them. "Were you able to copy the videos?"

"Of course."

"Have you seen them?"

"No. They're hanging onto them tightly. Editing and perhaps altering them I think. I was lucky to get them. Had to promise my body for the exchange."

"My little spy." She kissed him on the back of his neck.

"It's a dangerous course you've set me on."

"Your sacrifices are noted and appreciated," she said. " I'm sure we can put in for medals of commendation."

"Ma mère will be so proud! Her son the Mata Hari! I'll send out the invitations."

Nicola laughed. "Perhaps we better wait to see if the paper-work goes through."

"Alright. I'll wait. But just a few days!" René darted in front of a taxi. The horns blared behind them and they both laughed. As crazy as the boy could be on the little bike, they both knew Nicola was worse.

He shouted over the wind and traffic. "The American FBI were there all day. We could hear them arguing."

"About what?"

"Hard to know exactly. People don't pay much attention to the clean-up guy, but I was trying to be careful. "

"And?"

"I think MPD is trying to point fingers at your American."

"He's not my American. And he just got here. What could he have done?"

"Besides the shootings and stabbings and last night's murders?"

He could feel her tighten behind him. He loved her dearly but couldn't help but rub it in. Besides, in three years, it was the first time he could remember ever knowing something about anything more than her. He wished he could look at the face behind him.

"Seems he's on the run. They say he murdered even more in America. Chicago, I think. Just last week. They shot him last night at the club, but he got away."

Jesus! Had she been so taken with his charm she couldn't see it? *A psychopath!* She played it in her mind. Remembered the card she had given him. She might as well have given him a key.

She needed to call Ruth to warn her.

"I need to use your phone."

"What? Now?" He shouted over his shoulder.

"Right now!"

"It's in my pocket."

She tried to reach into his pocket. Not happening while he was driving the motorcycle.

"What happened to yours?" he yelled.

"Dead from last night." She was running backward and forwards in her mind and feeling stupid.

No, she'd spoken to him. He was here for the girl. He wasn't a psychopath. He wasn't hiding behind his charm, and she wasn't some school girl with a crush. She'd read his files. *He has a talent for violence.*

"Pull over," she said.

She could feel him shrug, but he slowed down and pulled to the side of the street. Pulled out his phone.

Black sat at the table. Scarred and heavy, it could easily fit ten adults—or as now, two adults and a dozen children. The children, he couldn't begin to remember all their names, seemed to have adopted him and wouldn't stop bringing him food until convinced he was full.

Their new puppy. A bunch of elfin helpers in Grandma's kitchen. Grandma was teaching them well. The food was delicious, fresh and simple and fragrant, bursting with the flavors of the island.

A young girl, Rayln he remembered, brought Ruth the phone. Ruth excused herself.

He couldn't remember when he'd had so much fun, the children trying to outdo themselves as they vied for his attention. The hardest part, trying not to laugh as that pulled at the threads holding him together. Almost worth the trade he thought.

Ruth hung up and returned with more coffee. Rich and smooth, as complex as any he remembered, filled with undertones of vanilla. He let the steam and flavor fill his senses and was reminded of Nicola. Nicky.

"Nicky likes you. You could have never made it here if she didn't. That's all I need to know."

He struggled for the right words. Something that would make her understand.

Nothing about this had been a part of his life for the past twenty years. He needed to be out hunting for Sam.

"I'm not the good guy here."

Ruth watched Aleeza trying to climb onto his lap. Black pulled her up, let her curl up in his arms.

"Maybe. But maybe good enough. Nicky trusts you. That says more than anything you can say."

He tried to speak, tried to find the words. He was overwhelmed with their trust and generosity, afraid of bringing harm or danger to them as he often had to so many others.

Ruth smiling at the little girl cradled in Black's arms, seemingly at peace for the first time in weeks. Black looked down at her, watched her eyelids flutter as she drifted off, and the way her hair danced under both their breaths, gentle and in time with each other.

Suddenly self-conscious. He looked back up to Ruth, her eyes filled with warmth and knowing.

CHAPTER
THIRTY-SIX

They briefed the team of cop-show techs on their time with the Mauritius PD, and were getting updates on what their crew had discovered. Lots of overlap. Lots of frustration.

"Maybe we let Black kill them all," Rodriguez offered.

Michaels and the tech posse just looked at him. In truth, they all thought it.

"Sure, great," Michaels said. "Who's all?"

"Fuck, I don't know," Rodriguez said. Jet lag, frustration, and the fear of never accomplishing anything while the fuckheads destroying the world ran free. "Maybe we don't have to. We run their IDs after he kills them. Case solved."

"Might put us out of work," Michaels warned. "Wouldn't really need us anymore."

"Exactly! We soak up the rays and drink Mai Tais or whatever they drink here."

Camille perked up. "TI's or coconut daiquiris."

"Or get serious with jalapeno punch." Clement's favorite.

"See? Lots of things to try," Rodriguez said. "Come on, Black's gotten more done in a week than we did in 2 years."

Michaels shrugged. "We play the cards we're dealt," Michaels said. "You start going down that road, and we're all fucked."

"Sure. But we're playing hearts, and he's playing crazy-eights."

"So... What? You want what?"

"An even playing field for once," Rodriguez moaned. "For at least five fucking minutes."

"We're all friends here." Michaels looked around the room. "But, you're walking a dangerous line with this kind of talk."

"It's always a dangerous line, but we only cross it for the cleanup." He took in the photos of the American victims. "For once—I mean, don't you ever want to take out the scrotes before they fuck everybody's lives up?"

A knock on the door and Julius jumped up to answer it.

Room service. He made room for the cart and silver trays the young porter wheeled in.

The porter looked around the room for a place to set things out. Tables and desks covered with laptops and modems. He glanced at the walls. What started as a few grainy photos taped to the wall was now a complete mural of reports, maps, and photos.

Alix took over. "I'll get it." She handed the bill to Michaels who signed it without looking. Gave it back. "Give yourself a big tip, okay?"

"Je vous remercie, Madame."

Two minutes later, plates full, they returned to their tasks.

Clement turned from his laptop and the monitor set-up created with the other flat screen. "You want to see it again?"

"Not much point if you think it's been fucked with," Rodriguez said.

They'd spent hours doing a team scrub of the videos. Pre-edited video from the night Sam and her friends were there. Only one angle showed a woman helping another who seemed to have fallen. A bit of concern from what must be their boyfriends, but nothing else.

The other video showed last night's stabbing and murder. Little business yet, Black could clearly be seen in the bar, maybe arguing with the giant bouncer. Forcing him toward the back. Unable to see much past the bulk of the security man, but presumably forcing him at gunpoint.

The feeds from the hallways proved useless. Curpen and his team blamed it on Black shooting and taking out the cameras, maybe on his way in. Michaels hadn't thought to look at the video last night. The one remaining angle showed a bit of Black struggling with the manager, maybe choking him out, before sprinting toward the back.

Moments later, Curpen rushed in, trying to stem the blood and save the man, and then striding back toward Michaels and Rodriguez.

"The first ones were obviously edited, not trying to hide it. Pretty shitty job of it too." Clement rummaged in the small fridge. Tossed a Red Bull to Julius that almost hit him in the face.

Alix handed her version of coffee to Rodriguez.

"This one's bogus too."

"How do you know?" Michaels asked.

"They're digital," Clement explained. "Should be perfect copies."

"You see pictures, frame by frame making up the video, but it's still just a bunch of ones and zeros," Camille said.

Julius took his turn. "When we break apart the data stream, reduce them to their digital components, we find some anomalies. You can't see any splices or glitches on the screen, but there are traces of uneven code, we can guess where the editing software added digital markers, and they tried to chop them back out."

"Then covered up by superimposing the time code," Clement said.

The agents looked a little lost.

"Think of the data like soup," Alix explained. "When they edited it, splicing and rearranging things, it added some new flavors. They can cover them up, but they can't pull them back out. Not perfectly anyway."

"Okay," Rodriguez said.

"Okay?" Alix asked.

"Okay. So, what are they hiding?" Michaels asked. "And why?"

"I might know." Julius scrubbed through the video. "I recovered some frames."

He played it. Black dropping the manager as he sprinted out of frame.

"Didn't we just see that?" Rodriguez looked around. No response. "Um... what are we looking at?"

"It's hard to see. If there's anything at all," Camille said.

"It's only a few frames but it's there," Julius shot back.

"Five to be exact," Alix said.

Michaels looked at Rodriquez and back at the screen. "I don't get it."

"Play it again," Alix said.

They did. No recognition.

"It might be nothing," Julius said. "But we think that there's a change in the light."

Clement moved and took over. Played it frame by frame.

"Harder to see like this, but we're thinking it shows someone else was in the hall."

"And Black was chasing them."

Alix played it in real-time. And again. "I know it doesn't look like much, but we're all convinced."

Camille frowned. "I'm not."

No one said anything. Running scenarios in their minds.

Rodriguez signaled to play it again. No one spoke.

"This is crazy," Camille said. "You think the Mauritius Police Department is involved in murder and kidnapping? For what? Human trafficking? A paedo ring?"

"No," Rodriguez said. "But I don't trust Curpen." He turned from the group to his partner. "I can feel it. He's playing us."

Michaels nodded. "What'd we get on him?"

"Nothing really. Sorry. We got caught up in tracking Black and the videos."

"Okay. I think this tells us most of what we needed to know. And where are you with Black?"

Clement beamed, couldn't wait to tell them this one. "We ruled out all the main hospitals and emergency clinics. Even an animal hospital, but we think he might have found medical care across the river in Sainte-Croix."

"Why?"

Alix took over. "We know Black used a lot of his military contacts to get here, so we set up a search including those parameters. We got a hit on a pub owned by a retired military surgeon. It's a hike, between Sainte-Croix and Vallée des Pretres, but doable on foot for a strong man."

"One who's been shot?"

Rodriguez grew up in the city. "Could have grabbed a cab."

Julius smiled at him. "In Port Louis in a storm?

The island team agreed.

Julius turned to the Agents. "This is Mauritius."

"We think the surgeon's ties might be to Alexandrescu."

Alix nodded. "Camille's right. We checked with the phone company. A lot of activity in the middle of the night."

Michaels frowned. "Pretty thin."

Alix couldn't help but smile. "At least two of the outgoing calls went to former corpsmen. FFL."

Julius clarified. "French Fucking Foreign Legion."

"Both who volunteer at the clinic," Clement said.

The geeks grinned. This was getting better and better.

"Okay," Michaels said. "Not as thin."

"Black's not there now," Julius said.

"How do you know?"

Julius shifted in his chair. "Ummm... we sent Clement."

The Agents turned to the boy.

Clement shrugged. Grinned. "I told them I ate some bad fish and my girlfriend insisted I go."

"Do you even have a girlfriend?"

"No," the boy admitted.

"*'My girlfriend sent me.'*" Rodriguez glared at them. "What are you? Fucking idiots? That's the kind of simple shit that gets you killed! *Something—just—that—fucking—simple.*"

"My fault," Alix said. "Seemed the easiest way."

Michaels shook his head. "Guys. You're not secret agents. You're not cops."

Clement slumped deeper into the chair. "Yeah, but—"

"But nothing. You can't—" Michaels stopped himself.

The dream team looked like they might cry.

"You can't do anything like this again. Okay? People are dying here, and we don't— Look. We need you guys here. Okay? No more fucking spy games."

He made sure he had their attention. "Black manages instant access with the girl. How? They looked pretty chummy. How do they know each other? What's their relationship?"

"You know she's a genius, right?" Camille asked.

"What's that got to do with anything?"

"I don't know," she said. "I think it's interesting."

Michaels shook his head. "Okay. Concentrate on the genius. We find her. We find him."

Julius turned back to his computer.

"Boss. You better look at this."

A photo popped up on the screen. He transferred it to the big flat screen.

Sam. Studio lighting. More photos. Wide. Close. Front, side, back, front. Closer.

"Jesus," under Michaels's breath. "When was this posted?"

Rodriguez stared at the photo. The defiance burning in her eyes. "And where the hell is it coming from?"

"Real-time," Julius said. "I'm monitoring some dark sites for chatter. Just came up." He hit a few keys and other pictures joined hers.

It could have been an art auction but this was children. Boys. Girls. From six to fifteen. A pre-announcement. Going on the auction block. The horror of what they faced sinking in.

Alix tried to choke down the anger. "They use the dark web voodoo shit for anything you can imagine."

"Not buying the kids. Buying the anonymity," Clement said.

Rodriguez felt his shoulders tighten; a full-blown headache was on the way. The kind that ripped the hemispheres apart. He knew what they signed up for but—it never got easier. No wonder his partner talked about getting out.

"But you guys can hack in right? Into the—this dark web voodoo shit?"

"Doesn't work that way," Julius said.

Michaels looked at them. "They have to say where the auction is taking place, right?"

Alix started typing in commands on her own laptop, her fingers a blur, her thoughts on how she might tackle this. Not a genius like Alexandrescu, but she might get lucky.

"Not yet, probably at the last second," Camille said.

"Can we find out when?"

The sound of forty fingers flying on keyboards.

"Got it!" Clement pumped. "Ten days from now!"

"Ten days." Michaels ran it forwards.

Rodriguez fought to keep his excitement in check. "I'd say there's a hell of a good chance we know where Black will be in ten days."

"Yeah. Sure. There." Michaels said. "But where is *there?*"

He scanned each face. "And where the fuck is he now?"

Alix was at the beginning of a dive deep, tuning them out, scouring the I2P network for any clue that told her where to begin. She needed luck. People's cruelty and perversions on full display, but she could be here a thousand years and never find the right thing. Too late for Sam. Too late for the children.

"Maybe you were right before." All heads turned toward her.

"We get lucky and find these guys, we let Black kill them all."

CHAPTER
THIRTY-SEVEN

Rícard couldn't believe his luck. Raced across the mountain on his bike back into the city to meet Curpen. He wanted paid.

He'd gone the extra mile last night. Not the first time he stabbed a man, but never a giant, and it was the first time doing it under the orders of a cop. He wanted the assurance that he wouldn't be hung out to dry.

His expenses were growing. Gustave was still crying about being mugged last night while on Rícard's payroll. Demanding more money. The man was an idiot. Still, he might be useful again, and this wasn't the time to bring anyone else to the party.

He fingered the knife tucked away in his pocket. The four-inch blade had almost been too little to take the big man out. Rícard reveled in his own speed and precision, four thrusts in the blink of an eye, not even time to enjoy the flesh parting beneath the steel as the blade sunk in. The giant had been so slow—it was like stabbing a cow—but the look of surprise almost made up for it.

He thought about the American. If he hadn't been sprinting full speed, the hand would have closed on his throat as he sped by. He still felt the fingertips grazing his throat, still saw the American's eyes boring into his. Impossible of course. He'd have been a blur, the moment lasting hundredths of a second.

Curpen was late, and Rícard began to have misgivings. And then, there she was. On a little motorbike across from the station and stopping almost directly in front of him. He had no idea of how she might be involved in this, but intuition told him there was more money to be made.

She waited for someone. He pictured her with the American the night before and had a moment to dream he'd won the lottery—the American would walk out, hop on the back of her bike, and he'd have them both. Curpen would have no choice but to pay him any amount he demanded.

A young man, a boy really, handed Alexandrescu a folder, kissed her in greeting, and climb on the bike as she moved behind him. There was a familiarity that told Rícard they were more than friends. He tried to imagine it. No, it was obvious. The woman was a gypsy witch just as they said. Using her beauty to ensnare beautiful, innocent young boys.

The boy darted into traffic and Rícard decided to follow. He would demand more money. Maybe let Gustave sit on her until they got paid. Then maybe he'd have a talk with the boy.

CHAPTER
THIRTY-EIGHT

"Let me take a look at that hole in your back."

"I'm fine," Black said.

"I'm an old lady. Indulge me."

Ruth helped Aleeza climb down from Black's lap. The little girl was shy, hadn't spoken once since she'd come to live with them three months before, but seemed to have adopted Black.

Ruth waited patiently as Black unbuttoned the shirt. He moved slow—hard to tell if he was feeling shy or just in pain. The shirt was tight on his shoulders, the pants a little loose. She'd have to search for a belt.

"That shirt's over twenty years old. My husband's," her voice soft. "I wear it sometimes," she admitted. Laughed at herself. "Silly I guess. The things an old lady does." She helped pull it from his shoulders. Smiled.

"It fits you better than me."

"I have clothes at my hotel. I'll make sure you get it back."

"I think you better stay away from the hotel, don't you?"

Black shrugged. "You're probably right."

Ruth adjusted her glasses. His entire side and half his back painted with dark blues and purples. A line of stitching sealed the gash across his ribs. She pressed on the bruised flesh.

"No sign of infection. Pretty remarkable." With her glasses, up this close, she saw some of his other adventures imprinted across his flesh. "It seems your body has a bit of practice."

She looked closer at the stitches and checked his other side. Aleeza seemed fascinated by the colors; blues and greens— already tinges of yellow—her little hands reached out to touch the black threads holding him together. No sign of redness and the swelling gone.

"Of course, they do good work as well," Ruth said.

"Who's they?"

She ignored his question, helped him pull the shirt back on, Aleeza already maneuvering to be picked up again. "Nicky should be back soon."

"Hopefully, she can point me in the right direction."

"Hopefully, she stays away a couple days and you heal up first."

Black scooped the girl up, and she wrapped her arms around his neck. "Do you think there's time for that?"

Nicola swept into the room. "Probably not."

She dropped her backpack. Tried not to show her surprise at the sight of the little girl in Black's arms. Kissed Ruth and Aleeza on their foreheads.

"But you're not going to do anyone any good if you keel over." She reached out, put her hand on his forehead, checking for fever. Satisfied. "For someone who is supposed to be so smart, you're a real idiot."

"Ummm, sure. Thanks, I guess."

"Not only do you get yourself shot, they told me the infection from whatever damage you did to yourself from days ago could have killed you on its own."

"And who are 'they' again?"

"Friends. Real doctors. With real medicine and training. A little more advanced than vodka and electrical tape."

"Bourbon."

"What?"

"Kentucky bourbon and duct tape."

"Duct tape?"

"You know what they say about duct tape?"

"I know what these guys say about duct tape." Nicola forced a smile. "That you're an idiot and only a couple days away from the point of no return."

"Still here." Black smiled. Aleeza looked up and matched it with a sleepy grin of her own.

She tried to stay angry, the two goofy grins weakening her resolve. "Yeah. Still here. No thanks to your own efforts."

Ruth watched—not bothering to listen. A man, a woman, and a child. Wishing she had a camera. Hoping Nicky missed the silly grin stuck on her own face.

"I'm going to let you two talk. Dinner will be ready in a bit. The kids will be excited you're home."

"You did a great job," Nicola said. "Looks like he'll live."

"Fifteen years of hacking and cutting my insides away. Had to learn something."

Nicola watched the older woman hobble away; a sure sign she was tired and in pain.

She turned to Black, Aleeza asleep in his arms. She sensed it, could feel it, that this man would do everything with his considerable physical prowess to protect this little girl. To protect them all. She thought back, but couldn't remember ever feeling so safe.

Still, she had to ask, had promised herself she would, if only to hear the answer from his own lips.

"Are you a psychopath?"

CHAPTER
THIRTY-NINE

Kronmüller wanted to kill somebody. Actually, he wanted to kill a lot of somebodies. His father always at the top of the list. Maybe Ringer—too much loyalty to his father. He'd seen the man's hand gripping Lina's arm, dragging her into the stables. Could see the powerful fingers digging into— Not Lina. The American girl. Sam they called her. *What the fuck kind of name was that?*

No matter. Ringer was choosing the wrong side, and Kronmüller could imagine a time when the big man, a fucking psychopath for sure, would be forced to choose. If he chose his father, Kronmüller would have to kill him. If Ringer betrayed the father, sided with Kronmüller, he knew he would never be able to trust him. Better all-around if the man was dead.

He could add Curpen. Greed and arrogance were becoming a liability, but he could use his help, for now anyway, to deal with the FBI. Americans spent more time policing the world than their own at home. As if they were the sole arbiters of right and wrong. He put them on the list just for principle.

Curpen's man Ricard or whatever his name was. Why did he stab the gigantic bouncer and not the American? The bouncer might live and the American was in hiding. According to Curpen, the American soldier—a real killer—was there for the girl. Sam. *Yes, he was going to have to deal with this stupid name.* And who the fuck was this American? He had no claim. The girl belonged to him now.

The list went on. He felt his mood brighten as if his blood became richer and his limbs lighter. By the time he'd added a Canadian girl he'd met at nineteen in Brussels who rejected him outright, he was feeling good.

His mind spiraled with possibilities, and he started planning the means of each death. Knife, gun, poison, torture, drowning—maybe each one unique? By the time he got to whole-scale war, he knew he was getting carried away and had to rein it in. Soon, he found himself sinking into a quagmire of depression. Still, death was on his mind.

Kronmüller flashed back to the first time he'd seen a dead body. A boy, maybe six or seven, no older than himself. He'd been told to wait in the truck. His father made the rounds with Joffire at his side, stomping and kicking up dust like a wild animal as he surveyed the devastation of a small village. The village itself, a few dried mud and dung structures forming a loose circle, stood on the outskirts of their western properties.

The uprisings in what would become Namibia had taken twenty years to reach a fever pitch and two white African conscripts had recently been killed. Reprisal was swift, and though there was almost no chance anyone from this small Nama village had been involved, they'd been raped, tortured, and gunned down to rot where they fell.

His father didn't grieve for the village—he grieved for the loss of manpower and able workers to dig the small mine nearby. Not his most profitable, but one of the many concerns across his lands that fed the fortune from a hundred thousand hectares his family had carved with sweat and blood from the rock and desert over the past two hundred years. Land, wine, cattle, gold, and diamonds.

Kronmüller looked down at the small body. Arms and legs as thin as the spears the men had tried to defend themselves with, belly ruptured from a line of automatic gunfire, a feast for the bluebottle blowflies swarming across the boy's intestines, the smell of spilled feces and rotting flesh heavy in the desert air.

It would be ten years later, after his first ineffective fumblings with a nineteen-year-old girl from a village in the north, three years older than himself, that Kronmüller would see the close-up of another dead body. Her attempts at guiding him and reviving his frightened, frustrated body triggered an anger which he released by carving his name time after time across her smooth, dark flesh. It was one of the last times he'd written out his full name, *Niels Christiaan Kronmüller.*

He looked into her sightless brown eyes until her blood dried and their two bodies were stuck together, then climaxed as he pulled their flesh apart.

He loved the look and feel of smooth, dark skin but perhaps it was his father's incessant harping about the inferior races that initially confused him but pushed him toward the famed beauty of the mixed-blood Cape Town Coloureds. For him, the compromise satisfied all his needs and wants.

It wasn't enough. His father berated his choices, constantly found him wanting in his comparisons to Joffire. He ignored the abomination of his oldest son's of homosexuality and drove the younger Kronmüller away with both words and whip. To Europe. To an uncle who allowed and nurtured his fetishes and perversions. Discovering at seventeen, he wasn't the only one. Finding how profitable it could be to satisfy the darker impulses of Europe's elite. Twenty years of enterprise before stumbling across Lina.

Lina was truly the love of his life. A beautiful, intelligent, challenging companion whose inner light kept the dark impulses of his heart at bay. One with which he could carve out his own legacy and finally leave the obsessions and memories of his father's beatings and tortures behind.

He thought of the American girl. Beautiful. Willful perhaps, regal, much like his Lina. He had thought to keep her, but unlike his father, unlike his dead mother, he only needed one woman, one lover, to make him happy. But perhaps the girl would make a companion for his beloved?

He'd acted impulsively on the island, but killing her companions was only a mistake if he didn't take further action. The American would bring a high price should he let her go.

He knew a dozen men around the world with which he could stoke a bidding war, but for now, she was his, and he would decide her place.

With his father gone, there would be no need to risk his life and fortunes on what was becoming an increasingly dangerous profession in an age of instant communication between international police agencies and their sophisticated forensics. It was time to start thinking about his future. A family of his own. *Anything else would be crazy.*

CHAPTER
FORTY

Dinner long over. Dishes washed and put away. Grandma's kitchen elves well-trained. Nicola made her rounds, making sure clothes were laid out for the morning, teeth were brushed, prayers in a half-dozen languages delivered.

Black considered the psychopath question. Laughed it off to dismiss it. This wasn't the time. He agreed it merited serious consideration. Maybe in a distant future. Or in another life, but not now.

He'd asked a psychiatrist about it himself. A couple ranks above him, making the rounds as he went to check on one of the operators under his command who'd been shot up. After he got past her clinical answer, the remaining conversation, one which lasted most of the night through dinner in the mess hall and another couple hours before they fell asleep in her quarters, had been disconcerting, and in his mind, inconclusive.

She only pointed out what he already knew.

His ability to navigate violence. His lack of remorse for most of it, even when it ended in death. Antisocial behavior? He ran a small team of operators whose primary mission was to create havoc directed at people they didn't know. Certainly not to dwell on it or feel guilty afterward.

Nicola dismissed the question even before the words left her mouth. She could see the parallels, imagined they were nurtured by those who used and directed his abilities. *He has a talent for violence*—it made sense to her now.

She'd read the reports. Read between the lines. But she also knew he'd put his life on the line countless times. She'd heard the catch in his voice, the pride and love when he talked about his sister and Big Al and Dillon and his men. He wouldn't even be here if he wasn't risking his life for another.

Black sat propped up on a large sofa. Nicola, wrapped in a soft throw and curled in a chair across from him. They'd talked for hours. Mostly about nothing and yet—*everything.* The island. The storm. She told him stories about the kids. The shelter on the opposite side of the mountains. She watched minute by minute as he sank deeper into the sofa.

"So who are you?" she asked. "I mean, really?"

Black did his best to keep his eyes open. A voice in his head shouting to get up and get moving. Another telling him, as Nicola and Ruth had, to give himself at least the day to recover, to mend. It wouldn't last long, but a third voice gave thanks that he was taking their advice.

"I'm sure you know more about me by now than I do," he answered.

"I know what the files say."

"Which tells me a bit about you."

"How so?"

"Most of my files are bound to be sealed. My history on hold. If you were able to see them, any of them, you have exceptional access or exceptional skills. Since you live in the middle of the Indian Ocean, I'll go for skills."

"Skills," she quietly confirmed. "Which gives me access."

"So where did you go to school?"

She grinned. "Twenty questions?"

He swallowed back a yawn. "I have at least that many."

"Okay. We'll trade," she said.

"Okay. But no fair interrogating me in my sleep."

She laughed. "Deal."

She grabbed another throw, spread it over his shoulders. Sat back and waited.

"So, how did you end up in Zurich?"

"You already knew?" Shaking her head. "Somebody has a big mouth around here," she said lightly.

"She's proud of you."

Ruth knew more than anyone else and would never betray that trust. But there was so much Nicola couldn't imagine being able to share. So much Ruth could never know.

"I raced through school. Through Politehnika. Trotted out as a shining example. Somebody noticed."

"Sounds familiar."

She dove right in. "Why did you kill those men?"

"Chicago?"

"Chicago."

"I think I'm tired now." He was. But she wasn't about to let him off the hook that easy. She waited.

"They were threatening my sister. I'd just lost a good friend."

"Sam's father?"

"Sam's father."

"And now you're here for the girl."

"Now I'm here for the girl."

"Why'd you join the Army?"

"I was good at it."

"And what about the math?"

"Isn't it my turn again?" She shrugged. Smiled. Turned it up enough to make him laugh.

"I couldn't figure out what to do with it." It wasn't the real answer, but it would have to do.

"The math?"

"The math."

"So. The Army?"

"Yep. The Army. It almost never makes sense, but it's rare they ask me to think about it."

She didn't tell him how much she really knew. His childhood. His schooling. His adventures and misadventures in his chosen career.

Nor had she told him about the files or the videos. She needed to watch them first. See with her own eyes. She was sure nothing in them could damn him in her eyes. She'd seen him with Aleeza.

"One more question."

He smiled. Closed his eyes. She could tell he was done in. She wanted him to stay. To rest. To recover. A day. A day and a half. Thirty-six hours. It sounded ridiculous. He'd been shot for Christ's sake. And now she was pushing for more when she should let him be.

She watched his chest rise and fall. Maybe he was asleep. It could wait until tomorrow. Or never.

She started to say never mind. Had every intention to. But those weren't the words that came from her lips.

"You're in trouble, aren't you? I mean, when this is over. The FBI? The police? I guess the Army. You save the girl, you save Sam. *What then?*"

CHAPTER
FORTY-ONE

Flames undulated, snapped, and jerked in rhythm, throwing their light against high canyon walls and cliffs as the drums, calling to a distant chorus of ancestral heartbeats, reverberated back and forth off the ancient stone enclosure.

A cackle of hyenas paced the cliffs, the celebration below reflected in their eyes as they watched sparks and embers ride on plumes of twisted black smoke that carried the scent of their upcoming feast. More gathered and waited, word traveling on high-pitched barks and yelps across the arid lands. The bitch snapped at her pups, cautioning them for patience for the feast of refuse that would wait for them after the two-legged creatures left their land.

Below, fifty women danced as if a single organism, mimicking the flames. Bare feet, stepping, sliding, and stomping, raising the dust just as the conflagration raised the smoke, competing with increasingly complex articulations. Twisting, turning, leaping—the strength and grace needed for keeping body parts from flying off in every direction evidenced in her every step.

Dancing with increasing intensity in concentric circles from outside the women, fifty men. Their movements told the creation of heaven and earth, mimicked the hunt, the battles their forefathers fought and won, each gesture and complex motion a faithful retelling of their people's history as meaningful as any written word.

The celebration was further lit in the headlights of a half-dozen trucks. Leaning against them, rifles in hand, ostensibly to watch over and protect the ranch hands and their families, stood Grip and Ringer, along with a half-dozen of their trusted men.

Ouderling sat high on the hood of a Land Cruiser. Like the others, he watched the woman drive the frenzy from within the middle of the group, giving herself to the ecstasy of the dance. Her passions fed the spectacle as surely as the piles of dried wood and brush fed the fire. A magnificent creature, but something to rut and breed with her own kind to birth more workers, not infect the lineage of his heirs.

Leaning against the grill, Kronmüller accepted the cup of gritty umqombothi, a traditional beer made from maize meal and sorghum malt that women were pouring from a large gourd.

Father and son. Ouderling beaming. Kronmüller ready to scream. Both with eyes much like the hyenas above, reflecting the frenzy before them.

"You're going to tell me there is white blood flowing through the veins of that klonkie bitch?"

"I love her."

Ouderling snorted. "You only love the kaffir doos."

"You're wrong."

Ouderling slid down from the truck.

"Let's find out."

Ouderling nodded to Ringer. The huge bodyguard set down his rifle and reached for a machete. He crossed through the truck's beam of headlights and began making his way into the crowd.

"Let her go—or love her without hands and feet."

Lina spun and leapt, let her eyes take in the Elder. His hate. Tired of the fight, she knew her time was near. Her grandmother, a revered Sangomas from Swaziland, taught Lina as a young child to divine the future. She'd seen her death.

She looked to the fear of the Younger. The man who swore he loved her. Who was hedging his bets by finding her replacement.

Her eyes went to Ringer. The gleaming machete. Grip watching on. The ring of trustees fingering their rifles.

She watched Ringer come. Kept at bay by the furor of the writhing bodies. Shivered in revulsion and gave herself to the dance.

Kronmüller watched in horror as Ringer pushed his way forward. Glanced at Grip who returned his look with no hint of comment or loyalty. He turned back to his father talking on his phone.

Ringer was almost upon her. Bodies leapt and stomped, the ground shook and the superheated air around them shimmered and vibrated. A dazzling display of color, sweat-drenched bodies, and powerful limbs. The enormous bodyguard reaching through the throng.

"Okay! OKAY!" Kronmüller shouted.

The slightest of nods from Ouderling. Ringer, disappointed, released his grip on Lina's arm and returned to his post.

Ouderling returned his focus to the phone. "If the American is there, bring me his heart," he growled as he slid from the truck.

Kronmüller started forward, but his father slipped an arm around his shoulders and neck and dragged him back.

"Your last warning," the father spitting the words into his son's ear.

Lina paused in her movements long enough to watch Kronmüller shrug the arm off and jerk away as if branded. Father and son faced off, shimmering in the haze, distorted by hate as much as the superheated air.

The moment passed. Lina closed her eyes, renewed her attack on the dance with a fury and athleticism that left those around her staring in awe.

Ouderling and Ringer drove away, the truck throwing up a curtain of red dust and broken rock behind them.

CHAPTER
FORTY-TWO

Nicola spent the rest of the night watching videos. René had brought her a lot to go through. Special Operations, a division of the Mauritius Police Department, had confiscated hours and hours of the club's security footage. Multiple angles covered most of the bar and floor. She watched them all in triple speed, found what she might be looking for, copied the relevant parts to a new drive, and then watched again at half speed.

First up, the night of the American's murders. An altercation at the bar. A woman—even with the poor lighting and less than ideal angle of the cameras, you could tell she was beautiful. Probably mixed race, tall and elegant, at home on any runway in Paris or Milan.

She ordered a drink. The bartender smitten. Nicola pulled a screenshot in case someone needed to talk to him.

A man, face turned away from this angle, grabbed her arm, and stole her drink, then pushed her toward a huge, hard-looking man. The woman looked like a child against his massive frame, and she could almost feel his hands pinning her in place. Nicola took another frame grab. Not the greatest but now she had the time stamp, able to quickly locate additional footage and angles.

She watched it play out in slow motion. Pieces, some partially hidden, some as clear as a network television show.

Two women, they looked American, came to the first woman's defense. The man pushed one and brutally slapped the other.

The bodyguards intercepted what she assumed were the American's boyfriends. Confirmed when she recognized the politician's son, sent reeling to the floor. The girl, it had to be Sam, came to his defense. Spitting at the man who started it all.

The crowd and the quick actions made it difficult to see. She had the impression of a colossal man, club security, starting forward, and being waved off. The first man grabbed the elegant woman. The huge bodyguards daring anyone else to come forward. Then the cameras went dark.

At first, she thought it was a glitch, but she quickly confirmed that all the camera feeds went down at the same time. Powered down. VIP Protection.

Okay. She had the timestamps. Not so bad, just tedious.

She loaded all the feeds, six in all, placed them on six tracks of a single timeline. Synced the time codes and fed them all into multiple windows on her computer screen.

The sun would be up soon, but she was determined to find the best possible shots of all the relevant players of this little drama.

Worked her way backward.

There were the two women on the dance floor. Their boyfriends joined them for a short time and then left them on their own. Both having fun, the time of their lives. Further back. The four of them sitting at the table sharing drinks and laughs.

The elegant woman, no idea of her name so Nicola shortened it to *Ele*, made her way across the dance floor toward the restrooms.

Nicola played it back and forth. Ele passed the girls, and they soon followed. And shadowing them all, one of the huge, brooding bodyguards.

She rewound the tapes further. Not clear, but there he was.

The man who hit women. That would be all she needed to know to hate him.

She made a quick diagram.

Sam and her American friends.

The asshole holding court in the VIP section. A man coming to shake his hand. The woman searching for an escape.

She plotted the angles and sight-lines of the cameras.

Calculated his eye lines and could track his eyes watching and following the Americans on the dance floor.

She wound back further. Searched for a clear shot.

Watched him push his way into the club. The doormen giving his group, Ele and the two ogres—she'd named them *O-One* and *O-Two*—the royal treatment.

Nicola rewound it one more time. Fame by frame. O-One in the way. Back another frame. One more. O-Two in the way. Another. She stopped. A nearly perfect portrait. A head of wavy blond hair. Straight, Grecian nose. Defined jaw. He would have been handsome except for the predatory eyes.

She marked the frame. Printed the best shots of all the major players.

Could hear the roosters across the valley telling the islanders it was time to rise and in her case, time to grab some sleep.

She turned everything off. Ruth would be up soon, the children soon to follow. She was shutting down when she remembered she hadn't watched the video that should show Black. The shooting. No matter. She'd watch it later with him at her side.

She peeked in on him. Deep regular breathing. She listened for any sign of effort or struggle, anything that might hint at renewed infection.

Fought the urge to cross the room and feel for fever. It took more effort to not wake him and tell him she had their killer.

CHAPTER
FORTY-THREE

"**O**kay, sure, he's a great fucking guy," Michaels didn't try to hide his frustration. "Except for the killing everybody part."

The team, minus Alix sleeping in the next room, stammered and fidgeted at their stations but offered nothing new.

Michaels shook his head. "Fuck it. We'll deal with Black later."

He looked around the room. Camille at the coffee pot, Julius fucking with the air conditioner again, and Clement with his laptop resting on top of a pile of blankets he'd climbed under in one of the room's plush armchairs.

"For now, we need to concentrate on the children. On the girl."

Nobody jumped in with new information.

Rodriguez came back into the room, set down a large tray of pastries and fruit. For the first time in two days, no one jumped for them. They all needed real sleep and real food.

Camille brought the pot, poured herself a coffee. She added enough sugar to make the spoon stand straight, topped it with a little milk.

"I'll take one of those," Rodriguez said.

She handed him hers and started on another. Nodded her head toward the other room.

"Alix was up all night," she said.

"Not sure she got anywhere," Julius said.

Camille stirred her coffee. "Maybe Alexandrescu could help."

"And Black," Clement volunteered from inside his cocoon.

"Jesus," Michaels mouthed under his breath.

Rodriguez stared at the wall of fame. Pictures spilled over the adjacent walls. New photos of their counterparts at MPD added to the mix.

He looked at the photo of Alexandrescu. Breakfast at Tiffany's. Gypsy version. "She's like some kind of—what do you call them? *A white hat?*"

"That's a bit Hollywood. White hats and black hats—but she's not really," she struggled to explain. "She's—something else."

"Camille's right." Clement sounded starstruck too. "She's one of the people who invents the shit the white and black hats fight over."

"Okay. So we track her down," Michaels said. "And maybe we find Black."

"Can't be that hard," Rodriguez said. "The island's not that big."

Julius plopped down on the bed, his laptop bouncing up and almost hitting him in the face. "Population, 1.3 million," Julius affirmed.

Rodriguez was not impressed. "That's not even downtown Chicago."

"And that didn't turn out too well," Clement countered.

Michaels watched his partner. Cuban charm came with a Cuban temper. He kept it in check; he was learning. Maybe ten more years, he'd be good. Plus, it was hard to argue the point.

"Don't know what we're into yet, but I'm not looking for another war," Michaels said. "We don't know who's on our side."

Rodriguez downed the rest of his coffee. Found himself chewing on sugar. "I have another angle I want to pursue."

The frustration slipped away as Michaels began to focus.

"Okay. And I want to go back to the club. With everything that happened there, maybe somebody will be in the mood to talk."

Julius twisted from his makeshift desk on the bed. "What about MPD?"

Michaels paused. "I want to limit our interaction with them until we know who's who."

Rodriguez put his cup down. "I hope to get you some of that today."

"Curpen?"

Rodriguez nodded.

"Need me with you?"

"Not yet. Working out my thoughts." Turned to Camille. "Be nice to have anything you can add."

"Got it."

"Okay." Michaels slipped on his jacket. "Keep at it. Take a break when you need to. We've got nine days."

CHAPTER
FORTY-FOUR

Late morning. One of those days when the air was so clear and bright it hurt. Black had escaped the children. It would be too easy to let himself enjoy their antics and revel in their youth, their sheer vitality. It was time to start thinking of darker things.

He walked through the narrow streets and made it to a narrow strip of sand framing a small lagoon. Too remote and unimpressive for the tourists, but three men stood knee-deep with broad-brimmed hats shielding their eyes and long cane fishing poles in their hands.

One turned with a tentative wave then turned back as he got a strike, his pole bending and dipping forward. The others encouraged their friend and soon he pulled up a good-sized blue jack and added it to their common string of silvery snappers and needlefish.

Black stripped off his shirt leaving him in a pair of shorts Ruth had found for him. The men glanced at him long enough to take in the tortured flesh across his back and side.

Black wasn't here for swimming or sunbathing. He was here for the remedial effects of ocean and sun, to test his range of movement, to clear his head, and plan his next moves.

The water beckoned him forward, and he waded in chest-deep. He could feel the warmth of the sun on his shoulders and the water massaging his back. Watched as a school of tiny red mullet darted by, the cloud of silvery red streaks below moving as fast below as the reflections of sunlight off the gentle waves above.

He floated on his back, stretched his arms as wide as they would go. So tempted to just float away. Spun in place, held his breath as long as he could, then spun again and floated his way back closer to shore. Again on his feet, letting them dig ankle-deep in the shifting sands below. He twisted and stretched to both sides, letting the weight and resistance of the water keep him in check.

He could feel the sutures pulling at his flesh, but the strong synthetic filaments held.

The three men tried to ignore him, but shook their heads and smiled as they watched. To anyone watching, Black looked like a crazy white man slow dancing in the ocean. In reality, he moved slowly through a full routine of tai chi-like postures, testing his strength in the shifting currents and then stretching and extending his range and boundaries.

He let the water determine his directions and speed. To move as slowly as he was in the constant pressure from the limitless ocean was more difficult than moving quickly. As one of the revered combat instructors he'd trained with asked him—a man half his size and twice his age—if he couldn't move slowly, control his body with absolute precision in stillness, how could he ever hope to move fast? He'd laughed it off until he saw the man clear out a bar of Marines on leave in Cebu.

A never-ending journey, but Black's constant quest for more power and speed had eventually been found in stillness and the control of near-infinite slowness.

An hour later, exhausted from apparently doing nothing at all, the three men watched him head back to the shore. He sat at the water's edge and let the sun recharge his body and bake away the pain. Nicola should be up by now. She'd evidently been up late into the morning, searching for information that could benefit his search.

He already owed her so much. Not least of all, for the reminder that there was good in the world as well as evil. If not, then what were they struggling for? He'd given up trying to judge himself years ago. Perhaps that was only in the hands of the gods.

He wasn't convinced there was a single god—one supreme being overlooking every happening and instance of all Creation—one that would have reason to be concerned with *his* existence.

If there was, maybe God had set himself up with some help. He liked the ancients' belief in multiple gods and could imagine that some minor deities were taking it on themselves to play mischief with his fate. *They were certainly putting some effort into it.*

There was something happening on this island and Nicola had access, skills as she told him, that he didn't, that could help shed some light. He could sense a growing sense of urgency telling him that Sam's time would soon run out. Though injured, he wasn't afraid of meeting the physical challenge or even finding her —his fear was not being there in time.

Sam had been taken four days ago. Almost five. He'd managed to travel across the world, get himself shot, and add another police agency looking for him.

"You save the girl—you save Sam—what then?"

He tried not to get ahead of himself. In his world, that had always been a mistake. Still, he was human.

If he lived, and there was no guarantee of that, he'd go to prison. There was no getting around the fact that he had killed people. Civilians who fancied themselves combatants, armed themselves as such, but in the eyes of the law were still civilians. And to bring Sam home, he had no doubt, as sure as the sun would rise again tomorrow, he'd have to kill more. *"—what then?"*

He could run. Had been running in some ways his entire life. He thought of Dillon. It's not like they saw each other or talked more than once every couple of years, but his heart ached to know they never would again.

He thought of the choice his friend had made. To protect the integrity of the memories his daughter carried. Could he have been as strong?

What memory would someone carry of him? *"Do you think we ever did any good out there?"* What had any of it meant? He didn't have accomplishments. He did things that should never have to be done and so were best buried and forgotten. No one even knew who he was.

He was sure Nicola, she said as much, thought she knew a lot about him. More than he would have volunteered. Details. Dates. Events. She'd never heard his name until two days ago, and yet now knew as much as anyone in the world. More than friends. More than family.

He knew none of the same about her, and yet, all he needed to. She was beautiful. Not important in itself, but the way in which she used it, and didn't, told volumes about who she was. Her love for the children. Equally mirrored in her efforts for the abused women. He wasn't sure where she got her money. How she funded the efforts. Donations didn't sound right; more likely she did some type of remote consulting with her computer skills.

Anyone could look up someone else on the Internet. Pay a few dollars and have access to potentially empowering or embarrassing details. But he knew that's not what she'd done. To have access at a level to read his files, files the world's most powerful government was afraid to destroy but afraid to have known, meant her skills were at the very highest of levels. Levels that made her a dangerous person, and vulnerable herself.

Vulnerable. Fragile. He found himself wanting to protect her. Knowing she was as damaged as he was.

CHAPTER
FORTY-FIVE

"**H**e's fucking crazy!" Sam was starting to lose it.

"That may true, but you need to listen to me. Things are changing here quickly. You'll have a chance, but not if he lets you go. Not if they take you away."

"This is insane. What kind of people do these things?"

"These kind."

She tried to make sense of it. She'd grown up in one of America's most racially charged cities, where violence and death on the streets could be an hourly occurrence. Gone to school to study the root causes, the factors that shaped people's thoughts and perceptions, originally hoping she could help her father. She knew he still dealt with things he'd done in the war, things he'd seen as a cop, things he would never tell her,

She knew she'd been reaching for something, anything, the knowledge she could use to help others deal with their own demons, maybe help shape lives before things were set in stone.

Lina told her what she knew of Christiaan. The father. The mother. The making of a monster.

Sam didn't feel sorry for him. She was too angry. And in truth, too scared. She grew up with a loving mother. A father, who was powerful and strong and good. Who doted on her and would fight to the death for her happiness. *It's what fathers were supposed to do.*

After being dragged into the stables to be photographed, she'd been returned to the house. It had taken hours to stop shaking. It played over and over in her mind. The lights, the camera, the computer. The children. She could guess what it meant for them all. She knew how terrified they were. Had seen the signs of disassociation and withdrawal. Felt guilty for being able to sit in this beautiful room instead of the cages she imagined for them.

Christiaan, only Lina called him *Christiaan* she told her, was out flying or hiking or maybe even killing someone. She didn't know for sure, kept in a gilded cage herself, but suspected it was what he did when he needed to release the pressure his father exerted on him. Ordering the deaths of people like Allan wouldn't begin to have the same effect as wielding the knife himself. The two women had the night and little more, but she knew he wouldn't come back until his thirst was sated.

Ouderling, the Elder, was equally evil and Lina was caught between their battle of wills. He relished the leverage he kept over his son, and constantly threatened her with torture and death. Short of killing herself, she was forced to live the nightmare.

Lots of things went into creating a monster, but nothing had prepared her for actually being caught by one.

"You must find a way to survive."

"And what about you? You can't just—you can't just give up."

Lina smiled. "I think it's too late for me."

Sam reached out to shush her, to stop her from speaking, but Lina pushed her hand away. "No. It's okay. I knew when I was very young, my life would not be a long one."

"I don't believe in that. Fate. Our paths preordained."

"Things exist even when we don't believe in them."

Sam stammered. Her entire world was upside down. She had no idea what to believe anymore.

Lina smiled. Reached for Sam's hand. "So you don't want me to tell you your future?"

Sam laughed. "Sure. Do your worst. Or best. Or whatever it is."

Lina held her hand. Traced the lines with her finger and studied it closely. She felt as if she was looking and holding her own hand. The women could easily have passed for sisters.

The gentle grasp was the first bit of warmth Sam had shared in days without malice or evil intention. Lina felt the same but instead of days, it had been years.

"Do you have a family?"

"Not of my own, I'm not married. I'm still in school. I thought—I mean it's why I came to Mauritius."

"I'm sorry."

"No, it's okay. It wasn't going to work out anyway but, but he didn't, you kno—" Sam saw the blood flying from Allan's throat, the look of surprise in his eyes. Choked back the emotion.

"But my parents. They're divorced. My mother has a new husband, he's a good guy, adores my mother. And somewhere along the line, my dad lost his mind and moved in with a crazy bitch girlfriend." Sam smiled and shook her head. *Crazy bitch?* That was being generous. "And what about you?"

"My mother. My sister, Lesedi. They think I'm dead."

"That's horrible. We can try to contact them! If they know you're here, they'll come for you."

"Which is why they can never know!" Lina squeezed so tight she threatened to crush Sam's hand. "Their lives would be in danger. Terrible danger. It's why I can never leave."

Lina's grip softened, but she held on, unable to let go, imagining for the moment that it was the hand of her real sister. Hoping at the very least Lesedi's life was filled with joy and laughter with a man who truly loved and worshiped her. Maybe her children brought their grandmother tears of happiness to replace the ones she surely cried for Lina.

Sam considered it. Maybe Lina was right—maybe fate was as real as the sun and the moon. Tried to reason it out, extrapolate the threads that bound them together. She had the feeling looking at the hands that held hers, that maybe, somehow, there was more, something beyond the whims of a madman that thrust them together. Sam fought her tears as she looked at the two thin scars lying vertically along the woman's wrist.

"So. What does my palm say? Am I going to make it?"

Lina laughed. "I can't read palms."

"What? I thought you said—"

They both started laughing. Five days in and Sam had thought she might never laugh again. How long had it been since Lina had a moment of real joy in her life untouched by fear?

Lina sensed her thoughts "My grandmother was a Sangomas," she said.

She reached for a bag at her feet. Pulled out a pair of jeans and a t-shirt. Tipped it over and a pair of combat-styled boots felt out, red patent leather and chunky lug soles.

Sam looked at the clothes. It took her a moment to process, then she jumped to her feet and hugged Lina.

"Oh, my God! Thank you so much!"

"I hope they fit."

"Are you kidding me?" Did her best ghetto voice, low and deep. "We gonna make dat shit fit!"

Lina laughed, caught up in Sam's excitement.

Sam stripped off the dress and reached for the jeans. Lay back on the bed and slid her long legs into them. Perfect. The girls the same size. Moments later she had the t-shirt on and worked the speed laces on the scarlet combat boots.

Everything fit as if made for her.

"Again, thank you." Sam stuck her legs straight out to admire the boots. "So a—San-go-mas?"

Lina smiled. "Sangomas. A healer. I think you Americans would have called my grandmother a witch doctor."

"We wouldn't—well—yeah. Yeah, we would. Where is she—oh, you said, was—"

"That's okay. I stayed with her a while, for two years, after my father died."

"I'm sorry."

"It was a long time ago. They live in here," she pointed to her head, "and in here," hand over her heart. "And in the people. He was a huge part of the political revolution."

Sam nodded. She could hear the pride. "And you always lived in South Africa?"

"Oh, no. I had two years in Paris."

"Paris? Wow. I'll go someday—" Sam caught herself.

"You will."

"Were you in school?"

Lina laughed. "No. Modeling."

"I can see why."

"It's where I met Christiaan. Or he—found me. On the runway." Lina tried to smile. "At first it was nice. He was handsome and charming, I suppose as psychopaths are."

"Not always handsome, but charming can be a trait."

"He loves his designer clothes, the shirts. The gaudier and flashier the better, and of course, loved to come to the shows."

"I've never seen one. Well, not a real one anyway."

"They can be fantastic affairs—full-scale productions, like the Phantom of the Opera. I saw it in London. Lights and music. Runways are like going to the theater. And of course, filled with young, beautiful girls."

"You're one. I mean, a beautiful girl."

Their beauty a curse, Lina tried to smile. "You are too." She took both of Sam's hands. "Listen, your only chance is if Christiaan keeps you for himself."

Sam tried to pull away. Lina kept on.

"No, listen. You'll have to navigate his father. He's crazy too. A vicious racist. As much a killer as Christiaan. I've seen it. I've seen him—" She stopped herself, the images too gruesome to share.

"Here, in the middle of nowhere, he lives with absolute impunity. He tries to keep Christiaan under his rule, but the time will come. And soon."

"My father will be coming for me. He'll bring the whole army if he needs to. He's a cop, a policeman in Chicago."

Lina took a deep breath, pulled out a folded piece of paper from her pocket.

Sam read it. Printed from a computer. A newspaper article, Chicago Tribune.

Lina watched Sam's face fall, tears welling in her eyes then running freely down her cheeks.

"I'm sorry. I heard Ouderling on the phone. I thought you should know."

Sam's heart shattered. She fought for breath. Could feel her throat closing, a physical ache that touched every part of her being. Her mind raced until it couldn't and her body began shutting down.

She fell back on the bed. Curled into a ball. Gasped for air.

Lina reached out with trembling hands, then lay down to hold her as Sam's heart-wrenching sobs lasted deep into the night.

CHAPTER
FORTY-SIX

Nicola woke in a panic ten minutes after laying down, knowing the day was over and Black was gone. She'd missed her chance. To help. To point Black along a path that would save his young friend. To make her case for... *for what?* She didn't even know the man.

Now he was out there. Taking on the world. Tilting at windmills. She could have at least pointed him in the right direction. Told him what to watch out for. Peel back the masks on friends or foes... who to trust... who not to.

Saddened by her failure, she closed her eyes again and let herself drift.

Noon by the time Nicola's eyes opened again. No concept of the time—it felt like days had passed.

Like her room at the shelter, her bedroom had an en suite bath and toilet, and an outdoor shower fashioned from lava rock and enclosed with tropical plants.

She tried to wash away the sadness, would look forward to the children lifting her day. The hot water did its magic. By the time the hot water ran out and she dressed, she was humming a song that danced at the edge of her consciousness. She could hear the children laughing and playing, the sound sweetening her melancholy. The smell of cooking fish carried in the air, and she realized she was starving.

Nicola walked into the huge main room and stopped.

Ruth announced Nicola's entry to the rest of the room. "Good morning, sleepyhead."

Aleeza was standing on Ruth's lap, looking over her shoulder into the kitchen, but turned to wave.

Other children giggled and echoed Ruth's greeting. "Good morning, sleepyhead." A few gathered for hugs and greetings.

More dicing and chopping. Rayln and Joelle setting the table. Aleeza turned back to the kitchen.

Cooking the fish in a huge, oversized iron skillet, Black worked at the stove.

He glanced her way, added his own, "Morning, sleepyhead," then turned the fish. It sizzled in the hot pan, the room fragrant with the steam.

She shuffled to the table. Hugged Ruth and Aleeza, kissed them both good morning, and plopped down in a chair.

Ruth shrugged and smiled.

Nicola sat and Rayln poured her coffee just as Black came with the fish.

Moments later, everyone was finding a seat where they could, making room for Black at the table across from the women. The children giggled and whispered, their eyes bouncing back and forth from Black to Nicola.

"Bon appétit," Black said, lifting his fork in a toast.

Aleeza climbed down from Ruth's lap long enough to climb up on Black's.

Nicola looked to Ruth who shrugged again and grinned like a daft fool.

Black took a sip of coffee, started in with his fork, and realized the children were taking the moment to give thanks. He waited until the sound and laughter started up again.

"Bon appétit," Ruth echoed.

Thirty minutes later, she was stuffed on the fresh fish, steamed and then flash fried, covered in a mango and chili chutney Black served over a bed of greens and rice.

The children contributed fresh fruits and vegetables and breads and more rice. It seemed they'd all wanted to help this morning.

Ruth helped the children clear the dishes and Black and Nicola were left alone.

"So. You cook."

Shrugged. "Sure. I eat."

Nicola laughed. "I see that."

His plate had been filled with what would have been two days of rations for her.

"It was delicious. I mean, where did you learn to do all this?"

"I don't know anything except that when things are this fresh, you just have to put it on the plate."

"And you went fishing?"

Black laughed. "Well, I thought I could swim out and wrestle back a tuna, but settled for splashing around in the lagoon. I think the locals paid me off with fish just to quit chasing their catch away."

"You're crazy. And obviously feeling better. How's the—you know? The gunshots?"

"Almost as good as new."

She frowned.

"Well, maybe forty, fifty percent, but I'm holding together, so that might have to do. Unless you have more duct tape?"

"Yeah, but no bourbon."

"Could make it difficult."

"So what now?"

"Now is, I find Sam."

"Pretty sure I can help you with that."

CHAPTER
FORTY-SEVEN

Windswept cliffs jutted out in huge, horizontal curves of near faceless rock above him. Kronmüller paused and looked up. Perceptions distorted from this vantage point and were hard to gauge. Maybe fifty, sixty feet higher, the edge pushed out at least twenty feet from the vertical face.

He looked down. It had taken him two hours to get this far, but he didn't consider himself a rock climber. To this point, it had been three or four-hundred feet of near-vertical bouldering. From three kilometers away, a glint of noonday sun bounced off the truck he left parked in a cleft at the edge of a small canyon.

Took the last of his water, little more than a few drops, and left the canteen behind. Looked up and grinned, relishing the challenge. Now it was going to get tricky, especially with the rifle over his shoulder.

Kronmüller stood beneath the overhang planning his route. Within the obvious layers and strata of rock, a crack opened upwards and across it, maybe the result of an ancient earthquake or an underground eruption. It jigged and jagged like a strike of lightning, and looking at it closer, seeing what he thought must be scorch marks and melted rock, he decided that was exactly what cracked the quartzitic sandstone. It had taken hundreds of thousands of years of constant, near-microscopic erosion to create the cave-like overhang, and a few microseconds to split it open.

Hands and arms and legs screamed in protest. Too much time in the clubs. He wasn't here to relax. He was here to test and torture his body, the self-punishment meant to clear his mind.

Kronmüller looked back down. *Fuck that.* He was going up.

The two men were having a time of it. They'd driven out in the earliest of morning hours to be in position long before the sun came up. Trespassing for the past fifty kilometers, but they could honestly claim they were lost. Easy enough to turn around at any time and follow their tracks back. Hook up the Garmin if needed. They'd be fine.

The promise of Africa's big game coming together for water at an obscure watering hole they'd been told about worth the risk. They'd bag one of the big cats for sure, maybe a cheetah or even a lion. They weren't smart enough to be poachers. Weren't even experienced hunters; shooting pheasants on the Downs could hardly count. No, just stupid.

Both had visions of bragging rights and were already spinning tales in their heads, envisioning the looks and envy of the fuckwits back in London. They'd shoot the biggest thing they could find—field-dress it the best they could. They'd watched dozens of Internet videos. How hard could it be? They'd take the head and the skin, and the claws for sure, and then find some native they could pay a few quid to clean it up and help them smuggle their prize.

They pretty much had it all worked out. And then their radiator hose burst. Steam started slowly, then filled the windscreen and soon they were driving blind in the night. GPS in their mini-sat didn't seem to work out here. Maybe the blasted metal content in the rocks they'd been told to watch out for, or some such horseshit. The stars had never seemed so bright but meant absolutely nothing to either of them.

The last time either of them had given any thought to astronomy was in middle school when Brendon—*the more successful of the two, now vice-president of a bank*—had borrowed Robert's telescope and was lying in a field with Sara Jacobson hoping to at least get his hand in her shirt and maybe even under her bra.

Then it got worse. Robert hit a deep rut in the dark and over-compensated by jerking the Range Rover into a boulder, bouncing across a deep furrow. He nearly flipped the vehicle and came down so hard it cracked two of Brendon's new implants, the jagged edges slicing into his cheek and filling his mouth with blood.

They staggered out, fell to the ground. Took a moment.

"You alright?"

"Yeah. Sure. Tits."

Brendon spat out the blood, made it to his feet, dusted himself off. Looked at their vehicle; one side stuck deep in a foot wide crevice, the other a meter off the ground.

He looked at the sky until Robert joined him. Neither had a clue. Couldn't begin to guess which direction they were facing. Brendon tried to laugh. He should have paid more attention in school—he hadn't even got a kiss out of the deal with Sara.

Robert tried to think. The sun was an hour away from giving them some sense of direction. "Yepper, we're pretty much buggered."

The two were halfway through their water and realized they needed to slow it down. They knew to stay with their vehicle, using it for shade as much as they could. Neither were mechanics, but it was obvious that would have made no difference.

Their wives were off on their own for an overnight dime store safari. They'd get close enough to the tamed wild animals to take pictures that wowed the grandkids and then buy some mass-produced trinkets to take home and brag to their friends how they'd bargained with real live natives and in the end, helped support the people's pitiful efforts at livelihood.

No one knew the men were out here, no one would be missing them or know where to look if they did.

They had several liters of water, some protein bars, and plenty of ammunition. The sun was now straight overhead, one o'clock. They would wait until it was cooler, maybe four or five they decided, and then start walking. Brandon began plotting their course and could expect to be reasonably accurate when he factored in the direction of the sunset.

The hard part would be walking in a straight line. The air was most times still, but Brendon occasionally felt the subtle tugs and pull of warm desert gusts, and knew they'd lost the tire tracks before they started. Besides, the ground was mostly hard rock, not soft beach sands.

He remembered that a man tended to walk in a circle when left to his own devices; the strength of the dominant leg typically causing a strong deviation to the left. Most of his daily math was simple accounting, but he was trying to work out a formula based on the facts that Robert was cack-handed, five-inches shorter, and not in as good as condition despite the man's incessant desire to prove otherwise.

And that's when they saw the man coming their way.

At first, Brendon thought it was a mirage. Heat shimmered off the sand and rock and made the figure seem at once both far away and close enough to touch. It seemed the figure was moving but it took an inordinate amount of time to determine that he, it finally was a *he*, was actually coming their way.

Robert watched Brendon rise to his feet, dust himself off. He turned to follow the bigger man's eyes, and he too saw the man striding their way.

The stranger was maybe handsome—wavy blond hair blowing in the strengthening wind, a strong jaw, and a slim athletic build. His colorful shirt, incongruous to the highveld of the plateaus, set off his deep tan, but he was white, which he knew would give Brendon some relief. All in all, Robert thought, a splendid looking fellow.

Brendon lifted his hands in greeting. "Cheers, mate! You really couldn't happen along at a better time."

Robert watched as the man unslung his rifle. Carried it easily and low. Couldn't process it when the man worked the bolt, aimed from his hip, and shot Brendon in the chest.

Like a bursting water balloon, blood sprayed as Brendon deflated and collapsed to his knees.

Robert knew he should go for his rifle, propped up against the vehicle just three meters away, but he couldn't make himself move. Wasn't sure if he was breathing or not, his mind frozen as the man, he really was a handsome bloke, kept coming. Relieved for a split-second when the man moved toward Brendon, still stuck on his knees, his brain not catching on to the fact that he was already dead.

The man pulled a knife and with one smooth motion, if asked, Robert wouldn't have been able to say if it was incredibly fast or incredibly slow, sliced it across the sunburnt flesh of the vice-president's throat.

Kronmüller turned to the smaller man. Hard to say if the man even knew what happened to his friend, still a mystery to be unraveled. He stepped closer as if to whisper the answer, and let the blade pierce the man's soft belly. Close enough to embrace, Kronmüller pushed it in to the hilt, sawed the blade back and forth from left to right, then waited as the final light of understanding flickered in the man's eyes. He stepped back as the Englishman's guts spilled onto the dust at his feet, let the man fall.

Kronmüller turned back to the cliffs overlooking his family's lands. His mind clear and filled with purpose. This was their legacy. Land and Blood.

He looked at the distant reflection of light that must be his truck. From this vantage point, he could see a gentle slope to the left. An easy hike back, no more than four or five kilometers. A few more hours of daylight. Plenty of time to field dress his kills.

CHAPTER
FORTY-EIGHT

"Let me see it again."

"Okay."

They were in her room, curtains closed but daylight creeping around the corners. A wall had been opened up to house four huge monitors along with a twelve-bay raid array, three wireless keyboards, a roll-out desk, and chairs. Her own private command center. Nicola scrolled an open timeline as separate video feeds populated three of the monitors.

They watched the security feeds of the altercation at La Caravelle again.

Black watched the big man hit the smaller American. Maybe six-three, two hundred sixty pounds. From the way he moved, and as much from how he stood when he stopped moving, Black knew he was former military. The precise placement of a left hook to the liver that dropped the American, the punch tight and economical, hinted at advanced close-quarter combat training and any one of a dozen different special-ops teams.

Though the man holding the girl was even bigger, the men moved as a single unit. It's what teams trained to do. "Can you go back?"

Nicola smiled. It had only been an hour. "Of course."

They started with the night Black came to the club. *Just thirty-six hours ago!* Almost the same video the FBI watched of Black coming into the bar, talking with the server, and then Oscar.

But this was the unedited version René had smuggled out. Nicola had needed to see it for herself.

Black and Oscar, the giant security guard, entered the hallway and headed toward the back offices.

Oscar turned back and Black continued on, entering the office. Nicola noted the time, scanned another angle, cued it up, and they watched from inside the office as Black opened the door.

The next few moments were frightening in their speed and intensity. Black reached out to shake the manager's hand, smashed his elbow into the man's chest, and somehow spun and slammed him into the door. The frame rate couldn't keep up with Black's speed, but it was clear he smashed Bradley in the head with his gun, shoved the barrel against the man's head, smashed him again, said or asked something and then walked out.

She glanced at the man sitting at her side. No effect, no apology—he might have been watching the weather report.

Nicola had no illusions of what Black was. She'd imagined the violence he would be capable of, but witnessing it, knowing the man beside her was capable of such ferocity, shook her deeply. Fractured and poorly captured, but the most important part of the video was clear. When Black walked out of the office, the man was alive.

They watched as Bradley went to his desk, pulled out a gun, then visibly tried to psyche himself up to pursue Black.

Back in the hallway, Ricard stepped from a door behind the giant and stabbed him in the back.

Oscar whirled in the narrow hall and lunged for his attacker like a wounded bear, but the little man was remarkably fast. He darted forward like a fencer with a dagger and stabbed the big man again and again, then danced back as the giant toppled to his knees.

Another angle showed a man coming into the hallway, gun drawn. Nicola's shoulders tensed.

"Peter Curpen. MPD Special Operations." Nicola scrubbed the video back and forth, stopping the frame on his face. She knew Black caught her reaction. "It's a small island. We've crossed paths before." She turned back before he could ask.

She captured a frame grab then hit play.

They watched Ricard sprint past Black as he exited the office.

Curpen stepped over Oscar just as two more men, the American FBI agents, came into the hall behind him. Curpen disappeared around the corner and Nicola switched camera feeds yet again.

Curpen fired and hit the hapless manager who spun and fell back against the wall. Chunks of plaster and concrete exploded from the walls as Black slipped by him, then turned and ran. Curpen fired, she counted at least five shots as Black dodged and spun, rolled, and bounced off the walls of the narrow hallway until he sprinted out the door.

Switching to another angle and camera feed, they watched as the older of the FBI agents ran into the hallway just as Curpen turned away from Bradley. The younger agent stayed with Oscar, apparently keeping him calm and assessing the damage until further security came through the door. They were soon joined by Curpen and the older agent.

It wouldn't have taken Nicola long to edit and assemble the various feed into a coherent sequence, but they could piece it together in their minds even faster. Black was anxious to see the night Sam came to the club.

"Can you go back?"

"Of course."

A moment later, they began watching the night a third time. These video feeds were clearer, high-definition footage that put them in the club.

The group came into the club. People gave them room and the club security guided them through the crowd. Black took in how the men moved and worked to secure their boss. The bigger one clearly in charge. Black could sense, not explain, the resentment between them.

"Okay."

"You good?"

Black nodded. "How about you?" He'd have had to be an idiot not to feel her unease after watching his night at the club.

"I'm okay. It's just that—" She shrugged. She wasn't sure what she wanted to say.

"Yeah."

She surprised herself when she put her hand over his, her smile tight but eyes filled with warmth. Grateful, Black closed his eyes for a moment, absorbed the touch and comfort.

"Okay, you're not supposed to know I can do this," she said, "but then, who'd believe you?"

She picked up the printouts of the various players. Laid them out in a line. "O-One, O-Two, and Asshole."

Asshole. Black shifted in his chair. *Could she know?* No. That was impossible. Still, it made him wonder how much she did know.

She caught his unease. "You alright?" A soft grunt was all she was going to get. She turned back to her task. "I already have these stored on the computer." She tapped in a few keys and the faces popped up on her desktop. "Who do you want?"

"Only one that matters. We find him, we find them all."

She moved Asshole to the front. Typed in a few commands and a screen flashed by. Only a fraction of a second, but Black recognized the logo. He'd worked with their agents and been in their offices many times. And she was right, nobody would believe him.

"We'll use their database and my software."

Working in command lines, her fingers typed so quickly he couldn't begin to follow. He'd spent time on computers, watched enough elite software engineers and programmers to know she could only be classified as a savant.

"Should be simple enough. We'll start with the international travel database. Narrow it down to recent entries."

The image broke apart as if shattered into a hundred crystal facets. They lined up on one side of the screen as each separate facet was compared to others residing in some massive database.

Seconds later, Black watched them reassemble into the photo and face it had been.

IDENTIFICATION FOUND: KRONMÜLLER, NIELS CHRISTIAAN. SOUTH AFRICA. AGE 39. KRONMÜLLER INDUSTRIES. CAPE TOWN. PORT LOUIS. AMSTERDAM. NOVOSIBIRSK.

Black scanned the rest. Mother deceased. Brother deceased. An uncle in Munich.

Nicola typed in a few commands. Switched databases. Immigration and Passport Control. "He flew back to Cape Town, four days ago."

"She's there."

"Or not." It was hard for her to look at him. She felt the anger rolling off him in waves.

"I know you want to take off now. This minute. I get it. But what if Sam is not a 'one-off'? There's no way she could be, right? That means he's taking girls, maybe other children too, into and out of the country."

"What's the local address?"

It only took her moment.

"Got it." She kept typing and searching. "It's a big operation. International shipping and transport."

With that infrastructure, they both knew it would be easy to smuggle anyone almost anywhere. Black pictured the cages on the fourth floor in Chicago just five, now six days ago.

"I've got everything I need."

"No, you don't. Not even close."

Black started to protest, but she cut him off. "You're not thinking it through."

"Okay." He waited.

Nicola took a deep breath and started in. "You take off. Who knows how? Evade all the authorities. Get to South Africa. But let's say you do, and you get killed."

"I'm not going to—"

"What happens to Sam?"

It only took an instant to know she was right. She could see he knew it.

"Look. I'm asking you, let me help you dig just a little deeper. One day. Then if something happens, happens to you, I have something—we have something I can call in to bring the cavalry."

"One day?" He was on his feet. "I could have her home in a day."

Nicola smiled. His confidence was infectious but she shook her head.

"Or lose her forever." She saw him pause. "I get it, and you're right. I have no doubt you can storm the beaches on your own and bring Sam back. But I think something else going on here. I'm not trying to be insensitive. Something bigger. You don't know me. But this is what I do. Why can I connect to Interpol? I write half of their software. I taught their software to *write* their software. This is what I do. For your government and half a dozen others. But it's always been about the children. For me at least. It always has been."

She took his hands and pulled him back down. He felt her trembling. Her eyes wet. "I grew up in the worst way. I was one of them. The children. I know the horrors. I know what Sam is going through. What waits for her. And I'm asking you to let me help you end this. It's a fucking hydra and it'll only be one head of the snake, but let's cut it off completely."

Long moments went by. Black was torn, he was here to save Sam. Right now, he didn't care about doing something bigger. He was sick of abstracts. But if it increased his chances to bring Sam home? His mind flashed on a million images, faster than any computer. *Sam, the children, Nicola.* Somehow, they were going to be alright.

"So, you're as fucked up as I am?"

Her eyes glistened but she laughed. "You have no idea."

He sat back and smiled. "Well—maybe a little bit."

"Listen. The docks. The warehouses. They're gonna have records. If they're on a computer I can break in." She pictured the way he would do it—kicking through doors or knocking down walls. "Different than you, but I can do it. But if they aren't online—if they're handwritten, in ledgers or coded notebooks— I could miss them."

One day, he thought. He hoped the gods fucking with his life went after someone else. Some cosmic vacation. Twenty-four hours.

"Okay."

"Okay?"

"Okay. One day. That means I go tonight."

"No. We go tonight."

"No way."

"What if you can't just walk out with their records? What if they are on a server the size of a refrigerator? You're going to load them on your back and walk out?"

"I'll figure it out."

"I'm going. Or I'll call your FBI and go myself. You can't stop me. I'm not some little girl that hides in the dark."

"I can tie you up or just knock you out or something."

Nicola rolled her eyes.

"Jesus, you're fucking stubborn."

"Yeah. Well."

"Yeah."

Her eyes wet, he reached out to wipe away a tear, she held onto his hand. Kissed it. "Thank you."

"You're still stubborn as hell."

"Yeah." She chewed on her lip. "You up for it?"

"You being stubborn?"

"That too. But— I'm putting my life in your hands." She pointed to his side. "So let me take a look."

"I'm fine."

"It's my life." She stood, reached behind her, and locked the door. Reached for his shirt. "Let me take a look."

She could hear him grunt, deep and low, a soft rumbling from his chest, but he stood up. She pulled the shirt over his head.

The room felt dark, but the computers threw a lot of soft light. She liked that she could see him.

He was built in hard slabs and sharp angles.

Black didn't give her much time to see how he was healing— he was already reaching for her shirt. Wrapped her in his arms and slid it up her back. She let him pull it over her head.

She was built in gentle lines and soft curves.

He smelled of the sea. Salt and sun and brine.

She smelled of the island. Cinnamon and orchid and vanilla.

He pulled her close, let her curves fill in the angles. Let her warm breath dance across his chest, the smell of her filling his lungs. Could feel her heart pounding against him. Her body trembling under his hands.

She liked that she could feel him shaking too. From need or the same fear of not being perfect. Her head against his chest, his heart beating strong and loud in her ears. She felt him breathe her in, matching each rise of her chest, making her rhythm his own.

"How much time do we have?"

"Two, three hours I guess."

"Damn." He grazed her lips—his first taste of her. "I guess we better get started then."

CHAPTER
FORTY-NINE

Rodriguez had spent most of his afternoon in the company of an independent taxi driver, who seemed to have heard English for the first time that very day. He did say *excuse me* and *sorry boss* a lot and got lots of practice as he belched and farted back and forth across the city. The FBI agent was thankful for the island's moderate temperatures and ocean breezes, opting to keep the windows rolled down instead of gagging on the man's flatulence and listening to the death rattle of the under-powered air conditioner.

The taxi driver, in a faded blue Corolla as nondescript as any vehicle could be, was adept at weaving in and out of traffic and seemed to relish that they were following a cop.

Curpen led them back and forth across Port Saint Louis; he didn't seem to be in a hurry to get anywhere and was content to do much of his police work on the phone sitting in his SUV or in various cafes.

Rodriguez watched the cop sit down for dinner and spied a car rental only a block away. He was almost sorry to send his driver away but was soon sitting in a new SUV of his own, the smell of new plastic and fabric a welcome relief from the day's gaseous adventures.

Night had fallen and Rodriguez was convinced he'd wasted the day. He looked at his watch. Half-past nine. The past hour and a half waiting for the cop to come back out of the police station.

...

Curpen had spent the last hour talking with the elder Kronmüller; the South African had tasked him with ending this tonight.

He came out of his office, jumped in his official vehicle, and darted into the traffic. Scanned his mirrors.

He'd plenty of reasons to feel paranoid and suspected someone had been following him for most of the day. The moment Rodriguez rented a vehicle, the service manager had reached out. The protocols that found Black had been sent to hotels, car rentals, and escort services; to look for anyone who looked like they could be a contractor. Military or private. Official or shady. Especially for an American.

Curpen wove through the traffic and checked the mirror again. Yeah, the agent was still behind him. Good.

The dream team was balanced on the edge; they needed sleep and hung on by sheer force of will. Everything else had been put aside, but they hadn't been able to find anything on the auction. They knew enough to know they might never find anything, floating on the near-infinite DarkNet and missing the actual dark web sites they needed to mine.

Alix wanted to contact Nicola directly. She could reach out through a dozen forums and then be sure Alexandrescu would take up the hunt.

They couldn't discuss it with Michaels. Her team lobbied for it the night before and were shot down by both agents, and now Rodriguez was AWOL.

Except for one cryptic text—

ON 2 SMTH — SYS

—Michaels's partner had been out of touch the entire day.

Julius said he'd seen the senior agent popping pills— *they didn't even want to imagine what that was about.*

CHAPTER
FIFTY

It was dark when Rícard left the house, the streets settling for the night. He needed to hustle if was going to make it to the docks. He was calculating how to spin what he'd learned, admittedly not much, into a bigger payday. Curpen was bitching as if it was Rícard's fault the American hadn't been killed. He could have finished the job if Curpen had done his part with the FBI. And if the cop aimed better, this would have been behind them.

The boy hadn't known much, but Rícard wanted to make sure. Besides, he was beautiful, which opened the evening up to more possibilities. Rícard didn't have time to wine and dine the boy. The knife brought compliance if not enthusiasm, the boy's fear a powerful stimulant for one of them.

Rícard had showered, congratulated himself for his foresight to bring a change of clothing. He wasn't worried about forensic evidence. Curpen would take care of that or find himself answering questions about his own adventures. Rícard had two years of detailed ledgers and photos, several of which he thought were artistic enough to be sold in high-end galleries, not hidden away as blackmail material. No, it was only that Rícard was a bit of a dandy and abhorred the idea of blood on his clothes.

What Rícard did have for Curpen was confirmation of what the boy passed on to the gypsy witch; duplicates of the original club security tapes which if seen by the wrong people, could prove tricky for both of them.

The boy also told him she'd never met the American, Tommy Black she called him, before two nights ago in the market.

Rícard recounted that night to him, the way the two hung on each other, slobbered and groped each in the streets, and laughed at the boy's transparent jealousy. How he had watched her pass on her phone number and address in hopes the American would come.

The boy's instincts and reactions confirmed what Curpen had told him—besides being a witch, the woman was a whore.

Rícard still had time. He'd stop and get a drink, give himself a few minutes to think about how he might leverage what little he found. He fingered the knife in his pocket. If nothing else, maybe Curpen would pay him to visit the witch.

CHAPTER
FIFTY-ONE

Kronmüller returned from his hike, refreshed and feeling stronger than he had in years, emanating power and confidence. You could see it on the cowering faces and demeanor of the help, the way Grip stood and addressed him when asked after Lina, the way Ringer hesitated to tell him Ouderling was waiting.

His father could wait. He showered, dressed, and thought to spend time with Lina. He knew she no longer loved him, but she was smart enough to pretend affection and passion. His mind was clear. He knew what had to be done to win her back. Soon enough, he promised himself. He unlocked the door.

Lina heard his arrival and rose from a chair to meet him. His blood was up, and he barely greeted her before spinning her and bending her over the bed. He fumbled with her jeans; how he hated her in anything but a dress. Pulled them down and ripped her panties off. He didn't take time to undress; he barely undid his own pants and entered her roughly from behind.

She cried out, and he pulled her by her thick hair until her back was arched and he could stand tall while biting her shoulder. His teeth brought blood. She cried out in pain, used her hips to buck backward and knock him away long enough to spin and fall back to the bed. If he was going to rape her she would at least force him to look her in the face.

Kronmüller looked at her and froze. Her eyes gouged and burned from her head. Nose and lips and breasts had been hacked away, the flesh still raw and oozing. Her arms, once long and elegant, now ended in stumps of cauterized flesh. He looked down past her jeans. Her legs still smoldered and the smell of burnt flesh made him gag and fight not to retch.

Kronmüller staggered backward, tripped and crashed to the floor. Lina sat up, and he crabbed further, scrambling to pull his pants back on. She stood, pulled her jeans back up, and pulled away from him.

Lina watched as he tried to rise, his mouth open in a silent scream as he pawed at the door. Using the doorknob, he pulled himself to his feet, slipped past the door, and was gone.

Heinrich waited in the shadows behind his truck, phone to his ear, assault rifle in his hands. Burke and Kappas were arming themselves. Both were hard men in their fifties who'd seen and taken part in unspeakable atrocities as part of the Rhodesian Security Forces counter-insurgency efforts in Zimbabwe and the Congo. Knives, sidearms, and a pair of Remington tactical shotguns.

Gustave jacked the slide on a Glock, grabbed for another magazine just as a fifth man, his arms and neck covered in Russian ink, joined the group. He traded his spent cigarette for another.

"Put the fucking cigarette out," Heinrich hissed. Suraav was by all accounts a psychopath with an appetite for children, but forced on them by the South Africans.

Suraav pinched out the flame, tucked the butt into his pocket. Looked at what was left in the back of the truck, grabbed for a knife and a Ruger. Did a quick takedown of the weapon, reassembled it, and slapped in a mag.

Heinrich took in the rag-tag team, mostly squared away, and if anything, overkill for their objectives. "This should be an easy trek." Gestured to the little informant. "The squirrel says the primary is injured."

"The kids?" Burke asked.

Heinrich looked at them one by one; he wanted to make sure they understood, especially Suraav. "The kids are outside the objective. The man and two women are the mission."

"I watched him trying to swim in the lagoon this morning," Gustave said. He hated being called the squirrel—the intelligence source—but in this case, admitted it was the role he was playing.

He smiled to himself. It was painfully obvious he was the only one with any intelligence here. "Looks like he's been shot and could hardly move."

"Keep your wits about you," Heinrich said. "Intel says he's one of the NATO pukes. Special Ops. American."

Suraav spit. "Americans are pussies."

"So are Russians—" Burke grunted.

Four actions happened so fast it would be hard to tell which came first. Suraav's blade snicked out of its metal scabbard and pressed against the big merc's throat as Kappas jammed his shotgun into the Russian's gut while Burke's .45 shoved Suraav's head aside only to find the weapon pulled from his hand, spun back in place and pressed against his own forehead.

Gustave clapped his hands. "That was awesome! Do it again. Do it again!"

They all glared at the annoying little squirrel. "Just saying. The American won't have to be too impressive if you kill each other first."

The weapons were being returned to their places when Heinrich's phone vibrated.

Kronmüller sat in the chair placed front and center of his father's desk. He could feel Grip and Ringer standing guard behind him as Ouderling perched on the desk's front edge in front of him, phone in hand.

The image of Lina fresh in his mind, Kronmüller was still shaken. He'd arrived home with renewed confidence, ready to take on his father and the world, but now, couldn't even listen as the elder Kronmüller told him what was happening.

Instead, he was doing his best to transfer the gruesome image—*he'd known it wasn't real*—to his father. He almost had it; was in the process of burning out his father's eyes when the old man kicked him in the shin to get his attention.

"You're shutting this down. After tonight, after this final transfer, you're done. Your bitch, the American. It's over. No more. Do you understand?"

Kronmüller couldn't hear him much less care what he was saying. He ground himself down into his chair as if it would protect him and tried not to laugh out loud when he looked at his father. It was almost over. *Eyes were gone, and he was lopping off his hands and feet.* Ouderling kicked him again.

"Yeah, sure. I understand."

"You'll put this perversion behind you or I swear to our Lord, I'll bury you in the ground beside your brother."

"Got it." Kronmüller had been thinking he might have his brother dug up and burned. He wanted no trace of him to exist. Or maybe he'd chop him up and scatter his corpse, let the hyenas grind his remains, their shit spread across the lands until it dried up and blew away on the wind.

Ouderling looked at Grip and Ringer to make sure they were on board. Undid the mute button and spoke into the smart phone's speaker.

"No half-way. Get it done."

CHAPTER
FIFTY-TWO

Nicola perched on the rooftop of a dock warehouse taking in the show of force at Kronmüller Industries and Shipping. She counted a half-dozen armed men through the pair of binoculars in her hands—tough-looking dock workers and shoremen with assault rifles and compact submachine guns. There had to be at least that many more she couldn't see, either inside or simply out of view.

She had no idea of the dock's usual activities. Except for one industrious driver on a forklift, work seemed to be on hold. As much as their weapons, the men's body language and their curt orders and replies told her they were on special alert. *Had they known they were coming?* That didn't seem possible as until just a few hours ago, neither had she.

She hadn't known she'd spend the afternoon and evening the way she had either. The four hours exploring and sharing each other, in and out of near sleep and wrapped in each other's arms, mirrored the past two days—surprising, intense, satisfying.

Both were generous, yet cautious, maybe in fear of setting the bar so high it could never be met again. Four hours began stretching to five, and she'd only wanted to drift and luxuriate in the glow when he whispered it was time to go.

Nicola dressed in silence in the dark and tried not to be hurt as Black's actions became more terse and efficient. She knew he was planning his departure and knew she would help, but was thankful he could neither see on her face nor hear in her voice the realization that sometime tomorrow, they'd be parted forever.

She double-checked the headphones in her ears and their connection to her phone. Still on, battery near fully charged. Somewhere on the other side of the digital tether, Black. The binoculars inexpensive, but they worked for the children's bird watching in the rainforests, and they worked well enough for her to see Black would be facing overwhelming odds to break in. She scanned for him in the shadows. Nothing—no sign of him. She was beginning to panic. How had she ever talked him into letting her come along?

"Everything will be fine," Nicola whispered to the night, the distant boats and barges. "He's done this a million times. No sweat."

She forced herself to breathe. Felt her heart racing. Threatening to explode from her chest. "This is fucking crazy."

There! She saw a shadow uncoil from the surrounding darkness. Black making his way toward an armed guard.

"Tommy? Can you hear me? This is crazy. Let's just go to the police. Your FBI. Tommy?"

She watched Black move closer, then held her breath as he traded his phone for a knife.

Black slipped the phone into his pocket and drew out the blackened tactical blade. He lunged forward as the guard passed, slammed the heavy steel butt of the knife into the base of the man's skull.

Black caught him in one hand as he dropped, his other catching the assault rifle just before it would hit and clatter on the pavement, then pulled the man deep into the shadows.

Nicola was lightheaded—she tried to breathe but instead found herself gulping huge chunks of air. She knew what they were here for, what the stakes were, but she hadn't wanted to witness a murder. She couldn't be sure that she hadn't just seen exactly that. Black had struck with the speed of an Olympic fencer and the man had fallen.

Her phone vibrated. Set as dim as possible and still be read, she looked down at the text. Ruth.

STAY AWAY CALL POLICE

The words hit her as hard as Black had hit the armed man. She dialed her phone.

It rang, but no answer. One ring. Two. Three! Voice mail. Damn it! She sent back a text.

CALL!

She redialed. *Nothing!* Tried Black. No answer.

Found him in the glass but lost him again as he slipped like a wraith back into the shadows. "Come on, Come on—"

Nothing! She was shaking so bad, she had trouble pressing the buttons. She tried Ruth again. "Please, please, pick up." She listened to it ring. Voice mail.

She started to dial for Black again, scrolled back further, and dialed René. Whatever was going on, he could reach out and bring cavalry long before she could.

The small house was quiet. No movement other than a cell phone vibrating on a small table. The phone lit the dark and the vibration spun it in circles, around and around as it danced near the edge.

Another ring and it toppled to the floor.

The phone continued to vibrate and spin on the simple hardwood floor, the blueish light casting a dim glow across René's naked and mutilated body.

Nicola fought her panic. This wasn't a case of intuition or some nebulous premonition. She and perhaps the most violent man she'd ever met were at the beginning of tearing back the cover of an entire enterprise of perversion and horror, much the same as she'd grown up with and then dedicated her talents and intellect to destroying. And now, the woman who in nearly every way had become her mother was reaching out to tell her something was very, very wrong.

She searched the shadows, forcing herself to be methodical, fighting against the fear that threatened to burst the heart within her chest. Nothing. No sign of anything or anyone other than the workers who continued on, oblivious to the violence that stalked them. She looked at her phone. *One last try.*

CHAPTER
FIFTY-THREE

Heinrich waited in the dark as Gustave picked the lock on the back door. The little man seemed to know what he was doing and the tumblers shifted and fell into place. Heinrich looked upward. Suraav perched three stories above on a fire escape waiting for the sign to enter. Burke cut the phone and electrical lines as Kappas silenced the dog next door. Heinrich nodded once and the five men entered the shelter.

They took in the huge room. No other light than their flashlights and the glow from a few battery-powered electronics. Heinrich gestured with his light for Gustave to investigate the second floor.

Suraav stepped from the fire escape through a third-floor window into a room stacked with boxes and racks of clothes on hangers. Storage. Each step placed and chosen, yet the floor creaked and groaned in protest as he crept toward the door.

He entered an empty hall. Closed doors lined both sides, and he cautiously approached the first.

Burke and Kappas moved into the locker rooms; their flashlights reflecting and multiplying off the mirrors to light up the lockers, shower rooms, and the bathroom stalls. It had been years since they contracted out their skills for more than a bit of intimidation, but they still moved as a lethal unit.

...

Heinrich made his way toward the back, threw open a door, and leapt to the middle of a small bedroom. His flashlight swept the room and lit up rolls of gauze and bandages, rubbing alcohol and antibiotics. Maybe the squirrel was right. The American had been shot.

Gustave entered the last room on the second floor—his fifth. Two neatly made beds, stuffed animals against the pillows, posters, and photos tacked to the walls, a small desk and table. He moved to the closet, the gun in his hand ready to fire. He stepped to the side, used the wall for cover, and opened the door.

Sitting in the dark, a wide-eyed young boy huddled against a teenage girl; the boy maybe ten, and the girl no older than fourteen. She held a huge kitchen knife above her head as if to ward away the Devil.

Rayln held the knife with both hands, ready to defend herself and her ten-year-old charge against the man who stood in the open closet door. She could hear someone else upstairs, cursing out loud, stomping, and throwing furniture around.

Gustave turned back to the waif-like couple, the girl's huge brown eyes reminded him of his long-dead sister, his hand raised to his lips warning them to silence. He could hear Suraav coming down the stairs and Gustave closed the closet door just as the Russian stepped into the room.

"Anything?"

Gustave shook his head. "Not here."

The Russian glared at him and Gustave thought he might have to shoot him just to make it out.

"Fuck." The Russian spat on the floor and stomped out.

The intruder's boot steps echoed off the tile walls and floor while their flashlights swept back and forth over the girl's showers. A hint of light crept through small cracks in the walls to a hidden boiler room where most of the children crowded around a single candle near the back. Aleeza at Ruth's side clutching her leg.

Ruth put down her useless phone—no signal could get back here—and reached for the one weapon they kept in the shelter, a thirty-year-old Remington shotgun.

She could hear the men kicking open the bathroom stalls and cursing under their breath before moving on to the other side and doing the same. As best she could tell there were at least two men. She knew more were bound to be spread throughout the house. She guessed five. More would be too cumbersome. She assumed they were here for the American. Even injured, Black was a trained soldier, so any less might be inadequate.

She hadn't wanted to message Nicola but didn't have time to call and explain to the police what she thought was happening.

Ruth hugged the little girl, disengaged her arms, then pushed a shell into the chamber. She wasn't a soldier like Black, but was no stranger to violence. "Stay very, very quiet."

Heinrich took in the computers. He couldn't imagine what they were doing in this setting. He touched one of the keyboards and all three screens came alive. Front and center was a still of Kronmüller. He'd love that. Heard shouting from the main room.

Gustave was at the stove with a spoon in his mouth when he heard Suraav dragging the boy and girl down the stairs. She was kicking and twisting like a banshee until he threw her down the last steps. She crashed to the floor, and by the time she scrambled away on hands and knees, he'd shoved the boy to land beside her, snatched her hair, and pulled her back to her feet.

"Look what I find in room you told me empty. Maybe we go back top and check again all."

Suraav's eyes were glazed. Besides the annoying English, the rumors were true.

Gustave looked at the children. In his own creed, as twisted as it might be, his not turning them in was as much a promise of their safety as if he'd put it in writing and signed with blood. "It's not what we came for."

"Yeah, yes. I make do."

Heinrich came from Nicola's room—Burke and Kappas from the locker rooms.

They took in the frightened children and the two men facing off.

Certainly more than the one injured American and two women, this was exactly what Heinrich had been afraid of. "So what's this?"

The Russian kept his eyes trained on Gustave. "He say is empty but then I find this two."

"Fuck you," Gustave said. "Let her go."

"Nope. I not think so." Suraav turned to Heinrich and the mercs.

"Anything?"

"A few supplies," Heinrich said. "Looks like the squirrel's right. He's hurt. " Turned to the other. "You?"

"Nothing," Burke said.

"Not down here," Kappas added.

Heinrich pointed to the girl. "They have to be somewhere."

Suraav jerked her off balance by her hair, pushed her down to her knees and ground her face against his crotch. "Leave her me. She will tell them up."

She twisted to look up at him in horror.

Gustave pulled his gun, loosely pointed at Suraav, and crossed the room to help the girl from the floor.

The big men were impressed—the squirrel had balls, challenging the psychotic Russian. Suraav just grinned.

"Get out of my house!"

Suraav spun to see the old woman stepping from the shadows and a shotgun pointed at his chest. She moved it back and forth between him and the squirrel. Her hands shook, but at ten feet couldn't really miss.

"Let her go!"

Rayln tried to pull away but Gustave held on.

"Hey hey hey." Suraav put his hands up. "We leave. Is good. Just is mistake. Please to put gun down."

Ruth heard the patter of little steps behind her. Fought her instincts but turned to glance backward when Aleeza crashed into her legs from behind.

Gustave pushed Rayln behind him. Ruth saw him from the corner of her eye, jerked back in panic, and pulled the trigger. Nothing. She looked down, flipped off the safety, and in that instant, Suraav darted forward, his knife stabbing deep into her soft flesh.

Staggered by the pain, she fell back another step and the shotgun went off, the blast high and wide but making the other men dive for cover. Gustave ducked and pulled his own trigger, the hurried blast grazing Suraav in the shoulder. The Russian, as fast and smooth as the American cowboy movies he grew up on, pulled his gun with his other hand and shot Gustave in the face.

Blood and bone exploded backward and Rayln's wannabe protector fell at her feet. She scrambled backward only to crash into Heinrich.

Suraav turned back to the old woman. She lay on the floor gasping and clutching her side, blood pouring from her hands. Suraav scooped up her shotgun, looked at the other men, daring them to say anything, pumped another shell into the chamber, and blasted her in the chest.

Rayln screamed and Heinrich pulled her up and pushed her behind him, strode across the floor, slammed the Russian in the head with the butt of his rifle.

The Russian took the hit. It rocked his head back, and he could feel blood pouring from a gash, but stayed on his feet. It had been worth it, and like usual he thought, he was the only one who was accomplishing any part of their objective.

Heinrich stood over the old woman. Shapeless and bloody like a bag of meat. Pushed her over with his foot. Aleeza lay on the floor, covered in the old woman's blood, wheezing for air.

Heinrich dialed his phone, hit the speaker so the others could hear, and moved his assault rifle to cover Suraav. Suraav stood tall in defiance.

"The American and his bitch aren't here. Your Russian fucktard killed the old lady."

"Not mine. SA's. Sure she's dead?"

"Yeah. No doubts. Got a little kid here." Heinrich poked at Aleeza with his foot. "Still breathing but she's not moving much. I think she's shot."

"Anyone else?"

Heinrich looked at Gustave. Half his face missing. "Your squirrel's gone. The fucktard again."

The big man looked at Rayln and the boy, both shaking and pale, both in shock. "No one else here, but you were right— signs you clipped him. Hospital supplies. IVs and shit. What about the fucktard?"

Heinrich, Burke, and Kappas covered him, but the Russian just grinned.

They could hear Curpen's heavy sigh on the other end. *What the fuck was is it with Russians?*

"Off-limits. Leave the kid. Get back to the docks."

The mercs eased their weapons. Suraav, the side of his head drenched in blood, grinned like an idiot, spat on the floor toward Gustave, and stormed out.

Burke and Kappas looked at the devastation without judgment. Both spent their years destroying the lives of others, whether as soldiers or hired mercenaries. The dead squirrel, a dead woman, and dying child—no reason to waste tears any more than would be cried over them when their time came.

Heinrich nodded approval to Rayln as she darted forward and knelt over Ruth and Aleeza. He saw the grimace on her face as she looked away from the old woman; saw the spark of hope in her eyes when she realized the child, pale as snow, was still alive.

It was out of his hands now. *If the little girl died, she died.*

CHAPTER
FIFTY-FOUR

E xcept for the forklift, the docks were quiet, work on hold, and the men on edge. The brilliant floodlights set to light up the night blew out the detail and color of vast expanses of empty pavement and high steel walls but served to blacken the shadows, leaving a colorless landscape in high contrast.

Ships lumbered into the harbor, while hulking silhouettes waiting their turn sat on the horizon. The flow to and from the outside world never ended. Incredible, Whank thought, that two-hundred years ago, with ships riding on sail and oar, the port was even busier.

The forklift was loud. Bearings were grinding and on their way to melting into a solid mass of steel in the rear end. Another thing for him to worry about. Leaking diesel with a tire that had to be filled every time they wanted to use it, but, as long as it got through the night.

The men with guns, armed on Heinrich's orders, had him second-guessing his decision to stay on. Rumors and gossip spread quickly on an island. Police, agents from the FBI, and now, the *American*.

Whank wasn't ready to retire. Like most of the world, he couldn't really afford it, but was thinking seriously about getting back to the continent. He'd known this would catch up with them someday. Maybe it was time to take the job his wife's uncle offered him in Albania, helping run his shipping operations out of the port of Durrës.

Somebody was spooked. They'd been told to destroy everything, and then burn it all down. No chance of records or breadcrumbs leading back to the South African. Yeah. It was a sign to get the fuck out of here.

He turned from the forklift he was directing to the big dually pick-up pulling up behind him.

Tiaan parked in the middle of the pavement, shoved a gun in his belt, took a shotgun from behind the seat, and stepped from the truck.

"Says to be alert," he shouted over the grinding forklift. He racked the shotgun for emphasis.

Whank gestured toward both sides of the warehouse. Hard looking men with AKs. "Think we're good!"

Curpen sat in a dark SUV, watching the warehouse from afar. He scanned the shadows, finding nothing, and watched Tiaan get out of his truck.

He couldn't hear from this distance but imagined the conversation as Tiaan chambered his shotgun and Whank responded by pointing to the men with his M4. The men were cocky, itching for a fight, and why not? There were half a dozen men, armed to the teeth, and they only had one American to worry about.

He watched as Whank and Tiaan destroyed the records and physical evidence of Kronmüller's secret export business. Slow as fuck, but getting it done.

Angry at himself for not killing Black at the club. He'd let himself get rattled by the FBI breathing down his neck, but Curpen was sure he must have hit him at least once, and maybe more. He'd fired five times.

Of course, one round caught Bradley, tearing out his throat. It hadn't been planned that way, but it would have come eventually. The American had rolled and bounced off the walls like a rubber ball. Surely, some of the rounds had hit. So, one *injured* American.

The phone lit up and vibrated on the leather passenger seat. He played it through the vehicle's Bluetooth system. "Yeah?"

"The American and his bitch aren't here. Your Russian fucktard killed the old lady."

Shit. She was on the list—his list anyway, but don't blame the Russian on him. "Not mine. SA's. Sure she's dead?"

"Yeah. No doubts. Got a little kid here. Still breathing but she's not moving much. Looks like she's shot."

"Anyone else?"

"Your squirrel's gone. The fucktard again."

Fucking Russians, even more incompetent than Americans— no wonder they're always at each other's throats. *Really just a contest of who fucked up the world the most.*

"No one else here, but you were right—signs you clipped him. Hospital supplies. IVs and shit. What about the fucktard?"

The American had snuck away, a fucking coward, and now remained a threat. Curpen sighed. He wouldn't be going home early tonight. "Off-limits. Leave the kid. Get back to the docks."

He watched Whank direct the forklift. They were moving any and all office equipment, records, and computers, any physical evidence that might link them to the trafficking to the middle of the lot, where a bonfire would make sure every last item was destroyed. Orders from the Elder. No records. No DNA. So far, it looked like the failing forklift had managed only a few empty barrels.

Whank lifted his radio before realizing it was his phone that was ringing.

"Yeah?"

"Stay on point. They missed the American." Curpen hung up. If the gypsy was as good as they said, she'd have pointed him here. Curpen looked forward to the chance of emptying an entire mag into the American's heart.

With Heinrich gone, these two were in charge. *They're all fucking idiots.* Not smart enough to know he was out here watching.

He wouldn't have been surprised if the crippled American sauntered past them and stole the evidence they'd been tasked to destroy.

He laughed when he thought about the other one. The FBI agent. *Mister Million-Dollar-Smile.* He looked exactly like a guy he remembered from an old black-and-white American TV show. Just as hapless and just as helpless. Curpen had lost him in a parking garage. Oldest, easiest trick in the book. Drive to the top, the agent could only follow so far before becoming obvious, then walk down and drive out in his own vehicle. Hard to believe something so simple worked, but here he sat.

He reached into his pockets, pulled out a small vial of uncut coke. Snorted a bump, and even before finishing the inhalation, felt the rush energize his entire being. It was going to be a long night, but Curpen was ready for anything.

Rodriguez took photos of the warehouse and the men outside it. All armed. All on alert for something. Guarding what looked like a pile of steel drums and cardboard boxes in the middle of the night couldn't be normal.

Not the greatest camera, but adequate. He'd picked it up in the tourist shop across from the hotel. A long zoom, but worthless in the dark where Curpen sat. He thought how he might get closer, but wasn't seeing it.

He let the man think he lost him in the parking garage. Not that difficult. He used the tradecraft drilled into him by his instructors in Quantico and more valuable, the lessons learned from his partner chasing bad guys across the streets of Chicago. Some of those neighborhoods were as much foreign countries to him as was this island nation in the middle of the Indian Ocean.

What was Curpen doing? Why was he hiding from the men on the docks? Staking them out? Rodriguez started having doubts— one of the dangers of working alone. Maybe he'd been wrong.

He wanted to call Michaels, the senior agent was going to be pissed. This was going against all protocol and training, but his phone died hours ago; no chance to charge it or buy a charger as he'd been afraid to lose his quarry. He'd play his hand and see this through.

Jian heard... *something.* A rhythmic tapping of metal on metal, coming from the shadows behind him.

He turned back to the forklift. The driver set down a stack of steel drums they were destroying—who the hell knew what that was about?

Sure, they cut a few corners loading and packing the huge containers, but in the three years he'd been working in this yard, he'd never witnessed any real wrongdoing, certainly nothing criminal. But there they stood, Tiaan and Whank, making sure it got done. Both armed, Whank with an assault rifle like the one Tiaan now held.

None of the others knew what was going on but everyone knows people aren't ordered to carry guns unless trouble is coming. Jian was the kind of guy who did his job, didn't ask questions and kept his mouth shut, and triple pay for the night bought a lot of silence from the others. He wondered if it was enough— this felt like a war was coming.

The tapping continued. *He couldn't place it.* Then it stopped.

Jian stepped into the inky shadows and into Black's fist—the blow caught him high on the temple. There was no need for a follow-up. Black pulled him deeper and took his radio.

Whank answered his phone. Heinrich.

"On my way. Keep your eyes open. The American got away."

"How?"

The call clicked off.

Tiaan saw Whank's face tighten. Signaled to the forklift driver. *Cut it!* The driver stopped in mid-turn, cut the engine. It coughed and sputtered, welcomed its respite. The driver reached for his own gun.

Tiaan keyed the radio.

"Jian? Come back."

The radio squelched, the sound scraping the chalkboard of a nearly silent night. A distant barge answered with a mournful bellow, but the radio only returned static. Whank and Tiaan looked at each other. Shrugged.

Whank tried his own radio. "Markus. Come back." Nothing— "Markus? How you doing out there, buddy? This is Whank. Come back." Static.

"He's here." Tiaan jacked the shotgun, the clack-clack echoed off the steel structures across the docks.

Tiaan looked to the far side of the warehouse. Keyed his radio. "Gordo — come back."

The radio squawked. "Yeah, boss?"

"Get back here now."

They saw the man a hundred meters away at the far end of the building, assault rifle in hand, jogging his way back.

Black slipped through the maze of shadows high in the rafters of the warehouse. An enormous vertical I-beam made an easy ladder for him to climb down. His movements obscured in shadow, hidden by the lifts and electric winches, the worktables, welding torches, stacks of barrels, and steel drums.

From the back of the warehouse, he could see the forklift driver reaching for his own weapon—a Chinese Mac-10 ripoff. Maybe not as dependable as the real thing, but potentially just as deadly.

Black looked at the two-inch-wide strap holding a row of tall steel Argon canisters lashed to a rolling metal rack. Each one a potential three-hundred-pound bomb of steel and gas, but unlike the movies where a single shot resulted in a fantastic cinematic explosion, Black might unload the entire magazine without anything happening.

Luck was just another tool to be used, but in Black's experience, only showed its face when coupled with action. A single slice from the razor's edge of his tactical knife released the six canisters.

A roll of the dice.

The tanks, sixty pounds of steel each, toppled over, bounced like a set of bowling pins onto the floor and into each other, narrowly missing Black's legs when two of the canisters' valves exploded off. Spinning like a deadly top across the floor, the first tank scythed into workbenches and toppled machinery, crushing everything in its path.

The second one could never have been planned or repeated. *Physics in random motion produced random outcomes.*

The gas, pressurized to six thousand pounds, pushed against the back wall, overcoming its inertia. An instant later, the steel cylinder rocketed across the floor as straight as a torpedo.

The men outside heard the steel ringing on the concrete and had just seconds to respond. The driver jumped from the forklift as the three-hundred pounds of steel tank and gas, a high wake of sparks trailing it all the way from the warehouse, slammed into its side.

Diesel from the tank ignited in a roaring ball of flame, flipped the massive five-ton machine high into the air and catapulted chunks of metal and shrapnel two-hundred feet away.

The explosion burned the oxygen and sucked the air from Whank's lungs and bowled him off his feet. Tiaan, equilibrium gone along with his hearing, tottered on rubber legs, and emptied his mag into the warehouse before realizing his mistake.

Another tank exploded as yet another spun its way toward the wide dock door, tearing out part of the block wall and spinning across the street.

Ean staggered to his knees. The warehouse still in flux—a curtain of dust and debris filling the air. Another part of the front wall gave way as machinery continued to topple, but the steel tanks, nearly empty, slowed to a stop. He looked back as Tiaan fell to the ground but locked his eyes in horror beyond him on Gordo.

The man staggered, still on his feet, a jagged piece of metal the size of a dinner plate sticking from his neck, blood squirting in successively shorter and shorter arcs from his throat. The man trying to hold his head on until he fell face-first onto the pavement.

Whank was just getting his feet under him, his right knee unwilling to support his weight, when Black cracked him on the head with the AK.

Tiaan twisted from the gruesome sight of Gordo's nearly decapitated head to the even more terrifying sight of Black standing over him with an assault rifle.

Curpen saw the flames, heard the thunderous boom, and felt the ground shake beneath the SUV. He saw Black, it could only be him, literally black, a silhouette against the flames, slam Whank in the head with the butt of the assault rifle.

Prodded at gunpoint, Tiaan staggered to his feet. He pulled and dragged Whank through the smoke and debris back inside.

Curpin thought to get out, to take on the American. He'd have the element of surprise, but his arms and legs stayed in place, heavy as stone.

The rational thing to do was wait for Heinrich. The man should be back at any moment. Together they would end this fucking American.

CHAPTER
FIFTY-FIVE

Nicola stepped across the dark shelter floor. Shadows and silence, coupled with the fear of what she might find, thrust her into an alien world. She turned her phone on for the light. Tripped on Gustave, fortunate not to see his face but slipped on the blood, crashing to the floor.

She cried out when she saw Ruth—the flesh ravaged from the shotgun, her face frozen in rage and defiance. The image triggered a thousand more that came in a blinding rush; sights and sounds and the smells of Hell from her war-torn youth. The pain multiplied, Nicola felt her heart clench and threaten to crush her past and future from existence. Condemned to spend eternity with horrors she thought were behind her.

Eternity lasted moments, and Nicola slowly became aware of life around her.

She turned her head and saw Rayln and then Samut, but it took moments more to realize they huddled over Aleeza.

Nicola willed her heart to work again, pushed the horrors and pain back inside, crawled on hands and knees to the children.

"Hold the light on her," she said, handing the phone to Rayln.

The small child was covered in blood, but she was alive, her breath labored and wheezing. Nicola ripped the tiny t-shirt, wiped at the drying blood to assess the damage.

She turned to Samut. "Find some water."

He sprang into action, ran to the kitchen, fumbled in the dark for the sink, and came back with a steel pan half-filled with water.

Nicola tore a part of her own shirt, soaked it in the pan, and wiped at the blood. She heard the girl's struggle for air whistling in and out and soon found the source. A small shard of bone had pierced the girl's chest. She'd seen enough in her life to imagine what was going on inside.

She didn't dare remove it, the surrounding flesh bruised and swollen, the girl so pale in the waning light as to be transparent.

Somehow, word of Nicola's arrival traveled, perhaps simply the energy of good versus evil, and soon the room filled with the other children. Candles were lit and soon a lantern and then another.

Horror was nothing new to any of them yet all hearts broke at seeing Ruth and with fear for their newest little sister.

Rayln returned from the dark and covered Ruth and Gustave, then tried to quiet a couple of the others, hyperventilating and on the verge of hysteria.

Nicola, tears in her own eyes, scooped up the tiny body. Grabbed for her keys.

She sped through the streets. Her hands twisting and turning the wheel, pounding on the horn when needed, and stroking the sweat-drenched hair of the little girl on the seat beside her.

She bounced off a car parked on the street, pin-balled off another, feathered the brakes while stomping on the gas, urged the little truck forward, willed the lights green, and the intersections clear, and fumbled to text Black.

CHAPTER
FIFTY-SIX

Whank and Tiaan were taped and gagged. Some kind of industrial duct tape. *Where was the good stuff when Black needed it?*

Tiaan gained consciousness bound with packing wire—the thin steel cutting into the flesh of his wrists and ankles, his knees and elbows.

Black returned and dropped a dozen large folders, three cell phones, and a laptop onto the scarred wooden desk.

"What's the password?"

Tiaan couldn't process what was happening. The wire was excruciating and his limbs were swelling.

"What's the password?" Black's voice as calm as if he sat at a cafe ordering coffee.

"What?"

Black cracked him in the head.

There was no escape. He'd entered Hell and was now being entertained by the Devil himself. What could it matter if he told? Damnation was just beginning. Tiaan had trouble making his voice work but finally got it out. "Password."

Black flipped open the clamshell and typed in the letters—

PASSWORD

The computer lit up and gave him full access. He scanned the obvious. A dozen labeled folders. Shipping routes and transportation orders.

Accounting. International shipping schedules and regulations. One on the lower right side.

BEELDE

Black clicked it open. Icon view. A long list; a hundred or more. Command A. Enter.

Images, identical in size, taken with a low-resolution digital camera tiled across the screen. Same distance. Same setup. Same photographer. Glaring light. Young boys. Young girls. Pushed down and stuffed into steel drums. A half-dozen of each taken until the horror and terror became overwhelming. A photo of each drum with holes punched in. Markings and identification for each.

Black scanned the photos. Three years of dates. His hands shaking and eyes tearing, he forced himself to see them all. Working his way from oldest to latest. Reminded himself to never underestimate the cruelty of man—that people were worse than anything you could make up.

Black stopped. The image knocked the wind from him as hard as any punch. His heart stopped; the pain and swelling in his throat impossible to swallow. *Sam.*

Tiaan watched the man. He saw the breath catch, the powerful, calloused hands grip the table and fight for control. He tried to meet the piercing blue eyes that held him with murderous rage and found his own eyes tearing up from the onslaught, yet couldn't look away. There would be no mercy—death was just moments away.

It took all of Black's willpower to not shoot the man outright. He slammed him in the head with the butt of the assault rifle, rending flesh and shattering bone. Mercifully, Tiaan's world went black.

...

Rodriguez was torn. He'd seen the explosion, the forklift thrown into the air as if a giant, invisible hand tossed a toy to flip through the air and crash upside down in the lot. A roaring fireball ripped the fabric of the night and then raced toward the heavens.

Like the men picking themselves off the ground, he cringed in horror as another man vainly tried to hold his head to his shoulders before losing the battle and slamming face-first onto the pavement.

He'd watched as one of the big dockworkers staggered to his knees, scooped up an assault rifle, and unleashed a torrent of steel into the open warehouse door. A heavy steel cylinder spun back in answer, crashing through the block wall near the giant roll-up where part of the supporting wall collapsed.

A man strode from the building, slammed one of the men in the head with the butt of a military assault rifle, and then forced the other to drag the first back inside. Though rendered in silhouette, Rodriguez knew it was Black. It was the fluidity of his movement, the ease and confidence carried in the midst of the violent chaos unfolding around him. He'd seen glimpses in Chicago. Watched him on tapes from the club. It could be no other.

Rodriguez couldn't see deeper into the warehouse from where he sat. He couldn't take on Black by himself; the man was a maniac. He looked to Curpen. He looked frozen. Maybe he'd been wrong about him. Perhaps they should team up? This could be a chance to put an end to the devastation that followed the rogue American everywhere he went.

He was about to start his vehicle and approach the cop when another vehicle, a big dually pickup, flashed its lights and pulled up behind the islander.

Heinrich wheeled into the narrow street behind Curpen and took in the chaos. He nearly rear-ended the cop before slamming on his brakes at the sight of the flipped forklift; the smoldering tires and burning plastic seat filled the night air with black smoke and the acrid smell of burnt rubber. A body lay nearby the rubble. He grabbed his shotgun and met Curpen as he stepped out.

"The American?"

Curpen swept his arm toward the chaos. "This in just five minutes."

"Jesus Christ."

"Yeah."

"You good?"

Heinrich jacked the shotgun. The past few hours had pushed him to the edge—he wanted it over. "Let's do it."

The big South African focused on the landscape in front of him. Tiaan's truck stood empty, the headlights the only remaining light, raking across the wide lot and hinting at further destruction. The driver's door open but the window shattered from the force of the explosion.

As Heinrich came closer he saw Gordo lying reflected in an impossible amount of blood; the man's head flopped to the side and barely attached.

The warehouse dock doors were open, large enough that the biggest of trucks could drive in, but one side of the walls now broken and crumbling. Beyond, the cavernous warehouse stood dark except for the sulfurous yellow light spilling from the back.

Curpen, Glock in hand, moved to the left side of the gaping entrance as Heinrich took a position on the right.

They could hear movement and suddenly the darkness filled with blue electrical arcing and the amplified sizzling, crackling sound of a welder. Both men looked to each other for answers— Heinrich's imagination firing in time to the electrical arcing as to what it might mean.

Black saw the headlights pull into the far lot. Turned back to his task.

He looked at the big man, still out of it, blood seeping from where the wire cut deep into his flesh as Black hoisted him on block and tackle then lowered him into a steel drum. A tight fit for a two hundred-sixty pound man. Black picked up a five-pound sledgehammer and broke the man's arm. Better. Black lowered him in. It took some more work, but he had the tools at hand.

He looked down at the man in the drum. The breaking of bones had left the man unconscious, but Black gave him credit, he was strong and beginning to wake up. Good. Black wanted the man to know what was happening.

Black watched as the man gained consciousness, then waited until the full measure of pain and horror distorted the man's battered face as recognition of his fate sank in. The man began to scream; a hoarse, wet rasp filled with hate, fear, and blood. Black muted it with the steel lid.

Black pulled on the welding helmet. Welding isn't hard, just harder than it looks. So is killing a man. Easy enough, just harder than it looks, and impossible for some to live with the guilt. Black wasn't one of those. His conscience clear, heart filled with the images of children terrified beyond comprehension as their fate had literally been sealed. His welding crude, but he got it done.

He could feel as much as see the shadows cross through the headlights. Two men. Not the greatest tacticians. He knew they were psyching themselves up, trying to reconcile their imagination with what little their senses and information had told them, making their plan. He had time.

He gathered the laptop, a plastic lunch box filled with Polaroids of the terrified children, the ledgers and manifests. Stuffed it all in a canvas bag he strapped across his back.

Saw the roll of industrial duct tape. He could tell without looking that he'd torn out some of the stitching holding his injuries together. Added the tape to the haul.

A dull banging started in the first drum, then progressed to the other two. The pounding and screaming muffled behind the steel. They'd soon run out of air and suffocate without holes for air punched in. One of the drums nearly toppled over, but the man inside quickly lost the strength to affect it.

He couldn't imagine someone would want to save any of the three but it was possible. Maybe they were someone's brother.

Someone's husband. Maybe they had a family. Like the children they had shipped in cans like packaged meat around the world.

Black pulled out his phone, thought to take his own pictures of the steel drums. Let the others know he was coming for them all.

Fuck it. *He wasn't cruel.* He pulled the big .45 and punched two holes for each.

The gunshots startled them. Three sets of double taps into steel rang out, echoed throughout the warehouse, and rolled across the docks as if thunder from the gods. Curpen and Heinrich, needlessly using hand signals to communicate, hugged the walls from opposite sides and slipped into the shadows.

Climbing the I-beam, Black moved along the eaves of the high ceiling and watched the two men enter. The cop from the club. Curpen. Nicola had hinted at the animosity between them. That in itself was reason enough for Black to kill him. *Jesus!* Nicola. She was out there waiting. He tried to playback the last few minutes as he imagined what she might have seen and heard from her vantage point. She must be going out of her mind.

The men worked their way through the shadows of broken wooden crates and toppled, knocked-out-of-place machinery. He'd wait until they discovered his night's industry and then shoot them both. Four shots from his high position. Realistically, less than a second.

His phone vibrated in his pocket. Nicola for sure; no one else had this number. Needed her to stay put.

He pulled out the phone, shielded the light from spilling into the warehouse.

Saw the texts, the frantic messages. One just in.

RUTH DED LEZA HOSPITAL

The corrupt cop and his oversized henchman were cautious, taking too much time. Let the FBI deal with them. It would give them something to do besides chasing him. Black slipped through the eaves and into the night.

Rodriguez hid in shadow, the long lens putting him in the room, watching the big man use a torch to cut the lid off a large steel drum. He couldn't imagine what shipment would warrant checking on it in the middle of a gunfight. Maybe drugs. What else could have enough value?

He'd do his best to get closer, grab a few pictures, and then get the hell out of there.

The bright lights that turned night into day had been cut as soon as Black forced the two men back inside. Dark clouds raced across a darker sky. Only the ambient light from the distant harbor and the spill of light from the back of the warehouse could expose him. He navigated the shadows and used the cover of Tiaan's abandoned vehicle, the pile of rubble, and the forklift to approach closer.

Black needed to get away from the docks, to find a cab, or better yet, an old car or pick up he could hot wire. He entered a side street and saw them; a modern SUV and a new pick up. The big dually was ostentatious on docks where everything by necessity was oversized.

The interior light beckoned him like a lighthouse. Black stayed in the shadows as long as possible as he moved closer; the distant chimes letting him know it was worth checking out.

Door open, key fob hanging in the ignition.

Rodriguez snapped a couple of pictures as the big man toppled the drum over. They rocked and levered the drum back and forth to free whatever was inside. Rodriguez, spying with the long lens, was as startled as if he'd been in the room. He jerked back as a man slid out onto the concrete floor.

Camera in hand—he fired off a shot. *Click.* How the hell had the man fit? *Click.* The big man poked at him with his boot. Obviously dead. *Click.* Time to get the hell out of there!

Rodriguez turned as Curpen shoved a gun in his face.

The blast filled the night as the Agent's head exploded—bone and blood drifting on the wind as his body crashed to the ground.

CHAPTER
FIFTY-SEVEN

Nicola saw him jump from the truck, ignoring the ambulance drivers and cops in his way. She couldn't stop herself from running to him.

Absorbing the emotion racing through her, he wrapped her in his arms, tried to quiet her sobs.

"They killed her. She died protecting the children."

"Aleeza?"

"I think she got caught in the middle."

Nicola clung to him, holding it together, finally able to release the tension and let someone else carry the burden for a moment.

"The doctors are operating on her. Won't let us in until they're done."

Black held her until she quieted. Fought his guilt.

"What?"

"This is on me," he said.

"That's fucking bullshit."

Black wasn't convinced.

"You didn't kidnap your friend's daughter. You don't murder old women and sell little children around the world. This is me. My fault. I thought I could save them. Protect them. Hide them away. *Jesus Christ!* We're at the end of the fucking world. The only way this ends is going after the bastards. This is Kronmüller. This is all the scum just like him."

They held on, finding strength in each other. It was a tropical emergency room in the middle of the night. Slow but not empty. Those around them ignored them, isolated by their own worries.

"She's going to be alright."

Nicola looked up at him. "Yeah?"

He held her until she pushed him away, guided him to the empty chairs away from everyone else.

"What about you?" She tried to look him over. Made a show of it. "You're not shot or stabbed? Nothing broken?"

He knew she was only half-joking. "I'm fine."

The image of Black taking out the first guard flashed in her mind. "Do I want to even know?"

He thought about it on the way here. "No."

She looked into his eyes. He was right. She didn't want to know. And yet, these were the people who had murdered Ruth. Who had left a child to die. A child whose life was in the hands of strangers in the next room. *Don't worry. We've got her from here. Be patient. Let us do our jobs.*

She began to understand the cost to someone like Black. She wasn't sure it was something she could do, but she could understand the why.

They leaned against the wall, each lost in their thoughts. She opened her eyes and looked at him. His eyes closed, breath steady. To anyone else, it might look like he was at peace, but she could tell, *could feel*, that whatever he'd done, whatever plans he was making for what still had to be done, was weighing on him.

She knew he felt guilty about Aleeza. There had been an instant and inexplicable bond from the moment they met, not unlike their own. She squeezed his hand, waited until he responded. A tight smile, then he opened his eyes.

"What can I do?" she asked.

He sat straighter. She noticed the blood seeping through his shirt as he pulled the bag from his back. Somehow, it gave her comfort, he was the same man she had known from the beginning.

What? Five days ago? She tried not to smile. She'd pursue the issue later. It wasn't a lot of blood, so for him was like scratch.

He opened the canvas bag. Pulled the laptop out. Showed her the ledgers. "This would take me a month."

She'd seen his files. You don't command a covert team of military operators without advanced skills in nearly everything and certainly everything to do with logistics. She appreciated his attempt to make her feel useful.

He opened the laptop.

"Give me a second."

She rose as a nurse, or maybe a doctor, came out from one of the operating theaters to reassure her. They spoke for a few moments, casting glances his way. The woman hugged her warmly and returned to the operating room.

"Nothing yet. She's in surgery. They act like it's no big deal. Still won't let us in."

It was the second time she had said 'us,' including him her plans. He knew it was a small word with huge implications. He flashed to the image of Sam, pleading as she stared up from the bottom of a steel drum. He'd have to leave soon.

"I'm sure they've got it covered."

"Yeah, I'm sure. It's just—" She took a breath. Aleeza would be fine. "It is a good hospital. I've been here so many times they should give me my own wing."

She saw the question on his face.

"Not me. Ruth. The kids. Mostly—just being kids. Sometimes the women we help."

Nicola grabbed the laptop and guided Black to a private room.

"Not my own wing, but we can work here. They promised they'd come for us."

She set the laptop on the bed, using it as a desk, pulled up a rolling chair, and looked at the ledgers.

Black added a couple of notebooks. "I grabbed everything I saw."

He caught her looking at the roll of duct tape. "What?"

She tried not to laugh. How could someone so capable be so completely childlike? "Nothing."

She grabbed the ledgers. Thumbed through them, then set the written material to the side. "They might be important. Let's see if we can give them some context."

She opened the laptop. A relatively high-end model.

Black pulled a heavy metal-framed chair beside her.

"Any chance you got the password?"

"Password."

She shook her head. "Well, that's okay. Let me see if I can bypass—"

"No. *Password* is the password."

"No wonder they're so vicious." She let the computer boot. "They're morons."

She typed it in. Scanned the desktop much as he'd done, blessedly ignoring the image folder. Gave a running commentary as she worked.

She brought up a command line window and set it to look for traps and rabbit holes while she continued with the system's GUI and scanned the directories.

"Let's get an idea of what's in here."

A dozen folders popped open and tiled across the screen. "Here we go." She brought a spreadsheet forward. "Here it shows... let's see... Six days ago was the seventeenth... a ship went out to Réunion."

She scanned the connections. "Should be able to get us online." She tried to connect. Waited as it scanned the local WiFi's. At five seconds, she thought of a better idea. "Let me just connect through my phone."

She made adjustments, connected the WiFi to her phone, and moments later, a dozen more windows began populating the screen. Just as a brush was something more to an artist, Nicola's dexterity at handling dozens of functions and threads at one time was impressive.

Soon he caught glimpses of bank records and shipping routes and manifests from the companies themselves that she verified and cross-checked with the records entered into the laptop.

Impressive became dazzling. Newspaper and magazine articles and press releases and then contracts and more business filings piled on top of each other across the screen. She absorbed it all as fast as it came.

She jumped back to Interpol. A quick search and she scanned the government filings and records for South Africa, distilling it down as she went.

"Kronmüller Industries is mostly legit. Two hundred years of expansion based from South Africa. Has hands in dozens of companies around the world. SA, Nigeria, Germany, Russia. Getting into Asia. Hong Kong. Malaysia. The father, Wilhelm Kronmüller runs most of it with an iron fist, though scanning I can see the younger, Christiaan, has been making some strategic moves to take control. First son Joffire killed in the Rhodesian Bush Wars.

"It's Christiaan who spends time traveling the world. And beating women. It looks like he's pushing for expansion here. Mainly textiles, taking advantage of duty-free access to U.S. markets. He has a minority stake in two Mauritian banks. Majority shares and partnerships in several clubs scattered throughout Europe. Interest in two major holding companies. Smaller stakes in a half-dozen more. This shipment went in as textiles. Split in two. Part of it to Durban and then a single container to Cape Town."

She paused. Thought of something else. Airline manifests. Passport controls.

"Christiaan flew into Cape Town." A second later, a photo of him and Grip coming through airport security. Security camera grabs. Immigration Desk and Passport control.

Black looked at the photo. It wasn't a face he'd forget until the man was dead.

"Can you get me a phone number?"

"Really?"

He offered no explanation. She dialed a number.

"Maddie. All good. How's Katie? Oh, that's great. I need a sec. Sure. Christiaan Kronmüller. C, H, R— Yeah. The same. Kronmüller Industries. Private cell would be great. Okay. Hit me back."

A knock on the door and the woman from the operating room entered. Smiling. Nicola picked up on it and was hugging the woman even before she got through the door. Black rose to meet her.

"Hi, I'm Doctor Geraci." She extended her hand and Black accepted it. The woman's hand firm and steady, much like the woman herself. Maybe fifty, stout but not big. Eyes that crinkled as she talked and more when she smiled. "Nicky says you're new to the island. Welcome."

"Thanks. How'd it go?"

"She's going to be fine—had a small puncture to her lung. Looks like a tiny shard of bone. Not her own. Our pediatric surgeon Dr. Russert is one of the best. Said it went fine. Doesn't see any physical complications. "

Nicola kept a brave face but couldn't control the momentary drain of color. The bone had to be Ruth's.

"Nicky, she's going to be fine. She'll have the tiniest of scars for a few years, but even that has a good chance of fading completely away, hopefully with the memory of whatever you're not telling me." The kindly doctor looked at them both. Made a point to linger on the blood seeping from Black's side. "Don't suppose you'd let me look at that and fill me in?"

"Sorry. I wasn't there. Two different things. A scratch from the brush on my way to the beach."

Geraci rolled her eyes, but Nicola jumped in. "Can we see her?"

"She's sedated. Gonna be out of it for a while and hopefully sleeps through the night. Sleep is almost always the best way for a child to heal." She looked pointedly at Black. "Really, almost anyone. But you can look in on her for a moment."

The two women hugged each other again. She kissed Nicola on the cheek. "And you need to come back and catch me up soon. Say hi to Ruth for me."

"I will. I promise."

They stepped into a small private room, but everything looked huge compared to the tiny girl lying in the bed. A huge bed. Huge monitoring equipment. Huge bandages across her tiny chest. One arm in traction lifted away from the side where they'd gone in through the axilla to complete the repair.

A nurse attached a set of sensors to her tiny arm, another to her chest, made notations on the charts, and hung them on the wall. She looked up at them and smiled. "She's a brave little girl, and everybody tells me she's going to be just fine. I think we'll have her out of here in just a couple of days."

"Thank you," Nicola said.

The nurse left them both looking down at the frail little body.

Nicola stroked the girl's hair and kissed her. "She likes you." She turned to Black and smiled. "That says a lot. She doesn't usually like men."

Black reached out, hesitated. He needed the reassurance of feeling the life coursing through her small frame. Let his fingers brush against the little girl's shoulder. She seemed so frail, so vulnerable. How did children ever survive to become young men and women? He found himself wanting to scoop her up, protect her from the world. From the bad things. But could he? He could feel his heart splitting in two at the answer.

Nicola wanted to comfort him. Paused with the rush of emotions sweeping through her. "You okay?"

He tried to hide his thoughts by turning to the room's solitary window, the sky beyond the blinds waking bruised and purple, hinting at the morning waiting to batter them all. Her phone vibrated in her pocket. She pulled it out and looked at a new text message. Showed it to him. Black dialed on his phone.

Kronmüller and his father sat at a massive dining table, the wood gleaming from generations of dining and subsequent cleaning and polishing. A maid filled the delicate china coffee cups from a silver coffee pot costing more than her lifetime salary.

She added the precise amounts of sugar and cream each favored and returned the pot, creamer, sugar bowl, and spoons to the silver tray before moving to the back of the dining room to await her next task.

Grip and Ringer sat in the shadows in the next room, out of sight but close at hand.

It was still night for Kronmüller, early morning for Ouderling. The elder dressed in bush clothes ironed with razor-sharp creases and looking like the white South African CEO of a multinational conglomerate that he was.

The younger looked as uncomfortable and out of place as a man can be; the designer shirt and slacks rumpled, a day of dirty-blond stubble darkening his face, drumming the fingers of one hand while alternately tracing fingers from his other across the lines of a gleaming 9mm and then his phone, both lying on the placemat beside his coffee.

He jumped when the phone rang. Ouderling set down his coffee. Grip rose to his feet.

"Yes?" Kronmüller voice betrayed his anxiety. He'd been expecting Curpen's call for hours. "Hello?" *Nothing.*

His father signaled for him to put it on speaker. Kronmüller hit the button and jerked his fingers away as if the devil might reach through and grab him.

Ouderling rose to his feet. Stood over the phone. "Who is this?" No answer. Both Grip and Ringer came into the room.

Kronmüller pushed away from the table and the phone. "How did you get this number?"

The men strained to hear any response. Only the sound from what might have been the intermittent beeping of a hospital monitor broke the silence.

Kronmüller stood, gun clutched in his hand. He stared at the phone, willing it to respond. Nothing.

He screamed across the silence. *"Who the fuck is this?"*

CHAPTER
FIFTY-EIGHT

This was now a full-blown nightmare. Three Americans were dead. Another one missing. The one thing they were sure of was that she alive, and in eight days would be sold to the highest bidder in an international auction of human flesh.

The fugitive from the Chicago case that made the agents heroes for seventy-two hours, was possibly—*no one wanted to admit it*—the best hope the American girl had, if any.

His bosses viewed his reports with skepticism and derision and finally gave the simple, direct order to get it worked out. Michaels figured he had twenty-four hours before they replaced him. Hard to imagine the pieces on the board weren't already being moved into place. They'd assign him somewhere north of the sixtieth parallel or more likely, begin pushing for a quiet retirement and obscurity.

And now, his partner had disappeared.

He paid for the pills, feeling better just having them in hand. Stepped out into the morning. The sky bruised, streaks of color fighting their way through dark purple clouds matching his mood. The smell of distant storms rolled on cool winds from across the ocean. Rain just hours away.

The streets were empty—a slow beach morning. People would use the coming rains as a respite from their forced vacation frivolities, seeking sustenance and recreation indoors.

Rodriguez. Eight years working with the man and this had never happened before. What the hell was he trying to prove? The handsome Cuban had become a friend as much as a partner. Maybe his only friend. *More like a younger, idiot brother.* Michaels pictured the beaming grin, suddenly hit with the thought he would only ever see it again in his memory.

He felt a stab of pain in his chest. He struggled to open the plastic bottle while dialing and juggling his phone in the other hand. "Where the fuck are you?"

Michaels stumbled, or thought he had. He was jerked off his feet and spun around the corner to crash into a brick wall. His phone and the pills went flying. He turned his head in time to save his face, but the impact on the wall knocked the breath from his lungs. He bounced off and spun to face Black.

It took the moments until his lungs half-filled before he could spit the words out. "Are you fucking crazy?"

"Yeah. Turns out I am."

Michaels clutched his chest. Slid down the wall to sit on the dirty pavement. Allowed himself to fall to the side and reach for the pills.

Black knelt down, reached for the orange plastic bottle. Warren Michaels. Nitrostat—Nitroglycerin. A few pills remained. He handed them to Michaels.

He waited as Michaels ground a couple of the pills in his mouth and pushed them under his tongue. Steadied his breathing.

"So. *Warren?*"

"Yeah. Warren. On my mother's side. Welsh, though she swears she's French."

Black reached for the cap, took the bottle from Michaels, and screwed it back on. Handed it back. "How long?"

"Ten years."

Picked up the agent's cell phone. Screen cracked.

Michaels looked at it. Shook his head. Spider-webbed from the bottom up. Could be worse—it still worked.

"Fuck."

"Yeah." Black pulled out his own phone. "This is not going to help."

Black pulled up a dozen fast snaps from the warehouse. Michaels struggled to understand what he was looking at. The computer screen with pictures of the children stuffed in barrels. Polaroids spread on the desk. Shots of the welding equipment.

"Jesus. You have all of this?"

"It's safe."

"Alexandrescu?"

Black nodded to hide his surprise. He shouldn't have been. This was the FBI.

"She's in the hospital with a little girl they shot last night."

"What the fuck is going on?"

"The children's shelter she runs was attacked." They both knew it was about him. He was stirring a hornet's nest, and people were suffering.

"Where were you?"

"Not there."

Michaels tried to get to his feet and Black helped him up.

"Do I want to know?"

Black ignored the question, pulled up pictures of the armed men moving about inside the warehouse. Not the best quality but recognizable. "Your man's a part of it."

Michaels zoomed in. Curpen. "Not mine. Local."

"Okay. You deal with him. I'm going after the source."

"I'm supposed to arrest you."

"Yeah. Well. Let me give you a few more reasons first, and then I'll let you do what you want."

Long moments. Black assessing the man, calculating the risks in using him as an asset. Michaels thinking out the consequences of letting Black go. Not likely he could hold onto him anyway.

There was nothing about the man screaming killer or crazy or irrational. Michaels looked in the clear blue eyes that gazed back at him. The determination and confidence rolled off like waves of heat, yet Black stood without pretense. Without posturing or inflated self-worth.

"I'm afraid to ask. My partner is missing. It's been twenty-four hours. Pretty sure he was tracking Curpen."

Black played back the night in his mind. He'd known someone else was out there, just hadn't made sense of why and hadn't stuck around to find out. He'd wondered at Curpen's agenda when Heinrich stayed in the warehouse and Curpen disappeared into the night.

Nothing crossed Black's face but that in itself confirmed the worst.

"I need you to look after Alexandrescu. Charlosta House. I need all your resources protecting them."

"That's a lot to ask."

Black's face never changed—no creasing of the brow or tightening of the mouth—and yet somehow the blue in his eyes shifted to gray and the intensity forced the Agent to step back.

"And what do we get?"

"She'll help you tear this apart."

"And you?"

Now Michaels saw the hint of a killer.

Michaels thought of Rodriguez. A pain that wouldn't be lessened by pills.

His technical team would be thrilled. They'd get to work with Alexandrescu. They'd been begging for it, and now he had the chance to make it happen. She could be an incredible resource, and very likely the key in helping destroy this web of perversion.

Time was racing and Michael knew this man—*soldier, killer, fugitive, hero*—was the best chance the children and the young woman had, willing to break every rule and any law needed to accomplish his task.

"How do I help?"

CHAPTER

FIFTY-NINE

It was in the air. The energy changed as if molecules in the air were giving off their electrical charge. She strained to see past her limited view from the window. Cars and trucks sat in the dusty courtyard, but no one came or went. No frightened maids with laundry. No gardeners. No visible men with guns.

She ran to the heavy door. Pushed her ear to it so tightly it threatened to bruise her cheek. She could feel more than hear movement from far away. The vibrations traveled through the bones of the house, the stone columns and heavy timbers that held the stucco walls and hardwood floors beneath her and the high-peaked tiled roof above. She couldn't be sure—her imagination creating sound where there might be none, but maybe doors slamming, voices, footsteps.

Abducted seven days ago; Sam had been here five. It had been three since she was paraded in front of the camera in the makeshift photography studio, two since she'd spoken to Lina, and one with no contact at all.

Her whispered conversation with Lina still filled her with dread. The children, most times plucked from streets where no one would miss them, other times bought from parents and families too desperate to hang on to or care for them, were to be transported and sold. *Slaves.* Sexual and otherwise. Property to be used and disposed of at will. Lina, though isolated from the actual workings of the transactions, had years to piece it together.

Possibly Russia. Perhaps China this time. Thousands of miles away. That meant flying for at least part of the journey, probably to an obscure airstrip before transport by caravan past any authorities and the scrutiny a major transportation hub would have.

Sam thought back to the terrifying dark hours in the steel drum, not knowing if she would be released, and how quickly fear became her only existence. She wiped at the tears welling in her eyes in shame—it only took moments of being trapped before she would have traded any indignity, any perversion or degradation, for a single moment of freedom. Lina had been trapped for five years.

Foretold in the stars or the rituals or the reading of entrails, Lina had divined her fate with the power of five-thousand years of African shamanism. It infuriated Sam. The acceptance that their destiny had been *written*. That some other force decided whether they lived or died.

She'd had only the briefest of moments to see the children, but she recognized the beginnings of their withdrawal, the processing of the actual events around them being pushed away in their minds. Defiance was not a luxury for them; shock and confusion their only companions. Of those she'd seen, at least two were physically sick, their immune systems as likely compromised by fear as the lack of nutrition and rest.

She'd been told there were sixteen children but had counted nineteen when she'd been trapped in the container. Somewhere in that short time, three had been taken away. Or escaped. Or killed.

Sam was probably seven or eight years the most senior. Where she thought only to escape, Lina begged her to find a way to stay here with the madman. To do anything and everything that would bond her to him so as not to be carried away to the unknown of the auctions. Sexual slavery was not the worst of what she had learned.

The thought of the South African looking at her, touching her, taking her for his own, nauseated her to the core. It made her bones ache, fear a massive fist squeezing her heart. Bile rose and boiled in her throat, and she fought not to throw up.

She moved back to sit on the bed. Forced herself to take stock. She had no real weapons. The door might as well have been to a bank vault. She couldn't pick the lock or knock it down. Windows were barred. If she somehow pried them off, she'd be left hanging three stories in the air, the high ceilings of the rooms meant it was closer to four, above the open courtyard where maids and servants ignored her and guards with guns passed back and forth below.

She sat in the jeans and t-shirt Lina had brought her. Thankful to be out of the sheer dress her captor had chosen. She had no money, and no opportunity as yet to beg or bribe or buy someone's help or loyalty. Her finger dug into the corners of her pocket. The earrings. They had to be worth something—maybe as much as three or four thousand.

Despite Lina's protests, her best bet would come from leaving. The auction could be 10,000 miles away. That meant planes or ships or trains, or as Lina said, a caravan. Trucks or even horseback. Surely there might come an opportunity to buy someone's defection.

She thought of the South African. Standing on the hotel balcony, she and Billie had thought the man handsome. *Jesus.* Would her family ever know what happened?

And the children. Did they have anyone waiting for word or news? Or were they so forsaken, that in the entire world, no one cared at all?

At least she had her mother and father. She corrected herself. Her father was gone. The thought slammed her as hard as a fist, and again she fought to breathe.

She struggled to focus and almost missed the door opening. Lina! She jumped from the bed as it swung open.

Kronmüller stood in the doorway. He'd somehow been turned around and entered the wrong room. Lina rose from the bed. It took him a moment to rearrange the image and see the American. *Sam they called her.* He didn't like the name. He knew it was the logical diminutive of Samantha and Americans idea of cute, but he'd have to come up with a new one.

Nothing masculine about her appearance though. In truth, the jeans and t-shirt were as revealing as the dress she had abandoned. Didn't have to guess where they had come from, the two conspiring behind him.

Her eyes shone with tears—her lips quivered. He stepped further into the room and watched as she shrank back, her fear a powerful aphrodisiac, and he felt himself harden.

Sam stepped back in spite of her resolve to remain defiant. Her father and mother, the streets of Chicago themselves, raised her to be strong. Lina, having lived through it for five years, reminded her that to stay alive, she'd need to focus on something other than fear until a time presented itself for escape.

She flashed to the children. Terrified. Confused. Alone. They needed her. They would be her cause, her reason to go on. She felt a quickening in her heart and the invisible hand around it relaxed. They needed her, and she realized she needed them in much the same way. Despite her fear, she would fight to the death if need be.

Kronmüller saw the trace of a smile on the American. Giving in. He knew she'd come around. He would keep her here. Fuck his father and his twisted ideas. He'd have both girls. He had the stamina for it. This was soon to be his land, his castle, the subjects here for his bidding. Lina would see a rival for his affections and reach back to him—it was human nature. He started forward, closing the door behind him.

The door stopped, pushed back inward. Kronmüller turned in anger. Ringer.

"Your father wants you in the study."

Again? This had gone on for too long. "Tell him I'll be there shortly."

"He says now."

Kronmüller was torn. Lust, fear, anger. He looked back at the American girl. Gave her his most winning smile, turned, and left the room.

Sam watched Kronmüller leave and looked at the huge body-guard. It was the second time she'd seen him since he'd murdered her boyfrie... Since he'd murdered Allan. The eyes stared at her now exactly as she remembered when looking up from the bloody knife, and again when he looked upon the near-naked children.

She watched him take a step forward, his weight and mass held in perfect balance. He was huge, trained, and experienced. If she were to have any chance against him, it wouldn't be because he overestimated his own abilities. It would be because he underestimated hers.

She forced herself to hold her ground. Felt the fork, hidden as she'd been shown, clutched in her hand. *No feint. No warning.* Right hand with power to the side of the neck. In and twist. Like her Uncle Tommy had taught her. Not about finesse or even stabbing—about ripping and tearing. Shredding flesh and the carotid artery. About surviving.

Ringer looked at the girl. She could easily pass as the sister of Kronmüller s whore, even a twin. He'd come back later when he could take his time. He left and locked the door behind him.

CHAPTER
SIXTY

S *eventy minutes—*

Black sat in the back of a venerable C-130 Hercules. Cruising at ten-thousand feet to give time for his body to adjust to the decompression demands he would place on it. A Hercules isn't the fastest of planes; the one he sat in was forty-years-old, and they'd been flying for the better part of an hour. Cold. Dark. The cargo loading lights on, encased behind thick, murky plastic. They didn't give much. Not that he could see anything more than what played in his mind. Non-linear, fragments and images, out of place and out of time.

Dillon, Aleeza, Big Al. The cheap Saturday night special pressed up against his friend's head. Sam. As a little girl, giggling and laughing on her father's broad shoulders. As a terrified woman trapped in a steel drum.

Nicola, the beat of her heart seen in the hollow of her throat. Her strong, white teeth biting at her lower lip. The pain in her eyes at the thought of her dead friend. A prepubescent girl, pointing from the stairs, eyes pleading for him to follow. Cops and reporters tracking his every move and gesture.

The flash of a blade in the sun. The crack of gunshots shattering the night. His mother, hanging off the bed, eyes dead and sightless, yet still accusing him of not joining her eternal slumber as he struggled to drag her from the flames.

Young children, so slight and slim they might blow away in the wind, trapped in cages.

He fought to put the images in order. The motel fire. Chicago. Big Al. Dillon. Jackie. Mookie. Mauritius. Nicola. Ruth. Aleeza. Sam. Nicola. Michaels. Nicola.

Sixty minutes—

He let the images run their course. Still disjointed. He tried matching them to a timeline. Chicago. Six days ago. That couldn't be right. *Six days?* It was—eight! *Eight days ago.* Sure, with eight days, it all made *perfect* sense.

He'd driven from D.C. to visit with the man who'd raised him, watched his friend kill himself, reconnected with his sister, took out a cadre of murderous thugs, uncovered a child sex trafficking ring, and evaded the Chicago police and FBI to hopscotch across the world and land on a tropical island.

Almost two days of travel. That meant he'd been in Mauritius... *five days.* He'd been shot and patched back together, traced Sam, fallen for a genius computer hacker, confirmed his primary target, killed half a dozen child traffickers, and struck a deal with the FBI agent tasked to put him behind bars forever.

Fifty minutes—

Michaels. Black knew the Agent was risking what might have been salvaged from his career simply by turning a blind eye. Michaels's twenty-four hours were gone. Rodriguez had been discovered and his body identified, and their replacements were on their way from Washington.

He'd had no illusions of how Black would handle things, nor did Black do anything to allay his suspicions other than a handshake agreement to turn himself in, if he survived, after he made the suicide attempt to rescue the American girl on his own.

Black made it clear that it was best for Michaels to stay out of his way and let him tackle this on his own. Besides, it wasn't as if they had time to make rational plans. Still, Michaels had jumped off a cliff when he helped arrange the plane Black sat in now.

Forty minutes—

Nicola. They hadn't said *"goodbye."* Neither had to say the words to know what was in their hearts. Black was determined to leave before the sun rose another day. Nicola was equally determined to use her considerable intellectual gifts to give him any possible advantage.

Having access to the world's online resources was an immensely powerful thing and one of the reasons Nicola lived in secret; routing her work, her payment, and her reputation through complex cut-outs and virtual intermediaries.

She removed Interpol's directives to search for, apprehend, and detain Black, Thomas Henry, United States Army, Major, and erased any record of the search in all relevant databases. After creating and backdating immigration records of his arrival in Mauritius, it was a simple matter to book him on a commercial airline to Johannesburg.

He insisted on paying for the economy ticket out of his own pocket but arrived at the gate with his US passport to find Nicola had upgraded it to first class.

Thirty minutes—

Black began his pre-breathing routine. Held the mask to his face. Drawing increasingly pure oxygen from the pre-breathing console to begin purging nitrogen from his body. Soon enough, they'd ascend to insertion levels. Nothing to do but wait. And remember.

It was as if he had entered an alternate reality, where time was truly malleable. He'd met Nicola just five days ago. That they bonded so quickly and completely, seemed impossible yet made perfect sense. One of the intellectual elite. Beautiful. Mysterious. Fearless. Compassionate. Dedicated. Damaged.

Every facet drew him in deeper. That he sensed she was broken in some way woke the primal instinct in him to protect her. A caveman and his mate. To ensure her continued safety and happiness.

It was in part, one of the reasons he had to leave. Another couple of days and he wasn't sure he'd have the strength.

He hated that Curpen still roamed the island but Michaels assured him he would use his considerable resources to protect her and go after the corrupt cop. With his partner dead, and the island cop as the primary suspect, Black was sure they'd make short work of it. If not, he might have to come back for the man himself.

There was no more time—what had somehow become fluid for him couldn't possibly be for Sam. As capable and resourceful as she might be, she faced a collective evil far greater than any one person could face alone.

Twenty minutes—

Nicola. 2500 miles and a world away. There had been nothing for either of them to say. If he lived, if he somehow survived the war he'd declared on the South African, on the man's equally ruthless father, and on anyone who associated with them, then he could count on going to jail.

A good chance it would be just long enough to be formally convicted before either being executed for his crimes or at the least, hidden from view in some obscure, dark hole.

Black made Nicola promise she would not use her powers to change the course of history. His own skills might have let him run free from the authorities indefinitely, but he was committed to facing whatever awaited.

He'd finished growing up under the care of a man who instilled the sense of right and wrong with both his faith and his actions. A former cop.

His sister, who he adored and admired and respected in every possible way, followed in her father's footsteps in the only way she knew how. As a trusted agent of the law. He would die rather than betray their trust in him.

He would honor his promise to Michaels. After he brought Sam back.

Ten minutes—

Nicola hadn't said anything, but he knew she felt it. That the lizard part of his brain had begun to take over. It was time to welcome his darker impulses and instincts—to put all other thoughts and emotions aside.

Everything was ready. The rucksack on his back had been carefully packed with the minimum of tools he'd chosen to wage war. Anything else would be appropriated from the enemy. His choices were refined from years of experience and his innate talents, and then narrowed further by expediency and availability.

He let himself play Nicola one last time in his mind. The sound of her voice. Her first touch. That damn lip thing she did. The hours they had explored and shared in bed. Her final brief kiss. The heartbreak and fear she tried to keep to herself as she held him one last time.

One minute—

Black rose, checked the straps, and hobbled to the door. Ninety pounds strapped on his back and chest.

The wind began to rush and swirl around him. The plane bounced and bucked on unseen currents—the force and turbulence matching the energy roiling inside him. Focused. Relishing the impossible odds. Traded the oxygen from the jump console for the supplemental tank. Positioned the mask. Tightened the straps. Felt the controlled flow of oxygen as he took his first pure breath.

Looked at the iridescent readouts of the altimeter strapped on his wrist. Thirty-two thousand feet.

"Fifteen seconds, Major." Removed the radio headphones, hung them on a hook near the door.

Beyond, near-infinite darkness beckoned him forward. He smiled as he had hundreds of times before at the thought. *Black on black.*

Five seconds—

No thought. Instinct and honed reflex.
He leapt.

And then it all went to hell.

CHAPTER
SIXTY-ONE

Dark, the children asleep in their temporary residence. It might be a few days, or even weeks until the police cleared the house for their return. The time might at least let the visions of the terrifying night dim before they returned to walk on floors now soaked in violence and blood.

Rayln was a huge help, stepping up as the elder. What a joke— *the elder*—not fifteen. Nicola knew the girl blamed Black, and by extension, her as well. Still, she was grateful. They would have to have a serious talk, and soon.

Black had entered their lives and a whirlwind of destruction followed. Nicola hadn't been able to wrap her head around it all. That would take time. She'd wanted him to stay, but knew it was impossible. She'd wanted to go. Equally, impossible.

Somehow inextricably linked, yet she knew she might never see him again. Black, she was now forcing herself not to call him *Tommy* as if that would help, had been gone less than a day. She was too logical and analytical to dismiss the possibility that a day would become forever.

Removing the international directives to detain and arrest him had been easy enough, though they both understood it was a temporary solution. She could rearrange the digital signatures and records, but not erase the human factor. Too many people in too many countries to imagine his exploits would soon be forgotten.

She'd held him, not even an hour. No words, no thought. Breath to breath, heartbeat to heartbeat. For those moments, they were one. And then it was time.

She arranged his flight, left him at the airport, and watched him walk away. Part of her mind screaming, as it did now, demanding him to come back.

They both had a good idea of what he was facing. However capable, he was one man. One man facing what might very well be an army. The South Africans knew he was coming. Hell, he'd baited and taunted them and told him he was on the way. He was waging war on their territory—on their lands.

He has a talent for violence. Despite his gentleness with her, she'd been witness to that truth. Still, she hoped for all their sakes the notation was a vast understatement.

Aleeza would be released tomorrow, the next day at the latest. Nicola dreaded her reaction when she found Black wouldn't be there to hug and hold and climb onto. The image of the little girl cradled in his powerful arms brought another catch to her throat. She swallowed it down.

She parked the small truck on the street just shy of the single amber streetlight. Most businesses closed; life still apparent at a small diner and two of the local bars. She was early but would wait ten minutes before going in.

Where was Black now? He was resourceful, but still, you counted on things to go wrong as much as right. Black and the FBI man, the Agent, no, Americans are *Special Agents*, the man she'd spoken too, were counting on favors from their vast off-the-books network to get Black close enough to use his talents and bring the girl home.

Nicola had agreed to meet a woman the FBI Agent insisted she talk to face to face, had made it a condition of letting Black go. She smiled. The man smart enough to know it was safer for the streets of Port Louis not to try to contain Black here.

Eleven o'clock. She sat as a couple of men staggered out the door. The bar was tucked between a hardware store on one side and an old fire station converted into a clothing boutique. She'd seen no one enter.

The children were safe. Or as safe as they could be, tucked away in a guest house on the other side of a deep inlet, miles away from their own home. She'd hired a couple of men she trusted to keep an eye on them. They'd already reported to her that there were others, capable-looking men working for the American FBI, watching out for them as well.

Nicola thought she might buy the guest house, move them all. Money wasn't an issue. Governments paid well for her services, and her investments had been lucrative, but she needed time to absorb the energy of the new place first and to see how the children adjusted.

For now, she'd find out what this woman wanted. Not that different from dozens of other women she'd met in strange, out-of-the-way places, many running from the violent men in their lives.

The scarred wooden door opened easily on time-worn hinges and Nicola was assaulted by a miasma of food and burned grease, of tobacco and sweat, of stale beer soaked into the wooden floors and fresh whiskey being poured from across the concrete slab of a bar.

Half a dozen men sat scattered across its length. Two occupied tables and a woman near the back tucked within a high-backed booth completed the small crowd.

A man at the bar, a couple of pints past better judgment, studied her in the mirror as Nicola came through the door. He saw the recognition on her face as she smiled at the other woman. He turned with his mates to follow her and take in the other woman.

Cute, petite. Pixie-like even. Two beautiful women. Little more than girls he thought. Probably in college somewhere nearby. Maybe in that experimental stage he thought. Yep. He would volunteer himself to be a part of that experiment—this could be a lucky night for them all. He turned back to the bartender and ordered three beers.

...

"Nicola."

The girl rose, offering her slim hand. "Alix."

Nicola took it and sat across from her. The girl's face lit up with excitement and Nicola couldn't help but smile back. *Pixie-like.* That's what she was. Cute but intense. Blue eyes shone bright with intellect and eagerness beneath bangs of straight, goth-like black hair.

Alix wasn't exclusively gay. She had her eyes on a guy now who seemed too shy to ask her out. *But, wow!* The legendary computer theorist was everything Alix had heard. Stunning. Unlike so many of the computer geeks she knew, *she wore that badge proudly herself,* Nicola was... *substantial.* Her hair naturally lush. Her skin radiant. Teeth perfect. Maybe five-six she guessed. Her arms and hands long and slim, but not slight. Jeez—*instant girl crush.* Oh, yeah. *And she's a friggin genius.*

Nicola laughed, the girl's excitement was contagious, even if she had no idea what it might be about.

"I read your thesis. Actually read it twice. I mean, once in college and then again a couple of days ago."

"You're kidding?"

"Nope. The Use Of Three-Dimensional Artificial Intelligence Models In Generative Adversarial Neural Cryptography."

The girl beamed. "I understood some of it. Maybe even most of it. You did a great job making it accessible. But to think your brain works that way, to come up with those theorems and implementations, is something I'm afraid I can only admire. I'm good at what I do, but I'm not there yet. I mean, obviously, I never will be. And that's okay. I mean, just to meet you is really fucking cool. Oh, shit, sorry about my language. Hanging out with the guys too much I guess."

Nicola laughed. "My language can get pretty fucked up too." The girl smiled, obviously relieved. "And what is it you do? That you're good at?"

"Well, I work with a team of cyber—"

"Excuse me." The man from the bar, having finally worked out his approach, set down two beers and grinned. "I was hoping you two beautiful girls might want the company of a man."

They looked up at him. He only wobbled a little bit, and his lopsided grin might have actually worked on some women.

"Wow, that really sounds *almost* irresistible," Nicola said. "But I think we're good for now."

The man didn't seem to hear. He lifted his own beer to show he was good too and was pushing his way into the booth when another man, in a higher-end, but still two-for-one discount suit and tie, grabbed the man's ear, twisted and dug his fingers into the bundle of nerves behind the man's jaw, and bodily lifted him from the booth.

The man went white from all-consuming pain; there and quickly gone when released. He spun to see the source of his torment; found himself trying to focus on the gleaming enameled badge shoved in his face. Federal Bureau of Investigation, United States.

The man tried to think of something clever. Twisted his face with concentration for a few moments, but then, thought lost when he looked into the gray eyes boring back at him, gave up. He was welcomed back to the bar with slaps on the back and good-natured jeers.

Alix moved over and Michaels sat down. Nicola had seen his image on video. The man was worn, beaten down maybe, still handsome, but he would have looked like a cop before he even thought of being a cop.

"Special Agent Warren Michaels."

Nicola reached out to his offered hand. "Nicola Alexandrescu."

"Alix is the smartest computer tech I've ever worked with," he said. "And she idolizes you."

"I don't idolize her," Alix stammered. She blushed, in part from the compliment, and in part at being outed to her new idol.

Nicola smiled to reassure her. "You can do better."

She kept her voice even, but Alix could tell what was behind it when she asked the Agent, "Have you heard from him? Major Black?"

She was good, Michaels thought. If he hadn't picked it up from Black's urgent request to protect and keep her from the fallout, he'd have never heard it now. Michaels gave nothing away, and Alix's respect for him went up another notch.

"Jo'burg to Durban. He made contact with a private contractor for further transportation and went dark."

"Is he supposed to check in?"

"It's his show. If he's successful, he's promised to contact me."

"For you to put him in prison?"

"To arrest him," Michaels said.

Alix squirmed beside him. She hadn't been told about that part of the deal.

"You know they'll bury him in some obscure black site," Nicola said.

"He'll stand trial like anyone else would."

"Do you really believe that?"

Michaels looked at them both. "I have to."

Alix couldn't imagine the woman would let Black *'stand trial like anyone else.'*

Michaels wouldn't be able to fathom the power someone like Nicola commanded with her abilities. Of course he wouldn't. He'd *think* he knew. Most people thought they had a grasp of the Internet, but only the people who studied it, who really dedicated their lives to it, understood how powerful and interconnected it had become in our daily lives.

And if by some miracle he survived, Alix couldn't imagine the man would turn himself in. Black was a lot of things but not a saint. Surely Michaels didn't believe him?

Alix shook her head. "So if he survives, if he brings down this South African trafficking ring, if he saves the girl, you really think he's gonna call and have you come arrest him?"

Michaels said nothing. It sounded naive to say it out loud, but there was something honorable about the man. His entire record said the same. Michaels had little doubt. If Black survived, he'd get the call.

Nicola answered for him. "If he said he would, then he will."

"Well, I think they should give him a medal," Alix said, "just for trying."

"Yeah." Michaels fidgeted and growled. "Me too."

Nicola could see why Black liked him.

The Agent stood. "I need a beer. Anyone else?"

Neither woman had touched the beers in front of them, they were tainted with stupidity, and they both pushed them aside.

"Whatever you're having," Alix said.

"Same."

Nicola pushed the bottles toward the Agent who scooped them up and headed toward the bar.

They watched the men at the bar shift and give him space. Michaels didn't push his way around, he nodded politely to the men and waited until the bartender addressed him before ordering.

"I like him," Alix said.

"Yeah. I can see that."

It took the girl a moment. Nicola laughed as Alix stammered. "I don't mean like that!"

"Hmmm... hmmmm..." Nicola smiled. "Don't worry. I like him too."

The girl blushed deeper—*eeeeshhh*—outed twice in one night! Rolled her eyes and shook her head. Nicola smiled and reached for her hand to let her know it was okay.

They waited for the Special Agent to bring three ice-cold beers back. Made room for him again. All clinked bottles and took a welcomed sip.

Alix knew that Michaels had already written Black off. He'd told them all as much. As romantic as the team thought it sounded, *'maybe we should just let Black take care of it,'* the chances of a single man actually being able to get in, accomplish anything at all, and then make it back out alive were virtually nonexistent. Which is why they were here.

She was convinced the best chance Samantha had was in them recruiting Nicola to pinpoint the auction and let the combined resources of a dozen relevant agencies intercept and recover the children.

"We need your help," Michaels said.

"I've given you what Black found and more. You have dates and names. Manifests and shipping routes. Vessel IDs and bank accounts and transfers for dozens of officials who are actively complicit. I'm also forwarding everything I have on Curpen. Bank transfers and cross-referenced activities coinciding with a half-dozen unsolved island murders over the past ten years."

Michaels hadn't said a thing about any of Nicola's information, probably to keep them on task. Instead, he had let them know there was a good chance, *a near-certain chance,* that he'd be removed from any active investigation. Without making some real progress, Alix knew there was just as strong a chance that Michaels would be drummed out of the Agency.

Alix pulled a backpack out from under the table. Nicola waited as she opened a laptop. Fired it up. She accessed a folder. Dozens, maybe hundreds of images.

Nicola pulled the laptop around in front of her. Screen-shots from at least four or five different computers documenting a detailed search through the dark web. Rabbit holes and cutouts, dead-ends, and wormholes. She recognized the beginnings of heuristic searches, three-dimensional quadratic cells, and an aborted attempt to implement estimated AI search maps. They were looking for the origin of something deeply buried.

Alix peered over the screen, reached around to hit the keyboard and brought up another folder. "We were recording when it flashed on. Up a few moments and then vanished without a trace. Like Snapchat in the deep."

Nicola opened the folder.

More images. They hit hard. She tried to turn away.

The tears welling in her eyes threatening to boil in anger Nearly naked children. One after another. Maybe as young as six or seven. Boys, girls. White, Black, Asian. Their new, snow-white underwear emphasizing their youth. A girl maybe sixteen or seventeen. Another. A young boy, maybe twelve. And another.

She stopped. A stunning young black woman, still a girl in Nicola's eyes. Maybe twenty-three or four. Hair perfectly coiffed. A sheer designer dress. Eyes burning in defiance.

"We need your help," Michaels repeated.

CHAPTER
SIXTY-TWO

Mathematicians, physicists, theorists frequently use the complexities of turbulence to describe hidden patterns within randomness and chaos.

Black had studied some of the same, and while part of his brain broke apart equations and searched for coefficients to explain what was happening, another part was fighting for his life.

As Black jumped, the C-130 skipped off a three-dimensional thermal plane as if it were concrete, a six-centigrade temperature variation, and shot upwards sixty feet, the wind draft sucking him skyward to fill the sudden void. He rocketed upward, equations forgotten, twisting, and spinning out of control. The plane, weighing more than a freight car, slammed back down nearly one hundred feet and Black was smashed under the wing like an insect beneath a giant hand of steel and iron.

The plane steadied itself and flew on, but Black was left spinning and tumbling end-over-end, skipping like a stone across invisible strata in the air, fumbling to pull the chute. Dazed, every bone aching and feeling crushed as if he had indeed been hit by a train, he mistimed it and pulled the cord. The chute ripped past his risers, caught him on the side of the jaw, ripped the oxygen mask from his face, and wrenched his spine.

The pain and blinding light felt and sounded like a gunshot between his ears and Black fought for consciousness.

In seconds, lungs screaming from the sub-freezing temperatures and the low air pressure at thirty-two thousand feet, his brain fought for oxygen, and finding no source, began shutting down.

Pummeled from the force, snapping and twisting as he hurtled toward the ground at nearly one-hundred-fifty miles per hour, Black's brain struggled to reconnect.

He tried to move his head. It felt hopelessly ripped from its moorings and was twisted to the side. The trailing, unopened chute whipped and pounded at him, and he gradually became aware. Black walked his hand across his body, fingers pulling his hand along, struggling to remove his knife and cut the fouled chute away.

Twenty-eight thousand feet and hurtling toward the earth at two hundred-twenty feet per second. Black, his body still unable to find oxygen, replaced the knife by instinct. Tried reaching for the mask hanging on its lines and buffeted around his head. It took a half-dozen tries before he willed his fingers to hold on long enough to pull it toward him.

Head still twisted to the side, he was afraid to even try to straighten it, but carefully fit the mask to his face.

It took a moment before his body realized there was air to be had, and he took his first deep breath, giddy with the thought that he would stay conscious all the way until he slammed into the earth below.

Twenty-six thousand feet. Black reached up, slowly turned his head forward with both hands, then flattened out his body to slow his descent. He was afraid to pull his hands away, afraid his neck wouldn't support his head, yet knew he had to try.

His head stayed on straight. His neck wasn't broken after all. Black looked out through the clouds below him, hurtling through a white mist that became one with the limitless fog in his brain and for the briefest of moments, time stopped.

He reached for his reserve chute, pulled the ring. Exactly as it should, it shot out and Black's momentum jerked him upright, pain shot through his body at the speed of light as the multiplied

G-forces rattled his skull again. The dazzling white light in his head gradually faded to the black sky he floated in.

He was going to be in pain, his head threatening to explode, but he'd live.

He checked the altimeter. Twenty-three thousand feet. Checked the GPS. Off course. He did the calculations, simple trigonometry. He had at most twenty minutes to try to make some of it up but figured the fifteen seconds of chaos had cost him approximately ten kilometers.

The gods were still fucking with him. In the heat of the desert, with the weight of his equipment, and now behind the rocky terrain he'd been hoping to land in front of, they'd cost him a minimum of three hours.

Pulled and adjusted the risers, began taking control and steering the big RAM chute, the massive black canopy silent above him. The night air was warm. The dark sky further blanketed under even blacker clouds, a thick nimbostratus shelf stretching as far as his eyes could see.

The only stars he'd found were the ones dancing behind his eyes when he'd slammed into the Hercules wing. Rains might come soon. If they did, they'd help shield his approach but cost him more time. Of course, rain was just as likely to blow on by. After all, this was the African desert.

CHAPTER
SIXTY-THREE

L ina led. Sam followed. The night fled with frightful speed and any plan of escape would soon be exposed in the coming light.

Lina had come to her minutes ago, waking and urging her to get dressed. "We have a chance," she whispered, "but if it goes wrong, an even greater chance we die today."

Sam didn't have to consider it. She finished tying the speed laces of her boots, pulled a cap over the mop of wild curls. "I'm ready."

They slowly opened the door, ducked back in as a house-keeper stepped onto the landing. Housekeepers and maids came and went. Lina never knew who she could trust, only who she could not, and Affina was the latter. The woman had been there for years, certainly before she'd come, and whether from fear or some mechanism of bribery, her loyalties lay with Ouderling.

Sam, clutching for any option other than those horrifyingly presented over the past few days, put her trust in Lina.

They crept down the stairs. Solid like the house. No sound gave them away.

At seventy, Ouderling was still always the first to rise, but today they heard him leave the house an hour before first light. Wherever he went, Ringer would be at his side.

Lina knew trouble was coming, it crackled in the air like the distant lightning. The urgency in the way Ouderling and the guards moved. The tension in Christiaan's eyes.

She'd sat in the dark watching Christiaan sleep. He'd had more to drink than normal last night and Lina had been especially accommodating, doing her best to ensure he'd sleep late. She could still feel his hands around her throat, his teeth drawing blood from her breasts and shoulders.

She'd waited until she felt the energy change outside. The vibrations of a big four-wheel drive more felt than heard.

Not quite five a.m. Already a hint of light in the eastern sky. Lina dressed quickly, lifted Christiaan's keys from his pocket and slipped out the door.

They made it to the first floor. Impossible to go out the front or the back, posted guards on alert. Their only hope a service door off the huge kitchen.

The cook was up early and carving a roast from a huge side of beef. The heat of the ovens filled the room and steam rose from huge pots on the stove. Though she was maybe forty or fifty, she was new to her post, and they had never spoken. Nothing to do but walk past and hope the woman wouldn't turn them in.

The cook turned, knife in hand. No expression, her black eyes never leaving Lina's as she watched them cross the floor.

Hands shaking as they turned the handle. Sam thought she might throw-up as fear and adrenaline coursed through her body. Though she hadn't given up hope, it was the first time in the past eight days, since the moment she'd been taken from the beach, when she wasn't confined in a cage.

She followed Lina through the door and breathed the fresh air. Sixty degrees, but a chill ran through her. Her knees almost buckled, and she reached for Lina's hand.

Whatever happened, even as her voice choked and tears came to her eyes, she'd be eternally grateful to the woman who was risking her own life for hers. "Thank you."

Lina squeezed Sam's hand as they knelt in the shadows, holding their breath as a guard approached.

Sam looked past the guard, her concentration on a point a meter beyond him as her Uncle Tommy had taught her. Any psychic energy would be directed past him and less likely to give warning.

The man went by, on radio and with assault rifle in hand. The squawking radio covered the sound of her heart which must surely be pounding across the compound like a drum.

There would be other armed guards posted around the property. Lina had the barest semblance of a plan beyond the simple hope the guards would be focused on whatever they anticipated arriving rather than what might be escaping, but it was more than they had before.

She'd caught small snippets of conversation, barked orders and demands on the phones. New men had arrived and been warned to stay away from her, the children, and the house. Ouderling was becoming increasingly demanding and Christiaan increasingly agitated and defiant. They always fought, that's who they were—always at each other's throats, but she had never seen them like this. It couldn't last, the pressure too great, and she knew both she and the American were the collateral.

"What about the children?" Sam whispered and instantly realized how meaningless any answer would have been. The children's best chance was for her own escape. That Lina, who owed her nothing, was willing to put her life on the line for all of them broke Sam's heart, and yet, filled her with resolve and even pride. As horrible as people could be, they could also be heroic and brave.

Lina eyed the stables. A guard in shadow near the barns, his cigarette gave him away. Nothing to do but stride across the dark lawn with purpose as if they belonged. Both in boots and hair confined as well as they could, wishing they had guns in their hands like everyone else.

Nothing to do but do it. Halfway across, another guard passed them but tilted his head and continued.

They made it to the door and went inside. Flipped on a single overhead light. It was enough. She knew her way around. The stirring of the horses, a dozen thoroughbreds, a half-dozen Arabians, soft snorts and nickers, hoofs pawing and gently kicking at their doors and walls, making it known they too would be happy to escape, gave her a new-found sense of hope.

"Do you ride?" Sam's hesitation was all Lina needed to see. They'd forego the big horses and go for the smaller, sturdier Lesotho ponies in the back. The original breed strengthened in recent years with Irish and Arabian blood to be even better suited for the desert hardships and mountainous plateaus. She reached for a saddle and tack. Another advantage in that it could stay smaller and lighter too. "Grab another set."

Sam grabbed a duplicate of everything Lina had. Bits and bridles, what seemed to be a thick coarse blanket, stirrups and leathers. The leather saddle seemed huge, more cumbersome than heavy, but heavier than she would have guessed.

Lina hoisted it to her shoulder and opened the back door.

A guard was reaching for her and without hesitation she kicked him hard. Her boot connected between his legs, and he folded with a grunt as all air and fight went out of him.

She looked up to see another guard running out from the dark. She dropped the tack and grabbed for Sam's hand.

"Back to the front!"

Halfway across the stables when the wide double-doors of the structure rolled open.

Lina reached for a stall door. And then another. Sam copied what she was doing and opened two more. Flipped the latches on more as she passed. It only took the huge animals a moment to realize their chance at freedom, and with snorts and neighs they stepped out while those that remained kicked their stalls and stomped at their doors. More stalls opened and the equine revolt was on.

Two guards entered the wide doorway. Lina sprinted toward a side door. She almost made it before a guard tackled her, and they both crashed and bounced off the wooden walls. The guard spun and lifted her off the ground.

The other guard fired off a three-shot burst in a call for reinforcements, and the horses panicked, reared up. The man fell back as a huge white Arabian galloped by and knocked him on his ass. He rolled and covered his head as yet another thundered by kicking up dust and straw inches from his head.

Lina kicked and clawed, her nails searching for the guard's face. He screamed out, and she scrambled from his grasp as he fell to his knees.

Lina gasped for air and watched Sam pull a pitchfork from the guard's back.

Sam dropped the pitchfork and they sprinted outside.

Half a dozen jeeps and trucks. Sam followed Lina as they ran to a Land Cruiser. Jerked the door open. No keys.

"Go! Go!" They split up and scouted two more vehicles.

Lina pulled a truck door open, clawed at the visor, ran her hands along the floor. *Nothing!*

Sam found keys in the ignition. The big Toyota roared to life, and she found herself giddy and shouting in relief. She might not know how to ride a horse—*fuck this country shit*—but she sure as hell knew how to drive!

She spun the vehicle around, a 360 that kicked up dust and gravel, and slid to a stop for the second and a half it took for Lina to dive in. Sam gunned it and spun the wheel again. The big truck spun in another circle, dust rising, gravel shooting out like bullets from the radius of the spin. Stones raked across men and horses alike, blinding one of the guards, further panicking the horses.

Kronmüller stepped from the house, his clothes barely on and was soon joined by Grip. Shouted orders over the noise that Grip tried to relay on radio.

More shouting and accusations and scrambling out of the way when a horse was hit with gunfire. It reared up and fell backward in the middle of the melee. Its piercing scream of pain and the snorts of distress cut through the night as it kicked and fought to rise, only to crash back onto its side and lie still.

Sam spun the vehicle, the rear-end fishtailed into a guard and crushed his ribs before she found her direction and aimed it at another. The guard let off a stream of bullets that shredded steel across the grill and shattered the windshield before jumping out of the way. As he spun and found his feet, ripping off another stream of lead before Kronmüller shot him in the back.

No one in front of her, Sam took off into the night.

The Toyota bounced and bucked harder across the unforgiving ground than any horse would have, and steam was rising from the engine block and making it hard to see.

Lina pointed her toward the mountains. There were wide ravines and narrow canyons where they could hide. And further out, dozens of small villages and camps where people loyal to her would give their lives to help her.

She turned her head and saw headlights far behind her, the entire compound lit and glowing against the dark.

They had a chance.

CHAPTER
SIXTY-FOUR

After the horrific start, the landing was anti-climatic. High above wide-open grasslands, descending past a herd of springbok that veered like a school of fish. They seemed to levitate mid-stride, watched him float by, then dropped back to Earth on their previous track.

He hit the ground hard with ninety pounds on his back, felt the expected compression in his spine, but rolled through the impact to protect his knees. Cut away the chute and let the soft breeze pull it from his hands. Watched it undulate with the wind in fantastic phantasmagorical shapes until it took off across the grasslands. Eventually it would be found and utilized, perhaps as shelter for some tribal nomad—San hunters or the pastoral Khoi.

Tall grasses rolled like waves, flowing around him as if he bobbed and floated on a vast sea reflecting the first blush of day.

He fell onto his back and looked at the heavens, dark clouds raced overhead against a brightening sky. Lighting danced somewhere along the far edges of his vision. Smelled more than seen, the distant air itself split and transformed into ozone, then rode past him on the wind.

Everything hurt, but he smiled, thinking as he always did of his very first jump. It hadn't gone well either, and was done far north of the equator where winter winds meant cold and ice. He was lucky he hadn't ended up crippled or worse. Still, it was one of the most exhilarating three seconds of his life.

...

It started with a kite. Like nearly every child, Tommy had at least seen them flown even if not actually holding the string in his hands and flying one himself. Plenty of people flew kites along the beaches, *yeah, the Great Seas had beaches,* long stretches of sand formed along Chicago's eastern borders. The full coastline, always in flux, spanned more than ten thousand miles, forty-five hundred of it in the United States alone, twenty-six of that in the city of Chicago.

Fifty miles east, in Indiana's Dunes State Park, people took kite flying further and would hang-glide off the 190-foot Mount Tom or one of the park's living dunes like the 125-foot Mt. Baldy, but Tommy knew nothing about that. Instead, he had seen the paper and plastic kites flown on Chicago's north shore beaches.

The beaches, only rough brambled coastline and marshland before city expansion, began forming as sand stirred from the bottom of Lake Michigan was trapped by Chicago development and newly constructed breakwaters. By the early 1900s, more breakwaters expanded the beaches with additional fine textured sand brought inland from places like Antioch and Waukeegan, where massive, seemingly inexhaustible sand pits were formed from glacial retreat fourteen thousand years ago.

Fully embraced by the 1930s, the beaches became a draw for rich and poor alike. Swimming, sun bathing, volleyball, and Frisbee were the beach sports of Tommy's youth, but kites, flying high in the ever-present Chicago winds and breezes, danced over the narrow strips of sand all year long. Simple diamonds and deltas, an occasional box kite and once, he'd seen a long-tailed dragon, its colorful ten-foot tail trailing under diaphanous six-foot wings.

Tommy and his friend Billy Gaston decided that it would be easy enough to build one for themselves. And not just any kite, *but the Mac Daddy of all kites!*

First the design; a simple diamond. Done. Then construction. While climbing on the steel-grate catwalks above the boiler room in an abandoned paint factory they'd found a set of twelve-foot, one-inch diameter aluminum poles. Two would do.

They used packing wire to bind them together. A large piece of scrounged canvas attached by sewing with the same wire and soon they had something that looked like a kite. The diamond soon became one huge square with a surface area close to the full 144 square-feet their structure afforded. They'd already found a half-spool of quarter-inch braided nylon rope. 300 feet.

They assembled their masterpiece in the shelter of the warehouse courtyard. No wind. By the time they drug it around the corner to the cracked parking lot, they knew it was something special. Years later, after some study of aerodynamics, Black realized their inability to tighten and ratchet down the canvas gave them the lift the kite needed to fly, essentially creating a flexible airfoil.

The kite began rocking and pulling and it took all their strength and weight to keep it down and drag it back. Obviously, they needed an anchor for the tail. They tied a four-foot log about six feet from the designated bottom and brought it back to the parking lot.

Moments later, Billy was lifted and dragged across the lot. A puff of wind, and he was suddenly ten-feet in the air. Tommy held on, fought the kite as best he could and soon found his own feet bouncing two and three feet from the ground. The wind shifted and the kite returned the boys to the ground.

They were giddy with relief before another gust tore it from their hands and sent it out crashing into the tree-lined wire fence that was supposed to have kept them out.

"Holy shit!"

"That was fucking amazing!"

They tied another log onto it—four-feet like the last one, but this one six-inches across. It took twenty minutes of all out battle to pull it back the fifty meters to the protection of the warehouse walls.

By the time they got it back, the skin from their knees and elbows left on the broken pavement from where it dragged them across the parking lot, Tommy already knew where they were taking it next.

With a third-story wall to shield them, they used the rope to haul it up to the second-floor rooftop. Placed a half-dozen concrete blocks on it to hold it down while they worked. Created what they thought was a genius set of stirrups he could stand in while holding onto the struts. Cut off the two-log tail. A quick scare when a small breeze almost tore it from their hands. The wind died and the boys dragged it to the edge.

"So not a kite?"

"Better," Tommy grinned.

Tommy's gut was doing some kind of crazy gymnastics routine, and he prayed he wouldn't throw up. Or worse.

"Your sure about this?" Billy asked.

"Hell, yeah."

Tommy worked his feet into the stirrups, swallowed hard, lifted the kite above him, and waddled to the edge. No wind.

Billy made the sign of the cross. "Holy fuck."

Tommy glanced back and winked. Billy sweating. Turned back. Shit!! Too late now. Took a huge gulp of air.

Tommy jumped.

Chicago winds can gust to fifty miles per hour even when there is no storm. Strong currents raced off the cooling waters of Lake Michigan and sped through the city. They were lucky, this wasn't much, maybe ten or fifteen miles per hour. A single puff that lifted him.

Tommy's jump was more like a step, but for a few seconds, four to be exact, it seemed he was really flying. He sailed out twenty feet. Thirty feet. Forty. Began rising.

He thought he might make it, just sail over the trees and buildings and keep on going.

In the split-second that followed, the kite twisted and plunged thirty feet to the concrete pavement below. It flipped and crashed on one corner, folding the aluminum strut and ripping the fabric as Tommy was flung from corner to corner. It stayed up on its side for what felt like a minute, then finally tilted and flopped over.

Billy ran across the gangway, shimmied down the crows-nest ladder, and raced to the parking lot.

Tommy, exhilarated, filled with joy. Already planning his next attempt, and trying not to laugh. Every bone hurt.

The crippled kite was restless, flapping and pulling in the wind, and Tommy kicked free of the stirrups. He rolled over and the kite flew away. It skitted and flittered until being trapped by the fence.

They heard the police sirens coming, but Tommy couldn't be bothered to sit up.

Billy was speechless. Torn between loyalty and self-preservation. Waited as long as he could. His friend was alive.

"Sorry, Tommy."

He sprinted across the parking lot, fought his way through the hole in the fence, the jagged metal clawing and ripping at his jeans and t-shirt, and took off.

The two cops watched the boy run, saw the other lying in the middle of the lot. Watched the huge trapped kite flip over the fence, and then fly across an abandoned lot before crashing into another building down the block.

One uniform got out to break the rusty padlock, then strode across the lot as the other cop pulled the cruiser in behind hi Tommy looked up. Laughing hurt too much, but managed a grin.

The big cop looked down at the boy. A good-looking kid. A mop of black hair and blue eyes above a goofy grin on his face. Shook his head. A few scrapes and bruises, but no blood. Nothing looked broken. Looked up at the roof line of the abandoned factory. *Kid was crazy!*

Tommy looked past the baseball glove-sized mitts reaching for him to the small metal name tag on the cop's uniform. *Lobinski.*

...

Black sat up. Rolled his shoulders. Turned his head left and right, up and down, testing his range of motion. Better than he would have thought. A few clicks and cracks in his neck, but they might have been there before. No time to worry about lasting effects They'd just merge with all the other aches and pains.

CHAPTER
SIXTY-FIVE

They bounced over rough terrain for most of ten minutes before settling onto a smoother stretch of hard-packed earth.

The distant mountains were no closer. Sam swore they were moving away from them at the same speed of their vehicle.

Night nearly over, they drove without headlights. The land, normally browns and golds, showed color from the recent rains, and was tinted with the rose gold of early morning light.

Sam thought they had a chance. Lina knew it was hopeless. Distant headlights and the glow of the compound faded. Lina pointed them toward a ravine, maybe thirty feet-wide. The truck slid across the loose rock until Sam got the feel of the land, slowed enough she didn't fishtail into the stone walls.

Sam knew there must be thousands of empty miles to hide in. Lina knew there were thousands of empty miles to die in. They had no food, no water. Their only chance was to get as far away as possible, then hike overland until they found one of the small villages or encampments loyal to her.

Sam rounded a corner, the truck tilting and grinding over the rocks of a dry river bed. As she maneuvered around the curve, she was hit with a wall of dust and flying rock. Gravel skittered into the steel and peppered the windshield.

The chopper roared overhead, the down-wash and *thwump thwump thwump* of the rotors amplified between the narrow stone walls over the whine of the engine and the spin of the rotors.

Lina didn't have to see who was above them; it was either Ouderling and Ringer, or Christiaan and Grip. Christiaan preferred his plane, but any of the four could pilot the two-man Robinson.

A high-powered round tore through the engine block. Steam mingled with dust and the vehicle seized and bucked. *Christiaan.* Lina knew Ouderling wouldn't have aimed for the engine.

Both women were out before the engine ground to a halt. No way to climb the steep ravine walls of razor-like quartz, they were forced to run back.

Throats and lungs filling with dust, both women gasped for breath. Lina grabbed Sam's hand, and they stumbled back around the corner.

Armed men were piling out of the two trucks blocking their way, and gunshots raked the walls around them in warning.

No escape. Any dream of freedom gone.

CHAPTER
SIXTY-SIX

Michaels watched the Airbus roll across the steaming runway. Heat-shimmer rising from the reinforced concrete surface let him hope, for the briefest of moments, that it was all a mirage. Maybe it had never happened, but minutes later, as the massive jet began to pick up speed, the roar of the quad-engines matching the roar of anger threatening to blow a hole in his heart, Michaels was again forced to acknowledge reality.

They'd worked together for eight years, his counsel and loyalty counted on as much as the ground they walked on. The fact that the man was dead, encased in a translucent body bag filled with ice-packs hidden inside a simple wooden box in the hold of the fading plane, proved the war on crime was as real as any other.

Rodriguez had been found near the dock warehouses where Black told him to look. Seven other bodies were found, Black's work, but it was hard for the Agent to care. Let the locals figure it out.

Michaels had steeled himself for what he'd find. Had been in the war, a Marine, two combat tours before coming home to finish a degree in finance and finding his way into the FBI. The reality hit harder than he would have imagined.

A federal agent; they'd fly Rodriguez home to complete the autopsy. Stupid. Michaels knew exactly how he'd died.

Powder burns and stippling. The 9mm bullet entered under his right eye—*leaving little doubt the shooter was cack-handed—*

punching through the handsome face and out the back of his head in less than a thousandth of a second.

Michaels was expected to go home, do a full debrief—multiple times to satisfy multiple agendas—everyone who could, jockeying for their piece of him. Write up the dozens of reports. They'd set him up with mandatory counseling, demand he take time off while they debated amongst themselves where might be the best place to hide him.

They'd hope out loud enough for him to hear and then strategize in secret how best to ensure he'd go quietly, praying he'd opt for a pension and binding non-disclosure agreements so departmental secrets wouldn't end up in a book or splashed across the Washington Post or New York Times.

If he fought them, they already had a complete set of procedural steps, specifically tailored to him, fully calculated and vetted to make sure he finished out his time as discredited and far away as possible.

Fuck 'em. He wasn't in the mood to accommodate any of them.

He needed time to decompress. Just a few hours for Christ's sake. *To be human.* Humanity was the one element the military and law enforcement agencies did their best to replace with procedure and protocols designed and voted on by boardroom committees.

The team was waiting on him. The dream team. *Yeah, they were dreaming all right.* Dreaming he had answers. He'd told them to disband indefinitely until he knew what the hell was going on and there was at least a semblance of a plan to bring those responsible to some kind of justice. But everyone adored the handsome Cuban. Always had. And with the specter of the auction looming? He knew they weren't hearing him. And now Alix wanted to make a pitch to continue.

He'd have to come clean; tell her the team they'd assembled, ostensibly for logistical support, had been set up without formal authorization from ITB, the bureau's Information Technology Branch. The agents would have been expected to liaise with an IT tech to set up their emails and secure communications, not to create a team of civilians for deep cover dives and investigative work. The agents had followed their off-the-record playbook from a successful operation they'd run on a Serbian crime boss in St. Louis. Michaels hadn't told his replacements they even existed. Wasn't sure he would.

Nicola was also waiting for him. She had access into the agencies in ways he couldn't have dreamed. Of course, if anyone thought about it, they'd know there must people like her somewhere. The problem was, like everyone else, he didn't think about it.

Black was off the grid, and she'd be desperate for news. Not that he had any. He'd done what he could; pulled a few strings, made a couple of calls and stayed out of the man's way.

He now understood the man's all-consuming anger. The anguish at seeing his friend's daughter—her horror and the growing realization of her fate, captured and preserved on film.

Black was a virtual war machine, the Olympian talents God-given to him honed by the world's most elite military forces. Forces that shaped and compressed him into something hard, something relentless and unforgiving. The man already proved he'd trade his life and maybe his soul to save the girl.

Michaels could have at least *tried* to bring him in. That the girl was trapped in a pit of many-headed serpents, as evil as any mythological monster, meant Black would likely be saving others, perhaps as he had when killing the Chicago crime lord.

They hadn't had much time to piece together the man's motivations in Chicago. But the dream team uncovered enough background they could start guessing. A foster sister working as the public defender of record for one Clarence "Mookie" Williams. The murder-suicide of a Chicago cop who turned out to be the kidnapped girl's father.

They made the military connections, but met dead-ends when trying to learn the task force's objectives. Missions cloaked in judicial legal opinions, Congressional intelligence committees, and war-college precedents. Anything so the objectives wouldn't have to be stated out loud or found through a paper trail. To kill those that someone higher up had decided were the bad guys.

Black was surrounded by death. He'd been in Chicago thirty-six hours and eight people came to violent ends, six at his own hands.

Three murdered before he came, but less than a week in Mauritius and you could add ten more. Not all his, but Black was a catalyst of chaos.

Michaels wondered how he lived with it?

Thought of the girl. The children. The old lady. And Rodriguez.

Michaels was a cop. A Federal Agent and before that a Marine, but he was suddenly thankful that there were people like Black. Willing to sacrifice their humanity for the lives of others. Rodriguez had his name for them, brought from the islands, which now seemed appropriate. *Soul eaters.*

Curpen was out there. Or, maybe not. Maybe he'd already left the island. Normal channels were blocked. Airports and commercial shipping. A couple of thousand registered ships and boats, but probably twice that could be put on the water, sailboats and skiffs and surfboards for all he knew. This was the rogue cop's island. Michaels was the outsider.

From what they guessed and pieced together, Curpen worked with the South Africans, running interference for the lucrative child trafficking ring Kronmüller controlled. The records and photos Nicola had passed on hinted at the scope of the operation. Ripped from the streets, but none like the young Chicago woman Samantha Dillon. *Why her?* What was the motivation? No answers, only that her companions were murdered as she was brazenly taken under the direction of a madman.

Was this what the world had become? Or was it always this way? Cavemen bashing each other over the head. Leaving bodies where they fell across the prehistoric landscape. Evolution favored the strong. Civilization defined by language and interpretation, not progress. Michaels had a lifetime of working up close to see the worst in man. Not that he thought he was any better.

He wanted so much to put a bullet through the man's head. Maybe film it, so he could watch it over and over in slow motion. The 9mm, 124-grain steel jacketed hollow-point exploding from the muzzle, entering under the bastard's eye like it had his friend's. The handsome face distorted as the maxilla and zygomatic sutures on the front of his skull and the lambdoid and sagittal of the back were torn apart by the ballistic shock wave, eyes blown from their sockets, micronized fragments of bone—collagen and calcium phosphate—nerve ganglia and brains and cerebrospinal fluid exploding from the back of the skull in an exit ten times the size of the entrance wound to leave bone and blood and brain matter across the streets.

Michaels was shaken, literally. His hands shook, and his chest felt tight. Reached for his pills. The vision had been too clear. *The color and smell and sound and taste of it.*

Looked at his watch. Two hours to clear his head.

CHAPTER
SIXTY-SEVEN

Nicola watched the nurse fuss about, make a show of it before she finally moved on. She pulled the metal chair closer and sat. Little free room in the small hospital but Nicola had made arrangements for a private room. Second story, eastern windows and light. No color—walls, ceiling, and tile floor blinding white. The color of—*what?* Cleanliness? *Insanity?*

Nicola settled on insanity. Not that she needed any help to get there. The chaos, the extremes of emotion left her drained, arms and legs impossibly heavy, yet her mind raced. Aleeza, Ruth, Black, the girls, the women at the shelter, the children trapped with the madman in South Africa.

Forced herself to breathe. Not close to being over, and she still had her part to play.

The little girl slept. The breathing machine and catheters had been removed. They said she'd been awake for a short time. Nicola imagined the girl's fear. Could feel it as if it were her own. Waking in terror, an intubation tube down her throat. Monitors and tubes attached and inserted. A sterile white room that would drive anyone crazy. Strange people in masks and the inhuman, mechanical sounds of life-saving equipment she couldn't possibly understand. Nicola was furious with herself that she hadn't been there to comfort the little girl as she wakened and heart-broken that she had to leave her again now.

She tried not to cry. To scream and rage. Forced herself to take a long, slow breath.

Nicola looked up to see Dr. Geraci watching her from the open door. Started up.

"No, no. Sit."

Geraci checked the charts and double-checked the nurse's work as Nicola watched the girl sleeping.

"She's so tiny," Nicola's voice breaking.

Geraci smiled. The first sign of warmth in the cold room. "She's going to be fine. Lots of time to mend. How are you doing?"

"Going insane."

"I know you better than to ask if you want anything."

"A mallet to the head?"

"I'm thinking of something a little less traumatic." Pretended to check her schedule. "But I can maybe get you in later this afternoon for a lobotomy."

"Perfect."

Nicola stood. Wiped away the wetness blurring her vision. Geraci reached for her hand.

"Seriously. She's going to be fine. I'm sorry about Ruth."

Nicola started to speak, couldn't find the words. Turned away. Couldn't risk looking at her.

One didn't need to be a doctor to see the pain it caused her. Geraci knew some of the story, how Ruth brought Nicola to the island to heal. She pulled the younger woman close, held on for just a moment. All she could offer.

Nicola turned back to Aleeza. The tiny chest rose and fell with each small breath. Desperate for contact, she stroked the small, perfect face.

"Does she have a favorite doll or a toy. Maybe a Teddy bear?" Nicola's throat tightened. She worked hard to keep the tears from coming back.

"Yeah." Flashed on the little girl cradled in his arms. Tried to smile. "But he had to leave."

"Yeah. I saw that." Smiling. "Wasn't sure if he was hers, or she was his."

Nicola turned away, couldn't face her. Covered by kissing the girl. Reached for the tiny hand.

"She's like you. Tougher than she looks."

Nicola searched for words.

"I'll be back in a couple of hours."

CHAPTER
SIXTY-EIGHT

He followed her from the hotel. An easy day for walking. Fair, southeasterly trades blew the humidity away, the cloudless blue skies and warm sun above a reminder of why the narrow streets on the island stayed filled with tourists.

Watched her slip past a gaggle of overweight women. Duck into a cafe. She wasn't looking for him, and he could hide if needed. He had a good idea of where she was going and an even better idea of who she was meeting.

He viewed her through the windows from across the centuries-old cobblestone street. Standing dutifully in line. Unlike everyone else who studied their phones, she focused on the overhead menu as if she could will the caffeine into her system faster.

He tried to think if he'd ever seen her without a cup of coffee. If not in her hand then at her side, on the desk or the closest table or chair. Realized for the first time, he watched her a lot.

Clement hadn't defined it for himself, only had a vague feeling he wouldn't have been able to articulate. He not only wanted to keep working on their mission, but wanted to work on it with *her.* Just the same, this wasn't about that. They all acknowledged she was the leader, the one who'd brought them together, but it wasn't fair for them to be cut out now.

...

"Bonjour. Je voudrais un double espresso noisette s'il vous plaît."

The tall, slim barista, the color of the coffee itself, kept his eyes hidden behind heavy lashes but watched the woman as he worked. The girl a mix of the islands, African and Indian and Chinese, definitely European. A bit slight for his taste, almost tiny, but her goth-black hair and oversized glasses framed her delicate face perfectly. That she had no idea the effect she had on him or others casting glances her way, made her more attractive and intriguing.

She'd been here every day for a week. A local but not from this side of the island. Even without the huge book bag hanging off her slim shoulders, you could tell she was smart. She must be working close by—he'd wait until tomorrow to ask her name.

"Merci. À plus tard!."

Alix left the cafe, sipped on the steaming double-espresso. The handsome barista behind the counter made it much better than she could. Coffee had been her friend since she was ten and found herself staying up all night, coding, creating little games and apps, and traveling through the internet.

She craved the freedom—the romance of it all. There were no boundaries, no oceans or borders, no need of money to prevent her travel, just an unlimited universe to explore as far as her intellect would take her.

Yeah. Sure. Real fucking romantic. Rodriguez was dead. All you had to do was look at Michaels's face to know how bad it was.

Alix didn't want to fight with the team, but they'd been assembled under her watch and were her responsibility. Lives were at stake but with the death of the Agent, she couldn't justify keeping them together.

She had wanted to meet with them on her own but there was no stopping Michaels.

"But we can help," Clement pleaded.

"Just some time to regroup," she said.

Camille ground her teeth. "What about the kids?"

"We're working on it," Michaels said.

Julius asked the obvious question. "And who's we?"

Alix glared at him, trying to warn him off, but Julius wasn't ready to let go. "We know they've taken you off the case."

Michaels paced the room. The double-suite suddenly felt very small.

"This is about your safety. There is no way I can protect you."

Julius crossed his arms, hands balled into fists. "Well, that's fucking comforting."

"Do we know what happened?"

They knew the basics but wanted it to seem like they didn't.

"Not really." Michaels didn't have time for this shit. "You know as much as me."

"And Black?"

"Gone."

Clement couldn't keep the excitement from his voice. "He's going after them, isn't he?"

"At least for now," Michaels admitted.

"This is bullshit," Julius said. "He's going by himself?"

"Can you think of a better way?" Alix asked.

Camille pulled at her hair. "So you know where they're taking the children?"

"Not exactly. But we are narrowing it down."

"Come on guys, you'll all be paid—"

"Fuck you."

"—and this is not open for discussion," Michaels finished.

"So what about the kids?" Clement looked from the group back to Michaels. "What about the girl? Sam?"

"What if he doesn't get there in time? SA right? What if it's not like the movies, and he gets himself killed?" Camille looked around the room. "I mean it's pretty fucking likely, right?"

No one offered an answer.

Michaels knew they wanted to help, but this was going nowhere. "I'm being sent back."

"Yeah, well," Julius rolled his eyes. "We knew that before you did."

Alix groaned—she preferred that Michaels didn't know everything.

Camille shut down her computer. Closed the clamshell as delicately as possible. Afraid if she gave in, she'd throw it against the wall. "We're down to seven days."

"Look. I appreciate—"

"Bullshit!" Clement stood but there was nowhere to go, and he stumbled backward into his chair. "Look, I'm not trying to be an asshole here but this is not about you. It's about the kids."

"You don't get it." Michaels felt his heart pounding. "This is not a fucking video game, shooting bad guys running away in your chat rooms. This is the real world. You've seen what Curpen does. I'm not having one of you get hurt, or shot, or your fucking head blown off. No. I'm not fucking doing it. Shut this the fuck down!"

Michaels slammed the door on the way out.

Alix couldn't meet their eyes. Gathered her computer, threw the bag over her shoulder. It made her look like a kid off to school.

Camille had known her since she was sixteen. "Bullshit again. You're working with Nicola. We might not all be geniuses, but we can help."

"I'm asking you to give me a day. Make a plan. After I meet the new team, we—"

"So you are still working on this?" Camille zipped her bag. "You know what? Fuck you." Stomped to her feet. "This is you trying to carry this shit on your own. Those kids are now on you."

She stormed out.

Alix hitched her back-pack higher and looked at the two guys. Both older but really just boys.

What else could she say? She shrugged and walked out the door.

CHAPTER
SIXTY-NINE

G rowing crowds spilled onto the streets, so Alix cut through the market toward the waterfront, across the manicured walks and past the casino, the clothing shops, and jewelry stores. Put her head down, determined to wait, but couldn't help but glance at competing espresso bars on each side of the street.

Tired of running the conversation through her mind. Bottom line—she could only do what she could do. The main thing was to make sure her team stayed safe.

Nicola sat at the waterfront restaurant. Watching sailboats and skiffs in the marina, the birds diving and skimming off the nearby surf.

No different from having lunch at any high-end marina hotel in Miami or Capetown or Nice, though because of the bright confectionery colors and endless streams of tourists from around the world, it was probably closer to Disneyland.

Nicola had strong reservations about continuing to work with the girl, especially without assurances from Michaels that he could arrange adequate protection. She couldn't see that happening, she'd seen the correspondence from the Bureau telling him to stand down and turn over all relevant materials to the team of Agents they'd sent.

She could tell him their plans for him as well but hadn't made up her mind about that. She had to decide on whether they should let the girl keep working on this. Plenty for Alix to do, and they were running out of time, but would concern for the girl's safety only become a distraction? She had Aleeza to think about, the children at the shelter, and Black.

Nicola sipped at her wine. Not tasting it.

Closed her eyes and listened to the sounds of the harbor.

Gentle waves lapped against nearby hulls. Tall masts creaked and the bell-like ringing and jangling of taut rigging carried on the breeze.

The chatter of aerobatic sea birds to her left and the dozens of languages and laughter of distant crowds to her right. Music drifted from a dozen different storefronts and mingled into a euphony of sound while words and hints of melody tugged at the corners of recognition.

Breathing deep and steady, she tried to quiet her thoughts. Opened her eyes and forced a smile in hopes a lightness might enter, even for a moment, but the cheerful sights and sounds around her gave her no comfort.

The distant crowd parted, and she saw the girl coming, huge book bag over her narrow shoulders. Straight black hair reflecting the tropical sun. Bug-eye glasses, probably chosen as the nerdiest ones she could find. Trendy. They looked good on her. The girl was cute. And maybe too smart for her own good.

Alix was coming to make the case on why she should stay involved. Why the team should stick together. Nicola looked at her watch. On time. Michaels on his way. She'd give them thirty minutes. She'd listen and make her decision but Aleeza needed her and Black was due to check-in in a few hours.

The smile stayed on her face but Nicola fought a deep, overwhelming sadness. No vague sense of apprehension, rather the certitude of a coming storm that had nothing to do with the weather.

Clement watched Alix work her way through the crowd toward the sprawling hotel. Saw her pause in mid-stride and followed her eyes. Nicola. So far, he'd only seen photographs and listened while

Alix gushed on about her. He'd reserve judgment until after he met her, give them a moment before introducing himself, then make his case for why the team was still needed. Stronger together and time running out and whatever else he could think of.

Pain exploded in his back. He tried turning but couldn't move, the agony so complete he couldn't even scream. His legs buckled, and he had the sensation that his bladder gave way. Strangely, the warmth ran down his back as much as his front but was soon replaced with a deep chill running through his entire body.

He hit the ground hard, felt his head bounce, his scalp separate and split. No problem. If he could feel all that, Clement knew he was going to be fine.

For the most part, people ignored him. A few disgusted looks as they realized he'd pissed himself. For the briefest moment, he saw himself through their eyes and hoped Alix wouldn't find out.

His eyes rolled back, and he saw a man hovering over him. Narrow skull, weak jaw, gleaming eyes set deep above a beak-like nose. He seemed friendly enough, thin lips pulled back from his yellowed teeth in what Clement assumed was a smile.

The man backed up with a light jig in his step, and Clement thought to rise and join in the celebration. He frowned when he saw the man wiping blood off a long, slim blade onto the back of his thigh, then fold and slip the knife into his back pocket.

Clement's eyes filled with tears, and he found it hard to focus. Tried to make sense of what was happening but gave up and concentrated on the warmth at his back, wondering if he were sinking into the pavement below. The warm trade winds of the morning shifted, and he shivered in the bitter cold.

A scream. Then another. Nicola looked up, grabbing for her things as she stood. She tried to catch Alix's attention, shouting, flailing her arms, trying to warn her, but the girl was already turning away.

Drawn by her movement, Rícard saw Nicola track a skinny goth-girl running toward him.

"Well... hello, Princess." Watched her come. Waved to the gypsy witch and grinned.

CHAPTER
SEVENTY

E ndless savanna shimmered with late morning heat beneath a shapeless white sun. A tower of giraffes crossed the near horizon where a trickle of water cut deep in the rock and pooled into a shallow watering hole bringing zebra and impala, and where a small family of oryx, their long, straight horns reaching high above faces patched in quilts of black and white, stood guard over their smaller cousins.

Their ears flit up, wary at the distant sound of a pop-top Land Cruiser as it crested and stopped on a gentle rise a half-mile away. The driver, well-muscled even in silhouette, his Vector R4 assault rifle close at hand, stood tall, scanning the hills and grasslands beyond with a powerful set of expensive binoculars. A distant pride of lions lolled about, sated from their kill. Hyenas frolicked and tussled with their young, bowled over like tumbleweeds and rolled through the tall grasses while they waited nearby for the leftovers.

The man's head exploded in a mist of red as he flew backward from his truck. The subsonic shock wave caught up, ripped the fabric of the air; the echo quickly absorbed by the hills and grasslands, and scattering the game.

Rising from high grasses a thousand meters away, Black remained unseen in the grassland camo-patterned poncho. Nor was his primary weapon recognizable; the Truvelo SG-1 sniper rifle and optics were shapeless and invisible within a cover of their own.

Back in his element, all pain forgotten, adapting, and making plans at the speed of thought. The planning and logistics in the fluid theater he was now creating, were as much the waging of war as the actual engagement. He'd proven exceptional at both. It was planning without the subsequent action that had never been his strong suit.

His adrenalin was up, but some would have argued it was something deeper. An energy that, like the marrow that created the rich red blood cells that now quickened in his veins, began somewhere deep inside him and was carried to every fiber of his being. The yogis called it *prana*—the Chinese, *chi*. The fusing of forces around us with those within. Black didn't try to name or understand such power, didn't dream of harnessing it as his own, but learned long ago to embrace it.

The sentry wasn't the first man Black had seen scouting the vast landscape.

He'd remained concealed as the first had driven by two hours before, easily avoidable, still out at ten klicks. A second man ninety minutes ago. The frequency was enough he could start making concrete decisions.

The third sentry had been inevitable and gave him some sense of how many men he faced. Simple calculations of their radius and overlapping grids of deployment. Much of it guesswork but the two mercenary bodyguards he'd seen on video had vast amounts of military experience between them. Strategic allocation dictated that operational procedure would get more disciplined as he neared his objective.

Terrain was stark and he'd made good time. And now he had a vehicle.

Examined the man's weapons. The hand-held two-way Motorola. The water stores. Grabbed the binoculars and scouted the same landscape they'd scanned just ten minutes before. Nothing that didn't belong.

Still six klicks out. Within that radius, simple calculations meant sentries had to surveil 113 square kilometers or nearly 44 square miles.

The sprawling ranch house, a mansion within a compound of out-buildings, sat unencumbered in a vast, virtually flat landscape. No geological cover other than a plateau some distance away that tempered the storms and accounted for the valley's fertility. The real danger would come a couple of kilometers from the house—less than five square miles. Then he'd face the small army Kronmüller had waiting for him.

Black pulled out his gear. Laptop, GPS, Iridium sat-phone. A desert-brown grass-patterned ghillie suit. Concealment options would prove crucial. Paint restructured his face into unrecognizable forms of shadow and light, but he took a moment to redo it. Hiding in plain sight meant patterning into unexpected, negative space as much as finding physical cover.

Three primary weapons—the South African sniper rifle, a suppressed H&K MP71, and his trusty .45 1911. People argued over each weapon's merits but much of it came down to what he could carry and what was available.

Confirmed his position against the satellite maps Nicola provided. Taken less than 24 hours ago, what she culled on his behalf was as close to being wired in with SatCom as he was going to get. He was on his own. No government cover, no cavalry if he bit off more than he could chew.

The photos showed dried river beds and shallow ravines two kilometers west of his target. He'd stage there, check with Nicola for any updated information, and approach his objective with the sun at his back.

The Land Cruiser moved easily over the broken terrain. Forced himself to drive slow and steady. Turned up the volume on the hand-held radio. If his path threatened to overlap with another, he should know in time.

Black felt good. Invigorated on a cellular level. Psychiatrists would have a field day. Probably sell out an entire convention just for him. Old Doc Gallagher could be the star. Standing straight as a flag pole behind the podium, his soft Tar-Heel drawl flowing over the mic like molasses over gravel. Adjusting the antique Benjamin Franklin bifocals at the tip of his nose to read from his own meticulously printed observations and footnotes. Slides and supplemental materials available.

The adrenalin mellowed into a high he knew he could sustain for days. The roller coaster had started in Chicago, so this was pushing it. He was human and the ride had to stop sometime.

He considered going at night. Planned for it. Tactically it made more sense; human's natural circadian rhythms made most people less effective, especially during the witching hour, but they'd be guarding against it.

So, he'd go when it made no sense at all. It had served him well so far. *He could hear the scratching of Old Doc's pen.*

Winter in Chicago, summer in South Africa. The solstice due in just days and golden and blue-hours meant there would be plenty of light even after his attack. Not long now. Besides, he'd either succeed or fail in a matter of seconds or minutes, not hours. Speed was his friend, not time. Rape or torture or the degradation and sale in some distant auction all took time. Minutes or hours or days. But the transition to death happened in a single instant. There was no more time.

Black's only strategy was to locate Sam. *Kill everyone in his way and take her home.*

CHAPTER
SEVENTY-ONE

L ina was locked in her room. Back in a dress. Everything else had been taken.

So far, nothing. No shouting, no slamming doors, no movement in the house, only the pounding in her chest, threatening to shatter her ribs from within. She wasn't afraid for herself, there was nothing more Christiaan could do to her. She feared for Sam. Their failed attempt at freedom was as she had seen, yet, she knew she still had a role to play in the fate of the American.

Sam clenched her hands, but couldn't stop shaking for more than an instant. The tension in her limbs threatened to tear muscle and crack bone, to throw her from where she perched on the edge of the bed. She'd thrown up thirty minutes before. Nothing left inside but fear. Her heart lurched when she heard a key turn in the lock. Knees promised to buckle but she forced herself to stand.

Kronmüller entered. Eyes hard as blue-gray slate, without expression or animation. Voice gravel and low.

"Strip."

No comprehension of his words, only the mental search for escape. None to be found.

"Get your fucking clothes off and get in the bath."

Frozen, all thoughts short-circuited by fear, her mind unable to function.

He stared at her for long moments and walked out.

The taste of terror, like battery acid on her tongue, burned at her throat and made her stomach twist in revulsion.

A moment later Kronmüller stomped back in dragging a child, maybe seven or eight, his hands digging into the little girl's arm. He pulled a gun from behind his back.

The little girl cried out and fought against him, but he pressed the gun against her head hard enough the surrounding flesh turned white.

Tears in Sam's eyes, ashamed she could think of no way to fight back, she moved to the bathroom and began taking her clothes off.

"Fill the tub."

She turned on the faucet and steam filled the small room.

"Take them off."

She looked at him. Face to face. No mercy. His eyes flat, even the light of the room caused no reflection. If he lowered his guard enough, she could bite his throat, rip out his jugular. She took off the rest of her clothes and stepped into the rising water.

Kronmüller threw the child aside, and before Sam could react, grabbed her hair, and shoved her under the water. She thrashed and clawed at his hands, her strong body twisted in his grasp but there was no give in his powerful grip. Her lungs screamed for air but found only water.

Drowning. Every fiber fought against it but Sam lost strength and the kaleidoscope of water and furious bubbles began to dim. Darker and deeper, blacker and further than any night sky. A sudden burst of light that shattered into a million shards and twinkled at the edge of her consciousness until that too faded. It was peaceful. *Death wasn't so bad.*

An instant later, her mind revolted. She bucked and twisted against his grasp, clawing and trying to spin in the water, her strong legs kicking but finding no purchase, her head cracking against the side of the tub.

Kronmüller jerked her above the surface. Throat and nose already raw and drowning in mucus and acid and bile as much as the water. A half-gasp of air and he shoved her back under.

Only seconds this time and she lost strength. He waited until she stopped. Dragged her out again. Limp. Held her by the thick mop of wild curls and slapped her face. Again. His hand cracked against her cheek and snapped her head to the side on a neck too weak to hold it. Slapped her again. Waited. Long moments.

Her eyes shot open as her entire being lurched for air.

"You will learn to obey me."

No fight left. No thought or time or meaning. He shoved her back under. Ground her face into the bottom of the tub. Shook her under the water. Nothing.

He dragged her by her hair over the side of the tub and let her flop to the floor. Blood ran from the side of her head, blooming like a watercolor across the wet tiles.

He towered over her. Prodded and kicked and shook her with his foot until she finally coughed and threw up. Left her where she lay and walked out the door.

CHAPTER
SEVENTY-TWO

Rícard looked from the witch to the skinny girl running toward him. Her oversized backpack bounced on her shoulders and jerked her body from side to side. *Alix.* He knew their names from the photos of the FBI's tech team he'd been tasked to remove.

The boy, Clement, had been inconsequential but irresistible to a psychopath like Rícard. The girl, *the leader,* was the one that mattered. *Cut off the head of the snake—*

The crowd regrouped, drawn to the boy lying on the street. Morbid curiosity bound by some psychic connection spread like a plague, and the once parted sea of humanity rushed back in.

Blood was mostly absorbed into the pavement below but began to pool out from the saturated ground. One brave man knelt and felt for the boy's pulse.

"Call an ambulance!"

Rícard tried to keep his eyes on the girl but two cops on bicycles changed direction and peddled his way to see what the fuss was about. Shrill whistles and shouting people added to the chaos. They stepped off their bikes, one reaching for a squawking radio as the other pushed his way through.

Rícard fingered the knife in his pocket and backed off.

Nicola watched the assassin melt into the crowd spilling from the market.

Saw the police. Alix was safe, at least for now. No idea if the boy was alive but it made the point for her. No way could she allow the team of amateur hackers to continue.

Who was the boy and who was he to Alix? She'd find out, see if there was anything her resources could do to help. Make sure Alix had somewhere secure to go. Why would Rícard risk attacking the boy in broad daylight? Why had he focused on the girl? Distraction or not, the girl's safety was now Nicola's obligation.

She crossed the empty restaurant floor until she was nearly jerked off her feet and dragged into the narrow hall leading toward the toilets. Nicola dropped and twisted, trying to use her weight to break free. Desperate for balance as she was pulled backward, her feet scrabbled for purchase on the polished wooden floors. The attacker stopped pulling, and she recovered her feet, spun from his grasp and whirled around to face—

Curpen, handsome face distorted by hate, jammed his gun against her chest and forced her backward down the hall.

She tried to control her fear, searching for any chance of escape, but with the maw of the gun just inches away, the dark hall offered none. Nor any to be found in the savage glare of the dirty cop.

Too much violent death, and hers would be just one more. Her thoughts jumped to Aleeza. The children. Black. *What would he have done?* Probably snatch the gun away and beat the man to death.

Nicola's eyes darted past him and lit with hope.

Curpen, spun to the left, made it half-way around and froze.

The 3.9-inch steel barrel of a SIG Sauer P229, switched out to accommodate the .357 rounds in the magazine and chamber, pushed hard against his forehead. No hesitation—only the moment given for recognition of what was happening and why.

Nicola dove to the side just before Michaels pulled the trigger.

CHAPTER
SEVENTY-THREE

Heat from the afternoon sun was tempered when the housekeeper opened the wall of bi-fold glass doors and fresh air swept through the lower rooms. Ouderling glanced up. Grunted. Returned to his reading.

The antique cup and saucer rattled in her hands but the new cook, still shaken by the events of the morning, dared not spill a drop. She'd heard the stories and already witnessed the cruelty of her masters.

Whereas the Younger's whims changed as often as the wind, the Elder was simple and devout in his routines. She worked the evenings, had been there most of a month and had yet to see any variation.

Warm milk in the mornings, the cream scraped from the top just before drinking. Custom blends of unfermented rooibos and honeybush teas in the afternoons, and spirits after nightfall, but then he poured his own.

Ouderling—*the Elder,* Wilhelm Jakob Kronmüller, expected the highest levels of discipline from those around him, imposed by force when needed, and demanded equally from himself.

Mornings were for physical work, and he began each day long before the sun came up. Had since he was a boy and been forced to rise and complete a long list of demanding chores—his father and grandfather before him harsh taskmasters of some repute. Had risen early when he'd served in the Army and trained alongside the Soviet and Cuban advisors in the 70s for the bloody conflicts along the borders of Angola. Had when his father died and it became his turn to expand the empire he commanded today.

Afternoons were a time for business. Daily letter writing with quill and well and the ever more present electronic communications and research. The world outside the boereplass was changing and his vast holdings constantly challenged. Here he could resist, still fight to maintain some control.

Reflection and prayer filled his evenings. If not in the library behind his massive desk translating antique Franconian tomes where he sat now, then in his rooms upstairs in the Eastern wing. Last night he'd prayed for strength and guidance on how best he could make up for his son's failings.

His day had begun when bruised predawn skies still held empty promises of a coming storm sweeping across the land. The clouds fled without a tear but left the heavens painted in pinks and golds. God's sky. His land. Thousands of hectares his Protestant ancestors won with blood, discipline, and destiny.

A three-hour drive to deal with a minor crisis near his Eastern borders. His holdings, crops of wheat and barley to the west and Macadamia to the south, vast herds of cattle and sheep, the mines of gold and diamonds, palladium and uranium, worked by tribes who traced their ancestors to the time when the mountains and valleys were still being formed from clay.

One of the chief's sons had bedded the wife of another. Petty disputes generally caused no concern, but this had grown and persisted far too long, threatening the security of the mine. Here, Ouderling was law and Ringer would lay out the options. *One bullet or three?*

Three hours back. Ouderling used the excursion as an excuse to look over the lush valleys, the protective tablelands, and the distant mountains. Reminding himself what they fought for. Besides, he wanted to see for himself the readiness of the men Ringer and Grip had brought in.

He'd only met three. Two on their way out and one on the way back. Tough men. High-powered sniper scopes and weapons and radios, with military coordination and discipline working back and forth over assigned strategic grids and concentric circles. As disciplined as those appeared, Ringer assured him the best of the men were being kept close to the house.

He sipped at the bitter tea. Watched the new cook leave. Returned to the folders on his desk.

Curpen had supplied what information he had on Black. Military and police files and the reports and observations from the man's brief time on the island—from landing on the island to threatening his son five days later. *The man was a fucking menace!*

He'd played the video from the club multiple times, watching for Grip and Ringer's reactions. That told him more than any report.

Grip and Ringer had listened in when he'd called his military contacts in Bloemfontein. Nothing added to what they already knew except the awe and respect that carried across the phone's speaker. Ringer scoffed but agreed when Grip suggested additional men. Hard men for hire they could both vouch for.

Who the fuck was this man? It was clear he wanted the American girl. Not family but a personal relationship. If it could have been that easy, Ouderling would have sent her back. On a plane or in a box. Maybe in pieces in a lot of boxes.

Christiaan had put them all at risk. Weak like his mother, and an idiot, but still his son. And who was now being threatened by a mad man. And now Curpen couldn't be reached.

He handed the files to Grip.

"What do you think?"

"American."

As if that explained everything. His men considered American military, even their Special Ops teams, physically capable but emotionally weak. Their entire society was soft, not something you could train out of them.

"Show me."

Grip spread a large, topical land map over the desk. Went over the markings, thick black circles and X's made in black and red markers, pointing out the stationed men and overlapping responsibilities.

"Another twenty spread within a kilometer of the house."

"And you raised the bounty?"

"Yes, Sir."

Ringer's idea, but it was a good one, meant to combat any lack of diligence or wandering attention. A half-million rand to the man who put a bullet through the American's head.

"Ringer?"

"Back before midnight."

"Any problems?"

"None. He should make the handoff in the next couple hours and head back."

Ouderling walked out past the windows to stand on the silver-blue slate of the patio. He'd had his father's library moved from the Eastern side of the residence and then the glass walls put in so he could enjoy the spectacular sunsets. He gazed at the plateaus. How hard it must've been to carve out an empire from this unforgiving wilderness. He wasn't going to lose it.

"Okay. Bring her down."

CHAPTER
SEVENTY-FOUR

"You should be okay in here."

Julius looked around. The room was small but nice enough. Better than the one he grew up in. Hell, it was better than the one he lived in now.

"Cool." He dropped his bag on the floor and followed the girls down the hall.

"And you guys are over here."

A bigger room. Four empty beds.

Camille knew she was being a bitch, but it was too much effort to be nice. "Perfect," she managed.

"We already ate, but we can find you something," Rayln said. "Food's always good around here."

Camille nodded. Dropped her bag on a bed. "Yeah. I guess I could eat."

Alix sat on a bed closer to the corner. Let the weight of her backpack pull her over. Curled up into a tight ball.

Camille wasn't sure what she felt—anger, fear, confusion, sadness, so stuck with anger. Julius just stared at the floor.

Rayln, not even fifteen and more grown-up than either of them, pushed them out of the room. "I'll be down in a minute."

Julius let Camille pass, and followed her back down the stairs.

Rayln closed the door behind them, pulled a blanket off one of the other beds, and wrapped it around Alix. She sat beside her until the bed shook with the older girl's sobs. She lay with her and held on while Alix broke down.

Hot water beat on her shoulders as she washed her hair for the third time. It might not be rational, she knew it wasn't, but she could still feel the mist of bone and blood in the air. The scorching heat of the gunshot across the side of her face, ears still ringing from the concussion in the small space, eyes blinded by the explosion from Michaels's gun.

Part of her understood she hadn't seen any such thing. It happened in thousands of a second, and she'd fallen to the side before the gun went off. The rogue cop between her and anything she could have actually seen. But her mind filled in the gaps, and the images, no less real, played over and over in an endless loop.

She dried and dressed. Jeans and t-shirt. Even that was a struggle. Stood frozen in the dark, thoughts racing in place and going nowhere, her body refusing to work for what seemed like the longest time. Couldn't think so sought comfort, settled on the bed behind the little girl, feeling for the girl's heartbeat as she wrapped herself around her. Faster than her own, but the breath slow and even and tickling the fine hairs across her arm.

She let her eyes drift toward the pull of the digital clock above her monitors. 6:42. Stared until the two changed to a three. She'd give herself a moment to close her eyes. *Five minutes maybe.* Breathed the little girl in, letting the warmth of the small body seep in and quiet her thoughts.

They'd come home an hour before where Black waited for them. Cooking at the stove, a pail of fish in the sink, and fishing poles in the corner. A dozen children cut and chopped under Rayln's command, adding their work to a pot large enough to feed an army. *Okay, maybe not that big, but bigger than any she remembered.*

Aleeza squealed in delight by her side. Nicola knelt down to caution her to take it easy, but the girl was gone.

The little girl sat on the island counter behind Black. Turned and waved.

Nicola waved back.

Rayln didn't bother to look up. Continued showing a seven-year-old boy exactly how she wanted the vegetables cut. "Hello, sleepyhead."

A chorus of young voices. "Hello, sleepyhead."

Aleeza stood on the counter and added her own. "Hello, sleepyhead." Giggled and jumped into Black's arms.

Black held Aleeza in one arm, and brought her a glass of wine with the other. Kissed her as the kids giggled and oohhhed and aahhhed.

She lifted the glass to take a sip. Empty.

A waiter came from around the counter with a bottle and offered her more. "Ai dori mai mult vin?"

"Da, te rog."

Black was back at the stove. No shirt. She marveled at the hard lines of bronzed muscle but saw the stitches in his side had torn open and blood ran from the gunshot down his side.

He ignored it, toasted her glass, and turned just as Aleeza jumped off the counter into his arms again.

Nicola was having trouble keeping up.

"Hello, sleepyhead." Black kissed her again.

He fell back on the bed and pulled Nicola down. Let his warm breath push away the hair from behind her neck, nipped at her ear. Pulled her into him. She felt herself melt, his chest at her back, felt him push in from behind and pass through her.

For a moment—*one heart*—stronger than hers had ever been. *Undamaged. Unbroken.* And then she was behind him holding on tight as he held onto Aleeza.

Nicola opened her eyes. The monitors were black. The clock above at 6:43 when she'd closed her eyes. Now it was 6:52.

Jesus—she'd been sleeping for 24 hours!

In her mind, she jumped up in panic, but in reality, she disengaged from Aleeza as gently as possible. The girl sound-asleep. Breath smooth and steady.

Black had been counting on her, and she'd let him down. Let her frailties betray them both. Checked her phone. Nothing. Checked her email. Nothing from Black.

What had happened? Had he rescued Sam? Was he still alive? She felt her heart skip and stutter with the dread of what she might find.

She'd failed him. Wanted to scream and cry and hit something. *Anything.* Forced herself to breathe.

Camille and Julius at the big table. They both glanced at her. Returned to their food. Maybe they already knew the answers she sought. Afraid to relay the worst.

They hadn't said five words to her on the way here, in shock over Clement's death, pissed and maybe scared to find their own lives in danger. They didn't know her, but Michaels and Alix agreed the team needed to bunk here until they were safe.

Ricard was still out there. She saw him in her mind lording over the boy, leering and waving at her, waiting on Alix with the knife. She knew in her heart he was the one who'd murdered René. And of course, there might be unknown threats. This wasn't over.

She poured herself a coffee, noted her hands were steady. Filled her chest with air, eased it out. Lives still depended on her; she'd face whatever had happened. Whatever was still to come.

They waited until she plopped down across from them.

"Feel better?"

She nodded and sipped the strong brew. Hackers brew. Wondered which one had made it. "Sorry I was so out of it. What'd Michaels say?"

"You said he was coming later," Julius said.

"Yeah, but that was yesterday."

Camille glanced up from her plate, frowned. The woman was clearly struggling to hold it together.

"What are you talking about?" Julius asked. "We just got here."

"Yeah, like, thirty minutes ago." Not that Camille owned a watch, and Nicola had made them give up their phones on the way here so they couldn't be tracked, but a half-hour sounded about right.

"What?" Nicola tried to make sense of it. "What day is it?"

"Thursday."

"That's imp—" Shook her head. "Today is Thursday?"

"Um... yeah," Camille said. Julius nudged her under the table with his foot. *Maybe you had to be weird to become a legend.* She kicked him back.

He glared at her, shifted in his chair. Turned to Nicola. "You okay?"

"I thought I'd slept for 24 hours."

"More like 24 seconds."

Nicola went for more coffee. Thinking it out. 6:43. 6:52. Nine minutes! *Impossible.* And the dream? Of course, it had been a dream. *There was no Romanian waiter pouring wine. Aleeza still hadn't spoken.* And Black? She could still feel their hearts beating as one. *Strong.*

"So how do we help?" Camille asked.

Just after seven. Black due to check-in within the hour. Nicola had promised to update the reconnaissance. New intelligence might be crucial to his success. She knew nothing would stop him, but they'd talked it out. He wouldn't go until the earliest hours of the morning when humans were slaves to their internal clocks and at their most vulnerable. The witching hour. Three to four a.m. She had time. She could give herself a few minutes.

Nicola sat down. Saw the hacker's near-empty bowls, and realized her stomach was growling. Got up and looked in the pot. Served herself a bowl of rice and rich bouillon Poisson; a fish stew that someone, probably Rayln, had added prawns and Moringa leaves.

"Let me regroup a moment." Nicola took a bite as she sat down. Reached for the spicy coconut chutney on the table. "Where's Alix?"

"Upstairs."

Camille saw Nicola's concern. "Rayln's with her."

Nicola was grateful, sad, and filled with pride. "A lot of these kids are tougher than we are."

"Anything from Black?" Julius asked.

Shook her head.

Camille stacked Julius's bowl on her own. "Okay. What can we do?"

"What've you been doing?"

Camille took the lead. "Searching the DarkNet for a response to the auction and—" She stopped herself.

"Michaels had us digging through Curpen's records," Julius said. "Trying to confirm the links to Kronmüller. Guess that's dead now."

He deflated as he realized what he'd said.

They heard the soft padding of bare feet as Rayln came from upstairs.

"She's sleeping," she answered before they asked. Gathered their bowls.

Nicola joined her at the sink. Held her close, kissed her on the head. "You okay?"

"Sure." Rayln pulled away and started on the dishes.

Nicola stopped herself from pushing, poured herself more coffee, and turned back to the two techs.

"Can you see his work?" Nicola asked.

"Clements?"

Nicola nodded.

"Yeah, maybe," Julius said.

"Okay. Let's get you online."

Comforted by the glow of her computer as it searched through thousands of satellite images, some of them taken just minutes ago, Nicola sat quietly at her desk. Nearly eight o'clock—nothing from Black.

Aleeza woke long enough to be helped to the toilet and was now sleeping behind her beneath a light blanket.

No word from Michaels. Between the Mauritian Police Department and the Agents sent to replace him, she imagined he was having a time of it. She'd reached out once to remind him she could be there tomorrow if needed. Hadn't heard back.

The quick program she'd written pulled commercially available sun-synchronous images from hundreds of earth-imaging satellites orbiting the earth.

As imaging capability had grown, so had the uses and needs. Mining and oil exploration. City and infrastructure planning. Weather, climate research and mitigation. Housing and farming and species migration. That in turn fueled greater innovation and advances in what collectively made up a trillion-dollar industry of ever-present surveillance.

Current technologies for low earth orbiting, or LEO, satellites were pushing past theoretical limits of light diffraction, image acquisition, and data transfer, but Nicola didn't need to tap into the intelligence agencies of the dozen countries with multi-billion dollar spy-satellite capabilities, or the university research programs under their purview.

Anyone could jump on the Internet, punch in geo-coordinates, and look at images taken from space of our cities and farms and neighborhoods. Even Google Earth came close for her purposes, but she could do better.

Her talents let her pull from the back doors of satellites with massive mirrors, 2400 millimeter apertures, and previously unfathomable resolutions and data-transfer rates.

Captured from hundreds of kilometers above the earth traveling at twenty-seven thousand kilometers an hour, the ultra-high-resolution cameras circled the globe every ninety minutes, scanning in swaths fifteen and twenty kilometers wide as they mapped the entire surface of the Earth as fast as every three days. Arrays of lesser resolution micro and nano CubeSats updated full global coverage on an hourly basis.

Nicola was only interested in relevant pictures from a small portion of the earth but there were still a lot to pull from. This was not about acquiring more information—it was about making sense of the massive quantities she had in hand.

The legal resolution of commercially-available images was capped at thirty centimeters. Her computer sorted through relevant degraded images then reacquired the original data at resolutions as fine as ten and fifteen centimeters per pixel.

Not close enough to recognize anyone but Black only needed an overview, an idea of their positioning to best make a strategy to get in and out.

She looked at an image that made her heart stop. Just for an instant but the pain from what it showed burst in her chest and sent a chill out to her limbs that raised the fine hair across her arms.

The house. A massive sprawling "Y" shaped mansion in the high-veld of the desert. Jeeps and trucks scattered. Barns, warehouses, and what must be stables. Horses grazed in a corral nearby. Jeeps and trucks and huge farm equipment. Combines and tractors. A helicopter on a small pad. Two-thousand meters away, a small airplane hangar and runway.

What made her stop wasn't only the vehicles absent on the images she'd given Black just twenty-four hours ago, it was the number of people, armed men, at strategic vantage points stationed across the property.

An hour late—*why hadn't he checked in?*

Her mind attuned to computers that made trillions of calculation in seconds; even a one-minute delay seemed infinite, the agony unbearable.

She had to reach Black. Warn him off. This was suicide.

CHAPTER
SEVENTY-FIVE

Lina didn't fight against the massive bodyguard. Considering he could break her arm with a squeeze of his hand, maybe he thought he was being gentle. They descended the steps, no one else visible in the house nor seen from the front windows, but something was happening. It was carried on the air currents that flowed through the house.

Grip led her to the library—not the gallows but it might as well have been. Shoved her to the middle of the floor where she tripped on the thick hand-knotted carpets.

Ouderling stood on the stone deck with his back to her looking over his lands. The horizon beginning its first transition to the golds and coppers of the sunset just hours away, the deepening colors in the sky mimicking the elements buried under the rock and soil. Soon enough it would be night's turn, far off galaxies reflecting rich mineral deposits of platinum and uranium and diamonds hidden deep under the lands he now surveyed.

His voice low. "Do you think I would let my son's perversions destroy this?"

His arms spread as if in an invocation to God. The pose no different from those working the land and praying for deliverance from his tyranny.

He turned, and loathe to touch her, stepped wide before sitting behind the desk. Reached for his tea. Cold. Spat it back into the delicate cup.

"You will go back to your people." He tossed her a small embroidered purse. Perhaps gold coins—it jangled as it hit her chest and fell to the floor.

"Pack one bag. Grip will take you tonight. I'll not have you becoming Christiaan's martyr."

Despite his words and the token of money, she knew she'd never make it off the property. "What about the American?"

"Fucking kaffers. Always you demand more."

Ouderling rose to pour himself a drink. The single malt shimmering in the cut crystal matched the golden light of the afternoon.

Kronmüller stormed into the room. "What the fuck is going on?"

His wrath directed at his father, but he glared at Lina and searched the eyes of his bodyguard for any sign of betrayal.

There were decisions to be made, and father and son seemed determined to force his hand. Grip was a soldier, not a general. He'd seen twisted fucks before. Men dangerous to all in equal measure. Both these men were ready to erupt.

He wanted to let them fight it out. Victor takes the spoils. They didn't need him for this shit and his mind was on Black. The man was out there stalking them, drawing closer. His blood quickened at a challenge that might finally call upon his talents.

The younger was sick. Impulsive—the reluctant grasp of his basest instincts tenuous at best. Obsessed with the woman. Had been since they'd first seen her on the runways of Paris. *Who the fuck was he to say?* Maybe this is what love is.

No. Psychotic bullshit is what it was. *All of this for a woman?*

The fucking voodoo witch made his skin crawl. She met your eyes but never looked at you. She looked into you. He would soon change that. She'd cry and beg and wail like all the others; the stench would come in waves from the stale sweat of terror as much as the puddles of piss and the shit she'd void from her bowels when the time came.

...

Ouderling ignored his son, looked up at the bodyguard, the heavy chest and shoulders blocking his view of the late afternoon sun. Inscrutable. They'd arrived from the same army on the same day but it was infinitely easier to work with Ringer, an equally powerful machine but without the intellect or aspiration to cloud his loyalties.

His hand threatening to shatter the glass in his grip, he looked at the man he was forced to call son.

"I'm making right what I never should have allowed to begin."

Kronmüller stormed around the room, looking for something to strike at. Pulled a leather-bound volume from the shelves, stared at the title without reading, and threw the book across the room.

"What you allowed? You're as irrelevant as the relics I dug as a child." His arms swept toward the mountains his father gazed at day after day. "You think your failing farms and empty mines support this land? They don't even pay off the dinosaurs in Pretoria so you can go on pretending you're not their puppet. They pull your strings and you dance for the applause. It's my support that allows you to pretend you have any relevance at all."

"You have no idea what the fuck you are talking about."

Kronmüller colored with hate. "Sure. And Joffire wasn't on his knees sucking off his lover when I slipped behind him and cut his throat."

Impossible! His son had been killed in the border wars fighting to keep what was theirs. Fighting for his country. For his family.

Ouderling looked in the eyes of the abomination standing before him. Memories rushed in as if the room imploded. The denial crumbled and threatened to crush him under its weight. He staggered, fell back into the shelves behind him.

"But why? He was your brother."

"That implies that I am also your son." Spittle against the afternoon sun flew from his snarl. "You killed my mother because you never accepted it. Why change now?"

He held out his hand. "Lina, come here."

Ouderling couldn't process it, clung to what he knew. "I can't imagine you're mine because your head is packed with shit. This ends now. The evidence is being disposed of and you'll begin acting like a man. The man who would be my son."

"Evidence?"

"Taken away."

"What have you done?" His voice betraying his panic as he ran the possibilities.

Kronmüller looked to Grip. Fists tight. Shoulders hunched. Looked like a bull gorilla ready to charge. But at who?

Black was torn between attacking now or waiting until the earliest morning. Lives depended on his decision. Hadn't reached Nicola as promised but what could she tell him? He could see with his own eyes and guess what waited. She didn't have time to hold his hand.

Sun at his back. Three painstaking hours to move out of the ravine and closer to the house. They weren't expecting him now; you could see it in their posture and their lack of operational awareness.

The energy inside his veins thrummed and vibrated until it threatened to explode, yet comforted him like a drug. He knew others called his talents *addiction*.

He scanned the outer buildings. Cover for those waiting but also for his movements. He moved the pieces of the puzzle in his mind. Adjusted the approach. Noted the helicopter beyond the house. A chance it would be his way out of here if he didn't take the plane.

He counted a dozen men. Which meant there would be twice that between him leaving with Sam. Soldiers honed and culled from some of Africa's most brutal conflicts. Some fuck-ups for sure, like the idiot smoking outside the barn flipping the safety on his assault rife back and forth. But there'd be others as professional as any he'd served with or fought against.

He scanned the house, a massive, sprawling stone affair. A central structure and two newer wings on opposite sides. Certainly, the satellite photos didn't do it justice. A fortress. Or a prison. He noted the bars on the upper windows. He could have admired the fortitude taken to carve it from the wilderness but for the blood spilled from the thousands they'd stolen it from.

The optical glass of the scope crossed the open room when he saw Sam—the dress, the wild cascade of curls—held in the unrelenting grip of the Elder. The blond man in the crazy shirt storming back and forth in the room must be Kronmüller. He grabbed and threw a book that seemed to stop in mid-air—frozen in time—long enough for a single extended exhalation. Black's finger flicked the safety and caressed the trigger.

"You think that every one of those stolen children is not another noose around your neck? And for what? How much fucking money can they bring?"

"You're the idiot." Kronmüller shook his head. "It's not about money. It's about influence."

Ouderling grabbed at Lina, jerked her into his arms. "You think your whore won't dance to see you on the gallows or slide a knife across your throat in your sleep?"

"Get your hands off her." Tears welled in his eyes as he struggled for control.

The moment hung in the air until both men looked to the inscrutable bodyguard.

"Time to decide."

Ouderling confident. Grip was a soldier and soldiers carried out orders. It wasn't in the man to betray him.

Nothing seemed to happen, no muscle in the mountain moved, but Ouderling recognized the shift of light in the man's eyes.

"You ungrateful fuc—"

He turned and reached for the sjambok, the traditional rhinoceros-hide whip lying across the mantle.

It happened so fast that one would have thought Grip had the gun in his hand all along. An ear-shattering clap of thunder echoed off the high walls of the tight room and Ouderling staggered back. Looked down in shock at the blood coming from his chest. Held on to Lina as he tried to stay on his feet, his other hand reaching for the gun on his desk.

Kronmüller pounced. The gun in his hand roared. Losing it. Three more shots as fast as he could pull the trigger threatened to blow out their eardrums.

The force of the rounds shredded his father's chest, shattered the arm raised to fend them off, and drove him back into the wall. Dragging Lina down with him. *BANG!*

Kronmüller dove across the room and nearly landed on top of them. Pulling her away. Until he saw the blood, the torn flesh in her side. He jerked away in revulsion and stared.

CHAPTER
SEVENTY-SIX

He'd waited too long! *Had his inaction killed Sam?* Black replayed the shots.

Calculated the possibilities in an instant. It made little sense.

The two-dimensional view within the glass flattened all perspective and sense of depth as a vehicle slid to a stop near the house. Gravel and dust took away his view.

He concentrated on reconstructing the room beyond the cloud. Hints of light and shadow that he assembled into a target six-hundred meters away.

Black lined up the reticle on the massive man, made larger than life in the pristine optics of the scope, just as the man turned.

Grip spun toward the mountains at the sound of a jeep sliding to a halt and waited as the driver emerged and lurched his way toward the house.

Radio filled with static but echoed what the man was shouting. "He's here!"

"Who? Who the fu—"

The man's head exploded! One moment there, and in the next it was gone. No longer under control, the man's body dropped where it stood.

A second tearing of air registered in Grip's subconsciousness as he dove to pull Kronmüller to the floor. They bowled over, slammed into the walls; books and crystal raining from above.

Kronmüller snapped out of his fugue, shook the bodyguard's hands off. Spun and scrabbled across the rug to reach for Lina.

Color fading, her body already covered in a fine sheen of oily sweat.

"It's okay," Kronmüller whispered. "I've got you. You're going to be alright."

Lips trembling, she looked into his eyes and smiled.

Scrambling behind the walls, Grip listened to two dozen shots from as many different types of guns echoing across the estate, the concussion rattling the huge windows above him.

He glanced at Ouderling. Chest torn and ravaged, bone and raw meat visible under the wash of slick crimson blood. Face colorless as dust. He watched Kronmüller lift Lina's limp body.

Grip fell back, twisted, and emptied half a mag blindly toward the mountains in the time it took for him to roll across the floor.

Lead peppered the hills and landed around him, but none close enough to worry about. Black sighted on the truck, put two rounds in the engine block before putting one in the gas tank. He repeated on three others, took out two men near the stables.

If he was right, the children were there, and he needed to be careful with his shots.

Another armed man sprinted across the lawn. A single round took the mercenary's arm off, and he bowled over and tumbled across the lot.

The scope literally narrowed Black's focus, so he tracked with naked sight. Took out two more.

The earth kicked up around him.

Black concentrated on the room. The big man rolled and fired blindly, and the ground around Black exploded. He ignored it, put his eye back to the glass, and watched Kronmüller scoop up Sam. Limp in his arms but surely he wouldn't carry her out unless she was alive. At least that's what he hoped.

More rock and dirt danced and jumped up around him, close enough to spit and pepper his face. Time to move. *But first—*

Vehicles rarely exploded like the movies from a shot in the gas tank. But once the fuel was spilled, all bets were off. Black fired twice more into the first jeep. Sparks hit the puddle of diesel beneath it and the jeep leapt into the air. The fireball and concussion blew out windows on the upper floors of the house fifty meters away and shrapnel took out another man. Smoke roiled across the lot and Black fired at the other two jeeps. One sat disabled but defiant while the other exploded.

Black crawled behind the cover of a 5-inch ridge of hard dirt. Better than nothing. The advantage of the rounds kicking up rock and dust that floated backlit in the late afternoon sun was that they helped hide his actions. Eyes were more sensitive to movement than pattern and the billows of oily black smoke added to his cover.

He scrabbled full-speed on hands and knees. Thirty meters later, he dropped to his belly and killed two more. Spun on his back and aimed at a pop-top jeep coming his way.

Black needed to get to the stables. Save the kids. Ran the odds—made himself focus. Their best chance was for him to continue his assault, save Sam, and deal with them later.

He changed mags and took out the tires on two more vehicles.

A bullet whined by close enough air rippled against his cheek.

Black tore away the remains of the ghillie suit and unleashed a stream of steel-jacketed lead toward the barns as he ran flat out for the stables.

A vehicle emerged from around the house, careening wildly and heading toward the helicopter. Kronmüller!

180 degrees away, at the edge of his vision, another truck spun out from the opposite side of the house. The bodyguard.

Black turned back. Kronmüller's jeep bounced and jerked across the broken ridges like a bike riding across a plowed field. He could have tried to take out the tires on Kronmüller's vehicle but was afraid of hitting Sam.

...

Kronmüller was pissed. And scared for Lina. His fucking father! He should have killed him years ago. And how did the fucking American shooting at them get this close?

Lina looked bad. Her skin wet and waxy like figures of celebrities he'd once seen in an amusement park in Paris. She was strong. He'd get to the chopper—it wouldn't take long to get her help.

Fifty more meters—everything would be fine. Then the helicopter in front of him blew up. Steel and glass-like shards of the polycarbonate canopy shot out in a sphere of potential destruction, the blinding flash and superheated air scorching his eyes. A piece of razor-sharp acrylic sliced his cheek. Kronmüller twisted the wheel, slid the jeep in the dirt until it stopped, took a breath, and then gunned it toward the hanger.

Black aimed past the bucking jeep and emptied the magazine into the helicopter. Glass shattered and metal flew from the onslaught of lead. A small explosion and a burst of flame. Kronmüller's jeep slid to a stop. Black sighted on the tires just as the ground around him kicked up, rock and metal shrapnel ripping across the back of his legs.

He spun back to the bodyguard's jeep. Pulled the .45 and put two rounds through the windshield and three more in the engine block. The jeep's engine seized and the big man turned hard on the wheel. The tires dug into a heavy rut of packed earth and the jeep twisted on its own before flipping up and over. It seemed to hang in the air for long moments, then crashed onto its side. The giant never hesitated. He leapt from the jeep in mid-air and was up and running for cover. Moved well for a big man. Probably a rugby star in his youth.

Black fell onto his back as three more soldiers entered the fray and unloaded in his direction. He twisted his neck long enough to see Kronmüller veering away from the helicopter and begin driving toward the hanger.

Black eyed another Land Cruiser. Two men taking shelter behind it and firing his way. He fell onto his back, minimizing his body. Kronmüller a hundred meters away and heading toward the hanger. The bodyguard rallying the troops near the barn—they were just seconds away from mounting an all-out assault that he couldn't possibly survive. He needed that vehicle.

Black rolled and spun, got off three rounds into a large kerosene tank next to the barn. It was enough that the peeling baked steel ruptured. He aimed at a tractor, and watched the men run when sparks started flying. Too late. The fuel caught and the tank blew, slicing one man nearly in half and drenching one of the others in flaming kerosene.

The screams only lasted moments as the burning liquid was inhaled and he melted from the inside as much as without.

Black turned back to the two men firing from the cover of the Land Cruiser.

Four figures as black as death against the flames rushed the men from behind. Machetes, a pitchfork, and an axe sliced through the air. The mercenaries decimated before they even knew they were in danger. Their weapons swept up and turned on other soldiers near the barn.

More men and women, the rightful heirs of the land entered the fray, scooping up automatic weapons from those who had fallen at Black's hands. *Maybe the gods were on his side for once!*

Soon it impossible to tell where the most danger lie and Black was up and sprinting for the lone vehicle.

He ran, stumbled, dove, rolled, and leapt as the battle raged around him.

Kronmüller twisted his head to look back and nearly flipped the jeep as he hit a ridge of hard-baked earth and the wheels jerked the steering from his grasp. He slowed enough to navigate the broken ground. The war was behind him. Impossible to think the American could survive it. He knew Grip wanted his piece of Black, and had two-dozen men under his command. Lina's only chance was for him to get them airborne. Let them battle it out below.

CHAPTER
SEVENTY-SEVEN

The American dove and shot another merc even before he came out of the roll. Ridiculous and improbable but Grip registered how easy Black made it look. The American twisted as he ran and took out another.

Black made it to the Land Cruiser. It roared to life and as Grip unleashed a torrent of lead, a wide blade sliced at his head and grazed his shoulder. He pivoted, ducked and came up under the man charging at him with a long curved blade. His legs exploded upwards and the man was launched into the air just as a crude spear was hurtled through the air. Destined to pierce his heart if not for his superior reflexes, he twisted and batted it down as it sped by. Shot the man who had thrown it. Then turned to deal with two more as he registered Black spinning out and rocketing after Kronmüller.

Grip calmly dropped the mag and popped in a new one, chambered the round—actions that took him just over a second.

He dropped the two men advancing on him, one with a wicked-looking scythe, and the other with nothing more than a plow handle.

Black had somehow taken out half the men and the remaining soldiers were fighting for their lives against what seemed to be an open revolt. Grip registered the new cook coming from the house, stabbing at one of the Rowanden mercs from behind.

Her gleaming butcher knife caught him in the side of the neck. Even from this distance Grip saw the geyser of blood rise high against the low afternoon sun. Grip fired at her from forty meters. Half of her head disappeared and both she and the merc dropped where they stood.

The American's vehicle was heavier than the one Kronmüller fled in. It had the power and weight to handle the uneven terrain better, and Grip knew it had the chance to catch him.

The Land Cruiser was following the same route of broken earth that Kronmüller traveled. Kronmüller in a panic and the American not knowing better. Either could have gone the long way around on the actual road and cut the time in half. It's what he would have done.

Fuck that! It's what he was *going* to do!

Grip ran for his own truck on the far side of the barn. He still had a chance to cut the American off.

Black was gaining. Nine hundred meters. The Land Cruiser growled and whined, bucked and jerked across the hard-packed ridges of earth, baked and solid as cement. The rise and fall rattled his bones and snapped his head to and fro. He'd once been dared to ride a 1700-pound bull when visiting friends in Texas and was now even more thankful he'd passed.

The battle raged behind him, and the psychotic trafficker fled in front, determined to reach the plane. Black had no idea of what Sam's injuries were, but if Kronmüller was taking her, he could only pray they weren't desperate. He wanted so much for her to sit up and look back, to know he was coming. For her to know she'd soon be free.

Six hundred meters and Black still gaining. He was afraid to shoot. Bouncing and bucking he'd be lucky to hit anything at all. If he somehow managed to hit the fleeing jeep, the steel-jacketed rounds could tear through the light metal and kill or injure Sam.

He ran through the procedures that the South African would have to take to get the plane off the ground. It wouldn't take long.

Kronmüller slid to a stop. Was up and out. Black saw him carry her to the plane. Limp, but it proved she was alive. *Hang on Sam.* Sixty seconds more.

The plane roared to life and slowly emerging from the small tin hanger. Black pushed the powerful 5.7-liter engine harder. *Thirty seconds.* Once he was on the runway, he could outrun the plane and stop it from taking off. He was already calculating his next steps—seeing his hand lift the big .45 into view, blasting a hole in the plane's engine. Slowly coaxing it off the runway. Shooting Kronmüller. Ripping the door free and lifting Sam into his arms.

Damn it! He couldn't shoot at the plane. He might need it to save Sam's life.

Ten seconds. He heard the engine of the Beechcraft whine and watched as it began to roll down the runway. He could have kept pace on foot at this speed, but soon it was moving faster.

The Land Cruiser bounced once and launched into the air, then fell back to earth and snapped Black's jaw shut. Teeth rattled and the breath went out of him. The back-end bucked off the packed dirt ridge as his front tires gripped the heated tarmac like gum on a shoe, and he skidded across the runway. The rear-end fishtailed and Black fought for control. Willed the front end toward the retreating plane. Moments away.

Then a blinding flash of light. Sound so loud he couldn't hear it, and he was hurtling through the air as the heavy Toyota flipped and rocketed sideways across the concrete runway.

Black slammed into the packed earth. No graceful landing, arms and legs attached but not under his control until moments later. Still, instinct had him rolling and contracting his limbs, pulling his head and chin in tight and stumbling to his feet.

He would have sworn under oath it played out over several minutes as he lay looking at stars twinkling above. *Fucking Guacamolians*—little green creatures that danced in the lights at the edges of his vision. That he staggered on legs of rubber for long seconds until they finally supported him. That air refused to fill lungs compressed in a broken rib cage as he swam for consciousness and learned to live without.

In reality, he bounced once, spun and fired twice with the end of his rounds at the windshield of the huge Dually that had rammed and T-boned the smaller Land Cruiser, dove to the side as the truck's rear end spun in a 360 and missed him by fractions of an inch, and then cartwheeled to his feet.

The Beechcraft was a hundred feet away and picking up speed. At 70 knots, it would be lost forever.

The door on the Dually opened and the nimble giant stepped out. Nowhere to hide, Black dove and rolled toward the man, the heavy .45 Gen4 empty in his hand, and leapt high into the air.

Grip was not even out of the truck when the American launched himself into the air. No gunshots—the .45 empty. Still, more than a pound and a half of steel that Black brought down with tremendous force with his right hand as his left was pulling a knife from behind his back.

Grip got off a shot before the American crashed the gun into his forearm, getting just enough of an angle on it to deflect most of the blow. Grip felt bone crack and the searing heat as the jagged gun-sight ripped a long gash in his arm. It was enough to knock him backward into the truck where he used his weight to bounce off and shuffle-step forward.

He parried the slashing knife even before Black had fully brought it around, the blade just missing his throat. Never felt his weapon being stripped from his grasp until he registered the missing weight after it was gone.

Black dropped straight down, stabbed the steel blade down in time to his motion. Grip managed to pull his foot back as the blade slid off the steel toes of his boot and bit through the leather to tear through the side of his foot, severing tendon and cracking bone.

Grip, impossibly fast for such a big man, punched down and caught Black on the side of the head with a blow that would have caved his skull if it had hit flush.

Black saw stars but exploded upwards, the top of his head just missing Grip's jaw. Instead of shattering bone and separating the man's spine as it was meant to do, it only grazed the side of the granite chin, cracked teeth, and staggered him back.

His feet kicked forward. Black pushed off the big truck, sending himself backward eight feet through the air to where he crashed onto his back and rolled to his feet to face the giant.

Only two hundred meters between them and the promise offered by the endless sky. The 500hp Rolls Royce engine filled the little cockpit with the gentle growl and vibration that lifted his heart as much as the plane. He could feel the plane lighten and at seventy knots, the first lift of the structure, the Beechcraft as anxious as he was to be back in the air.

He tipped the rudder to counter the prop's leftward pull, pulled back on the stick, and let the inherent physics of the design lift the two tons of plane and fuel off the end of the six-hundred meter runway.

He knew Grip had his back, behind him and soon far below, as he climbed gently into the golden sky. The turbine conversion gave him the power to climb at rates and speeds impossible without it. Dark clouds gathered and billowed in the distance. They could gather with frightening speed, and he could see the horizontal bolts of lightning common above the metal-filled land, but he was heading left and racing toward Cape Town to where hospitals and doctors would take care of his beloved.

She'd be on her feet in no time, and he'd treat her to a visit with her family. Maybe it was time to move them to the ranch. First, he'd take her away from here. She talked about Paris. Where she could recover and fall in love with him all over again.

Grip would have erased the memory of the American by then, and he would do the same with his father. Africa reclaimed itself with frightening speed. This was his land now. His destiny. He'd begin to use the capital and equity of influence and information he'd built over the years to take his rightful place within the future of South Africa.

Laughing, overwhelmed with the thought of how they'd welcome him into circles his father had never been a part of. His father was an ancient relic and would have never been accepted. Always a Boer riding his donkeys and forced to tilt at windmills.

The American. *How fucking arrogant.* And stupid. To challenge him on his own lands? *And by himself?* He pictured Grip snapping the American's neck and then ripping the skull from his spine. He hoped the loyal bodyguard would have the sense to bring him the body. Like a cat leaving its kill in offering on the doorstep.

Why hadn't the American shot at him? If positions were reversed, he wouldn't have hesitated. He may have gotten lucky and disabled the jeep or even the plane as it taxied down the runway. For Lina? A woman he didn't know? No matter. Americans were unfathomable.

Kronmüller looked at Lina. Tears welled in his eyes and rolled down his cheeks even before he realized why.

Light in her eyes gone, the gentle smile frozen on her lush, but colorless lips, the love of his life reduced to a broken doll in a thousand dollar dress and shoes. Her hair a cascade of curls over her waxy visage—long limbs hanging limply over the seat.

She looked so much like the American girl he'd dragged from the tub. How had he never seen that? They could be sisters.

He laughed. *That's why the American hadn't shot*—he thought this was *his* bitch. *Sam.*

Everything had gone to hell since he'd first spied her. Teasing and openly beckoning for his attention on the balcony. He could picture himself captured between her thighs, bucking and grinding and being pulled in to his doom.

He'd last seen her on the floor of the tile bathroom. She looked as dead as Lina until he'd shaken her, and she sputtered back to life.

Kronmüller scanned the gauges. 1000 feet. He set the Garmin autopilot. Lina was still alive. She *had* to be.

Like the American, she only needed encouragement, perhaps more gentle than a stomp and a kick as this was the woman he loved and adored. He would never hurt her. He felt lightheaded. Giddy. *Everything was okay.* Lina was going to be fine.

He let the automatic flight control system take over. The million-dollar plane, well over with the modifications and engine conversions, really could fly itself. Kronmüller reached for Lina, wanting to tell her everything was okay.

He jerked his hand back in revulsion. *No.* It couldn't be true. He swallowed hard and forced himself to shake her gently. Trying not to touch her ashen skin. His laughter began to change to tears. Gut-wrenching sobs. Mind leaping from the two whores on the balcony to their defiance of him in the club to his father to the fucking American mercenary surely dead 1000 feet below.

He saw the pool of blood on the cream-colored seat, already thickening in the dry air. The infinitely deep red wetness seeping from her side.

Kronmüller screamed at her. Beat on his legs, tore at the custom leather seats. Ripped at his hair. Lina—the most beautiful thing he'd ever seen. He'd done all of this for her. Everything. *Why would she desert him now?*

Hate coursed through his body as if electrified, and he fought to stay conscious. His view swam before him as he clawed and kicked up from the black. Fought not to throw up. The acid burned his throat, and he spit it across the cockpit.

The American. This was his fault. He'd keep the head on his desk for all time. When the blow-fly maggots had finished feasting and there was no more flesh to be found, the bleached bones would give him comfort all of his days.

He released the autopilot and without realizing he was doing it, turned to go back.

Grip feinted to the side, slid forward on his ruined foot, and pulled his own knife before kicking low to close the distance. Black turned enough that the strike was caught in the crook of his knee. Instead of fighting against it, Black let the kick buckle his leg long enough to trap the big man's foot and pull him off balance. He dropped to the ground on his knee for a split second—enough for his knife to find flesh behind the big man's leg. Black bounced up in an instant and used his momentum to spin the South African mercenary away.

Grip used the momentum to torque his body around. Faster than Black could have imagined for such a massive man, the African slashed out with his knife. The slash aimed to take his head off and Black had to use both arms to roll and parry the gleaming blade.

Black pulled back and his razor edge again found flesh, this time slicing muscle and tendon in the crook of the giant's arm.

Grip roared in frustration as much as pain. He was rapidly being dismantled. His other hand swung in a tight, compact hook that was meant to decapitate the smaller man.

Black took the punch high on a forearm braced against his skull. He rolled with the blow while letting his blade gouge a deep furrow through the man's massive bicep and it still took him off his feet.

Grip sensed his opening and darted forward, but his leg, the tendon severed behind his knee, buckled, and he began collapsing to the side. Black stepped up on the big man's thigh, launched himself into the air, and stabbed back and down with all his might as he dove behind him.

Black landed hard, spun in the dirt, and rose to face the huge man.

Grip still on his knees—trying to rise. Made it to one foot. He clawed at the steel buried to the hilt in the back of his skull. With both hands, he pulled it out, fell back to his knees. Looked at the knife and then at Black in disbelief, and toppled over.

Kronmüller dropped to 600 feet. Not close enough to see the fight but close enough to see his man fall. He turned hard on the rudder and climbed high against the golden sky.

Impossible! Grip was a force of nature. As elemental as the distant mountains. And yet—

All this to save the girl? Even he didn't know where the fuck she was.

Ringer. *Of course!* His father's lap dog. She was probably dismembered by now and in the belly of the wild dogs. And the American below had no idea. Kronmüller started laughing again.

The American thought the woman beside him was Sam. *The American with the fucking ridiculous name.*

He looked at Lina. Minutes ago, certainly less than an hour, she had been the love of his life. The most beautiful part of this godforsaken land. Now his stomach lurched at the thought of her corpse, rotting from the inside in the seat next to him. The cloying smell of death filled the small cockpit of the plane and made it impossible for him to breathe.

He pulled on the stick and rose in the sky ever higher. Circled back. Put the plane back on autopilot. The American wanted her so fucking bad? He could have her.

Black staggered to his feet, fell to his knees as the giant crashed to the ground in front of him. Tilted his head up at the plane roaring overhead. His head swam, threatened to crack. The light of the sky hitting the back of his eyes nearly took him out, and he grasped at his skull to keep it from splitting open.

He knew he had a concussion. The big man hit like a train and though he'd blocked and blended with the attacks, he imagined his forearm was broken, the ligaments behind his knee ruptured, the cheekbone beneath the balloon-like swelling on the right side of his head likely cracked and fractured.

Yet none of it ached as much as the force of knowing he had failed. Sam was still out there, alone and afraid and perhaps mortally wounded.

He heard the plane making its turn and flying back. Taunting him. He glanced up but the pain nearly made him blackout. Maybe a 1000 feet above him. Held his head and shut his eyes tight. Opened them to see drops of blood falling from his nose and ears onto the colorless dust. Forced himself to breathe and then look back up.

Black couldn't fathom what he was seeing for a moment that stretched into hours. The sight burned into his memory for all time.

A dark figure against the billowing, golden clouds. A white dress. A flash of red-soled shoes. Tumbling from the sky, hurtling toward the earth. The real-world resistance of the heated African air beating and twisting and pulling at the figure to stretch the entire fall to maybe ten seconds. Speed increasing to 120 mph.

His mind balked at the sight. His heart literally stopping for the moments he forced himself to watch through tears distorting and overwhelming his vision. Part of his mind processing the physics of a 115-pound body falling from a thousand feet. Another part of his mind screaming in silent rage and pain as the only daughter he had ever known smashed into the earth just fifty feet away. The sound of flesh rupturing and bones breaking slammed into his ears and wiped out all thought, echoed in his heart until gasping and throwing up, he tried to stand and fell flat on his face.

The sun, ashamed at witnessing the cruelty of man, fled below the horizon. Distant thunder rolled across the Matroosberg plains, and the heavens split open to splatter the desert below with tears

Black lay in the blood-soaked earth and cried.

CHAPTER
SEVENTY-EIGHT

Like the other five men of his detail, he kept his distance. Not his place to question orders, but it didn't look like their charge was in any shape to make a run for it. He'd been only polite even if distant and remote, and this small excursion was no different. Unless he ran and jumped off the two-hundred-foot cliff onto the rocks below. Suddenly, it seemed like a possibility.

"Sir? You might want to be careful near the edge."

The Mediterranean air was achingly clear. Turquoise waters broke against geological rifts and folds that took their current form some three-million years ago. Millennia of wind and rain further shaped the softer limestone cliffs while polishing the pale green schist and rich yellow phyllite into a lustrous sheen.

Deeper inland—craggy mountain peaks tipped with winter snows stood guard 8000 feet above shallow caves and deep ravines—the birthplace of Zeus.

The narrow pebbled beach below might have been popular enough on its own but not enough to compete with the attraction of the island's famous pink sands. Not forbidden, but lovers or sunbathers who might find their way to the remote inlet were quickly encouraged to move on. Besides, even on the sunniest winter days the temperature rarely made it out of the 40s— not exactly beach weather.

A Beneteau 50, sails filled with the Aegean breeze, gleamed in the near distance. Somewhere, close enough to carry on the wind, the sound of singing; perhaps from wayward hikers in one of the rocky gorges or canyons stopping for a picnic, accompanied by laughter and the assured plucking of a four-string baglamas.

The radio on his lapel squawked, and he responded with a circling on his finger to the rest of the detail.

"Sir? It's time."

Their charge gave no sign he heard him but just as he gave up and started forward, the man turned around and began the 1000 meter walk back to the vehicles waiting at the church.

A chopper kept pace high above.

The man didn't look that impressive. Arm in a sling, slight limp. Side of his face a riot of colorful bruises. The Captain noted the thick calloused knuckles and smiled. Whoever he was, he was sure to have given as much as he got. Maybe more. He was here.

Decommissioned tiger-striped BDU's. A Navy Pea coat, ill-fitting across wide shoulders and short in the sleeves. Perhaps on loan. No hint of the branch, nationality, affiliation, or rank. From the way he carried himself—an officer. And by the deference being shown, a fairly high ranking one. A bit young to be a General. Too hard and active to be a Colonel. A Major at best.

They entered the vehicles without incident or comment and turned away from the little church. A short ride on the winding perimeter road and they were welcomed back through the gates of U.S. Naval Support Activity Souda Bay just as the sun slid below the distant mountain peaks.

"I'm to see you to your quarters, Sir."

The door locks snicked into place behind him. They sounded like any other electronic hotel lock except you could tell the door was solid steel. No hollow doors here, nor a handle on the inside to open it. It was a secure, if comparatively glamorous, prison cell.

He knew the comfort wouldn't last long and was being extended only until they figured out what to do with him. A way-station on his march to court-martial and prison, or just tucked away in one of the dark sites without the formalities.

He was surprised they'd let him out for the walk. Not surprised at the snipers hovering above or that they had kept their distance. Probably hoping he would dash himself on the rocks below and save them the embarrassment.

Didn't bother to turn on the lights. Right now he preferred the dark. Closed his eyes and slumped to the floor, back against the door.

Black knew he wasn't alone but didn't have the energy to deal with it. Didn't deserve the distraction.

He watched Sam fall the thousand feet to her death below. Memorized every undulation of her body as it was pummeled by the thin African air, each ripple of her tattered, bloody dress. The improbable twelve-hundred dollar shoes being torn off in the shearing forces and tumbling on their own paths a hundred feet away.

He felt the vibration through the earth as clearly as when her body slammed against the red African dust, and had to clutch the concrete floor where he now fought to not pitch over.

The same scene he had replayed hundreds of times in the past forty-eight hours. The kind of torture a man condemned to Hell deserved for eternity. He cued it up and started from the top.

Michaels watched from the one chair tucked into the shadows. No windows, no illumination beyond a naked bulb throwing light from the nearly closed bathroom door.

He could have checked his watch, but he was content to let the moment play out. Imagined the second hand ticking away. A minute became ten, then ten became twenty. Pain radiated like heat from across the small, sparse quarters until he could take no more.

"It wasn't your fault."

Second hand working its way around the dial.

"Fuck you." So softly Michaels wasn't sure he hadn't imagined it.

"It wasn't your fault," he repeated.

Maybe this was part of the torture of Hell. People spitting out platitudes. It's what he imagined would come from Nicola when they had told her he failed. Sam dead. Children gone. Sincere, but the same words. *Not your fault.*

Black slowly opened his eyes. The acute slash of naked, white light from the small bathroom cut across the twelve-foot room and just touched the polished toe of the Agent's right shoe. As his eyes adjusted, he saw Michaels's face painted with genuine concern.

He didn't have any more pearls of wisdom to offer besides another, "Fuck you." Any additional words would have to come from Michaels.

Both men stood. Black had nothing to pack other than a toothbrush. He grabbed it, slipped it into his pocket, then held his hands out when Michaels offered up a pair of handcuffs. The Agent gave him the decidedly unprofessional courtesy of keeping his hands in front, and knocked on the door. Two quick raps that were expected as the door opened almost immediately.

Black followed Michaels into the night.

As the only deep-water port in Southern Europe capable of harboring a Nimitz-class supercarrier, Souda Bay occupied a strategic launching point for Euro, African, Middle East, and Central Asian deployments and logistical support for American and Allies' interests.

Sharing the Hellenic Air Force Base with commercial as well as Allied and Coalition forces, they taxied on the longer runway past U.S. F-15E Strike Eagles and the Hellenic F-16 Vipers with their distinctive Aegean Ghost paint camouflage, both squadrons anticipating further bilateral exercises in the coming days.

Their plane leapt into the sky, and the military base and the small port village were soon far behind. Still further out, U.S. gunships of various sizes and purposes floated in the protection of the bay.

Sparse crew. The spit and polished Gulfstream V was otherwise empty. Michaels must have had more pull than Black had known to score the DoD's VIP transport. Michaels uncuffed him and let him pick his seat. Two uniformed stewards made no pretense of being anything other than armed guards, but the one did offer coffee before returning to his station at the front of the plane.

He tried to tune it out, none of it of interest to him, but Black registered enough radio chatter to know they were heading north, he assumed to NATO Supreme Headquarters in Mons, Belgium where he'd be formally tried and court-martialed. Michaels tagging along to ensure the interests of the civilian agencies. Perhaps they'd negotiate. After the military had their say, they'd want to make a show trial in the States where some political appointee or other could further their career at his expense. Let them. There was plenty to go around.

Michaels said nothing and Black let the thrum of the engines block everything else.

Let his head fall toward the window, staring out at the endless sky, and rolled the film from the beginning.

Michaels was so far out on a limb here he might have been levitating, but they might have one more chance. It counted on breaking rules that hadn't even been written. And of course a lot of luck which had been in short supply.

He watched Black stare out the window and wondered if he was up for it.

Physically diminished, yet the Agent could swear that the limp seemed less with every step toward the transport, and after Black had discarded the sling, he looked almost normal. The swelling was mostly gone and heavy bruising on the side of his face appeared weeks old, the coloring wrong for injuries sustained just two days ago.

Okay, so the guy healed fast. The complete medical exam had shown some tearing behind his right knee. No fractures to his arm or his head. Certainly a concussion, but very little brain swelling or internal bruising. He may or may not be sensitive to light for a while. Predicting the effects of traumatic head injuries was iffy at best.

He'd sustained a couple of cuts, but they'd stapled him back together and removed the torn stitches from his previous wounds.

Michaels was worried. Black had seemed almost elemental to him before. Now it was obvious he was just a man.

"You okay over there?"

No sign of movement or recognition. Maybe the blow to the head had affected his hearing. If so, he wouldn't have heard the pilots discussing coordinates and flying times before locking the cockpit door. Wouldn't have recognized the name of the street where the two armed attendants were meeting friends to begin their search for a night of female companionship.

"Figured out where we're going?"

Nothing from Black.

As unlikely as it seemed, he felt a kinship to the man. He knew that was based on his brother.

Though they looked nothing alike, Michaels couldn't look at him and not see Robby. Sandy-haired brush cut, ruddy complexion. His brother a bit shorter. A bit thicker. Heavy shoulders, clubs for arms. A dusting of freckles across the back of hands scarred and calloused. Robby moved like a lineman and Black like a running back, but it wasn't about the look. It was about the energy. The confidence that drew men in and was born of extreme skill and competence in the arts of war.

U.S. Army Captain Robert Michaels served under Brigadier Allen Jefferies back when he was a One-star commanding British Army Intelligence and Security Command. Jefferies was the kind of commander who reached out personally to let Michaels know his brother had been killed in action while serving as the U.S. intelligence liaison with British Special Forces during the initial ground phase of the war, Operation Desert Sabre.

Michaels resigned his commission, went back to finish his degree, and let the pull of service lead him to the FBI while

Brigadier Alan Jefferies continued to rise. Commanding British and NATO forces during operations in the Persian Gulf, Eastern Europe, and the Horn of Africa.

Twenty years and two stars later, General Alan Jefferies now served as DSACEUR—Deputy Supreme Allied Commander Europe. NATO.

"You know I called in my last favors to get you here."

Black wasn't trying to be an asshole. Didn't put an effort into it. Breathe in. Breathe out. If it hadn't been automatic, even that might not have happened.

Noise was uniformly low throughout the fifty-foot cabin, but the pervasive vibration of the two massive Rolls Royce engines made it easy to ignore the FBI agent. He'd turned down the coffee but now found himself wanting something. His stomach rumbled and reminded him he was still alive, still human after all. He hadn't eaten since the small bowl of sour, protein-rich gruel he'd managed fifteen hours ago.

He looked at his clenched hands. Hands that had lifted Sam from the dirt. Hands that carried her far from the carnage at the house. Hands that had buried her deep in the desert until he could arrange to have her taken back to her own people. To a mother who would never forgive him. Torn between wanting revenge and wanting to crawl in whatever hole they'd throw him in, Black was lost. Adrift.

He looked out at the featureless black sky over southern Europe. Maybe Slovenia or Austria.

Five thousand miles away, a woman worried about him. It wasn't fair to her. But wasn't it less fair of him to stay in her life?

Black pushed her image from his mind but then found it hard to breathe. It took concentration to swallow, even more to bring his heart rate down.

He needed food. At least enough to keep going until he made some decisions. Letting his thoughts drift, but they kept returning to a theme. Revenge.

He realized part of his mind been calculating flight times, windage, coordinates as the pilots had readied the plane. Now he replayed snippets of conversation from the stewards that floated at the edge of his mind.

His heart slowed but his blood quickened—a force that danced like a memory at the periphery of consciousness. Turned to Michaels.

"What's in Berlin?"

What was in Berlin, besides the six-million people who lived there and the 14 million travelers per year, was the Berlin Hauptbahnhof. The Central Train Station. With 2000 trains and close to 400,000 people every day, as good a place as any to disappear to the far corners of Europe. They also had one of the most modern security camera and facial recognition systems in the world. About a half a day if played the Agent's way would be the most they could hope for.

"How far off the reservation are you?"

Michaels smiled and shrugged. "Not quite as far as you, but getting there."

Black smiled. "Cowboy up."

Michaels laughed. "My brother thought we lived on the Ponderosa until he was eight. Fuck the reservation—I was Geronimo until I was ten. You?"

"Tasunke Witkó." Black said.

The Agent nodded and grinned. "Crazy Horse."

Michaels bought the tickets. They sat across from each other in a first-class car of the EuroCity train. Went to the restaurant car and ordered food. Ignoring his heart—pasta, cream sauce, and truffles for Michaels. Pork Cutlet and spinach salad for Black. Comfortable. Nothing like a plane.

Black went back to his thoughts. They raced by as fast as the speeding landscape. Dark, fleeting images and impressions that like the Hauptbahnhof itself, led back to a single destination.

Kronmüller. He was out there somewhere.

Four and a half hours later the train emptied onto platform number 6, Prague Hlavni. The blast of frigid air that met them made the Crete winter feel tropical.

After a short cab ride, they stepped out onto Starý židovský hřbitov—outside the Old Jewish Cemetery. 12,000 tombstones piled on top of each other, the graves sometimes ten deep. Renaissance poets and scholars, astronomers and politicians, rabbis and congregants. They'd pay their respects in passing to 600 years of history while they were here.

Easy enough to move around the rest of the Old Quarter. Easy enough to walk on the quieter streets following the bends of the river. *Easy enough to see if they were being followed.*

CHAPTER
SEVENTY-NINE

The kids were trying to teach Julius to dance. The reggae-rap Afro-pop fusion of Cameroonian superstar Recky Dasha filled the room. Though the children flowed with the syncopated rhythm, Julius broke all stereotypes of innate African rhythm, and looked like a stork flapping on an electrified hotplate.

The kids couldn't stop laughing. Crisp island light was streaming through the open windows, and Nicola felt her heart lift for the first time in days. They were too young to have to carry the weight of the world.

Rayln was holding her own in a chess match against the genius hacker team of Alix and Camille. She'd kicked their butts the night before in spirited rounds of carom, having to purposely miss just to let them think they were in the game.

Breakfast was being put away while still others were coming from their baths—watching the chess match or joining in the dance.

The music was infectious, and even Aleeza, standing on Nicola's lap, was swaying and bopping to the beat.

Julius finally did a dance move that earned him cheers and clapping. Tried to repeat it and was back to groans and laughter.

"How did we miss that?" Alix groaned and turned to Camille shrugging and shaking her head.

Rayln scooped up the hacker's rook, rose with a curtsy into a pirouette that finished with a deep bow, and made her way to the kitchen where a kettle was starting to boil.

"And no cheating!" She shouted back.

Alix looked to Camille. "What do you think?"

"That we're getting our asses kicked." Camille considered the board. "NH6?"

"No." Alix pointed to their rook. "Then she'll have us here or... maybe here."

Camille's forehead scrunched in concentration. "Damn kid.

Rayln brought a cup of tea to Nicola and went to take Aleeza from her arms. The little girl held on.

"No. It's okay."

"You sure?"

"Thank you, honey. But I've got her."

Rayln held the tea for her while Nicola scooped up Aleeza and carried her to her room.

The computer room would be great when set-up. Generous space for the future, but right now it was a lot of equipment stacked against a wall and a single laptop on a small desk.

Rayln set the tea down, kissed Aleeza lightly, and left.

Nicola's knees were trembling. *What the hell?* She held her hands out in front of her. Shaking. *Worse than a schoolgirl confronting her first crush.*

She glanced at Aleeza. The child was too young to see her embarrassment, yet nodded as if to say *'carry on'*. Nicola smiled and let her fingers fly across the keyboard.

Moments later, a video feed popped up on her laptop. The resolution of the camera at odds with the higher resolution of her monitor, but enough that she could see the room.

A few more keystrokes and a second feed resolved on her monitor. Opposite angle. The one on the door and the other on the counter and cash register. The small square tables of the small cafe half-filled.

University students wrapped up in their studies and tourists refueling for their next sightseeing or old-world shopping adventure.

Morning. A two-hour time difference—fifteen minutes before eleven here. Now she'd wait.

"What are we doing here?"

"Beautiful city, right?" High spires and towers of the many churches and ancient cathedrals poking their heads above streets and shops filled with winter tourists.

"You want some coffee? I could use some. Let me buy you a cup of coffee."

Black knew he was being set up for something but couldn't quite figure out what.

"Spent a few days here a couple of years ago. Great place up the street. The man's Hawaiian, and his wife's from Jakarta. They import the beans from Indonesia and Kenya. *'Toraja'* I think he said. I guess Hawaii is somehow too far away. Roasts them every Tuesday so you can stick with the single-origin or try one their blends."

Michaels was as transparent as the frosted glass of the shops but Black couldn't figure out what he was looking at inside. Didn't know if he should laugh or just beat it out of him.

Shrugged. *What the hell?* It was better than sitting in a twelve by twelve-foot box on the Naval base in Crete or the eight by eight cell he was expecting until his arraignment in Mons. Plus, he could use a good cup of coffee. Sulawesi, if they got that lucky, east of Borneo, was an Indonesian island that produced an exceptionally smooth, low acid brew—sweet and filled with complex earth notes.

Ten minutes. Aleeza seemed content to stand beside her, leaning on her leg. Though nearly static, the little girl stared at the black and white feed on the laptop as if it was the most interesting television show ever shown.

It hadn't been that difficult to discover where Kronmüller was taking the children. He needed buyers after all. Staying completely hidden defeated his purpose.

The three-person hacker crew camping out in the other rooms proved dedicated and were determined to see the children saved. They all knew that Black was still the best chance they had.

The team needed the direction and Nicola welcomed the company. A killer was still out there and though unlikely to come here, the distraction was welcome until he was found and put away. Michaels had arranged a gun. A Russian made 12-gauge Baikal that she only needed to point in a general direction and pull the trigger.

The children were a mixed bag but mostly fine. Even Rayln had started coming out of her shell and Nicola knew she'd have never gotten this far without her. As proud as if she'd been her own but equally dismayed that the fourteen-year-old seemed to be putting her childhood behind her. Nicola would have to search for a way to balance that.

Aleeza hadn't spoken, three-years-old and never a word, but seemed to have little physical effects from the shooting. If only adults could recover, physically and emotionally, as quickly.

As minutes had turned to hours after his attempt to save Sam and the children, her own heart was crushed beneath the certainty of his failure. She found herself praying, something she thought that was long behind her, that first he was alive, and second that he was relatively unscathed.

Twenty-four hours with no word or contact. Mind racing and transposing the horrors she had witnessed in her war-torn youth onto Black and the children. She knew it could only be bad.

She'd failed him. If she'd been able to marshal more resources or insist in some way that made him listen or reconsider his approach? She should have been able to help.

True to his word, he contacted Michaels and turned himself in to the authorities. She understood even before they'd pieced together how wrong it had gone. She'd been hoping he would run, but there was no chance of that now. He wanted to be punished.

As much as Black, she had failed Sam and her heart broke at the terror the girl had been forced to endure. Nicola knew how much Black had given of himself to bring her home. The bonds of war, the obligations he carried. The horror of watching the girl fall from the sky.

She understood on an intellectual level why he wouldn't want to talk to her, but emotionally she had the overpowering need to comfort him. She'd scanned the aftermath by satellite. Truly a war zone. Bodies strewn. Buildings still burning, vehicles destroyed. That he had lived seemed a miracle. Her heart split in knowing she couldn't help him deal with the defeat.

Men like Black used their gifts to expand and push boundaries—increasing the demands on themselves until they succeeded or broke. They were the ones who built the railroads, climbed the mountains, walked on the moon. They never accepted that some things were beyond their control. In his mind, the evil that Black couldn't destroy pointed to his own failings.

She felt guilty trading on that, but the kidnapped children were still out there. Confused. Terrified. *Alone.*

The team had tracked and traced, and she had searched for clues inside the dark web, but eventually, she'd been forced to reach out another way.

As fanatical as the tech geeks were in their secrecy, the analog resistance was just as strong and just as hard to track down. Determined to stay off all radars, many lived with only the rudiments of what we thought of as civilization. Not easy to find, especially searching from a remote island in the middle of the Indian ocean. Still, it had only taken her five calls before tracking down her old friend. He would never betray her. She could trust the children and Black's life to him as she had her own many times before.

Black sat alone after ordering as Michaels excused himself in search of the toilets. He looked around the cafe. Decorated with what could pass as a small museum of Czech film posters.

European cinema he'd never heard of and original interpretations by Czech artists of the 60s and 70s American films.

Black watched the young students on their computers. Many working, studying. Others reaching out to their friends around the world across social media networks.

A young server set down their coffee as Michaels returned. Even before he began pulling out his computer, Black knew. Was pushing away from the table.

"No. Come on, Black," Michaels said. "Sit."

Low but strong enough to carry. "Who the fuck do you think you are?"

"Who the fuck do you think you are? You fuck up—or not. Who gives a shit? The results are the same. Sorry, pal. Turns out you're human. You want to feel sorry for the kids? For Sam? Okay. You want to feel sorry for yourself? Then fuck off. And you have a woman who cares about you. Who the fuck knows why? Who's given as much as you, who's lost as much as you. Mister Badass Soldier Boy. Can't you suck it up for five fucking minutes to hear what she has to say?"

"I don't owe anybody anything."

Michaels snorted. "Of course you do. More than most."

Black knew he was right. He'd given much, but owed more than most. This wasn't over.

He was filled with anger, and yet hope had flickered through the night that they were heading to a place where Nicola would walk through the door. He wanted it. And he didn't.

He obviously couldn't think straight. *Couldn't they see that?* And was pissed they had played games to get him here. For what? Time was being wasted and Kronmüller was out there. Besides, he didn't have enough of a handle on his emotions to face her.

"Come on. Sit down."

"Or what? Shoot me with the gun you don't have? Call the cops? Why would you do that? They're probably just kids. They never did anything to you."

"God, you're an arrogant prick." Michaels laughed to hide his frustration.

"Fuck off."

People were staring, and two tables got up, one to move further away and one to leave. The manager was reaching for the phone.

Nicola watched on the security feeds as Black slid back from the table. Even 6000 miles away she felt the heat of his anger. The self-loathing in his eyes. This is not what she'd been hoping for.

In truth, she hadn't thought this through enough to be hoping for anything. Desperation and emotion. Not the best bedfellows for sure. Her right hand held Aleeza even as she held her breath. Her left squeezing her own thigh so hard it brought her tears. Focus. Black needed them as much as they needed him even if he didn't know it yet.

It played in slow motion as Michaels spun the open computer. Black tried not to look down. Tried not to look at the screen. It was as if everyone in the cafe was staring at him, waiting to see his reaction.

He tried to steel his face, freeze his expression so as not to give them the satisfaction. He registered Michaels's hand reaching into his coat pocket, the bottle of pills he clutched in his hand. The lizard part of his brain registered the reflections in the glass pastry cases of the two uniformed police officers stamping ice and snow off their boots as they came through the door behind him. The manager brightening at their arrival.

As clear as if looking in a window, the high-resolution screen filled with Nicola and Aleeza looking back at him.

His heart lurched, then broke as Michaels shut the clamshell, scooped it up, and led Black by the arm out the door.

Nicola looked at the monitor, willing the after-image to remain. Aleeza reached out, her hand pressing on the screen and spoke for the first time, her voice as clear and tinkling as a bell.

"Tommy."

...

The two Czech municipal officers, responsible for public order but with no inherent rights to arrest on their own, watched as the Americans left.

A collective sigh of relief went through the cafe as Michaels ushered Black into the street.

Michaels's phone rang. He didn't even bother to look. He handed it to Black as he further secured the laptop.

Black stopped. Closed his eyes, and hit the talk button.

"She spoke."

"What?"

"Tommy. Clear as a bell. Aleeza. She reached for you on the screen and said, *'Tommy.'*"

Now it was Black's turn to be stunned. As powerful as if he'd witnessed it himself. Images. Complete with sound and smell and pain came rushing at him with a force that nearly took him off his feet. A lifetime of pain and joy and triumph and regret, all over in a split-second. It paused and started again on the young woman falling from the sky. It stuttered and skipped as he first saw Nicola in the market stalking him. Her dazzling smile and first words to him at the outdoor cafe. The moment when a precious three-year-old had climbed onto his lap and changed him forever.

Michaels sat on a bench. Chewed on a pill. Let it sit under his tongue. Pushed the laptop back into its soft case. Put it back in the backpack that made him look a bit more like a college professor than a U.S. federal agent.

He watched Black on the phone. Standing in the middle of the street. Not much different from the tourists on their phones swirling like the mist of their breath around him.

Michaels had kept his anger in check long enough to fulfill his promise to Nicola. He'd gotten Black to Prague. Now it was up to her.

He smiled. She was every bit as much a force of nature as was Black. They might ebb and flow, but that's how forces were. Michaels was just a man and had played his part.

More than ten hours of travel. The Agent knew Black had needed the time to work it out. That the man was passing through the stages of grief at the same speed as he healed shouldn't be a surprise.

He knew what quest Black would focus on even while Nicola would try to guide him toward another.

The children for Nicola. Revenge for Black.

"You still there?"

Found his voice enough to grunt.

"Tommy. Listen. There's a chance we can still stop this."

She could hear the wheels of self-doubt grinding in his head.

"There's a man. He has information. I only need you to meet with him. Make up your own mind."

"Nic—"

"Tommy. Stop. Please. I can't be there. I can't tell you what to do and I can't pretend to know what you're feeling. Not exactly. Maybe not in a way that means anything to you. You want revenge? I get it, I do. But there's more to this than that. More to you than that. She spoke, Tommy. One word. She's in my lap now staring up at me and wondering why I'm shaking and crying. *That's what you do.* To me and to her. Listen, Tommy. You want to hate yourself. I've been there, for longer than I can remember, but there are still children out there waiting for you to bring them home."

No sound other than packets of ones and zeros that flowed across invisible airways.

She could hear his thoughts. He could hear her tears.

Finally. "She really spoke, huh?"

She laughed through the tears. "As clear as you and me. Like she's been talking all along. And maybe she has been, and we just weren't listening."

He could hear her kissing the little girl.

"Just hear what he has to say, Tommy."

"Okay."

CHAPTER
EIGHTY

B lack walked along the cobblestone streets of Old Town until he stepped past the stone tower onto the Vitava's oldest bridge, Karlův most, or the Charles Bridge. Begun in 1357 under the auspices of King Charles IV, the bridge, many times repaired and restored, was now one of the Czech Republic's most visited sights. Black felt none of the joy or wonder of the tourists and let them dodge and step from his path.

It was cold. Mist hung low above the slow-moving river as the sun heated the frigid waters. Visitors from around the world, bundled in scarves, hats, and mittens, crossed east into Old Town for shopping and food, or west to marvel at the obsidian-black spires of Prague Castle, or along the banks to feed the multitudes of white swans waddling and honking across the river's parks.

Black passed a couple of newly-weds; the bride braving the winter chill in a white dress exposing her back and shoulders, and the groom, looking a bit embarrassed and out of place in a borrowed, ill-fitted tuxedo, posing for pictures under the Baroque Statue of Saint John of Nepomuk.

Children ran to and from their families, the young mothers as likely to be taking self-portraits in front of the many statues and pillars as to be capturing photos of their children.

Black stopped just shy of the statue of John the Baptist on the north side of the bridge. The prophet foretold by prophecy, reaching out from his ministry, preparing those who would listen for the promise of the Messiah.

A man just feet away threw bread to the birds cartwheeling above the river, their antics and daring a delight for the small children watching on. Under the parents' keen eyes, the man divided a large chunk of bread among five children and then watched them do their best to follow his example and throw pieces into the air.

Black knew Michaels sat somewhere below in the warmth of one of the small cafes lining the southwest side of the bridge. He'd find him soon enough. They'd forego the coffee this time. Share one of Prague's famous beers and then begin the long trek back across Europe.

He opened his coat, hoping to feel the bitter cold coming from the north and across the river. Nothing. He watched the children cavorting and squealing in delight at the acrobatic exhibition above them. Nothing. Watched the birds diving and wrestling on wing in mid-air—a dazzling aerial display anyone in the world who once dreamed of flying could appreciate. Nothing.

He thought of Sam. Nicola. Aleeza. *She spoke, Tommy. She reached for you and said one word.* The weight of his thoughts was numbing as if they cut off all circulation and his mind and body had fallen asleep, now inured from feeling.

"Nicola described you well. A man whose eyes burn with self-hatred."

Black gave the man scarce acknowledgment.

"We'll get one chance," the man continued.

"There is no we," Black said.

"They'll march by caravan through the Altai toward Almaty. From there they have an area the size of Mongolia to hide on the way to Astana and then on to Novosibirsk."

"You know the starting point and the destination."

"Sure," the man said. "We can then maybe narrow down the search to the size of your Texas."

Black forced a smile. "Piece of cake."

Karlik handed Black the rest of the bread. Black shook his head, tossed it over in one piece, and watched the birds fight over it all the way to the water.

"They won't all make it. And those that get to Russia are lost."

Black took a moment to look at the man. No different from hundreds he'd seen and sometimes fought with, and just as often, against. Others who lived hard lives throughout the war-torn Middle East and Central Asia. The body spare, the face lined with hardship and deep-set black eyes that would be home among the Afghan or Iranian, Turkish, or Georgian, but Black placed his accent on the other side of the Black Sea, maybe Romania.

"Suntem cu toții pierduți—" Black said. *We are all lost—*

"Poate. Nicola a spus că vă veți ajuta." *Perhaps. Nicola said you would help.*

"Karlik, Nicola asked me to speak to you, and I am. But—she has too much faith in me. These are your lands. These are your people. I'm not the right man."

Karlik reached into his coat and retrieved a stack of poorly printed photos. Computer printouts pulled from the web. Young girls. Young boys. Some not even teenagers. He reached for a grainy black and white of a young girl.

"These came to me last night."

For the first time, Black noticed the man's right index finger was missing, the gnarled flesh shorn before the first knuckle.

"The daughter of my cousin." He searched through the stack for another. Stopped on a black and white of a young boy. Maybe ten. "Her friend from the same village." Black looked away. The girl's haunted eyes, and the boy's fear instantly seared onto his heart.

"Karlik, I'm sorry."

The man went for another. A beautiful blond girl. Maybe fifteen. Posed on display in her underwear against a simple white backdrop.

"We are military men, Mr. Black. Tempered in fire. Warriors."

Black turned away. Scanned the bridge and stopped at the column of aged sandstone on the south side of the bridge topped with the sculpture of Bruncvík, the mythical Bohemian knight, a lion in repose at his feet, long golden sword in hand.

"Like you, I grew up on the tales of better men. Legends," Karlik said. His eyes fierce. "Perhaps now is your time."

Ridiculous. Black had no use for legends. No other desire than to forget and be forgotten.

Karlik shuffled the photos to another girl. Crying. And then another. Shell shocked. On display. Maybe seventeen. The look on her face the same as the Africans.

"Did Nicola tell you I failed? That I—that my friend is dead."

Again Karlik shuffled through the photos as Black fought the vision of the girl falling from the sky. He could taste the dust and dirt and tears. Swallowed hard, and opened his eyes to the man's fierce gaze boring into his soul. Looked down to the photo now clutched in Karlik's disfigured hand.

The poor quality of the black and white printout did nothing to hide her beauty or the fire that raged in her eyes. *Sam.*

CHAPTER
EIGHTY-ONE

Mostly dark. With no windows, time quickly lost meaning. At least they weren't trapped without air in a steel shipping container.

Just over a week ago, Sam spent the morning locked in the throes of passion with the man she'd thought to spend her life with. Rich, powerful, handsome.

The same night, she'd gone out with her dearest childhood friend to a club filled with the flavors and rhythms of tropical drums and African reggae beats. They'd danced hard, channeling the energy of the islands and the melange of cultures that informed the island's history. She pictured Billie's sweat running from beneath thick tresses of blond hair down her graceful neck to run in rivulets through the valley between her breasts. The joy in Billie's laughter, following where Sam led since childhood, cut through the loud club music and heavy bass that rattled their bones and tickled their feet with the vibration of the floor.

Thirty-six hours folded into a steel drum with the stench of her terror and the super-heated, stagnant air followed by a day in a rusted shipping container locked in with a dozen children whose fears and cries amplified her own.

Three days locked in her gilded cage, threatened by the perversions of a madman and his equally vicious father before being dressed and coiffed in preparation for some far away auction of abducted child sex slaves.

Two terror-filled hours in what became their doomed escape attempt.

An hour waiting for the beating and torture that left her unconscious on a bathroom floor. Torture that she knew hinted at the future now waiting for her.

She sat quietly. They had been in southernmost Africa, so she assumed they flew north. Northeast. Lina had said Russia or China.

The only light came from the heavily encased bulbs signifying exits and further locations for maintenance controls and ground handling. After the hours of flying, gasping for air and shaking under threadbare blankets in the cargo hold of the plane, she and the dozen children huddling close for warmth were beyond exhausted.

Several of the children were sick. It would be hard to imagine they wouldn't be. Fear interrupted or completely prevented their sleep. Lack of nutrition, extreme variations in temperatures. Seven hours ago they'd been crammed in the back of a 5-ton truck, rumbling over ancient, long-dried river beds of rock in one hundred and twenty-degree heat, and were now huddled against each other for warmth and struggling to breathe.

Sam was as afraid as the children, filled with the known horrors as much as they were with the unknown.

The plane lurched and dropped and moments later, shot vertically upwards a hundred feet; the warm and cold currents along the coast bouncing the aircraft like a stone skipping across the water.

Some of the children cried. Others fidgeted back and forth in a restless, zombie-like sleep. Still others stared blankly, perhaps their thoughts mercifully short-circuited and now without fear.

Adeline cried out from her dreams, and Sam smoothed the pale blond hair back from her brow, made damp with sweat even in the icy cold. The little girl, no older than eight or nine, the only white child of the bunch, had adopted her during the surreal photography session, holding on tightly and crying out whenever they'd been forced apart. In truth, Sam knew she needed the child every bit as much as the child might need her.

"Where do we take us?" another girl asked. Sabina, if Sam remembered correctly. The girl maybe fourteen, had a child wrapped under each of her arms—a girl close to her age named Emiko, and a twelve-year-old boy named Milhail.

Sam felt helpless. "I don't know."

If she was going to come out of this or to help any of the children, she knew she needed to find a way to regain some measure of control.

"I'm scared," Milhail said.

Sam was thankful for the bodies surrounding her. She felt guilty absorbing their warmth. "Me too," she said.

Sam huddled inside her T-shirt, glad she at least wore jeans on her legs. She saw their breath condensing in clouds lit from the various colored notification lamps. She pulled the edge of the blanket further over Adeline and tried to think. She began compartmentalizing events, putting the things that had happened in one box, the things that needed to happen in the other.

And in between—*the unknown.*

CHAPTER
EIGHTY-TWO

The flight attendant finished clearing the glasses, dishes, and silver from the first-class cabin.

This part of the plane was nearly empty. It gave her time to create a complete history—a past and future for each of the fifteen people under her charge. A game she played where she imagined each person's life, assigning them the romance she'd sought when she first joined the airline.

Businessmen, oil moguls, an arms dealer, a wealthy poet from Leningrad, the matriarch of a royal family returning to the land of her birth. An actor perhaps, but not famous. No, a playwright researching his next London production. She frowned. The two men sitting halfway back in the cabin to her left were still a mystery.

Breakfast had been served, but neither of the men touched more than coffee on the five-hour flight from Istanbul's fabulous new airport to Almaty's comparatively shabby port of entry.

She knew there was no equivalency. Turkey had pulled out all stops to open their new twelve-billion dollar aviation marvel, and until China responded with something more costly and grand, Istanbul Sabiha Gökçen, or as the rest of the world called it, Istanbul's *"new airport,"* was now the largest in the world.

Both men were foreign. The older perhaps Serbian or Bulgarian. He hadn't spoken enough for her to place his accent. Perhaps Romanian, from Transylvania she mused. Piercing dark eyes shrouded beneath his heavy brow had the mystery and sorrow she imagined must be inherited from a bloodline of struggle and sorrow. He was missing a finger. No doubt lost when fighting the evil that lurked in the shadows of high stone towers and ancient castle walls.

The younger was surely American. His Russian flawless, but not his native tongue. Perhaps he spoke just a handful of words, albeit perfectly and without hesitation. His eyes also filled with sorrow yet hard as stone, as rare and unyielding as the gems in the small tanzanite necklace she wore beneath her uniform.

His face bruised. She first guessed he was maybe recovering from an accident. He also favored one arm. An automobile crash, or in her fancy maybe even a train, but when she noticed his hands, scarred and calloused and reshaped from what she imagined must be years of violence, the thin three-inch scar above his right eye, a slash of jagged white flesh just beneath his hairline, she decided he was perhaps a fighter. A boxer or the champion of some underground bare-knuckle fight ring.

The two were traveling together, and yet she had little sense that they knew each other. It paid to be attuned to the energy that emanated from her passengers. All fantasy aside, she was drawn to the younger yet knew in her heart this wasn't the time.

The men were colleagues. Maybe both warriors. Both on a mission. Secret agents or spies.

The two men sat on the right-hand side of the plane, now the south side of the Turkish Airways jet as it began its initial descent, where Black looked past Karlik to the mountains.

The ragged peaks of the Tien Shan rose along the back of Central Asia like the crest of a dragon from north of Afghanistan in the former Soviet republic Uzbekistan, to where the nearly 25,000 foot Jengish Chokusu stood on the edge of Kyrgyzstan casting afternoon shadows across the border of western China.

To the south, glacial fingers and ice-fed lakes crossed the borders and quenched the thirst of former Mongol strongholds once ruled and settled by Genghis Khan, until the vast grasslands and steppes met with deserts sands and rocky plains covering nearly a million square miles.

First shaped as part of the Himalayan orogenic belt during the collision of the Indian and Eurasian plates in the Cenozoic era, Kazakhstan was further shaped by still-rising mountains formed far from plate boundaries by faulting and uplift as recent as the Pliocene, between seven and two and a half-million years ago. The ninth-largest country in the world. The political borders stretched from Europe and the Caspian Sea to the east, China to the west, Russia to the north, and Uzbekistan and Kyrgyzstan to the south.

Vast mineral wealth and oil made it ripe for exploitation by their former Soviet masters and their current Chinese partners which in turn made the region a concern of neighboring Europe and their distant ally, the United States.

Mountain winds and thermals buffeted the mid-sized Airbus. At 20,000 feet, below the tops of the tallest nearby mountains, the air perfectly clear. Nine in the morning. A winter's day in Central Asia where the city below could have highs as low as 10 degrees Fahrenheit.

Visible only as geometric blocks of hard shadows and light, with dense forests of wild walnuts and the birthplace of the apple, where silver spruce perfumed the air above two-thousand meters, a home to bear, wild boar, deer, and the rare, almost unknown snow leopard, until higher into the snow belt, the Golden Eagles and Peregrine Falcons nested and raised their young under the protection of Khan Tengri—*lord of the spirits*—23,000 feet above.

As the plane tilted, Black saw the crust atop the thick soup of impenetrable smog that blanketed Almaty. Ranked high in the charts of the world's worst winter pollution. Beneath, a vibrant city of three million and the capital of the country until 1998 when then-President Nursultan Nazarbayev moved and built his vision of progress to straddle the banks of the Ishim River far to the north.

Caught between glaciation and the Indian ocean monsoon climate, with bitterly cold winters and sweltering summers, European and Chinese tourists came in the winter to ski in the purified air above 7000 feet, while the city's population below choked on the noxious combination of car exhaust, coal dust from the Soviet-style hydronic radiator system that heated the construction of the 40s and 50s, and the rural burning of anything combustible. Old trash and rubber tires. Synthetic fabric and plastic refuse from local manufacturing. Raw coal and harvested peat. The people, young and old, Muslim and Christian, Asian and Slav, wore masks for protection, and fought to breathe the air.

Black had been once before, in mid-April, when the harmful particulate of smog dissipated and the same basin that prevented vertical mixing of mountain air trapped the fragrance from the city's flowering trees, and a rich melange of perfume filled the air.

A short spring had blanketed the foothills with carpets of flowers rolling like ocean waves beneath jagged black peaks, and the pristine snow, shining atop the mountain and glaciers, released life-giving resources to the valleys and steppes below. Vast lands where according to legend, red poppies grew on earth soaked in the blood of heroes from a thousand years of battle, while delicate blues and lavenders flourished in fields of mourning.

Nicola had arranged the flights, booking and paying, while Karlik had arranged the passports. No direct flights from Prague to Almaty. The sheer size of Istanbul's airport where soon, an estimated 200 million passengers a year would transit across all points of the globe, made it the safest bet.

They estimated they had a small window of fewer than forty-eight hours, and every minute locked in the cabin of the plane was agony. Black pictured her face. The smell of her hair when at four, she'd fall asleep in his arms. The gleaming smile when she'd hugged him on her birthday at twelve. The squeal of delight when he'd had her graduation present delivered. The fierce light of defiance in the crudely printed photo. *Hang on Sam. I'm coming.*

Karlik remained silent, filled with his own thoughts, and Black was thankful. His mind raced as he tried to still his heart. Sam was out there, maybe just a few miles away in a city foreign to both of them. Black would need the grizzled warrior and his knowledge to point him in the right direction.

He had only the most general idea of what he was doing in this faraway land but it was enough. *Find Sam. Kill Kronmüller.*

The attendant made a final pass through the cabin. Secured the hatches and overhead bins. Strapped herself in with the 3-point harness. Looked out across her passengers. Stopped on Black. Smiled sadly and turned away.

The plane pierced the crust of pollution and landed without incident. Both men carried small bags of inconsequential clothes and toiletries. Just enough to make it seem they had a purpose other than killing whoever stood in their way.

They left the plane and walked through the small terminal where they were immediately inundated by the obligatory taxi drivers and hotel merchants and just as quickly left alone when those who approached saw the steely purpose in their eyes. A ripple went through the crowd of airport scavengers that these were not men to fool with.

A man approached Karlik. Even close up, they could have been brothers and Black would later learn this was nearly the case. Cousins. Younger but with the same haunted eyes and the strong, hawk-like nose, the same black beard sprinkled with white, and even similar scars across a deeply lined face.

"Bună ziua." A greeting of purpose, with little displayed warmth. First, a perfunctory hug, a kiss on each cheek, the grip of a powerful hand in Black's.

"Taras."

"Black."

The end of introductions. The man reached for both men's bags.

"Come."

CHAPTER

EIGHTY-THREE

S am sat in a truck, as cold as the plane had been. She worried about the children. The icy temperatures further lowered their resistance. They were weak and feverish. Perhaps this was planned. Certainly, none of them had the strength to resist.

She knew they climbed over mountains. Desert air became thinner and thinner as the truck ground through its gears. Winding roads she was thankful she couldn't see. The truck tilted precipitously, and she wondered if they should all be prepared to move their weight to one side or the other.

They went up and up, high enough they gasped for air, then down again and leveled off at what she guessed was five or six thousand feet. The guess was as much to keep her mind on something else as for any real purpose. She had no idea where they were. She decided the language she heard from the driver and guards was Russian, but in truth, could only compare it to films and television. Stereotypes of what Russian sounded like. It might have been anything but English.

Adeline slept. The other children barely stirred, huddled together for warmth under the coarse blankets they'd been given. One boy returned from the corner where the only concession to a toilet was an overflowing bucket of waste. Modesty and embarrassment forgotten—all human.

Sam thought they descended further, down to foothills or high plateaus. On the map she constructed in her mind, she placed them somewhere north, but south of Russia. She laughed at herself. *Easy guesses.* Lina had said Russia or China. Moscow was north. St. Petersburg and Leningrad were north. Or were those the same city? *What the hell did she know about Russia?* But wherever they were headed they hadn't arrived.

Okay. She was still capable of critical thinking. Kind of. She tried to construct a map. Africa. Then what? *Egypt?* No, that was still part of Africa. Israel. Turkey. Was there an ocean? No. The Black Sea. Or was it the Caspian Sea? *And then what?* Maybe Afghanistan. She'd looked it up once to see where her father said he'd served with her Uncle Tommy. Where her uncle stayed after her father had come home.

She tried to remember how the countries were laid out. Iran. Afghanistan. Turkmenistan. Pakistan somewhere. Lots of *'stans'*. She knew the suffix was Persian for 'land'. The Persian Empire stretched across much of the world at one time. *When was that?* She tried to remember more. She should have paid more attention in school. Couldn't concentrate now. *And how in hell could it possibly matter?*

She wondered where Lina was. Tried to remember everything she'd been told that could help in some way.

They hadn't spoken since their failed escape. She wondered if Kronmüller had beaten her as well. Kept separated until the giant who had killed Alan had rushed her from her room to force her into a truck with the other children in the middle of the night.

She played each moment again, from the moment of her arrival. All she'd needed was a fucking phone—how could something so common become so impossible?

"Lina, there must be a way to get the word out. I have people who will pay. They might not have much but—"

"Not as much as others to keep you."

The girl's words rang true and Sam shivered in horror. Fought the unbidden tears.

"But why?"

"You know why. They will sell you at auction. In Russia or China."

"I'll kill myself first."

Lina had grabbed Sam's shoulders. Pulled her close, held her fiercely, then pushed her back at arm's distance. The African's eyes boring into her soul.

"No! Someday, you'll find a chance to escape, but you must stay alive. No matter what."

"And you? We have to try."

"My fate is written, but you must find a reason to hope, to stay alive. Find something to hold on to. In death, there is no hope at all."

Russia or China, but they weren't speaking Chinese. She was sure of that. The truck slowed to a crawl, she heard the gears change and felt the transmission grind beneath the steel bed of the truck. Sam thought they were stopping. They inched forward. Stopped. Inched forward. Felt more than heard, doors opened and closed. Muffled voices. Perhaps a checkpoint or border?

She could try to call out, but what of the children? And it was likely there must be payoffs and established routes of corruption to allow this to happen?

Adeline stirred in her arms. Perhaps the little girl also sensed a new chapter in their journey. Find a reason to stay alive. Something to hold on to. Sam held the little girl close.

In death, there is no hope at all.

CHAPTER

EIGHTY-FOUR

Once again, Nicola found herself waiting on word from Black. How had it come to this? Feeling powerless as she waited on a call. There were differences for which she was thankful; this time he was not on his own.

Karlik. Her only family. She had no proof and very little likelihood they were related. Wishful thinking on both their parts. If he was, it would have been a score of generations ago. His people were fierce warriors and could be found in the battles and conflicts against the Germans and Russians, the Ottomans and Turks, even earlier fighting the Austria-Hungarian and Bulgarian Empires, and before that, Romans marching upward across the boot and Huns fighting their way through Mesopotamia into the country's earliest history.

Perhaps these lands had been at war since the beginning of man. Karlik came from a small village near a small town. Nicola would have never heard of it were it not for remains of Europe's earliest modern hominins found near his home. No doubt humans fought then too, robbed and raped and pillaged—40,000 years ago when modern-man walked with the last of the Neanderthals.

Nicola's people were unknown. Maybe they'd also been part of the land for generations, but more likely were Romani. Crossing from the Punjab and Rajasthani regions of modern-day India to become a part of Europe's population for over 1,500 years. Persecuted and forced into nomadic exile, they brought their traditions and ancient tongue wherever they crossed the globe, assimilating into local cultures until fear and ignorance and political machinations forced them to move on once again.

Karlik was the only family she'd known as a child. He'd found her in the rubble where she'd been forced to work for Serbian traffickers, locating and recruiting other displaced young children. Karlik killed her abusers, part of his life's mission for reasons she'd never learned or dared to ask about. It was he who brought her to the attention of NATO forces sent to mitigate the corrupt and horrific aftermath of a city and country at war. Those soldiers were long gone from her life, but he'd stayed in touch as she recovered, followed her education, and eventually introduced her to a former law professor on her own mission to make a difference. Ruth Blanton.

Nicola checked the time. Michaels's plane was due to land within the hour. His career over. Ready to retire, or more accurately, ready to be forced to retire. Still, he was determined to see her safe. To make sure she wasn't caught up in the international political machine he'd helped bring to the island. Like Black, Michaels would face whatever awaited him in his own country. She waited to hear what he could tell her of Black.

"We still have forty, maybe fifty minutes. Coffee?"

Alix looked out at the windows of a cafe and nodded. Coffee would be good. It was her first time outside the walls of the house since witnessing Clement's murder. Something she knew would never leave her.

They turned past the next corner and parked.

It hadn't been hard for Rícard to find Nicola's new house. It was an island after all, and she had very specific requirements that narrowed it down further. A few dollars exchanged and the woman at the real estate office searched through the island's databases. Houses for sale. Houses no longer for sale.

Some things in the world still needed to be done face to face, but it seemed all information could be found inside a machine.

Not that Rícard had any clue. According to Curpen, the witch was as facile with a keyboard as he was with a knife. The corrupt cop, who had no fear of him, said her skills made her dangerous.

Once he'd found the house and done a preliminary reconnaissance, he'd spent two days trying to talk himself out of it. The security surrounding it was lax, but he was definitely pushing his luck.

Everyone else was gone, even Curpen. He'd circled back to the hotel and had been close enough to hear the gunshot. Watched the scramble of tourists flee, and the police descend on the scene.

Now he was on his own. There was no payday waiting for him here.

He considered Réunion, but decided he needed to think bigger. His partner, such as he was, was gone, shot dead. There was no one to hold him back. Maybe go to South Africa or Europe. He spoke French and English and Creole and Russian. There must be work for a man of his singular talents in Europe. Maybe Canada or even the United States. He imagined he could command his own price, and with 330 million residents, there was surely work to be found.

Three days. He hadn't slept. Couldn't even shut his eyes. Saw her staring into him from across the plaza. Saw her in the dark. He closed his eyes and still she followed him. The gypsy had cursed him. What if she followed him to Europe or the United States? The curse following him but him unable to reach her?

He looked at the shops along the street. A woman in the window. *The same fucking face.* Music vibrating the storefront windows made him turn toward an open-topped jeep. Three college tourists laughing and singing their way to the beach. The girl in the back with the same black, soul-sucking eyes.

A small SUV parked. He recognized the vehicle—had spent days following it for the corrupt cop. The passenger door opened and a young, black-haired girl, thin as a reed, stepped out. Rícard knew she was familiar but his mind and breath caught as the other woman, trying to hide beneath a hat and oversized sunglasses, stepped from the driver's side. He stared at her in horror all the way to the coffee shop. He swallowed hard, tried to think. Slow his heart. They couldn't *all* be her.

Rícard ducked just before the witch saw him. He studied her reflection in a shop window until she was lost behind the cafe doors and wondered if she'd been real.

CHAPTER

EIGHTY-FIVE

Black sat in the back of the big SUV as they drove the wide boulevard through the city. Mostly three, four, and five-story buildings. A few mid-rise hotels and offices. Apartments. Coffee shops and cafes. Soviet-style block construction updated with plate-glass storefronts and modern window displays. Pharmacies. Banks. Restaurants set back from the road with wide walkways and room for open-air seating in the warmer seasons, now empty in the bitter cold. Even more coffee shops.

Taras looked at Black's reflection. Spoke to Karlik.

"On govorit po-russki?" *Does he speak Russian?*

"Nedostatochno, chtoby postavit' na eto nashi zhizni," Black answered for him. *Not enough to stake our lives on it.*

Taras grunted.

Black looked out the windows. Nothing really exotic, at first glance it looked like Pasadena or Denver—a city with nearby mountains. People and cars crowded the streets. Students in drab uniforms beneath brightly colored winter coats. Businessmen in suits, hats, and scarves. Muslim dress and head coverings. Lots of face masks on lots of Asian faces. Scores of Russian teenagers with blond hair towering over their Asian friends.

Electric and clean-energy transit buses mixed with the logjam of cars burning cheaper fuels in vehicles without the emission controls that prevented better gas mileage. They created more than their share of pollution. Kazakhstan was rich in resources, and poor on allocation and control.

Outside of Russia, Kazakhstan had the second-largest oil reserves of all the former Soviet republics. Politics of international trade agreements and sanctions imposed by other oil-producing countries and their main oil field's adverse operating environment under the Caspian Sea made it difficult to extract and keep the best of the oil for themselves. The people suffered in the quality of their air, their health, and their life expectancy. Slow progress was being made as global environmental groups and local governments began to heed their citizens pleas for clean air, but for now, even the snows that fell across the city were rarely white and never for long.

The two men in front spoke low in a dialect and language Black knew nothing about. It had little of the Turkic earmarks of Kazakh which he only recognized by comparison to the other languages across the region. He'd spent enough time in Central Asia to fumble his way with the languages of a dozen countries. He could get by in the two official languages of Afghanistan— Dari and Pashto. Enough to wage war when called to.

Here, he recognized the word patterns and rhythms more than any single word and assumed it was an obscure dialect imported from their homeland. He heard a smattering of Russian when it suited them, caught a few Kazakh words, and tuned them out.

They headed south toward the mountains. They passed Republic Square. The Mayor's office complex. The former Presidential Residence. Bare trees and the grounds deep in soot-covered snow. They crossed over an east-west thoroughfare and began twisting and turning toward the foothills.

A cable car slashed diagonally across the city to the small Kok Tobe amusement park and the scenic overlook above. Constructed on the hills beside it, its observation decks and aerial lost in the yellowed, low-lying mist, Almaty Television Tower; the world's tallest free-standing tubular steel structure stood as an ever-dependable landmark over the city.

The foothills presented a maze of twists and turns. A few small hotels and guest houses, a couple of restaurants—Italian and Greek, and traditional Kazakh way stations serving rich stews and sausages of mutton and horse. Houses big and small, partially hidden behind high walls of tin and steel, crowded the view but gradually thinned as the four-wheel drive of the SUV carried them on slippery, uncleared roads further up the mountains.

They drove high above the smog-filled basin below, higher than Medeu or Shymbulak, where the shops and slopes catered to tourists from other lands. Black estimated maybe ten or eleven-thousand feet, not even halfway up the tallest mountains of the Altai. In the middle of the far side of nowhere. Sam was out there, somewhere, no doubt far below, alone and scared.

"My skoro budem tam," Taras said.

Karlik needlessly translated.

"Soon."

CHAPTER
EIGHTY-SIX

"Davay, davay, davay! Potoropis." the rough-looking man bellowed. "S'yebat 's gruzovika."

The children did their best. Scared, weak, and stiff from the cold. Half a dozen guards dragged them from the truck, cuffed them on the sides of their heads, and pushed them into a roughly formed group. A guard jerked away their blankets and forced the children to stand under the frozen rain.

Sam looked out from the back of the truck. A huge warehouse behind the children. Adeline, still in her arms, feverish and whimpering.

"You're going to be okay. I promise." Sam held the little girl close. "I promise."

Sam climbed down into the ice and snow, her own knees locked and stiff, and helped others from the truck.

A guard grabbed at her. Shoved her to the side where she fell to the snow-covered gravel lot. He reached for Adeline, jerking her out of the truck and letting her stumble and fall toward the others. Sabina was reaching for the little girl when Petru, a foul looking man armed with an AK, shoved her from behind with his foot to slide face first in the snow.

"No!" Sam reached for Sabina to help her up, then pulled Adeline close. Another guard grabbed Sam's arm and tried to separate them.

Sam whirled and fought and kicked. The men laughed, dodging her blows and pushing her back and forth from one to another until she wound down and fell from exhaustion.

Petru pulled her to her feet. His hand digging into her naked arm, he glared long enough to make his point before shoving her to the side.

Other guards passed out a mishmash of coats and coarse sweaters. Worn and filthy but the children grabbed at them in desperation.

They stood in some kind of large compound. A series of warehouses, three and four stories high. Concrete block and corrugated steel or tin as if crudely patched or expanded. A high fence of metal grating, plates of steel, and what appeared to be old metal signs, anything to create a barrier from prying eyes, topped with concertina wire and barbed spikes.

The guards spoke Russian, she was sure of that now, but she saw Cyrillic, Latin, and Arabic script on visible parts of the signs. A huge smiling face behind a steaming cup of gourmet coffee. A sign announcing the construction of new luxury apartments. A car dealership. Almaty Renault. No idea if that was someone's name or the city, but she was desperate for something to latch onto and this felt like—something. A beginning.

Another truck pulled in beside them and immediately began off-loading more children. Maybe fifteen or twenty. Only a couple of the children were black. The horror grew as Sam realized this was bigger than she'd thought. The children brought from other parts of the world, perhaps Europe or the Middle East.

A boy and girl, no more than ten or eleven, perhaps brother and sister, both blond and beautiful, held hands for the briefest of moments before a guard knocked the boy to the ground then jerked him back to his feet.

The guard shoved his Chinese-made assault rifle under the boy's chin, grabbed the girl by her hair, and pulled her close.

She stood shaking as he ran his hand over her face, his thumb trailing across her lips, down across the flat chest, and let his hand slide between her legs, lifting her onto her toes. The boy stared in defiance and hatred and the young girl wept in shame as the guard spit in the dirt and walked away.

Two old women, shrouded beneath dark robes and the veils of their religion, began passing out chunks of dark bread and strips of dried meat from buckets they carried. The children grabbed at them and were herded toward the warehouse. Sam put her arm around Adeline and led her toward the meager food.

"Not you," Petru shouted.

Sam stood defiant in the cold— too numb and exhausted to speak or protest.

Another man brought his phone to Petru. He listened for a moment, snapped the phone shut. Nodded his head to the others.

A one-eyed man, his empty eye socket a mass of twisted flesh, reached out for Sam, trying to lead her away.

She grabbed for Adeline.

"No! She stays with me."

The man jerked Sam back by her arm. Only his iron grip stopped her from falling. She clawed and kicked until the man grabbed her by her hair and twisted her head back to where she thought her neck might break.

The man looked at Petru. Nothing to consider. The message had been clear. Petru shrugged.

The guard let go and Sam fell to the ground. She rose and scooped Adeline into her arms. The one-eyed guard sneered, his eye gleaming in disappointment, but stood silently as they were led away and shoved into a late model Mercedes SUV.

The girl, too weak to even cry, lay still in Sam's arms. Sam let her own tears run freely, and prayed she had the strength for them both.

Two men moved into the front of the SUV. It roared to life, the heat from the rear vents a relief across her bare arms.

The guard in the passenger seat turned and handed her a heavy black hood.

"Nadet' eto."

As they left the compound, she twisted her head to glance back.

The two groups of children, maybe thirty in total—along with Sabina, Milhail, and Emiko—vanished into the building.

She pulled the hood over her head and held onto Adeline.

CHAPTER
EIGHTY-SEVEN

He waited until she came out. Definitely her. The witch and her apprentice. Rícard watched them head back to the vehicle. There was no reason to follow. He knew where they'd end up.

Twenty minutes later he pulled into her neighborhood. He parked and made his way on foot. He passed a woman walking her dog. *Why the fuck would a person complicate life with a dog?*

He nodded politely and whistled a tune as if he was out for a walk himself. Of course, it was one of the more expensive areas. Huge old-growth trees overhanging the winding streets. Houses set behind imported plants—ficus and bougainvillea, sweet-smelling nutmeg and clove and tropical "sea almond" trees towering over huge, prehistoric-looking ferns grown massive in the tropical heat and rain. A witch had ways of accumulating significant amounts of wealth.

Rícard made the decision he would leave. He'd stop to see a cousin in Paris. He wondered if she was still beautiful—the way he remembered her as a child when they played together, or had time and distance, the vagaries of life, weighed upon her too.

He didn't know if his mother would technically have been called a prostitute. Maybe by some—her husband for one. He only knew she rutted with men in hopes of their generosity and seemed to have healthy appetites for all things money could buy. He never received any benefit from it. Nor did the man he called 'father' who was eventually found passed out in a rain-soaked alley with a split scalp and reeking of cheap alcohol. Pneumonia came quick and he died drowning in his bed. Cremated and ashes dumped in a gutter.

Still, he'd been relatively happy as a boy, running wild along the beaches among a constant flow of tourists who came and went as quickly as the tides. His cousin, his father's sister's child, had been just as free, and he remembered fondly their time playing on the beaches.

They'd practiced their pickpocketing skills at which they'd both been terrible. How many times had they run and scampered, adrenalin pumping, blood roaring in their ears as they fled through the crowds. Laughing at their ineptitude until the day she'd been caught.

Ricard followed the man back to his house, peered through the windows as he tied her hands to the bed and stripped her. In truth, he could have intervened some minutes before but wondered what she looked like naked. His own body shook and quivered as much as hers.

Her screams muffled beneath a pillow, Ricard found it both terrifying and exciting. When the man climbed on top, Ricard decided it had gone far enough.

Ricard slipped in through an upstairs window, crept down the stairs, clutching the small penknife in his hand. He stepped behind the man, let the anger consume him, and stabbed with all his might in the middle of the man's back. The small blade, no more than three inches long, barely made it past the fat, but Ricard still felt it, the infinitesimal moment of resistance and the feeling of penetration.

The man bellowed and spun in pain and surprise. Long enough for Ricard to slash the blade across the man's throat. He remembered the drag of the blade cutting through cartilage and flesh, transferring the vibration to his hand and igniting something deep in his heart.

Blood sprayed—the kill was his first, and he hadn't yet learned his craft. The man clutched his throat, blood overflowing his hands, eyes wide in surprise until they filled with understanding and then filled with nothing at all.

In shock, his cousin Emma lay still and silent as the geyser of blood pulsed in diminishing arcs across her naked body. Rícard sat beside her, watching until the man slipped off the bed and flopped to the floor.

Rícard looked into her eyes, gently wiped the blood from her budding breasts. Cut her free.

He led her from the bed to the tub. Helped her bathe. Helped her dress.

There was nothing to tie them to the murder. Rícard had never been concerned. Emma moved away within the year.

Rícard only knew she now lived outside of Paris. Had her own children now. He would visit her. They would talk about care-free days on the beaches, and he'd see what kind of woman she'd become.

Here, a house full of children waited. What kind of woman let youngsters run wild in such a dangerous world?

Hidden by the tropical foliage, he easily kept to the shadows and scaled the wall.

Rícard hoped to see the girl through the window like before. No more than thirteen or fourteen. Memories almost overwhelmed him, and he struggled to put them aside.

He estimated how long the witch would be gone. He'd learned to be conservative, let's say thirty minutes. There had been men watching the house, maybe cops, maybe not, but no sign of them now. It would take him only a minute or two to enter the house.

That there were others in the house meant nothing. Children. Still soft, their flesh little distraction for his blade. All together not more than ten minutes and more likely just one or two.

That would leave him at least twenty minutes with the girl. *What a surprise the witch would find when she returned!*

Then they would talk about what it meant to be a *real* mother.

CHAPTER
EIGHTY-EIGHT

The road became progressively steeper, more winding, and less visible. Late-morning rain on the low elevations changed to frozen rain on the lower slopes and finally to small, hard flakes that bounced off the glass of the SUV as they moved upward through the first layer of clouds. Forty minutes later, they pulled off what passed as a road onto what might pass as a foot trail and Taras stopped the truck.

They got out without explanation and Black followed the two men higher into a narrow pass where Taras led them through a near-vertical field of snow.

Black felt light-headed—he'd had no time to acclimate. Twenty-four hours ago, he'd been just above sea level on the cliffs of Crete. Here, his lungs worked hard to keep up. From his struggle for oxygen, he estimated they were somewhere above 4000 meters, close to 14,000 feet. Towering above them, high triangular peaks of black granite, so close individual rocks could be seen, jutting thousands of feet higher into the thick white clouds.

Deep ravines filled with snow above glacial ice led lower than the eye could see, where a rushing river, too steep and fast to freeze, could be heard echoing throughout the hard-walled valley below.

Taras led them beside a sheer, one hundred foot wall slick with ice. Striated cliff faces and fossil laden bedrock indicated that the land, polished in the millennia of retreat and re-advance of the glaciers, had at one time been temperate despite the present cold climate.

The hint of a shadow and Black looked up in time to see a golden eagle circling high in and out of the clouds. He looked away as fine, hard flakes, driven by the whipping, mournful winds sweeping through the canyons pelted his eyes and clawed their way in beneath collar and cuffs.

He was thankful for the heavy German combat boots they'd found in Prague. Resoled, worn, and broken in, they felt secure if not good on his feet and went well with the thick wool, peacoat-styled uberzieher. A slip onto the near-vertical slopes would have meant virtual free fall for a thousand meters where Black could have died looking fashionably Bohemian.

They rounded the cliff face and stepped through a small vertical crack in the stone walls. Narrow enough Black could touch both sides of the hundred-foot cliffs at the same time.

Fifty meters later, the walls spread and presented a wide, flat clearing. Two men guarded the trail from above. One perched on a boulder with a rifle and the other sitting opposite on a horse, the tip of a notched arrow visible in his hands from below.

Two more hard men strode out to meet them. One carried a bolt action Lee-Enfield, the other an AK-47, stock removed.

They led the three men around a jumbled wall of boulders and ice toward their camp and what looked to be a warm fire shielded by a high wall of rock, and a vintage, Russian made World War II jeep. Black assumed there was another road somewhere, but he couldn't see it or imagine how steep it must be.

The men from above joined them, a total of seven men; eight counting Black. A half-dozen horses nearby dug through the snow to graze, while two mules stood stubbornly alone.

A man came forward, impossible to tell his age. His deeply lined face scarred and partially hidden behind a beard so blue-black that Black thought it must be dyed. *Elvis black.* And yet he couldn't imagine such hard men succumbing to the vanity.

The man greeted Karlik warmly, pulled him toward the fire.

"Veni. Încălzeşte-te. Avem mâncare şi multe de discutat!"

He looked at Black. Changed language again.

"Vy govorite po-russki." *Do you speak Russian?*

Taras looked from Black and grinned, answering for him.

"Nedostatochno, chtoby postavit' na eto nashi zhizni." *Not enough to stake our lives on it.*

"Ahhh... good. I can English practice me."

Taras, his driver who had yet to say a word to him, stepped forward and surprised him with his perfect, nearly unaccented English. "Come. Get warm. We have food and much to talk about."

The men huddled around the fire. Behind their backs, the wind howled and snow fell. The horses crowded together for warmth in the shelter of the cliffs. The mules stood resolute and alone.

The grizzled Elvis-styled warrior beckoned them to sit close. Metal plates were distributed and chunks of meat and stew pulled from a large pot. Coarse black bread was torn apart and divided. They ate the scalding hot food with their hands. Black dug in, the first real food he'd eaten in twenty-four hours. The gravy made it impossible to know if it was mutton or goat or horse on his plate. Black didn't question it. He tore the bread as the men did, sopped up the gravy, and ate.

The men introduced themselves. Askar, Berik, Dima, Oleg, and Temir who seemed to be the leader.

Askar opened a leather purse and pulled out long links of traditional sausage. Used a wicked-looking knife from his belt to cut and distribute.

Black took his share. He needed the nutrition. He knew it was horse, but the alternating quadrants of meat and fat were welcomed and delicious.

Only the crackling of the fire and the grunts and smacking of lips and licking of fingers filled the air until the food was gone.

Oleg made a show of handing Black a beat-up tin cup. Pulled out a large leather flask, shook it once, and poured a heavy, frothy drink into his cup. Oleg nodded his encouragement.

Said something to the other men that Black couldn't understand. They added their nods and grunts of encouragement.

Black knew he was being set up, but figured he could play along. The men slowed down their eating to watch as Black took a sip.

He tried. Really. The smell was gagging him as he raised the cup, but he thought he did a good of keeping it off his face. Black didn't like fermented milks. Yogurt was as close as he could get. Kefir and its variants were something he'd drunk for the calories when necessary and there had been times he'd been happy to have it. Couldn't stomach kombucha. But this? Black knew what it was by reputation. Fermented horse or camel milk.

On its own, kumis was maybe three or four percent alcohol. Oleg had added cheap gin and lemon. The acid of the lemon, the heavy froth bubbling to the top, the fermentation and curdle of the carbonated milk with the near overpowering smell of local, homemade gin—juniper berry and coriander—was all in all as disgusting as anything Black could remember.

Oleg looked stricken, tried to hold onto it as long as possible, and then his face split wide in a grin, his missing teeth exaggerating his expression. The others burst out laughing.

They too drank the traditional beverage, mostly as a digestif after a heavy meal, or before the meal as a mild tonic to aid immunity. Kumis was part of the culture and the legacy of the Mongol's horse culture in Central Asia. It could be found in local upscale bars and grocery stores, but no one could drink Oleg's original cocktail.

Black took a breath—and downed the cup to the shock of the men.

They cheered while Berik offered him a Coke. Black shook his head and reached for the near-boiling cup of coffee Taras held out.

He hid his revulsion for Oleg's drink behind the cup of camp-fire brew, strong and filled with grounds like the strongest of Turkish coffees. The bitter drink a welcome cleanser of his palette.

"Our Brother we understand. Karlik's family is our family. But why here are you?"

Black pulled the folded photo from beneath his coat.

Temir looked at it for long moments, then passed it around. The conversation low and hushed. Moving easily in and out of a half-dozen languages and dialects.

Dima looked up. "This not your child."

"My friend died. He was a soldier. A brother. A warrior. His daughter is now my daughter. She was stolen on her travels. Like Karlik's family. Carried by force where they will sell her in Russia to evil men."

The men spoke in a low, sometimes heated mixture of Kazakh and Russian, Romanian, and perhaps Roma.

Temir offered more coffee. "You are a man of military in your country. A general? US of A?"

"A major."

Askar spat in the fire. "You have fought in our lands before?" His eyes narrowed but still reflected the flames. "Killed our brothers?"

No hesitation. "Yes." Black's eyes equally grim.

Sparks rose and danced in the wind. They all watched until they settled back down, listening to the trapped ice hiss and sizzle like distant cries of pain, the crackle of wood splitting and breaking apart like bones.

Dima looked up. "Will we kill Russians?"

Oleg looked at the others and waited for the answer.

"If they're there."

That seemed to make Oleg happy. The men talked amongst themselves.

"Why know Karlik you?"

Karlik answered. Black followed along enough to hear Nicola's name.

Temir reached for both of Black's hands. Like Karlik, he was missing the index finger of his right hand. Black had known

Russians and Taliban who sometimes chopped off the fingers of prisoners they thought were snipers.

Temir felt the ridges of hard muscle along the sides of Black's hands, turned them over and ran his fingers over knuckles pounded flat from years of constant work and training. Turned them back again to stare at his palms. Finally—

"Come."

Oleg lifted his rifle, Berik his bow. Grabbed a powerful set of Soviet-made binoculars. They made their way back to their posts high above the trail of entry.

Black followed the others to the back of the jeep. Dima pulled away a canvas tarp heavy with the freshly fallen snow.

New AKs, MP4s, Glocks, Sigs, a Soviet-made RPG, a variety of blades and knives.

Temir brought a separate canvas bag. Opened it to a .338 Stealth Recon Scout. Leupold Mark IV scope. A case of .338 Lapua Magnum.

Taras clapped Black on the back as he led him back toward the pallets and blankets around the fire. "Get some rest. We go tonight."

Black took in the epic mountain peaks now blocking a sun already dimmed behind falling snow.

He wondered how many tons of rocks were in each peak? Billions? *Trillions?* Began creating an equation based on simple visible geometry and calculations of size drawn from their estimated heights above sea level.

He knew the density of granite varied between 2.65 and 2.75 grams per cubic centimeter. Since the events took place later in the history of the planet, he decided that the plates that collided to form these mountains must be denser than most, so he put it on the high side.

He wondered if he should convert grams to pounds and centimeters to inches. *Might as well.* He needed to fall asleep somehow.

And what if he wanted to share with his American friends? All of his other calculations were based on estimates, so he thought it was fair to round things off. So— 170 pounds per cubic foot.

As Black began applying it to the geometry, he thought of Sam. Brought her face forward. Thought he saw Nicola in the clouds and swirling snow. Lay back and closed his eyes.

CHAPTER
EIGHTY-NINE

The maid stepped from the service elevator onto the 27th floor. Pushed the steel cart across the thick carpet to the end of the hall where a man sat outside the door of the final room. He made no attempt to look like he belonged. Foreign like most of the guests, maybe Russian, his clothes and style of dress said he wasn't rich. Certainly not enough to stay in a hotel like this.

He examined the cart with care, ran his rough hands through the towels, checked the folded robe. Looked with interest at the variety of complimentary toiletries. Lifted lids on trays of food.

Then he frisked her. She could see the gun tucked into his waistband. Her mouth clenched tight as he ran rough hands over her head and body. His fingers searched her hair through the cloth of the hijab before his hands crossed her breasts—his warm, sour breath in her face and the shame brought tears to her eyes.

Back down the hall, a door opened. A young Asian couple stopped in mid-stride and stared at the sight of the big man openly molesting the maid until they registered the gun sticking out from beneath his coat.

The young man swelled his chest but the woman deflated him with a sharp elbow and pulled him toward the elevators.

The maid was afraid her clenched teeth would break when the big man's hands slid down her back, across her rear and then back up across her hips. His hands fumbled in the pockets of her apron. Confiscated her phone. Found a small plastic bottle of aspirin. Nothing else of interest.

Sam hovered over Adeline, keeping her warm under the blankets while using a washcloth and water in the ice bucket to keep her head cool. Despite the thick covers and the heat being turned up, the girl was feverish—sweating and shivering.

The door opened to a rough-looking man and a maid.

The man stood watching as the woman, just a few years older than Sam herself, pushed a cart in. He pointed to the watch on his thick wrist. "Pyat' minut." Held up five fingers so there could be no misunderstanding.

He stepped back into the hall. The maid cautiously shut the door.

Sam rushed to her as she unloaded the cart. The woman placed the food on the table and the thick, luxurious robe on the bed.

"Please help me."

The frightened woman shook her head. Sam thought she genuinely looked confused. If she knew English, she did a good job of pretending she didn't.

"I need medicine." Sam pointed to the little girl.

The woman looked at Adeline and Sam was afraid she'd bolt from the room. The maid turned away. Sam watched as the woman fumbled in her pockets and turned back with a half-empty bottle of aspirin.

Sam was thankful, wanted to shout in triumph, but knew she needed more.

"She's sick. I need antibiotics." Sounding it out as if that would help.

The woman shook her head. Terrified. Her eyes wet.

"Do you have a phone?"

She mimicked a phone.

The woman shook her head no.

Sam was on the verge of tears herself. Dug into the pockets of her jeans. Fingers pulling out what could have passed as a wad of dirty tissues shoved up high in the front corner below the watch-pocket.

The woman watched Sam unroll the tattered paper. The diamond earrings sparkled in her palm.

"I have these." Sam tried to push one into the woman's hands. "Please, I need some medicine."

The maid looked at the diamonds. Her body racked with fear. Shook her head, grabbed at the cart, and left.

The door closed and locked. Sam stood in despair. Looked around at her new prison.

A luxury hotel room. Not a full suite, but a beautiful room by any standards. She looked out of the windows. They were high above the city. Twenty or thirty floors at least. The glass door to the small balcony locked. The windows iced, and the balcony and railing high with snow. Disoriented from the afternoon haze and snow, she felt dizzy. Seasick with no horizon. As if she stood in a tower at the bottom of an infinite bowl of white.

A huge, king-sized bed. A desk and chair. A seating area— a love seat, two chairs, and a table. She was hungry. Starving in fact. She opened the lid and grabbed a piece of meat. Took a bite, ripping flesh from the bone. The flavor so intense it hurt. Didn't bother with the plastic silverware. Used her fingers to grab at small potatoes broiled in sea salt and olive oil.

Opened another tray. Fresh fruit. An assortment of cakes and pastries. Bottles of water. Glasses of juice. A small bottle of wine for one. She flashed on the room in South Africa and knew she hadn't escaped anything at all.

Adeline moaned.

Sam ran to the bathroom. The phone removed from its normal place on the wall. A huge mirror above double sinks. If she'd seen the image staring back at her on the street she wouldn't have recognized it. She looked like the scared, desperate girl she was. She could pass for a junkie or a crack addict, and she jerked away as if scalded. Somewhere in mid-turn, she saw a glimpse of her mother. Maybe in the desperation and fear on her mother's face when her father woke drenched in sweats or shouted in his nightmares until he finally stayed away and quit coming home.

She turned back to find it again. Gone. It was only her. *What would her mother do?* What had she done when Sam was little and sick?

A large shower on one side, a tub on the other. She dropped to her knees and turned on the faucet. The water was icy, and she prayed there was nothing wrong with it. She let it run for what seemed like minutes but in truth was only seconds. Put her hand back under. Still cold. Icy. A moment later, it spit and sputtered.

"No no no..."

It sputtered again. A hint of warmth and then it came gushing out in with the steam and heat she sought.

She found the stopper and began filling the tub. As hot as she dared. She raced to the room's main door. Tried to lock it. The chain removed. Moved the chair and shoved it under the doorknob as her dad had taught her. The legs in her shoes as her Uncle Tommy had taught her.

She scooped up Adeline, stripped off the filthy clothes, and set the limp girl in the steaming bath. Refilled the ice bucket with cold water. Seconds later, her own clothes lying on the floor, she was in the tub behind her, holding the naked little girl in her arms, bathing her forehead with the cooler water from the bucket.

CHAPTER
NINETY

Most people never stop to think how much easier large trees alongside a house made it to break in. They hid entry and voyeurism from both inside and out, and in times like these, allowed a nimble person to search for ingress on the higher floors.

They were in the tropics with a house full of children. There were bound to be open windows somewhere, and he lightly stepped from the tree to the balcony. Surprised to find the sliding glass doors locked. A window four feet to one side was not.

Rícard pulled his body across the sill into the room. A child's room. He shook his head and smiled, relaxed, and in command. He'd made the right decision to come.

No sign or sound of anyone home. It was more like a hotel, and at one time, it had been. If they were here—*and where else would they be*—they were in hiding.

Had he given any misstep that would have warned them? No. He'd been perfect.

The witch. He knew she had somehow warned them all.

He wanted to laugh. If they were hiding, bunched together, his job would be even easier. Seconds, not minutes. People had no idea how frightful a knife, its tip and edges, even the butt and handle, could be in the right hands.

He watched his own feet move across the floor, enamored with his skills. He could have been a dancer. Master of *"The Tango of Death."*

Maybe he could stage a theater production after he made it to America.

The room was empty. An open door told him the next was as well. They were close, he could feel it.

Ricard made his way down the steps. Congratulated himself. Absolutely silent.

Made his way toward the kitchen. No one. Looked out the window in habit. They weren't outside. He'd scouted the lush yard before he scaled the tree.

The layout memorized at the real estate office, there were a dozen more rooms on the lower floor where they could hide.

He'd slipped past the hired security and walked the perimeter each of the past two days. He knew where a room of computers sat blinking and humming in the back of the house and shivered. Perhaps they all hid inside. *The witch's lair.*

He, Yves Ndiaye Ricard, would destroy her lair this very day. He wondered which would bother the gypsy more, the children or the tools and engines of her nefarious work? Maybe he should just burn it all down now.

No! *Concentrate.* The children. Then the girl. *Then the witch*

He entered the room and froze.

There she was, sitting in front of him, not fifteen feet away, eyes calm and clear. *Waiting.*

Icy fingers clawed at his heart and his vision swam. He wondered if he was having a heart attack. It took every bit of his strength to swallow and tear his eyes away. He looked at the shotgun cradled in her arms.

For the briefest of moments, he had hope. He was as light and fast on his feet as a fencer, a dancer with a blade. Within ten feet he could lunge and thrust faster than the best-trained man could draw and shoot.

He knew he had a—

Nicola pulled the trigger.

The fury of the .12 gauge shotgun blast overwhelmed the small room, but she would have sworn she could see right through it as two-thousand pounds of force-pressure exploded against Rícard's body.

Four of the nine double-00 buckshot pellets passed completely through him, displacing the flesh and blood in their way at nearly the same velocity they had left the barrel. Five of the .33 caliber pellets, 53.8 grains each, bounced and skittered off ribs and vertebrae, supplying the kinetic energy for atomized bone and splintered fragments to completely liquefy much of his insides.

Rícard's body dropped where it stood outside the door to her room.

The ringing in her ears stopped, the blood mist settled, and still she sat. The smell grew in intensity as the cordite dissipated and the stench of emptied bowels and bladder increased.

She had no regrets for the man. She'd first watched him stab the huge security man on video. Seen him from across the plaza as he attacked the boy and danced in glee while the young man died on the sidewalk. She knew without a doubt he had killed Renè. The police had prevented her from seeing the body but hadn't been able to prevent her from accessing the coroner's computers. The torture and trauma visited upon her once beautiful young friend was beyond understanding.

Nicola lifted her phone and made a call.

Alix reached for her phone. Listened. Turned to Camille. Nodded. A wave of relief washed over them both. Julius sat up from where he hid in the back. Camille pulled off the sunglasses, handed him the hat, and turned the vehicle around.

Nicola made another call. The men had been sent away but were expecting it. It was answered on the second ring.

"It's done."

Blood didn't bother her. She'd seen more than her share as a child. But the killing?

She thought about Black and others like him and wondered what it must do to them? How did they learn to live with it?

What right did she have to expect him to do her killing for her?

To give up his soul to save hers, to fight for children he had no connection to other than being human. There was a small chance he could still save his friend's daughter and that would be the end of it. It wasn't right for her to exploit his talents. He wasn't responsible for the world.

Nicola had been determined to end this chapter on her own. Had seen the assassin stalking her through town, staking out the house. She was resolved that the children would be safe and not forced to be a part of this. This was their new home, and until they were strong and capable enough to be on their own, she was their mother.

The men came in. No words were said, they understood their tasks. They wrapped the body. Scrubbed the floors. Searched for damage to the walls. Took away her gun. She said nothing, and they knew she'd thank them another day.

She looked at the time. Rayln would soon bring the others back from the beach. She wondered how Aleeza had done without her for the day. Nicola was filled with so much hope for them all.

Moments later, Camille and Alix and Julius entered. They looked at Nicola in awe, not only was the legendary hacker a genius, but she was also the strongest of them all.

They watched the men finish their tasks. Trembling, Alix asked to see the face and the men pulled back the edge of the plastic tarp.

Camille held her hand as they looked down. He didn't look tough. Didn't look evil. He just looked dead.

Alix nodded and they carried his body away.

CHAPTER
NINETY-ONE

B ody cramped and twisted on the love seat, she opened her eyes, stared at the gray ceiling, and wondered if she was awake. It was dark. She tried to remember where she was, difficult because she'd never known. A hotel room. Somewhere.

Sam twisted her neck to stare at the frosted windows and wondered what waited beyond in the distant glow of night? A good-sized city. She'd heard the traffic when they'd brought her here, blinded beneath the hood. Was it like Chicago? *No*. Not like Chicago.

This city was muffled beneath the blanket of falling snow.

Her hometown would be filled with the frustrations of an endless river of cars jockeying for advantage with horns and sirens, the roaring engines and squealing air brakes of city buses, the ceaseless bone-rattling rumble and screeching of metal on metal as trains weaved between and echoed off the high rises, the whine and hum of tires over the grates of the many bridges crossing the serpentine river.

Her arms and legs were numb. She looked down at Adeline nestled in her arms. Still sweating as occasional tremors rippled through the little girl.

She was failing the little girl just as she'd failed all the other children. Tears blurred her vision until the weight of her thoughts pulled her down into a deep abyss.

Big echoey BOOMS echoed in her head.

Eyes open but not really awake. She tried to sit up, realized Adeline was wrapped in blankets and asleep in her arms and cutting off her circulation. Put her tingling feet on the floor, pushed with her legs, and fell to her knees. Used her elbows to stop from crushing the girl. Rolled over and tried again. She staggered to the bed and set the little girl down. Pulled the blankets over her.

BOOM BOOM BOOM!

The chair had done its job. She pulled and pried until she pulled it away and the rough-looking guard shoved his way in.

The man scowled at the chair, one leg still inside one of her shoes. Glared as she clutched the robe tight, and stomped out.

Pushing in the cart, the maid pulled the door shut behind her. Handed two large plastic shopping bags to Sam.

The maid turned on lights as Sam dumped out the contents.

A flood of gratitude coursed through her as Sam took in the fresh jeans and long-sleeved t-shirts. A winter coat. It looked warm. Winter underwear. Thick socks and practical boots. The same in small versions for the girl. Tiny boots and a jacket.

The woman gathered up what was left of the earlier meal. Unloaded new plates of food.

Smiled shyly and pulled out a small bottle of pills.

Sam, almost afraid to look, reached for them.

"Oh, my God."

Cefadroxil. Sam hugged the embarrassed woman, and pried the lid open. She used the bottom of a glass to grind and smash the first pill. Dipped her finger into a glass of what she thought was juice. Apple.

Satisfied, she sat brought it close and sat on the bed. Dipped her finger in the juice and then the antibiotic, slid her finger past Adeline's lips and rubbed along her gums. Repeated it until the first pill was gone.

The women looked at each other and smiled. Sam kissed the girl and pulled the covers up to her chin.

She stood and reached into her pocket and pulled out the earrings.

"Please. A deal's a deal. They're yours."

The woman looked stricken, shook her head, and pushed them back.

"You keep. You maybe need."

Sam knew she was right.

The women looked at each other. Sad, unsure smiles. Really nothing to say. Both prisoners. Fear as their common language.

The door opened and the guard glared and grunted. The woman hurried the cart from the room. He grunted again and locked her in.

Sam sat long enough to feel for Adeline's temperature and kiss the little girl's cheek. Watched her sleep, willing her recovery.

Turned to the clothes and began to dress.

CHAPTER
NINETY-TWO

The street was quiet enough. A few dogs called to each other, the distant hoot of an owl, and the clucks of nervous chickens came from somewhere but no human voices.

Light reflecting off the dome of smog above and the ground below supplied plenty of murky gray light. Two, three, and four-story houses and buildings stacked on top of each other. Many seemed incomplete. Details, as if they were enough to make houses on their own, seemed out of place in the simple construction. A leaded glass window or a huge hand-carved door of imported hardwood, an ornate hand-forged railing or gate, sculptures and fountains and ornate mosaics that graced otherwise raw and unfinished homes. They gave the sense that some were designed and added in afterthought only to outdo their neighbors while others perhaps took inspiration from the illustrations of Theodore Geise, *Dr. Seuss himself.*

The compound took up most of the block. Four squat stories surrounding an open courtyard. Uninspired. The high fence made of a mishmash of metals and barriers topped with razor wire. A fortress.

Two men guarding from the roof. Two more staying in shadows outside the walls. Others, frozen and cursing the cold and their luck, posted at each end of the block.

Inside wasn't much warmer except within the small radius of heat coming off oil drums burning wood and raw coal. The air thick. At least they were shielded from the wind. Much of the massive structure was unfinished, an open design with cement block pillars and columns holding the upper floors. Armed men kept their own counsel but gravitated toward the heat.

Petru nodded and an armed guard unlocked and opened a large door on rails. Inside, a single weak bulb hung from above to light up the African children. More than a dozen, eight to fifteen. Huddled together for warmth and security, sitting or sleeping on reed mats and huddled under threadbare blankets.

One child sat cross-legged in the middle of the others—eyes preternaturally bright—staring back at him. Neither moved until Petru tore his eyes away and shut the door behind him.

He moved to another room where a man stood looking at the European cargo, separated to prevent information from being shared between the two groups. One never knew how it might come back to compromise them. The system had worked for eight years.

Petru stepped into the room, looked past the man, looking for what drew him. Two children stood out, perhaps a trick of the light or that they held each other close in their sleep.

Petru was responsible for the children's safe arrival in three days. This wouldn't be the first time he'd had to defend them until they were delivered from his care.

"They are not for you."

The other man said nothing.

"We leave in the morning. We do not need you here."

"Tem ne meneye ya zdes." *Nonetheless, I am here.*

"Those are not for you."

"Nor you, but perhaps I'll buy them for myself. Mozhet byt', ya pererezhu tebe gorlo ran'she, chem ya." *And perhaps I'll cut your throat before I do.*

"Udachi s etim." *Good luck with that.*

Petru turned and left. Just because they could speak a common language did not make them the same. Why had his bosses saddled him with the Russian enforcer? The man's reputation as

a rogue assassin for various factions of the Bratva preceded him—
his only loyalty was to the highest bidder.

Petru knew he could not afford to let his own reputation
be challenged. He'd been born in Kyiv, and was fiercely Ukrainian.
He had reasons to hate the Russians and decided then that
somewhere over the next three days and two thousand kilometers,
the enforcer would go missing.

Suraav was here to look out for Kronmüller's interest. The South
African paid him much more than his comrades ever had.

He was here because Kronmüller's men had lost control—
he'd heard in detail what happened. He should have killed the
American as he had argued for when they were both on the small
island, not having to wait on the slimmest of chances he'd make
his way here.

From what Suraav had found out, the American would spend
his life in a high-security American prison or in one of the not-so-
secret black sites, private facilities funded by multiple governments
to keep eyes and ears away from those whose secrets could bring
down those very governments. Stupid. Put a bullet through his
head and be done with it.

With pay-offs or threats, Suraav would make sure it happened.
In the meantime, a boy and a girl. Equally beautiful. Hair like
spun gold. Surely his efforts deserved to be compensated?

Petru watched them escort the man in and out of shadows as
they crossed the courtyard. Not even Kazakh. An Uzbek from
Turkmenistan. Holding his hands out toward the fire.

"He's here," Askar said. "The American."

It seemed impossible. "Let him come. When?"

"Before light."

"How many others?"

"Five. Six."

Petru nodded and one of his men pulled out a thick stack
of American bills. Lifetimes of money for a Uzbek peasant
turned spy.

"Let them come," Suraav said. "I hate Americans."

Askar nodded and grunted his agreement.

No one saw the Russian's hand move. The knife pierced Askar's throat and drove deep into his brain. Suraav held it there as blood poured over his hand.

"And spies." Suraav jerked the knife free, plucked the money from his hand, and let Askar fall.

The men were stunned, their eyes darting from one to another, hands tight on their weapons, and waiting for Petru's reaction.

The Russian tossed the stack of bills to one of the soldiers. "Share it."

Petru looked at the bloody knife clutched in the enforcer's hand and smiled, daring the man to attack. He didn't want to have to watch his back for three days. Better to end this now. The men surrounding them slowly inched away.

Outside, a guard was lighting a cigarette when a razor-tipped arrow went through his neck and severed his spine. He fell to his knees and watched his own blood pulse into the snow as he toppled over.

A block away, the other guard froze in place, trying to make sense of what he'd seen when the honed edge of carbon steel blade opened his throat, and he was pulled further into the shadows.

PHHHHITTT! Another arrow took out the guard on the right side of the opened doors. His partner spun toward Oleg drawing another arrow, and he let his assault rifle shatter the night. The light blinding, and the noise against the quiet echoed across the foothills. He was well on his way to emptying his mag when a single bullet spread the back of his head against the wall.

Temir was sighting on a third guard just as Black ran and leapt overhead from a nearby rooftop. He watched the American fly through the air. Heard a scream a moment later as another sentry was thrown from the roof and split against the razor topped fence.

The night exploded with gunshots from a dozen directions, the awesome noise and power of the assault rifles shattering and lighting up the night as steel-jacketed rounds tore through steel and concrete.

Three men pulled the heavy steel doors closed at the front of the warehouse, doing their best to stave entry.

More gunfire came from above and another man plummeted to the snow-covered pavement.

Men stormed up from the lower floors. One was almost torn in half from his men shooting from below, and Black shot two more from above.

Berik followed Black's leap across the gap between buildings.

A Russian soldier was charging Black from behind when Berik nearly chopped the man in half with a huge, curved Mongol-inspired sword. Black turned back in time to see the man fall and Berik grin.

Black returned the favor and emptied the mag of his .45 into two men entering from behind Berik. With too much smoke, floating debris, and bad light to know who he might be sighting on, Black reached for the blade tied across his own back.

He was almost to the third floor before he used it. The fearsome blade, as much a short sword as a knife, took one man's hand off and split another's head in two.

Karlik and Dima prepared to charge while Temir sighted on a man searching for targets from behind a wall on the second floor. The man's head exploded.

Perched on the second story rooftop of an unfinished building across the street, Oleg traded his bow for the Soviet RPG and sighted on the steel door.

Suraav was grabbing for a Kalashnikov as Petru shouted orders to his men when the front gates exploded inward, the thermo-baric blast igniting and sucking the air from the room while steel shrapnel and concrete rubble flying at 3000 feet per second took out another half-dozen men.

Petru was nearly blinded, no sound but the ringing in his ears and what felt like the grinding of bones in his skull. He saw

Suraav, somehow still on his feet, forgoing the assault rifle torn from his hands and scrambling for the blade lying on the floor. *Fucking Russians.*

Shadows were made huge against the smoke. Men—*real soldiers*—fighting their way in. His men going down in a horizontal hail of steel. His guards weren't soldiers—they were armed men. Those attacking were fierce warriors as good as any in the world. He'd fought against them in a half-dozen wars and conflicts. Gunshots rang out and more of his men fell.

Suraav was staggering on his feet, his hands on the blade when a shadow, like the specter of death, dropped from the sky in front of him.

Karlik saw the American seemingly drop from the heavens between the two foreigners. Black spun and his foot rocketed out, the powerful kick catching a third man across the jaw, the force snapping the man's neck. Black finished the turn and faced Suraav and Petru.

The three men with knives in their hands.

Dima's rifle was coming up when Karlik pushed it back down. Karlik and his men would save the children. There was no resistance left and no doubt at all.

Karlik knew the American needed to purge the self-hatred and the all-consuming anger, or he was dead no matter what.

Suraav darted forward, his thrust almost unseen and yet Black was no longer there.

Black parried and blended with the attack, his blade slicing deep across the Russian's thigh even as he twisted and his foot snapped out at Petru with the full force of his powerful legs behind it.

Petru's leg folded. He staggered back, the shock and pain too great to even scream as cartilage and tendon separated from bone yet still he slashed and caught Black's leg with the edge of his knife.

It was meant to slice deep, but instead scraped off a wide swath of skin and flesh along the American's shin but spared muscle.

Suraav slashed and thrust from the opposite side, searching for an opening while Black focused on controlling the blade. The Russian feinted with a kick, threw a tight hook, but Black met the powerful blow with an elbow strike that broke the man's hand.

Suraav slashed wildly, hoping to disembowel the American, but Black matched the speed and direction, folded the Russian's wrist back on itself, and drove the Russian's blade up and under his attacker's arm.

The Russian fell back, tried to take a breath but his lung was collapsing and already filling with blood. His vision swam but he wasn't done yet. He pulled the knife out of his chest and feinted, switched grips, and slashed it across Black's arm.

Like water—the philosophy behind everything he'd been taught—Black rolled the arm with the blow. Where it should have bitten deep it barely sliced through the nap of his thick coat.

Black dropped to one knee, driving his blade through the man's foot. As Suraav bellowed and fell back, Black rolled sideways into the Russian, continued upward, his blade slicing between the Russian's legs, severing arteries and flesh. Half-way up, Black dropped again, his blade stabbing Suraav through one knee then pulled it out to slice through the other. Black and the fearsome blade rose as one, and he cut deep across the man's throat.

Dead even as his brain raced to catch up.

Instead of stepping out of the way, Black circled the knife behind the Russian. Using both hands, he pulled the point through the back of Suraav's neck. Face to face, hot blood pouring over his arms, the knife's point fractions of an inch from Black's own throat, he held the man up until the assassin's eyes, first wide in shock and surprise, glazed over with the film of death.

Petru, unbalanced on one leg, hopped and tried to stab Black from behind. Black let the dead assassin in his arms fall, stripped Suraav of his blade, and stepped backward. Petru's thrust slipped past—Black trapped it with one arm and stabbed backward with the other. The blade, like a vertical scythe, gutted Petru and lifted him from the floor until the point stopped in his heart.

Black stood still and let the Ukrainian fall. Locked in place, vibrating with emotion and anger, adrenaline raced through him like a current and just as quickly, was gone. Emptied, he collapsed to his knees, gasping for breath and struggling to slow his pounding heart.

Oleg and Dima held their breath, unsure that what they'd witnessed hadn't been a trick of shadows. They fought to make sense of it until Karlik pulled them away.

Karlik lifted the crossbar that locked the door. Inside, huddled in the dark, a dozen children. Boys and girls. The Africans Nicola had tracked—some not over eight or nine.

A shout from Dima and he rushed to another room. Fifteen more children. Black-haired and blond. Pale and dark. In the back, clutching each other, two ten-year-olds from his country with hair like spun gold.

The men led the confused and terrified children from the rooms, searched for blankets and coats, anything to keep them warm. Reassured them they were safe. Led them through the burning debris, the air thick with black smoke burning their eyes and pulling the oxygen from the room.

Karlik came from the cells. Shook his head.

Black forced himself to stand, to watch the children leave. He had failed again.

CHAPTER
NINETY-THREE

S now stopped. The air clear enough that Sam could sense the
mountains in front of her, the gray foothills fading into the
mist. Still dark. Four in the morning.

Adeline was sleeping. Her fever had broken sometime in the
night. Sam dressed her in the new clothes and put her back to bed.

She'd moved the chair to face the door and sat in the dark.

Sleep hadn't come for her though she estimated she still had
about two hours before the door would open.

She was wired—strong and focused.

Playing it over and over again, trying to account for every
detail. She could see each footstep, count each breath. See the
shock and surprise and feel the triumph of success. She knew
she would only get one chance.

The dinner plate she held was broken in half. The smooth,
curved outside edge rested against her palm, while the broken side,
eight inches across and razor-sharp, faced out. Her other hand
cupped the bottom of a broken glass.

Now she had her claws and knew her only chance was
surprise and absolute commitment. She'd pause as the maid
pushed through the door using the woman and the cart to hide
her attack and then destroy whatever stood in the way of their
freedom.

She looked at the clock. Half-past four. She'd get Adeline to
safety. There must be hundreds of rooms below her. A desk clerk.

Police. People on the streets. Someone would help. She'd fight and beg her way to the American embassy.

No knock. The door burst open.

The huge silhouette blocked out the hallway and all reason. Sam froze. Her plan on hold as the man stepped into the room. He dismissed her and the threat of her improvised weapons, kicked her chair back as she was rising, and she crashed against the wall.

She scrambled up, spinning like a tiger for the attack. And stopped.

Ringer. The huge South African held Adeline in one hand as if she were a rag doll.

They rode down twenty-seven floors to the lobby. Sam tried to control the shaking. Ringer stood as still and calm as the statues in the lobby. Adeline cradled in his massive hands. The door opened and he guided Sam into the lobby.

"If you scream—she dies. If you run— she dies."

They crossed the lobby without incident. Only a young man and woman, both with smiling Asian faces, in dark blue coats and ties worked behind the desk.

This was Almaty, and a giant mountain of a man with a face set in stone, a stunning young black woman with a wild cascade of curls, a beautiful child asleep in the man's arms would have raised no undue alarm in any case.

Moments later, the doorman watched the three of them, one big happy family, pull away in the black Range Rover. He turned to the desk clerks and shrugged. Got a thumbs-up sign, then returned to his iPhone.

CHAPTER
NINETY-FOUR

Sirens in the distance. Shadows against the smoke. He could see the bodies. Smell death. Blood and guts and destruction. How many times must he be witness? How many times would he be the cause?

Why couldn't he have another talent? Be an artist or a writer? You could change the world that way too, right? Why did it have to be violence? He had some facility with numbers. Could see and determine and calculate geometric shapes and at least solve elementary equations. He could have been an engineer. Maybe an architect. Then he could have fixed these goddamned ugly fucking houses.

Fire and dead bodies. The smell of death. *The smell of his childhood.*

He watched the men load the children. They hadn't needed him for this. They would have found a way on their own. He'd come and more people died.

The stench of death clung to him like the smoke. He could cover it up. Try to wash it away, but it was a part of him. Had been his entire life. He'd embraced it, and yet, still Sam was gone. Dead or maybe wishing she was.

The snow stopped, and yet he felt currents on the wind as if it were gathering strength, preparing for the onslaught. He let it pass through him, breathed in the forces, and made it his own.

Oleg tried to get his attention. It took pulling on his arm before Black came out of his fog.

"Come!"

Black followed the man into the night. The children were being secured, trucks and SUV's pulling out. Karlik sat behind the wheel of a Land Cruiser holding out a satellite phone.

No doubt Nicola. He already knew the conversation. It took all his will to lift it to his ear.

"Tommy." Her voice broke his heart. Clear and strong and brave.

"I've got them, Tommy. Sam. Kronmüller. I've got 'em."

Stunned, all weariness was gone.

Nicola spoke as he drove. Kronmüller had booked a private charter. A two plane outfit out of Boraldai Airport, a regional strip outside of the city.

Nicola explained there were two storms destined to converge within hours or even minutes, and then there would be no way they could fly.

Monsoonal moisture from India was sweeping up from the south and east, and crashing into the sub-zero, polar vortex pushing down from Russia and Siberia to the two-thousand miles of Tien Shan mountains that defined much of Central Asia.

Alerts had gone out across a dozen countries. Airports and trains were told to batten down as record-setting blizzard conditions, thundersnow and electrical storms, stretched from the mountains of Afghanistan into the Himalayas.

From the west, a massive high-pressure front pushed from below the sub-Sahara equatorial belt, had driven super-heated dry air, absolutely devoid of moisture, into Northern Africa, Southeastern Europe, the Middle East, and now across the arid steppes of West Central Asia.

Soon, a five-hundred mile wall of a hundred-million tons of sand led by a prefrontal wall of toxic dust rose 15,000 feet and blanketed the sun. The haboob ebbed and flowed like a living creature and marched across a thousand miles of Kazakh desert toward the former capital city.

"You're twenty minutes out, Tommy. Kronmüller is in a black Mercedes Geländewagen. I'm locked onto their GPS. They're there!"

It had taken just five minutes to transfer extra gas tanks, plug in the 90s sat-phone, load weapons, first aid supplies, and blankets.

Taras did a one-minute patch job on Black's leg. A eight-inch strip of flesh had hung from his right shin, and his foot sloshed in a boot filled with blood.

The men, filled with respect and awe, surrounded him and said their good-byes as they worked.

Temir presented him with the sniper rifle. Oleg pulled off his coat and tossed it in.

"If you need for girl," he said. "You call, let us know me."

Karlik hugged him and kissed both cheeks, and shoved him into the vehicle.

Sirens and the first lights of the coming army of police were descending—thirty seconds out, but they would cover for him if needed.

Fifteen minutes away five minutes ago.

Nicola's voice urging him on. "It looks like they were trying to make it to Tashkent. But everything is being closed down. There is no way they can take off."

A small regional airport. A dozen small planes, two hangers, two separate airstrips. The bi-wing AN-2, an ugly, squat bug, waited on the runway. Not the prettiest of planes, but they had proved themselves for seventy years in some of the harshest environments on earth.

A black SUV entered the airport and headed toward the plane.

Sam in the SUV's passenger seat, holding Adeline in her lap. She watched Kronmüller step down from the plane. Waving and lighting up as if they were long-lost lovers.

"No!"

Sam jerked on the steering wheel, doing her best to turn it.

Kronmüller watched the SUV's erratic approach, it looked like it might crash into the plane but when he saw his beloved, he couldn't help but smile and wave.

He darkened when he saw Ringer backhand Sam. Watched her head bounce against the window.

Dazed, the girl continued to fight. Her nails broke as they raked across the giant's cheek. Unfazed, Ringer held her at arm's length and continued to drive.

Enough—he pushed her again, long enough to reach for his gun. Her head bounced off the glass, and she spun back to see him pressing the gun against Adeline.

Kronmüller saw the blood on Sam's lip. The swelling above her eye. Saw the little girl. Turned to Ringer.

"What the fuck is this?"

Sam held onto Adeline.

"So now I need a fucking kid? Do you ever do anything right?"

Ringer stammered but reached to take Adeline away and Sam went berserk. Kicking, screaming, trying to hold on to her.

Kronmüller looked across the runway at the airport—no one yet concerned or paying attention.

He looked at Sam and sighed.

"*Jesus Christ*—bring the fucking girl."

Ringer pushed them toward the plane. Sam resisting and slowing them down. Kronmüller pulled a gun.

"You want the kid alive? Get in the goddamned plane."

Sam picked her up and carried her. The little girl too confused, weak, and in shock to cry. "It's going to be okay. We're going on a little ride."

"And me?" Ringer asked.

"Yeah," Kronmüller said. "You're a problem."

Kronmüller shot him. Ringer had been his father's man. He shot him again.

He watched the man look down at the blood blooming across his chest. *The man couldn't even die right.* Kronmüller shot him in the head.

The pilot had no idea what to do. He couldn't see, but he heard the gunshots.

If he and his partner weren't always so desperate, he would never have come to work today. Reports had changed a dozen times in half that many hours, but all new information was telling him to stand down. Abort the flight. He interpreted the data, had some idea of how bad it might get. Dangerous at best. If the reports held, suicidal. And now he had a hysterical woman, a terrified child, and a homicidal maniac on board.

And a gun to his head.

"Get the fucking plane in the air now."

Twelve-hundred feet later, the AN-2, ten-thousand pounds of plane, fuel, and cargo, known for its abilities to take off and land on short, compromised terrain, left the icy runway.

No traffic, which in Black's mind meant no lights, stops, or traffic control. He sped through the city in time to see the plane lift off and head into what promised to be clear skies. Perhaps the meteorologists were wrong.

In perfect conditions, the plane had a maximum range of about eight-hundred fifty kilometers, over five-hundred miles. An optimum cruising speed of 120 mph. It could make the flight to Tashkent, the capital city of Uzbekistan eight-hundred miles away, in six and a half hours. Add in landing and refueling somewhere on the way—call it eight.

Nothing about these conditions were perfect, but they were in the air, and he was on the ground.

Black looked at the SUV, the door still open. They'd left in a hurry. A giant of a man, the other bodyguard, lay on the icy pavement, blood pooling from his head.

One less obstacle to worry about, but Black felt trapped in an endless loop of failure.

There were two security guards two-hundred meters away getting in their vehicle. He knew they'd be armed. He had no appetite for explaining he knew nothing and who he was, but was having trouble making himself move or even care.

Looked up to a clear window in the sky when the sat-phone rang. Signed and pressed the 'on' button.

"Tommy."

No strength to speak.

Nicola was at her computer. A half-dozen monitors up. Alix and the hackers surrounding her.

"Goddamn it! Tommy, pick up the phone."

Finally. "Yeah?" Black on speaker.

"We watched them take off. I'm tapped into satellite now. Looking at you I think."

"They're gone."

"No. Listen to me. They're going to have to put down. You've got two conflicting weather patterns converging. A blizzard behind you and a massive dust storm coming in from the west. Hell, you can see it from the space station."

The hacker team was indeed looking at the international space station feed of the earth's surface. The space station had passed the Prime Meridian just minutes ago and was over Northern Africa and Southern Europe moving east at 19,000 miles per hour. The demarcation of the rising sun had crossed China and was lighting up Kazakhstan and India.

A massive disturbance, captured as a nebulous cloud of pixels from two-hundred fifty miles above the earth, was no more than two-hundred from Almaty itself.

"He's suicidal for trying. They won't be able to turn around and the plane doesn't have the range to choose another airport."

Black ducked his head and looked out the windshield to the west. "The sky looks great out here."

"No! The storm is going to be on top of you in the next couple of hours. He won't make it more than a couple of hundred kilometers."

Black glanced toward the east. Where it should have been brightening, a wall of black clouds stretched across the horizon and lightning danced across the mountain tops.

"Head west. He can't cross south over the mountains. He's going have to stay in Kazakhstan."

Neither wanted to voice the obvious. *The plane could land anywhere.*

CHAPTER
NINETY-FIVE

They'd been arguing for ten minutes. The pilot was determined to stay within visual range of the highway below, set down on the nearest farm or oil field, and wait it out. Even that was going to be tough—nothing belonged in the air today.

Kronmüller was determined to push on to Tashkent.

Headwinds were getting stronger, gusting at thirty and forty knots. They hadn't even flown a hundred kilometers. The fuel was burning at a frightful rate, and they would have to set down regardless. The AN2-100 ran on kerosene rather that Avgas—it would be widely available, but it wasn't going to happen in mid-air.

"You want to fly the fucking airplane?"

"Yeah. I do."

Kronmüller put the gun against the pilot's head and pulled the trigger.

Sam was terrified. Had watched the mad man kill the pilot. The plane was bucking, riding the winds in ten and twenty-foot crests and troughs. The bi-wing design, eight-hundred square feet of wing surface, strained against strong crosswinds. She held Adeline close.

She knew they were moments away from death. She glanced at the cockpit—it looked like a space ship. Clinging to hope no matter how improbable, she was giddy with relief when Kronmüller pushed the pilot out of his seat and took over.

Kronmüller looked over his shoulder and shouted cheerfully. "Don't worry. I trained on this plane."

The noise—the groan of metal and stretched fabric fighting wind, ailerons and rudder stretching their cables, the straining of the one thousand horsepower engine driving the four-blade prop was as intense as the beating of Sam's heart. Adeline was shutting down and Sam couldn't imagine the terror she must feel being constantly bombarded with ever-increasing danger.

Sam laughed at herself. Of course, she could imagine the nightmare. She was living it.

"We can have a good life," Kronmüller said.

She shouted back. "You're fucking insane!"

"Yeah. I've heard that." He turned his head enough she could see he was smiling. "But you'll see. We're going to be happy, Lina."

The words chilled her as much as anything that had happened. "My name is Samantha—"

"No. It's understandable. You're confused. After we get home, you can rest and everything is going to be fine. Really just soooo... Perfect."

Sam sat halfway back in the twelve-seater. She could have backed up further, but there was really nowhere to go. She looked out the window, wondering what it would be like to jump and be embraced by the mists below.

She looked at Adeline. Tucked the girl's head under her chin. Clung to the smell of the little girl's hair and held tighter.

She watched the mad man fly the plane, seeming to dare the elements even more. Forced herself to look out the windows. She had no idea how high they were or in what direction they flew.

"I think maybe you should hang on."

Sam looked past him at what looked like a solid wall rising in front of them.

Like a living thing, sucking the light from the sky as it rose upwards from the ground. A massive wall of dust and sand.

Moments later they were in it. Bad and getting worse.

Sam locked both her and the girl tighter into their seats, held on and prayed, unable to tear her eyes away from the window though there was absolutely nothing she could see. No idea if they were still in the sky or buried under the ground. No visuals, like wearing a blindfold in the dark. Overcome with the sensation of floating as gravity ceased to hold her down.

She could have sworn they sat still, suspended in a sea of mud, or maybe even flew backward. The plane fishtailed in the air, shot up in the air fifty feet.

She heard something snap, the tearing of fabric against the metal. Seconds later, they were falling.

They hit the ground hard—her mind closed down—and then there was no sensation at all.

CHAPTER
NINETY-SIX

April 14th, 1935, Black Sunday. The defining storm of the dust bowl was a thousand miles long and a half-mile high, displacing 300 million tons of topsoil across Texas and the Oklahoma panhandles in a storm with 100 mph winds. Catastrophic drought along with decades of poor soil management and abuse helped produce the historic event.

Kazakhstan had many parallels, not the least of which was one of Earth's worst man-made ecological disasters with the virtual draining of the Aral Sea. The diversion of the rivers that fed what was once the fourth largest lake in the world for Russian irrigation projects 1500 miles away, left a vast sea of toxic wasteland, some of which blew on the winds slamming into Black's truck even now.

They'd lost communication. He fought to stay on the road. The divided four-lane highway had ended miles ago and was now two adjacent lanes. Safe enough if he could find it.

He stopped the truck. Pulled off what he thought must be the highway. It was as if he floated in a sea of quicksand, and in a very real way he did.

Black listened to the sand stripping the paint from the vehicle while he choked and fought to breathe as near-microscopic particulate was slowly forced into the cab.

He wrapped his face and nose, kept his eyes shut so the silica wouldn't strip his corneas and leave him blind.

Nicola had said this was the *smaller* storm, that a larger threat was bearing down on them from the east. Twenty minutes later, the mountain of sand and dust rolled over him, destined to crash into the blizzard she said was rushing up behind him.

The sky brightened. After the blacker than black of the storm, the dim light was blinding. The sky, a deep amber, with streaks of tarnished green, soon darkened again as clouds rolled in and the first flakes of snow and ice began replacing the dust and sand.

If they hadn't crashed, if Kronmüller or his pilot had been skilled enough to land the plane, he hoped they'd been smart enough to seek shelter. It not, he knew all he would find were bones scoured clean of their flesh.

He had followed the AN-2 west. Almaty behind him and nearly two thousand miles of Kazakhstan in front. Glacier valleys and snow-clad mountain peaks to his left. Vast steppes and rippled landscape to his right.

He was under two feet of sand, but the winds, still gusting at 30 and 40 mph soon cleared the windshield enough he could at least try to start the vehicle.

Nothing. He held his breath and tried again. Nothing. As if it had all been short-circuited. As if it waited for him to curse at it. He did. And the ten-year-old vehicle started up as if he'd been test-driving it at the dealer. Moments later, he found none of his instruments worked. No lights. No gauges. No GPS.

He couldn't tell if he was on the road or not. He normally had a remarkable sense of direction but with no bearings at all, would not want to swear on what was east or west, north or south.

The sat-phone on the seat blinked, the light drawing his attention.

"You okay?"

"Yeah, fine. Lost."

"Give me a minute."

Black sat as Nicola worked some obscure magic. He tried to think about what it might be. He could assume the sat-phone itself had some sort of signal that she traced back to its GPS location. That she had access to it made perfect sense. He wondered if she could commandeer a satellite to follow him. He felt like he should roll down the windows and wave.

"I've got you."

"Really? This is crazy."

"You want me just take control of the vehicle and steer it for you?"

"You can do that?"

He could hear laughter. "No."

Black smiled. Maybe his first in a couple of days.

"Listen Tommy. It looks like you're off the road, maybe four or five meters."

He began to pull forward. He had gone maybe twenty feet.

"Getting worse. Steer left."

He did and a moment later felt the tires find purchase.

He could see a patch of road as it blew clear of dust and sand but it was quickly turning to what must have been frozen mud. The heat of the sand was soon overwhelmed and began freezing. Snow began falling in earnest and soon he felt he was driving in a snow globe.

"I have no instruments, no lights."

"Shit."

"Yeah. Shit."

He kept his speed to about 10 mph. He was used to Chicago, where lake-effect snow squalls could dump a foot of snow in an hour. He thought he could safely pick up the speed. All the way to twenty.

He could hear the discussion. She seemed to realize it.

"Sorry. I'm here with Michaels's team. Alix, Camille, and Julius."

He heard a couple hi's and helloes.

"I'm not going to have access to visuals for the next few hours. Everything is being used right now, but we're tracking down another idea."

It never occurred to him she could *actually* commandeer a satellite. He knew they were up there of course and that someone controlled them, but it was so far beyond what he expected from a woman with a computer on a tropical island in the middle of the Indian Ocean that he was stunned.

"We're running scans for any ELT's broadcasting in that area."

"You think he'd run it?"

"He's an experienced pilot. It's probably as automatic as pulling on the stick."

He heard a shout.

"Got him."

"Jesus. We've got him, Tommy!"

"He's close. Maybe ten kilometers."

He heard another voice.

"Julius says fourteen," Nicola said. "Fourteen kilometers from your location, Tommy. But you've passed him."

He heard a younger woman's voice. "You need to go back about seven or eight kilometers, about five miles, and then head directly north. Pretty much at right angles."

Nicola came back on. "We're looking at the maps, Tommy. Doesn't show a road, but he's about a thousand meters out from a large farm, so there might be. And the ground should be hard enough if you take it easy."

A simple triangle. Hypotenuse at 14 miles. Right angle at 5. That left him with a little over 12 miles to cross what he hoped was hard-packed or frozen dirt.

"Tommy, I— —if y— —ry—"

Damn. He followed the cord back to the dead console panel. Holding no charge, the light faded out on the ancient sat-phone.

CHAPTER

NINETY-SEVEN

She came to slowly—then shot awake. Reached for Adeline.
The girl was still, and Sam's eyes welled with tears. It took all
her will to move her hand close enough to search for a pulse.

"No. No. No—"

Just as her hand rested above the girl's neck, Adeline's eyes
blinked open.

"Oh, my God." Sam unbuckled herself and then the girl. Let
her tears flow until they were gone.

There was light outside. And snow. The wind howled, and
huge flakes the size of saucers were driven across the sky.

"Stay here, honey."

Kissed the little girl on the head and staggered on drunken sea
legs toward the front of the plane.

Kronmüller leaned against the fuselage. He looked lost. No
sense of command or purpose. He wasn't dressed for the cold and
must be freezing but gave no sign of it. She glanced at the plane.
If it had been completely crushed it wouldn't have surprised her,
but except for crumpled struts and one of the lower bi-wings
cracked in two, it seemed intact. It wasn't going anywhere.
They were standing in a blizzard in the middle of what had to be
fucking nowhere.

She was off-balance. It had been blacker than black. Now
whiter than white. The snow came in sheets. Then stopped. Just
as she prayed it was over, it started again. Waves of white showers

in time with increasing gusts of wind. If it kept up like this they would be buried within hours.

"We're going to be okay."

"What?"

He looked at her, his eyes tender. She fought not to throw up.

"Someone will come."

"We're in the middle of nowhere. No one will come. Where the fuck are we?"

"About a hundred, hundred-twenty kilometers west of Almaty."

"Almaty. What's Almaty?"

"Biggest city in Kazakhstan."

"Kazakhstan?

"Ninth largest country in the world." She showed no recognition. "Central Asia."

"What the fuck are we doing here?"

"I came to take you home."

"Home?" Tears of frustration froze against her eyes.

"Lina. We're going to be happy. Me and you. My father—Well, my father's gone so you don't have to worry about him anymore. We'll have to rebuild, but we'll be fine. Better than fine."

"You're fucking crazy!"

He shook his head, disappointed. "You can bring the girl. Of course, she'll have to go once we have our own. Siblings can be so jealous."

The waves of snow stopped and Sam thought she could see a structure, white against white. Or gray against gray. Maybe her imagination.

The wind was picking up and she had to shout. "We can't stay here."

"Of course we can. Someone will come."

CHAPTER
NINETY-EIGHT

B lack tried to relax. He needed to estimate five miles. No way
of knowing how fast he was traveling or in what direction. His
only hope was a road that might exist at right angles to a highway
he might not be on. No way to see it.

The battery dead on the sat-phone, instruments and gauges
not working, no secret electrical connections to find. He tried
the cursing technique. *No luck.* Then the praying technique.
The gods were in rare form today.

Sam was out there. Maybe, just maybe, still alive. He had no
way to find her in the middle of the storm.

The bulk of the storm system was still hours away. He knew
it could last for days. They were in the shadow of some of the
tallest mountains of the world. One had to plan for snow beyond
imagination.

He forced himself to breathe. To think. He estimated he'd
gone a bit over two miles. Counting the seconds—he'd stopped at
eight minutes. Okay, this was bullshit. He knew he could already
be off a mile. He stopped the SUV.

Karlik and Temir, Oleg and Dima and Berik had loaded the
SUV. Temir had given him the sniper rifle and the sat-phone.
Dima and Berik loaded an assortment of weapons, blankets, water,
and food. A medic's first aid kit.

And Oleg? Tossed in his coat in case he needed it for Sam.
'You call, let us know me.'

He could picture it but was afraid to look. Got out of the SUV. Opened the rear door and looked through the blankets. Pushed aside the weapons and the first aid kit.

Underneath, Oleg's coat. Prayed one last time. Reached into the pocket. Nothing. *Still fucking with him.*

He cursed and slammed the door. The Land Cruiser rocked from the force. And stalled.

He scrambled to get to the gas, to keep it going but by the time he slipped and slid and fell behind the wheel, it was completely dead.

Black closed his eyes. His brain stopped. He couldn't think or yell or pray. Just... nothing.

He turned the key. The engine roared into life. The wipers and lights and the full instrument panel. The heater came on and the air blew. He looked down at the sat-phone. Eons went by, and then... BLINK BLINK BLINK.

Moments later it found the signal and almost instantly the call came in.

"Tommy?"

"I'm here."

Fifteen minutes later, he saw the silo. A white tower against a white sky. Thirty meters high, and maybe twelve-hundred meters ahead. Hiding behind a blanket of snow, but he'd seen it... he had a landmark.

"About a thousand meters east," she'd said.

The snow was blinding. A thousand meters was like a thousand miles. A ferocious squall hit the truck, and he drove blind until ten seconds later, he hit a wall—a ripple of frozen land a foot high and as hard as cement. It knocked his teeth together and he bit his tongue. Tasted the blood. And the lights went out and the instruments went down.

He laughed at the absurdity of it all. As impossible as the odds were, the blood in his mouth reminded him he was alive, that it wasn't over. He'd battled his way across the world to be right here at this exact moment—nothing was over. *Fuck the gods.*

Black got out of the truck. The wind howled and made it impossible to see. He turned his eyes east. Tried to calculate where a thousand meters from the farm might be. Stared. White on white. Stared. White on white. Took a deep breath, closed his eyes. Took another breath. Opened them and there it was. The smallest hint of *not white* against the storm.

His mind filled in the gaps. Kazakh blue. Thirteen-feet high. Forty-feet long. Sixty-feet of stacked wings. Oleg Anatov's original, insect-like design not changed in seventy years. *Beautiful.*

Black got back in the Land Cruiser and started forward.

Sam was still staring out at the storm. Willing the snows to part again and reveal what she had seen against the white.

Kronmüller was screaming. "We have to stay here."

Sam had grown up on the Great Lakes. She knew the rules. You never leave the vehicle. Everyone knows that. *You leave— you die.* But she also knew of people who had been buried in snowstorms in their cars in January and dug out in March.

She was a Midwestern girl, she knew a silo when she saw it. Rationally, it could have been her imagination, but she knew in her heart, it was there. A farm.

She could stay here and freeze with a fucking homicidal madman. *Or try.*

She was guiding Adeline from the plane when she saw them. Not her imagination. *Headlights.* If only for a moment. *Someone was out there.*

"We stay!"

"You fucking stay. I'm taking the girl."

He grabbed at her and threw them down. Pulled his gun and aimed it at the child.

Kronmüller staggered against the onslaught of the storm, found his footing. This was for the best, the child would only come between them.

His arm stretched out—

One moment he was standing and the next he was falling. No idea what had happened, the *event* lasted just hundredths of a second. No time to realize the bottom half of one leg was gone.

He hit the ground, crashed face-first into the snow. It knocked the wind out of him and gave him time to hear the distant thunder of a rifle report roll across the tundra.

Black drove toward the plane. Stopped forty meters out.

Sam stared out at the storm. White on white became gray on white. *And then Black.*

Kronmüller summoned the strength to roll over. The blinding snow parted enough to reveal the silhouette of a man, rifle in hand, looking down on him. He couldn't concentrate. Couldn't think. But he knew.

The American.

Black looked at the dying man. He'd die of shock. Of blood loss. Five, ten minutes at most. Let him rot until he turned to dust and the storms and winds blew his memory far away.

Black had done what he'd come for. There would be no red flowers on these lands—*no heroes died in battle here.* No fields of blue—*no one would mourn the loss.*

He looked at Sam, her tear-stained face, watching him in wonder and holding on tight to the little girl, trying to believe in the impossible as he reached out his hand.

Snow fell and the bitter winds howled, the moment frozen in time as much as the air, but when she smiled, Black only felt the warmth.

The End

A Special Thanks to My Readers

YOU MADE IT TO THE END, for which I am humbled and thrilled!

BLACK FIRE started as a trilogy of screenplays, and we're in talks with several production companies about moving forward with the feature films.

In the meantime, I write!

The sequel, BLACK STEEL is underway, and takes Tommy Black around the world again, this time to Paris, Mauritius, Nigeria, and then to the steamy swamps and bayous of Louisiana.

Since BLACK HEART will be guided by the screenplay, I can tell you now, that this third book in the Tommy Black series will put us in Asia — Thailand, Cambodia, and the Philippines.

The worldwide pandemic inspired me to write a sci-fi horror thriller, LOOP, full of hard-core action, off-the-wall characters, and a crazy premise unlike any that I have seen. As it also lends itself to film and a possible series, we're (my film partners and I) pursuing that as well.

Any on-line review you take time to write for BLACK FIRE would mean the world to me, and to the continued success of the series.

I'm starting an email list and website to keep people updated, and to share some of the news and progress. I can only do so much, so I promise not to drive you crazy with more than a few, periodic emails. To see early 'preview' chapters of the sequels, to buy or win a bit of *'Tusker's swag,'* please connect @

https://williamkelymcclung.com

Thank you again for the all support!

Acknowledgments

IT'S A STRANGE WORLD, and we have no guarantee of saying thank you unless we do it now.

Dad, you would've been convinced this was a biography as much as a story, and though you'd be wrong, your belief in the best of me always made me feel there was nothing I couldn't do. Mother, you somehow raised five of us, and encouraged all of our dreams. I'm blessed to have four brothers who are all just damn good people. Your inspiration and influence walk on these pages as much as I do.

To my friends in the military and police services around the world, there are not words enough to say thanks. The full list of my martial arts teachers and their contributions would make up one of the longer chapters of this book, but special thanks to Danny and Paul and Chai and Tim and Mike and Leo. I've been lucky enough to teach around the world, and must thank my core group of students, Lisa and Jeff, Erik and Beth, Jess and Scott. All of you taught me more than I ever taught you.

Boris, your faith in my abilities continues to push and inspire me. These pages can be traced directly to our friendship and your efforts on my behalf. Josef, your advice became the catalyst in one story becoming three and expanding that to this series. Always thankful! Rob, for your encouragement in all facets of my film and writing journey. Ben, my fellow scribe, your endless patience with my 5000 questions is inspiring in itself. Your simple words of wisdom resonate each time I found myself stuck, "Just write the story."

Amazon author page
add reviews, ask questions
and see what's next

williamkelymcclung
books, films, blogs,
and swag

Facebook
follow for an entire
community of creatives

Instagram
world travel
and adventures

YouTube
films, interviews, and
behind the scenes

William Kely McClung

AFTER TRAINING IN DOZENS of fighting systems around the world for nearly thirty years, Kely McClung was launched into the film industry after winning the brutal International Full Contact Stick Fighting Championships.

Working, traveling, and teaching martial arts, acting, and film production around the world, Kely is also an accomplished artist and photographer, a prolific screenwriter, and has directed three award-winning feature films.

His pen and ink portrait of Martin Luther King, Jr. and Mahatma Gandhi hangs at the King Center in Atlanta, Georgia, while his photography is represented by the Michael-Warren Contemporary in Denver, Colorado.

Kely has taught and trained with various military, police, and private security firms and personnel, and continues to train and teach martial arts around the world.

BLACK FIRE is Kely's second novel, behind LOOP, and the first in the TOMMY BLACK SERIES. Look for the upcoming sequels BLACK STEEL and BLACK HEART soon.

To connect and say hi, find Kely on a multitude of social media pages or at williamkelymcclung.com

Printed in Great Britain
by Amazon